Praise for

RONDA RICH

and

The Town That Came A-Courtin'

"Indescribably delicious! And now, Miss Ronda . . . may we please have some more?" —Jill Conner Browne,
author of *The Sweet Potato Queen's Book of Love*

"A wonderfully sweet, entertaining tale of goodwill and good people. True 'bliss.' " —Richard Paul Evans,
author of *The Christmas Box* and *The Perfect Gift*

"Southern fun with lots of heart as only Ronda Rich can write it." —Haywood Smith,
author of *The Red Hat Club*

"Sweet, funny, with all the flavor and charm of a good old-fashioned love story!" —Sela Ward, Emmy® Award–Winning actress

"Filled with romance and flirting, with courtship, plot turns and more charm than a debutante ball."
—*Asheville Citizen-Times,* North Carolina

"An endearing confection that offers romance and intrigue, a pleasant escape on a plane, a porch or on a beach towel."
—*St. Petersburg Times*

continued . . .

The Town That Came A-Courtin'

Ronda Rich

BERKLEY BOOKS, NEW YORK

THE BERKLEY PUBLISHING GROUP
Published by the Penguin Group
Penguin Group (USA) Inc.
375 Hudson Street, New York, New York 10014, USA
Penguin Group (Canada), 90 Eglinton Avenue East, Suite 700, Toronto, Ontario M4P 2Y3, Canada
(a division of Pearson Penguin Canada Inc.)
Penguin Books Ltd., 80 Strand London WC2R 0RL, England
Penguin Group Ireland, 25 St. Stephen's Green, Dublin 2, Ireland (a division of Penguin Books Ltd.)
Penguin Group (Australia), 250 Camberwell Road, Camberwell, Victoria 3124, Australia
(a division of Pearson Australia Group Pty. Ltd.)
Penguin Books India Pvt. Ltd., 11 Community Centre, Panchsheel Park, New Delhi—110 017, India
Penguin Group (NZ), Cnr. Airborne and Rosedale Roads, Albany, Auckland 1310, New Zealand
(a division of Pearson New Zealand Ltd.)
Penguin Books (South Africa) (Pty.) Ltd., 24 Sturdee Avenue, Rosebank, Johannesburg 2196, South Africa

Penguin Books Ltd., Registered Offices: 80 Strand, London WC2R 0RL, England

This is a work of fiction. Names, characters, places, and incidents either are the product of the author's imagination or are used fictitiously, and any resemblance to actual persons, living or dead, business establishments, events, or locales is entirely coincidental.

PRINTING HISTORY
Berkley hardcover edition / May 2005
Berkley trade paperback edition / May 2006

Berkley is a registered trademark of Penguin Group (USA) Inc.
The "B" design is a trademark belonging to Penguin Group (USA) Inc.

The Library of Congress has cataloged the Berkley hardcover as follows

Rich, Ronda.
    The town that came a courtin' / by Ronda Rich.—1st ed.
        p. cm.
    ISBN 0-425-20258-5
    1. Women novelists—Fiction. 2. City and town life—Fiction. 3. Obituaries—Authorship—Fiction.
4. Fiction—Authorship—Fiction. 5. Georgia—Fiction. I. Title.

PS3618.I3335T69 2005
813'.6—dc22   2004058318

PRINTED IN THE UNITED STATES OF AMERICA

10   9   8   7   6   5   4   3   2   1

For Mary Gay Shipley and the fine folks of Blytheville, Arkansas

Author's Note

When I wrote this book I thought I was making up Dexter, GA—and now that I've learned there's a real Dexter, GA, I hope it's as wonderful as the town I imagined!

Acknowledgments

This story, although elaborately embellished as is normally the case with fiction, was inspired by a true, personal experience. A book tour took me to a small Arkansas town where, to my delight, I found people who loved unconditionally. It was an experience for which I will always be grateful because it is nothing short of uplifting to see such a beautiful side to humanity. I was honored to become the center of their attention for the man who was the center of their affection. That said, I must throw handfuls of kisses and appreciation to Mayor Barrett Harrison, Teresa and Dale Hinson, Mary Gay Shipley and the many charming, gracious people of Blytheville, Arkansas. May God bless and keep you always.

No book is ever birthed by one person. It is delivered through the laborious efforts of many, such as my editor Susan Allison who bought it, edited it and loved it and publisher Leslie Gelbman who believed in it fervently. Jane Dystel, Miriam Goderich and Michael Bourret formed a formidable sales team on behalf of Dystel-Goderich Literary Management. Thank you, dear ones. Liz Perl and Craig Burke enthusiastically oversaw the publicity and the sales reps—the unsung heroes—bravely, boldly and strongly took on a new novelist.

Others in the publishing industry must be thanked, too, because to overlook them would be ungracious: Without Amanda Patten, who loved the story when she heard it told casually over dinner and said, "Write this as a novel. You must! You must!" this book would not have happened. Virginia Stanley provided encouragement and inspiration; Michael Morrison, Marian Lizzi and John Duff gave assistance and friendship. Richard Curtis was the first to believe in me as an author and that piece of faith will never be forgotten.

Travis Massey is a photographer extraordinaire who has been with me from the beginning and to whom much appreciation and friendship is owed. You're the best!

Personally, there are always many to thank but first for this must be Debbie Lunsford Love, Karen Peck Gooch, Fran Lewis, Kim Watson, Stevie Waltrip, Pinky Cabe, and my mama, Bonelle Satterfield—their prayers brought divine answers. Others who are often invaluable to me are Barbara Dooley, Cindy Owen, Sharon Pearce, Sam Richwine, Jim Whitmer, Barclay Rushton, Rickey Gooch, Mike Love, Rodney Nix, Edithe Swensen and the entire, beloved gang of Dixie Divas and my wonderful family.

Mostly, though, I am obliged to and completely charmed by Blytheville, Arkansas—*The Town That Came A-Courtin'*.

Prologue

Folks around Dexter, Georgia, where I grew up, always talk about how lucky I am. It is a subject that has found itself in the center of countless conversations in places like the beauty shops, grocery stores, post office, Wednesday night suppers at the Baptist churches and even the barbershops, when the old men stop grumbling about their wives long enough to talk about it.

They all say that, because how else can you explain all the good fortune that's happened to me over the past five years? How else can you find reason for an obituary writer for the *Dexter Tribune* suddenly finding fame and fortune as a world-wide best-selling author? My inclination is to agree with the town's consensus. I am, for the most part, lucky.

"That Abby Houston is the luckiest one woman I ever saw," someone around town is likely to say with a puzzled shake of the head. "She's luckier than Bimbo Barton at the downtown drugstore when a big epidemic of the flu hits. She just makes money hand over fist."

I am an author but not necessarily a writer because that hallowed title belongs to those who are truly talented at what they do. I am a storyteller, a simple creature graced with the DNA that permeates the bloodlines of most people born in the Deep South. I am nothing special, no different than most of my kinfolk, who can hold your attention with a spellbinding account of their trip down the driveway to the mailbox. The only thing that separates me from them is that I write my stories down, publishers make books of them, lots of people buy them, and Hollywood occasionally makes movies of them.

Mama, though, has a slightly different take on the situation. "Lucky in life, unlucky in love," she will say in a bittersweet tone, then sigh wistfully.

That's true, too. I've been getting my heart broken by the opposite sex since I was in the sixth grade and Gregg Nixon stood me up to take Beatrice Miller on the hayride at the Halloween Carnival. It's a tough lesson in love when you have to watch the one you adore crawl into the hay with another girl. That began a pattern that has followed me through a series of breakups including a husband who left me to crawl in the hay with someone else, too. Only this time, the hay wasn't in a wagon that was being pulled by an old blue Ford tractor. I can't complain because life is good, even pleasant for me. Every woman wants to be in love, though. It's one of the things we're called to do in life, but somehow the fate that otherwise blessed me so bountifully just didn't see fit to bestow a decent love on me. To be honest, I spent a lot of years shrugging it off because I figured that the good Lord had already given me so much in a lifetime that I couldn't and shouldn't complain. Plus, while I hate to admit it, love had left me too wounded and my heart had become brittle from the burn. I will admit, though, that I had naturally strong yearnings for kisses under a full moon and arms that held me tight after a long, tough day. I just pretended otherwise.

Other than the silent martyrdom of my lonely heart, the only thing else I could find to complain about would be my weariness of a hometown that has grown too much. Dexter is only an hour north of Atlanta, and unfortunately, our once small, sweet town now bustles with the population of strangers happy to commute to the city on a daily basis. The town of my childhood is no longer a simple country town where everybody knows everybody and whom they're related to and which skeletons reside in their closets. To tell the truth, had it not been for my family and friends, I would have already up and left Dexter and found a place that resembles the simplicity of my childhood memories. A place where folks still care if your dog dies, know the postmaster personally and will bake a casserole when you're not feeling none too good. A place where traffic is never a problem, Wednesday night is still considered a church night, the whole town turns out for a Friday-night football game because there's nothing better to do, and a viewing at the local funeral home is considered a social occasion. Now, *those* were the days.

Still, life for me was sweetly blessed and mostly good last autumn, when I was preparing to set off on an extensive book tour for my new release. I had flown to New York to meet with my publicist, Jamie Gray, about the tour she was arranging for my publisher. Through some light arm-twisting and some old-fashioned Southern charm, I managed to convince her, despite her initial objections, that we should add a tiny little spot of a town called Bliss, Mississippi, to an agenda that included major cities like Los Angeles, Chicago, New York and Dallas. I had no reason for going to a simple small town like Bliss, other than to keep my word to the owner of the town's bookstore. I had been promising Susan Marie Jackson for three years that I would do a signing at her store one day. That day, I decided, had come.

I was soon to discover that the day had come for much more than just that. I set out on a routine book tour, but in more ways than one, I discovered a big dose of Bliss. This, quite simply, is the story of a woman who fell in love with a town that had been in love for a long time.

Chapter 1

Using a pair of tweezers, I was cleaning the lint from the vent in my hair dryer when the phone rang.

"Hello?" I answered, tucking the cordless phone between my head and shoulder as I continued with my important task.

"Whatta ya doin'?" That's the standard phone greeting for me and Mama. Knowing that the conversation would probably turn into a long one despite my best efforts, I laid down the dryer and tweezers on the vanity top in the bathroom and headed toward the sofa in the living room. I stepped over the suitcase that, though unpacked from my trip to New York three days earlier, had not been returned to the attic.

"Cleaning the lint out of the vent on my hair dryer," I replied, flopping down amidst the collection of brightly colored cushions, then pulling my legs up and tucking them under me the way a hen settles down over her eggs.

"Oh." I could tell by the detached tone that Mama wasn't the slightest bit interested in the maintenance of my household appliances. I waited as she paused for a moment of reverence to my hair dryer, then plunged into the reason for the call. "I have the most wonderful news," she announced, her voice thrilling to an unfamiliar pitch of excitement. It takes a lot to get Mama excited.

"What?"

"Steve Marshall is gittin' a divorce!"

"Mother! That is awful news!" I chided sharply. "That's not wonderful!"

"Yes, it is!" she replied adamantly, her cheerfulness not interrupted one iota by my chastisement. "You always had a crush on him in high school."

"That was twenty years ago."

She talked right over me as she often does. "I'll never forget how you used to sit by the phone, hopin' he'd call and ask you for a date. But he never did because he was all tied up with Sue Ann. Now, she's run off with the pool boy and left Steve with them twins in that big ol' house. After all these years, you're finally gonna get a chance! Ain't the Lord good?"

I rolled my eyes, a frequent habit of mine when in conversation with my mama about my love life or, rather, lack of one. "Mother, I am not interested. I haven't even seen him in four or five years."

"He still looks the same 'cept his hair is thinner and he's gittin' older." She paused for a quick moment before adding "like you." The dagger was plunged firmly into my heart as she reminded me in her not too subtle way that the older I got, the harder it was to find a husband to replace the one who left me a long time ago. She continued, "And you know he's got plenty of money. He's made a killin' puttin' up them mobile home parks all over the state. Now, we're very lucky that Melinda gets hold of these things before anyone else. His lawyer just filed the divorce papers yesterday, so you're a step ahead of all the other single women who'll be settin' their caps for him, and you can bet your bottom dollar that they'll be plenty of 'em, too."

Melinda, in addition to being my older sister by six years and only sibling, is Mama's chief cohort in the conspiracy to marry me off. For twenty years she has been the clerk of courts in Dexter, running unopposed in the past six elections. Melinda, hands down, is Mama's favorite. She is the one that Mama considers to be the stunningly successful one in the family because she is an elected official and because she has been married for twenty-five years to Sanders Tyler, called Sandy for short. He is indeed a wonderful man, who owns one of the few full-service gas stations left in the country. He also has his hands full since he must take care of so many women—Melinda, who is a handful by herself, Mama, his widowed mother, me, and their daughter Claire, a senior in college. That is to say he gets an awful lot of calls about flat tires, leaking hot-water heaters, fallen trees in the yards, and once I called him to help me find a lizard that had skittered in when I opened the door to let in my dog, Kudzu. Melinda, knowing how much I adore my brother-in-law, points out that it would be in Sandy's best interest for me to find a husband and take some of the burden off him. Needless to say, she keeps a careful eye on all the divorce filings, for Mama's and Sandy's sake more than mine. In the ten years since my divorce, I have suffered through many such phone calls, blind dates, pleadings and badgerings. Mama worries that each year tacked onto my cumulative number edges me closer to the "high risk" category of growing old alone. She searches diligently for comfort where she can find it, often saying with a sigh, "Well, at least you did get married once, so it shows that you can do it again if you set your mind to it." My mama isn't the only maternal one worrying over the fate of her unmarried girl child. In the South, mothers determine their womb's worth by if and how well their daughters marry. Mama feels that I am compromising her reputation as a child rearer extraordinaire. When I sold my second book on the heels of the tremendous success of the first one, she had reason for celebration since that book sold at an auction for more money than I could make in twenty years of writing obits. I stopped by to see her one day and found her at her kitchen table working hard with pen and paper.

"What are you doing? Your grocery list?" I asked, pouring a cup of coffee.

She looked up and smiled broadly. "Oh, no!" she said excitedly. "I'm workin' on a list of all the men you've dated who still aren't married, and all the other eligible men I know."

My eyes narrowed and I immediately moved into that defensive, ready-for-battle mode where I place both hands on my hips. "Why?"

"Because I'm gonna call 'em and tell 'em about your book!" She beamed proudly.

I didn't know what was going on, but I knew I wasn't going to like it. My voice grew sterner. "*Why?*"

"Because," she said, grinning as if she had discovered gold in the backyard. "I just got to thinkin' that when they find out that you've got some money now, surely *someone* will want to marry you!"

Hope springs maternal with that woman. But as for me, I long ago adjusted to single life and accepted the fact that I have been blessed with so many things that there's no need for complaining about a lack of passion and romance in my life. After all, I did have it once.

And, boy, did I have it.

I was so in love with Terry Houston that I floated on a cloud twenty-four hours a day after meeting him at a tailgate party before a football game at the University of Georgia. I was majoring in journalism and he was majoring in parties with a minor in girls. Or maybe it was the other way around. At any rate, I thought I could rein in that wild heart of his. I quite simply adored the ground he walked on. And for a time, he adored my piece of real estate, too. That is he did until, for some unexplained reason, he fell into lust with a woman half my size and fifteen years older than he. She had yellow hair and pumpkin-colored skin from too many years in a tanning bed. Turned out that everyone in our social circle knew about it before me. Then, after she and her best friend had a big blowup over something, the best friend decided the wife should know. So she called me with details, including times and places. She may not have been much of a friend to the other woman, but she turned out to be the best friend I ever had, even though I never met her.

That's how, after six years of married life, it all fell apart, and to be honest, I bear just as much of the blame for the failure. I worked too late, nagged too much and cooked too little. I have seen the error of my ways, and if I ever have another chance, I'm going to do much better. That was almost ten years ago, a period of time which has been filled by teary recovery, nail-biting survival, heart-spinning success and the gradual dying of my beloved father. First, I buried my heart and then I buried my daddy. For a time it seemed that there was just not enough dirt in the world to cover those two graves and put the pain to rest. Although I did stop eating for a while, I never stopped breathing, so through many prayers and one breath at a time, I inhaled and exhaled my way to a new life. But just because I once, albeit briefly, dreamed of tearing the toenails from my ex-husband's size ten feet to show my displeasure at his brutal disruption of my happiness, just because occasionally I'd still like to pluck his thick hair one strand at a time from his head, please don't get the impression that I'm bitter. I'm well past that. Although I actually do have a small savory taste of revenge every Thursday when his current wife, a much plumper version of his marital infidelity, rings up my groceries at Winn-Dixie. Things, I figure, worked out for the best.

I learned quickly after my divorce that I did not care one iota for dating. What had been sheer torture as a teenager morphed into unadulterated hell as an adult. I'd like to have a nice sit-down with those psychologists who claim that our teenage years are our most difficult in life. Whoever came up with that brilliant conclusion never tried dating in her thirties after love has wrung her heart dry and relationships are complicated by exes, children, pain-inflicted skepticism and tremulous self-confidence. I grew so tired of those monotonous conversations over dinner when you yet again explain why you're divorced and why motherhood was bypassed.

"It just never worked out to have children," I have learned to say simply and truthfully.

Somewhere along the way, I just gave up on dating, doing it only sporadically and then only to reassure my mother that I remain heterosexual. The things I do to make my mama happy. You would think that she would appreciate my effort more than she does. Yet she always points out sardonically, "It don't count unless you have more than one date with the same guy."

Give me a break. So Mama, with Melinda's help, works constantly on finding me a husband.

"I was thinkin'," Mama continued, completely undeterred by my lack of interest, "that you could call him up and invite him over for dinner. The poor man's probably starvin' for a good home-cooked meal and this could be your ticket in."

"I don't have time to call him *or* to cook dinner," I replied firmly. "I'm leavin' on book tour in a couple of weeks and I have too much to do to get ready for that."

"You can't leave at a time like this!" Mama exclaimed, despair creeping into her voice. "You'll just have to cancel. This is much more important. You can go on book tour anytime, but it's not every day that a man like Steve Marshall becomes available. You know good and well that Imogene Dillard will be all over him like flies on a dead June bug when she finds out. That girl's even more desperate than you are, and you know what they say 'bout desperate people. You've got to stay here and stake your claim."

Anger swept over me. Quickly, I bit the inside of my mouth to keep the mean retort from slapping Mama in the face. I hate the way that she discounts my career in the belief that a husband would be better. There was only a brief second of silence before she continued with her plan.

"You oughta consider asking him to bring the twins, too. Joyce told Melinda that he's havin' a fit with those girls. You know, they're just at the age to be a handful anyway and what with their mama runnin' off and settin' such a bad example, there ain't no tellin' what'll happen with 'em. I guess they're 'bout fourteen or fifteen now."

Joyce Valentine, Melinda's best friend, completes the triumvirate working to push me down the aisle. She's an assistant vice president at Dexter's biggest bank, so she keeps an eye on the financial matters of Dexter's single and soon-to-be-single men while Melinda diligently watches the divorces, bankruptcies and probate filings. Together, they compose a formidable team of snoops. Joyce is also a first cousin to Steve Marshall, their mothers having been sisters, so she, undoubtedly, was proving doubly helpful in this venture. While Mama chattered on about the necessity of canceling my book tour and how Steve should be stalked and chased down like an animal in the woods, I tried to interrupt so that I could end the phone call. But, true to form, she kept talking and never allowed me to get a word in edgewise. Finally, I took the cordless phone and walked to the front door. I opened it, reached over and pressed the doorbell, then held out the receiver toward the chimes, which rang out in harmony. She stopped. "What's that?"

"The doorbell. Someone's at the front door," I lied without the slightest tinge of guilt. "Sorry, but I've got to scoot. Talk to you later." Mama was saying something as I clicked off but I don't have a clue what it was. I slammed the door shut, then dragged my bare feet to the big red club chair next to the fireplace. I tossed the receiver on the sofa, dropped into the spongy comfort of the chair and slunk down low. I rubbed my eyes wearily and thought about the conversation.

How, I wondered, could the world view me as such a success while my mama saw me as a failure because I wasn't someone's wife? The worst part of it all was that I didn't know who was right—the world or my mama.

♡

Frustrated, I rifled through my closet after lunch, overstuffed to the point that some clothes are able to hang without benefit of a hanger, searching for outfits to take on my book tour. I had a closet full of nothing to wear. At least, not anything that would look good on television *and* on me. Plus, I was still aggravated over the conversation with Mama that morning, which was doing nothing to help my mood. I was in a dither, growing more anxious by the moment. I yanked two dresses out and walked over to the full-length mirror at the foot of my four-poster bed. I held a sleeveless red shift with matching embroidery along the neckline against me, then, with disgust, tossed it on the bed into the "heck, no!" pile. At my age, I shouldn't be buying sleeveless dresses, let alone thinking of wearing them, but I have a hateful rebellion against middle age. I held up my arm, pinched the wiggly underneath of the tricep and thought two things: "I need to have liposuction. It's the only thing that's going to help," and "If I look like this even though I work out regularly, imagine how I'd look if I didn't work out." Both thoughts punched me hard.

As my mama likes to helpfully point out, I'm no longer a spring chicken. I am at that point in life that divides youthful stupidity from sedate wisdom, the point when conventional knowledge proclaims that half your life has been lived—the half where you're climbing toward the pinnacle—and that the half that lies ahead is the downward slide.

I detest that phrase "middle age." It smacks distastefully of images like thinning hair, slacking jawlines and expanding waistlines. There simply is nothing pretty about those two words when put together. You would think that those geniuses on Madison Avenue could come up with a better descriptive phrase, and if not Madison Avenue, certainly someone in Los Angeles. Those LA types are the ones who really hate to age, so I can't believe they, of all people, have let me down on this. But for the record, I'm not middle aged. I did recently turn forty to the delight of my *much* older sister who enjoyed throwing a big surprise party to celebrate the aging of her baby sister, never realizing how much older that made *her*. Other than my daddy, though, my family lives well into their nineties, several making it past the century mark. That would mean that I'm still several years away from my midpoint. Just so you know.

I've never been impressed with the way I look, and that lack of being impressed hasn't improved with age. In fact, it dramatically increased after those three months I spent in Hollywood, consulting on the movie made from my first book. They even gave me a bit part in that movie, but since it was as a worn-out, raggedy-looking waitress, it wasn't anything to write home about. So I didn't. That combined with the sheer, perfect beauty of those Hollywood mannequins made me feel worse with each passing day about my deepening crow's-feet and sagging skin. When I boarded the plane at LAX—first class, thanks to the studio—I resolved that my Hollywood days were behind me. I can stay home and feel bad about myself. I don't have to traipse across the country to do it.

It's puzzling to me but I do have people tell me from time to time that I'm attractive. Odd. I look in the mirror and wonder how others could see that when all I see is a pug nose that's off centered, a face too round without definition and a lopsided mouth, though my teeth are nice and straight. If you were to ask me what I consider to be my best feature, I would say—and even this would be with hesitation—my feet, even though they're a bit wider than I would like. I am never pleased with what I see, especially my hair, although I lightened the auburn in it to a golden red. Still, it has not looked good since 1989 when my hair was so voluminous that it kindly distracted from my face. Personally, I am living solely for the day when big hair returns in all of its split end glory. Meanwhile, I just do the best I can with what I've got, and fortunately some people see it as being a lot better than I see it. All I can figure is that pretty is as pretty does. I will say I have a good personality. I'm friendly, outgoing, witty, with my daddy's socially seductive sense of humor, and I treat everyone, regardless of social or economic status, the same, so apparently the beauty that others see is spiritually, not physically, influenced. But don't get the notion that I don't care how I look. I care mightily. I spend a good bit of time and money trying to look my best. Clothes and accessories, particularly high heels and purses, are a hobby of mine. My only hobby, in fact.

In an effort to improve my self-image which, after a divorce, enough one-time dates and my mother's constant disapproval of my single status, really needed improvement, I threw myself into my career. I swear I don't know which is worse—your husband leaving you for a beautiful woman who makes you look bad, or leaving you for an ugly one who makes you look pathetic. First I threw myself into my job as the obituary writer at the *Dexter Tribune*. In the South, it's considered to be an important job because death is big news in a small town. And if the deceased was able to hold off eternity until a long and illustrious life had been achieved, it's a front-page-making, above-the-fold story. In Dexter, where I was born and raised, my position as the town's chief chronicler of death was much more impressive to the local residents than when my first book hit the *New York Times* best seller list.

"Ain't nobody but them Yankees read that paper nohow, and why in thunderation would you care what *they* think?" cantankerous Cousin Cora sniffed, placing a perfume-scented lace hanky to her ancient nose. Cousin Cora's granddaddy was a Confederate colonel who died at Chickamauga. For decades, the family heralded him as a fallen hero in one of the war's bloodiest battles, until the newspaper in Atlanta did some digging and discovered that, in actuality, he died from diarrhea. Cousin Cora was in such a fit of disgrace that she took to her bed. That was twenty-five years ago and she hasn't left her huge, hand-carved canopy bed since that dark day. You can do things like that when your daddy was one of the original investors in a product known as Coca-Cola. She ceremoniously holds court from the monstrous bed, which is covered in silk sheets imported from France and trimmed in hand-crocheted lace from Belgium while her ever-attentive Lessie Belle flutters around, answering to Cousin Cora's silly whims and constant demands.

Despite the position of prestige guaranteed by my job as obituary writer, I needed more diversion from my pain and more help on my self-confidence. So I started working at night on a novel about a small Southern town and the colorful people who live there. It was published, became a best seller and spun off a series of books about that little town. Now, millions of copies later, my self-image is greatly improved. But not as far as Mama is concerned. She still thinks I need to be married, and all the money in the world isn't going to change that.

My life in Dexter, for the most part, is comfortable and at times cozy, particularly in the winter when I keep a fire burning constantly. I have a small, two-story stone cottage with ivy that climbs the chimney, roses that bloom beautifully in the spring and a kitchen that is used only at Thanksgiving when I prepare dinner and host my entire family. Mostly, I just eat peanut butter and crackers or whatever else I can find to nibble. I like instant grits a lot, too, particularly the ones with cheddar cheese and bacon bits. I worry only that there is coffee and cream in the house for mornings, and other than that, food is just not a big deal.

Lately, development has begun to crowd in on me and take my sense of peace away. Bulldozers hum, cars zoom and people noisily clatter by. I prefer the quietness of woods and rivers and people who stay away from me when I need solitude in which to write. Although I am mostly fine with just the company of my chubby red dachshund Kudzu, there's a sense of restlessness that seems to encompass me. I feel I no longer belong where I am, yet I don't know where I should be. I just want peace for my battered soul, which makes me no different from anyone else.

With just a couple of weeks to go before I was due to leave, there I was rummaging through my closet. Mostly, I was just fretting over what I should wear for which television show and trying not to duplicate the few clothes that make me look halfway thin on television. I'm telling you, if you have a full bosom, there's just no way not to look fat on that little screen. My nerves were already prickly over the excess of my flesh and my mama's busybody ways when the kid next door started roaring his minibike up and down the driveway, taking great pride in revving it as loud as it would go. I just wanted to scream. Then, the phone rang.

"Hello?" I tried to sound nicer than I felt. I didn't think it worked.

"You are not going to believe this!" The tone was incredulous.

"Good afternoon, Jamie," I replied tersely. "It's nice to hear from you, too."

She ignored the comment. "Listen to this: the president of the Rotary club in Bliss, Mississippi, called and requested that you speak to the club on the day you're in town for your book signing. Can you imagine? They want a big author like you, an author who gets a lot of money for speaking engagements, to speak to a little club?" She paused for a moment and then curiously asked, "What's a Rotary club?"

"It's a big deal in small towns," I responded. "It's a service organization dedicated to helping the community."

"How? By having bake sales and things like that?"

"Sometimes."

She snorted. I couldn't tell if it was a snort of sarcasm, thoughtfulness or disbelief. "Well, I felt compelled to tell you, but don't worry. I'll call and get you off the hook. Even though the guy did say that Susan Marie was anxious for you to do it in order to promote the book signing. Just leave it to me."

"You don't have to get me off the hook. I'll be happy to do it." I clearly remember the days when clubs like Rotary were the only ones that wanted me to speak to their groups. You have to be loyal. Besides, any time you have the opportunity to expose new people to your work, you should do it.

"Uh, excuse me? Did you say you would do it?"

"Of course. I'm happy to do it. Anything that Susan Marie

wants. Now, let me ask you what you think I should wear for *Good Morning, America* and the *Today* show."

It was that simple. One phone call, one "yes," one dismayed publicist and the wheels were set in motion for one troubled heart to find more trouble.

Chapter 2

Mama was mad, which meant she was pouting. This is not a pretty sight. I hope you never have to see it. I knew the moment that I saw her that trouble was hovering because the corners of her mouth were turned down into a hard line, and her dark eyes, normally lively and sparkling, were almost black with no reflective glimmer. As though that wasn't enough evidence, when she saw me, she slammed down her ceramic coffee cup, the one I brought her from Panama City when I was ten, on the cherry-stained table next to her recliner, and cream-colored coffee sloshed over the edge.

Kudzu happily scampered in and I brought up the rear, the screen door slamming behind us with a soft thud. Never suspecting that Mama's current spell of displeasure had anything to do with me, I said cheerfully, "Hey! Whatcha doin'?"

"Hey, baby," she greeted lovingly. She wasn't talking to me. She was talking to Kudzu, who immediately recognized her signal and flitted flirtatiously over to the dark-rose-colored plush recliner. I've heard that dogs take on the personality of their owners. I believe this to be true. Kudzu's as big a flirt as I am. She also sides with the one she believes is most inclined to give her the biggest treats. That would be my mother.

Kudzu lifted her long, reddish brown body upward and sat flat down on her big round behind. Preciously, she put both her paws into the one hand that Mama dropped over the armrest for her to touch. "Your maw-maw's sick, honey."

The clever canine played it for all it was worth, looking appropriately saddened at the news. She even managed to drop her head slightly. It worked. Mama reached down to release the footrest, saying as she did so, "You know where to come to get fed, don't you, honey? That mean mama of yours won't take care of the baby, will she, like your maw-maw does."

I rolled my eyes. I do this a lot around my mother.

"What's wrong?" I asked in a way that implied aggravation, not sympathy. In the two weeks since she first brought up Steve Marshall's divorce, we had managed to come to agreement that my pending courtship with the town's newest most eligible man would have to wait until I returned from my book tour. So I knew that wasn't the problem.

"Nothing," she replied curtly, shuffling toward the kitchen. I heard the "g" she added to that word and knew immediately that "nothing" meant "plenty." On the other hand, "nothin'" would have meant "nothing."

I followed her into the kitchen, folded my arms and took my battle stance. "You're mad that you're not goin' on this trip with me, aren't you?"

She refused to look at me as she pulled a new bag of doggie treats from a pantry shelf and tore it open. "I've got a sick headache." She looked as though she barely had the strength to open the bag. Her shoulders drooped, the front of her NASCAR sweatshirt—where she got that, I have no idea—had a coffee stain on it, and her silver hair, still liberally sprinkled with the black hair of her youth, was badly disheveled. Not that Mama has a lot of good-hair days anyway. "I'm sick on my stomach, too."

"Have you taken anything?" I tried to sound compassionate but I knew I was being played. When Mama doesn't get her way, she always gets sick.

"I haven't felt much like eatin' anything, but I did have a couple of sody crackers and a glass of buttermilk."

"Well, that shoulda helped."

"It didn't," she snapped. "I was havin' a weak spell so I was just drinkin' a cup of coffee when you come." She tossed a couple of treats to Kudzu, who danced around jubilantly on the blue-and-white tiled floor and then scooted under the antique breakfast table to enjoy them uninterrupted. I scrunched my face in annoyance at the miniature traitor, but she was too busy enjoying the fruits of betrayal to pay me any mind.

I looked back at Mama, who was fastening the bag of treats with a clothespin. "When I'm sick at my stomach, coffee is the last thing I can drink." It was an innocent observation. But let's just say that it didn't sit well with Mama. She whirled around, her strength suddenly and miraculously regained, pointed a finger crooked with mild arthritis in my direction and issued my comeuppance.

"Let me tell you something, young lady: don't you sass me! Especially when I'm in the sad shape that I'm in. I'll bring you down a notch or two."

It was starting to get funny because I knew that what she was really wanting was some attention. So I called a halt to the battle. Mama, I admit, can be mighty aggravating, but when all's said and done, she's my buddy. There are just times when I have to overlook her eccentricities because, after all, she was raised in the foothills of the Appalachians and those Scotch-Irish she is descended from are quite an interesting bunch of folks. They tickle me when they start calling each other "quaire," a mountain term for "odd." As though the one doing the name-calling isn't!

"Mama, why don't you go in yonder and sit down and I'll make you a bowl of soup. I've got some time before I need to leave for the airport." This mollified her—a little attention goes a long way with her—and she shuffled back to the living room. For a seventy-four-year-old woman, she gets around pretty good, except when it suits her otherwise. I made a bowl of chicken soup, placed it, along with a napkin, silverware and a cold glass of buttermilk, on a tray decorated with a Santa Claus with a Coke in his hand and took it to her. I found her fully reclined, shielding her eyes with a weary hand. She looked up weakly as I set the tray on her lap. Mama missed her calling. She could have been a great Hollywood actress.

"Thank you," she mumbled softly, as if they were her dying words.

I sat down on the faded floral sofa and leaned toward her, placing my elbows on my knees. "Now, what is this all really about? Does it have anything to do with me going on this book tour without you?"

She cut her eyes sideways toward me, puckering her lips into a pout and then answering as a sudden surge of strength swept over her body. "You know what a big help I was to you the last time. You said so yourself."

I nodded. "That's right, you were a big help what with all the entertaining stories you told as I was driving. It made the time pass by fast."

She straightened her shoulders with pride, and the small

fleshy pouches of too many biscuits and cream gravy that reside above and below her waistline, or what once was her waistline, thinned noticeably. "And don't forget, I was the dog's nanny." She pointed her finger for emphasis. "You can never say that I didn't carry my share of the load on that trip."

"That's exactly right," I agreed, my mind flickering back to the book tour that trailed across the state of Mississippi, a driving tour in which we visited seven cities in seven days, and my mother, who had rarely been out of the state of Georgia, had enjoyed each mile with supreme relish. The booksellers, too, had been intrigued by her folksy charm and chatty personality. It was definitely Mama, not me, who had been the star on that trip.

"I could have been a big help this time out. And you need it, too, what with you flouncing around all over God's green creation."

"But you know what?" I asked in the kind of tone that she once used on me when I was a child. The irony of the role reversal was not lost on me. "You're going to be an even bigger help by staying here to take care of Kudzu. That's an enormous help." It sounded patronizing but it was true.

Her lips puckered tightly again, producing an even, almost invisible row of those insidious lines around the mouth that appear with age or years of smoking. My mama, thankfully, was never a smoker and I suspect that is why her skin, which has seen seven decades of continual use, looks many years younger. It certainly has nothing to do with drinking water since Mama only manages, at best, to swallow a couple of glasses a week. I look at her and the strong health she enjoys and know that she is a living contradiction to the wisdom of modern medicine. Unlike me, who does everything that any expert in any magazine says I should do, she does nothing. Absolutely nothing. She religiously coats her arteries with generous doses of Crisco, never exercises (although her backside would benefit from a few miles of walking a week), never drinks water, never uses moisturizer or sunscreen, and the thought of watching her caffeine intake never crossed her stubborn mind. However, she is a staunch old-fashioned Baptist so she doesn't drink, smoke, play cards or dance.

One evening we were out to dinner, along with my sister Melinda and my grown niece Claire, when Mama picked up a yeast roll to butter. We three, health-conscious zealots that we are, watched in silent amazement as she smeared the roll with more butter than I would use in a month. We didn't protest or comment. We've learned better. The sense of it falls on deaf ears while the intrusion of such unwelcome advice only stirs up a bicker. The three of us, wide eyed and slack jawed, just shook our heads in united disbelief.

"Just think," I commented brightly to the other two, "we've got her genes!"

"Yes, I know," Melinda replied, nodding. "I've got her varicose veins and butt. Neither of which, I might add, is anything to brag about."

Mama continued to argue her case. She could have been a terrific lawyer as well as a great actress.

"We could have gotten your sister to take care of Kudzu," Mama popped up and pointed out. "Where's there's a will, there's a way. Clearly, there was no will in this situation."

I sighed. It made me weary to even consider the thought of pulling, pushing, prodding my mother through LaGuardia or Los Angeles International. I may be dumb but I'm not stupid, and I knew better than any of that. Goodness gracious, taking her to Wal-Mart is a major ordeal, and there she always has a cart she can hang on to as she meanders through the aisles. I envy the pace at which my mama lives her life, though. It is slow, deliberate and enjoyed, tasted thoughtfully like a chef savoring his finest creation. Unlike the pace of mine, where each morning begins with the mild remnant of the stress headache from the previous day of deadlines and the promise of a stronger headache to come. Book tours are stressful enough in their own right with before-the-sun-rises mornings, bewitching-hour nights and sometimes three airports in the light of one day. This tour to launch my new novel was twenty cities in twenty-five days, including four cross-country flights. Taking my mama never entered any crevice of my mind, not even the whimsical or idiotic crevices.

"Mama, please," I said in a pleading tone, closer to pitiful than I like to be. Kudzu, refreshed from her abundance of treats, leapt happily into mother's lap at that moment. Mama smiled, well pleased at the show of affection, and stroked the shiny coat of her best buddy.

"I'm only gonna say one more thing about it and that'll be that," Mama promised. I knew better but sometimes I like to live with naïve hope, so I nodded as though I believed that would be her last word. I also believe that all politicians are honest, the IRS is unceasingly fair, and all preachers have the Lord's best interest as theirs. "If I had had my druthers, I'd be goin'. But not for my sake, mind you. For yours." This I couldn't wait to hear. I didn't have to wait long. "It's obvious that you ain't no good in attractin' a husband. I coulda helped scrounge one up for you. I'm sure that in all the places we would have went, I could have found at least one decent one."

My head dropped forward so quickly in beleaguered despair that I felt the muscles pop, pop, pop like a cap gun as they released the tension that had stiffened them since I entered the front door half an hour earlier. Had it only been thirty minutes? My gracious, it seemed like hours. My shoulders sagged visibly from the weighty burden of Mama's matrimonial expectations for me. Sometimes it doesn't pay to argue. Other times, though, you have to stand your ground.

"Mama, I'm not looking for a husband." I was plumb tuckered out from all of these restatements of my intentions and nonintentions.

"Well, you should be." She jutted her chin upward.

"Why?"

"Because it's the thing to do. Everybody in their right mind knows it's the thing to do. It's normal."

I stood up and smoothed my red skirt, a movement which caught Mama's eye. "That's skirt's too short. I hope you're not plannin' on wearin' that thing on television and embarrassin' the whole lot of us by showin' your butt."

A spark of my daddy's temper flashed across me. I could hear him saying, "That confounded woman! She'd drive a sober man to drinkin'." I put my hands on my hips and retorted—brilliantly, I thought—"You worry about your butt and I'll worry about mine. Which, by the way, yours could do with some worryin' about."

"Abigail! You'd better watch the way you talk to your mama! How'd you feel if the good Lord came and took me home tonight and you had to live with the disgraceful way you talked to your mama today?"

That worked. It always did. Even though I had heard it two thousand, four hundred and sixty-four times in my life, it worked the desired, intended magic and I backed down. It's an interesting thing about mamas: no matter how old you get, they always know how to make you toe the line.

"Mama, I've got to go," I said in a suddenly gentle voice. "I don't want to miss my plane." I walked over to the recliner, bent down, and kissed her on the forehead, and then I leaned down and kissed the top of Kudzu's head and stroked her back. "You two girls be good and I'll call you when I get to New York. Don't forget to watch me on the morning show tomorrow."

Mama smiled. She likes to brag about a daughter who shows

up on television every now and then, even if she does think my skirt's too short and my hair's too red. One of her constant moans to anyone who will listen is, "I used to pray every night that I wouldn't have no redheaded children. And the sweet Lord saw fit to answer my prayers. Then whatta ya know? I get one that don't have no more sense than to make herself a redhead. Oh, Lord, what have I done so wrong in this vale of tears and heartaches to deserve such a thing?"

"We'll be watchin'," she promised with a smile, a smile that erased the memory of the previous tensions. "I wouldn't miss it for the world. I love watchin' my little girl on TV. It's a *big* deal." She paused for a second to study on something and then said, "If anyone asks why I didn't come along, just tell 'em I wasn't feelin' up to it."

I felt it was a pretty safe assumption that no one was going to ask but I played along. "If anyone asks, I'll tell 'em the truth. That *if* you had been invited, you'd been there in a heartbeat."

She laughed. "Well, I reckon that's right. No sense in tellin' anything different than the truth."

I smiled, threw up my hand in a wave, pushed the screen door open, and just as I stepped on the broad porch that runs the full length of the old, white-framed farmhouse, I heard her words ringing behind me. The same words I have heard since I was knee high to a grasshopper, the same instructions she has given every time I left our house for a date, a social outing or a trip.

"Now, you be sweet. You hear me?"

Chapter 3

I can be such a smarty-pants sometimes that I just aggravate the heck out of myself. That said, just know that the heck sure was aggravated out of me as I drove along a rural Mississippi back road trying to find my way to Bliss.

"Now, why should I be surprised?" I asked myself. I talk to myself a lot—my friends say that I'm my own best friend—especially when I'm driving alone in a car. For some reason, I find myself to be particularly good company during those drives. "I shouldn't be at all surprised that I'm having a hard time finding Bliss. I've been looking for it all these years and haven't found it. What makes me think I'd find it now?" I chortled sarcastically, and myself answered back equally sarcastically, "You're so clever that you should be writing books for a living!"

As my two halves brilliantly bantered back and forth in a sparkling repartee, they united in their conclusion that we were flat-out lost, somewhere in the backwoods of rural Mississippi where my cell phone had flashed "No Service" for twenty miles and where I couldn't remember how long it had been since I had seen a gas station or even a house, for that matter. Do you know that there is actually a twenty-mile stretch of road somewhere in the United States that *does not* have a McDonalds on it? It's an oversight, I'm certain, and will quickly be remedied as soon as the corporate office hears about it. I had, though, recently seen what I believed to be an armadillo, which gravely concerned me since I had never heard of armadillos in Mississippi. I was afraid that somehow I had really taken the wrong road and wound up in Texas.

Of course, if I were in Texas, then I deserved to be, since it was all my own doing. Instead of following the directions that Jamie's assistant had faxed to my hotel in Little Rock—that would have been much too sensible—I had devised my own route. Using the practically worthless one-page map that the rental car company had given me, I, with great bravado, had decided to take the "scenic route." My great bravado, I should probably add here, often segues seamlessly into what then becomes known as my great stupidity. I had yet to see one sign that said anything about Bliss or any other town in Mississippi.

I have another bad habit when I'm driving. When I'm not talking to myself, I'm thinking about myself. Pretty self-absorbed, I know, but the truth nonetheless. Since driving out of Little Rock on that bright, clear September day, I had been reflecting on the events of the past week since I left home and embarked on this whirlwind book tour. I had started with the *Today* show and *Good Morning, America* in New York, then flew to Chicago and Detroit for television and book signings and then to Los Angeles, where I had appeared on *Larry King* followed by *The Tonight Show* with Jay Leno. It's rare for an author to make an appearance on that show, but I had met his producer once at a luncheon to promote literacy. He sat at my table and laughed so hard at a couple of stories I told about my family that he said, "Here's my card. When your next book comes out, have your publicist give me a call and we'll book you for the show. Jay loves ordinary people who can tell a funny story and tell it well."

I was under a lot of pressure to perform well, since most of the New York publishing industry was looking for me to make a big splash and hopefully open the door for other authors. No one had forgotten how Truman Capote's regular appearances on the show with Johnny Carson in the seventies had kept his career thriving when it otherwise would have been extinguished in a haze of overindulgence. So I told some of my best stories. The one I told that tickled everyone to a delicious shade of pink was one I put in my first book, about my daddy's cousin Zoey. She's an old maid who's been in an old folks' home for close to fifteen years, but for the past thirty years, she has steadfastly clung to the belief that she's married to Burt Reynolds. She also claims that he visits her daily up at the home. She even believes that they have a son together, and when Burt's filming a movie, the son visits instead. I asked her one day what her son's name was.

"Why, Reynolds, of course!"

I smiled. "Yes, I know that, but what's his first name?" We like to play along since she has only these daydreams to entertain her in a life that is ebbing toward its end.

She smiled beatifically, the broad grin causing the deep lines and wrinkles on her eighty-five-year-old face to hang in fleshy folds from her eyes to her chin. "I told 'cha. His name is Reynolds Reynolds." Her faded blue eyes glistened with a faraway look of pride and love. "Ain't that the most bodacious name you ever heard in all your born days?"

When I talked to Mama the next afternoon after I told that

story on *The Tonight Show*, she was busting at the seams to tell me the latest news.

"You ain't never gonna believe what happened to Zoey today," Mama proclaimed.

"What?" I didn't know whether to be nervous or not. One thing I've learned about telling such things to the media is that you never know when they're going to backfire on you. Trust me, I have enough burn scars to prove that.

"She got three dozen roses delivered to the home! One dozen was red, one dozen was yellow, and one dozen was pink. And listen to this: each card was signed 'Love, Burt!' "

I was standing in the middle of the airport in Dallas and nearly dropped my cell phone. "What!" I exclaimed. "Are you serious? Mama, you gotta be kiddin' me!"

"Not a'tall. But who knows if it was the real Burt or someone just bein' kind to an old woman. Maybe three different people for all we know. But it don't matter none, because the newspaper's done sent a reporter and photographer up to the home, and tomorrow, Zoey's gonna be on the front page of the newspaper. You couldn't have give her a mee'on dollars and made her no happier."

I was thinking about world-changing things like that on the drive to Bliss, so between my distractions, my conversations and my improvised directions, it was quite possible that I had taken the wrong turn, or missed one. Just when I was becoming very concerned that I would soon be seeing the Rio Grande followed by the border of Mexico, and myself was doing nothing to offer reassurance of any kind to its other half, I saw a tiny gas station, so run down that I was certain it had been closed for years. I slowed the car, edging toward the clapboard building with dingy white paint, most of which had peeled off or just dissipated into chalk, leaving exposed gray termite-nibbled wood. The gas pumps were old, the kind with rotating numbers, not the kind I used on a regular basis with digital readouts and a nifty slot for placing my ever-handy credit card. Figuring it was a waste of hope, I pulled onto the somewhat graveled but mostly dirt parking area, giving a serious eye to the front of the store. There was a red metal banner across the front of the weathered screen door that advertised Wonder Bread and large round, rusting discs that hung on either side of the door. One advertised RC Cola and the other touted Pure Oil, long lost in a maze of corporate mergers.

"Oh, great," I mumbled. "Pure Oil. That's real encouraging."

I almost drove back onto the highway but two things stopped me. It looked like the door behind the screen was open and that the store building was long and rambling as though it had a living area in back. Pulled over to the side at the back of the store was an ancient pickup, a big black GMC from the 1950s with a cattle railing attached to the bed. It appeared that there might be some life around, so I got out of the car, pushed my sunglasses to the top of my head and took a few crunching steps on the bits of gravel to the entrance. The screen door squeaked when I pulled it open, and I heard a friendly voice call out, "Howdy do, ma'am! Come right on in!"

The room was dark, lighted by only the shallow natural light that trickled in from the door and small windows. The floor was old wood that had been darkened by years of oiling. When my eyes adjusted, I was a bit startled to see an older man, somewhere in his sixties perhaps, with a large barrel-thick waist, dressed in overalls and a white tee shirt. He had no hair on his head but plenty on his face, with a bushy gray beard that was a little too long and scruffy for my liking.

"Good afternoon," I replied, easing on in and gently releasing the door to close behind me. "I didn't know if you were open or not." I inhaled deeply and liked the smell that filled my lungs, the fragrance of tobacco, wood flooring soaked with oil, chocolate Yoo-hoos, bananas and hoop cheese in a red waxed ring that sat next to the register. It reminded me of the store near my granny's house that my cousins and I used to visit on Sunday afternoons while the adults sat around the living room and talked. If it was summertime, we came from the swimming hole, lugging inner tubes and dripping drops of the Chattahoochee River back into the hardened red earth. If it was another season, we sauntered the one-mile walk, entertaining ourselves with games of I Spy and tall tales of life as a kid in rural Georgia.

"Yes'um, we're open. The only place around for 'bout twenty-five or so miles." He chuckled and leaned forward to rest his elbows on the countertop. "Might not look it right now but we get a gracious plenty amount of business. What can we do ya for?"

I wanted directions but thought it too rude to ask without making a purchase. "Something cold to drink would be nice." I smiled and he returned it with a bigger, broader one.

"Help yo'self. Over yonder's the drink machines." He gestured to the corner where I found two refrigerated machines, both the old-fashioned kind that opened from the top with the drinks laid down on top of each other. Funny how something that simple can scoop you up and haul you back to a place you haven't thought of in years. Suddenly a nostalgic chill swept over me and I was transported back to those simple Sunday afternoons of my childhood, when I thought that Billy Gooch was the meanest boy I'd ever known in my life. That was about seven or eight years before he became the *cutest* boy I'd ever seen in my life. The McCorkles owned that old store, but Mrs. McCorkle closed it down about twenty years ago after her husband got killed in a tractor accident while he was getting up hay. She's in the home now with Cousin Zoey, but since she has Alzheimer's, she never recognizes Burt when he visits. That really rankles Zoey, who'll carry on and say, "How in the dickens could Ocie not know him? We've been married for years and she was at the weddin' and saw the whole thing happen. I'll never forget that she give me the purttiest set of dishrags you ever saw. You'd think that, of all things, she wouldn't forget that. Bless Pete!"

I shook myself out of the remembrance, although I hated to leave that moment in time and that uncomplicated life when so many, including my daddy, my uncle Samuel, my granny and my aunt Pauline, were still vibrant threads woven into the cloth of my existence. But time and death had unraveled that cloth, and now, although some of the yardage was still strong and beautiful, the edges were frayed from the pieces that had broken away. Back when I was that chubby-cheeked, freckle-faced kid, I didn't know, and I'm ashamed to say that I didn't care, how fragile those delicate threads were or how quickly and unexpectedly they could tear away from your life. One thing I've learned, though, is that when strong memorable times like that grab you by the heart, you need to just stop for a second and fully feel it again, live it again, if only for a moment. Standing in the corner of that light-deprived country store, I closed my eyes, took a deep, lung-filling breath of those smells of yesteryears and submersed myself in those happy Sunday afternoons of my childhood. When I reopened my eyes, I was still lost somewhere in Mississippi, but my spirit, tired from ten battering days of travel and demands, was completely revived by those days of long ago and many miles away.

I couldn't decide what I wanted to drink, so I chose a sinfully good chocolate Yoo-hoo, a Dr. Pepper in a glass bottle, for there were no cans in that little store, and a bag of Cheetos. When I travel, I devoutly believe that two things don't count—calories and money. I have never had any success convincing myself otherwise. At home, I would never go into a store and buy a chocolate drink and a bag of Cheetos, the big-grab size no less, but I didn't give it a second thought as I headed to the register. I placed the items on the counter, and then realized I had not brought my purse in.

"Oh, my gosh!" I said, slapping my forehead. "I left my money in the car. I'll be right back."

He had already rung up and bagged the items in a little brown sack by the time I returned. "That'll be $3.54, please."

I dug out four somewhat crumpled dollar bills that I had stuffed into the inside pocket of my purse and handed them with a smile to the old man. He took the money, but before turning back to the register, he cocked his head to one side and grinned with one corner of his mouth. "You ain't from around these parts, are ya?"

Instantly, I thought that I had been nosed out of incognito by my clothes, which were perfectly appointed, including a hot pink cashmere sweater with a wide neck that clung to the outer edges of my shoulders, a hot pink and bright green tiny floral-patterned straight skirt that narrowed further just above my knees, then stopped, and high-heeled sandals in the same shade of deep rose pink. Yes, I know I was traveling, but that *is* comfortable for me. Although I have been known to kick off my shoes and drive barefooted on plenty of occasions. I don't want to scruff the heels of those expensive things. So there I was, thinking that my elegant, gorgeous attire had caught his eye and singled me out as a nonresident of the area. I was pretty sure of myself, so I smiled confidently and asked, "Now, how did you know that?"

Before he answered, he reached over to the other side of the register, picked up a dirty white foam cup and spat a mouthful of disgusting brown saliva into it. I know I made a face. I couldn't help it. But he was so busy spitting that he wasn't seeing, so he didn't notice my disgust. I realized then that one of his hair-covered cheeks pouched out more than the other. How can anyone walk around with a big ol' wad of tobacco stuffed between his gum and cheek? When the old man turned back to me, I noticed that two large droplets of dark brown tobacco juice clung to the silvery hairs on his chin. I tried to divert my attention, paying a lot of attention to not paying attention.

"I knowed you weren't from 'round here, first, cause I know everybody in these parts. Second, I knowed it because the tag on the front of your car says 'Avis.'"

My fashion bubble busted, I mumbled, "Oh, I see." He handed my change to me and I said, "Now that my cover has been blown, I need to ask for directions."

"You headed down to Jackson?" He spat into the cup again while a big yellow cat with a big attitude jumped onto the counter. She bared her teeth, showing that one in the front was missing, and growled before the man patted her and she settled down.

I ignored the snaggletoothed varmint. "No, sir. Bliss."

"Bliss! Why, little lady, you done pass the road to Bliss 'bout thirty miles ago!"

My shoulders sagged. "Great." My book signing in Little Rock had been at noon, so I had had the luxury of a sunny afternoon of driving. I glanced out the door and saw that the shadows of the afternoon were growing long. I looked at my watch. Almost five. Still not bad since my activities in Bliss were scheduled for the next day, beginning with the Rotary club event at noon. "How far am I from there?"

He shrugged and stroked his beard, missing, of course, the brown droplets that still hung there. "It's 'bout thirty minutes back to where you shoulda turned and then from there, 'bout another hour. So, all told, 'bout an hour and a half."

I sighed. "Well, that's not bad. Sir, could you give me directions?"

"Homer's the name, miss. Just call me Homer."

"Thank you."

"Let's see. Just turn left onto this black top out here, follow it for like I said, 'bout thirty miles, and there'll be another black-top that turns off this 'un. You'll turn right. But there's a sign there big as day. Ain't no way you can miss it." Then, realizing that I had missed it, coming from the other direction, he grinned and said, "If you'll just look fer it. Big ol' sign. Says 'Bliss' on it and it has an arrow pointing in the right direction. Just follow that two lane for 'bout forty-five miles and you'll be there."

I picked up the little brown sack. "Thank you, Homer. I appreciate it."

I pushed the screen door open but was stopped by Homer's voice asking, "If'n you don't mind, could I ask ya what ya do for a livin'?"

"I'm an author."

His eyes widened. It sure looked like I had impressed ol' Homer. "That so? My boy, he's a writer. Wrote him a book. Yes'um, he shore did. Ain't had no luck gittin' it published yet. He wrote off to some of 'em folks up in New York, but he ain't heared back from most of 'em. One of 'em did write back and said in a mighty fine way, too, that he had talent and he should just keep at it. What's yo'r name?"

"Abby Houston. That's wonderful that someone thinks that your son has talent. New York publishers are mighty hard to impress," I said, forcing an unnatural smile onto my face. I said it mainly because I knew it was important to Homer. Pride just beamed all over his face, and I supposed he didn't have a lot of things to beam about. Since I got published, about three out of every five people I meet either write, have a book they've been meaning to write, or have someone related to them who writes.

"You ain't got no words of advice that I could hand out to 'im, do ya?"

I didn't have any that I could hand out in about thirty seconds, which was about all the time I had to expend on it. After all, I had unwittingly managed to put myself an hour behind schedule. Standing with my hand on the rusted screen of the ancient door, I happened to glance out and see three old, weathered rocking chairs situated under the wide overhang of the tin roof. I imagined three old men sitting there, rocking and talking about corn that wasn't growing, skies that weren't raining or women who weren't cooperating. I envy people who can live like that. People who can mosey through a day without a watch reminding them of things to do and appointments to keep. It was what I missed about the world of my childhood. I turned my attention back to the storekeeper.

"Homer?" I tilted my head toward him, then surprised myself with the words that followed. "How 'bout you and me having a seat out here in these rockin' chairs? I'll drink this nice, cold Yoo-hoo while I give you some advice to pass along to your son. Whatta ya say to that?"

The large, hairy cheeks plumped up to an all-face-encompassing smile. "Shore 'nuff? You'd do that, miss?"

I waved my hand airily as if the loss of time was no big deal. Again, I surprised myself. I practice religiously the art of packing each minute of the day as full as possible. But the feel, the smell, the look of that country store had taken my adult hand and led me, without resistance, back to the lazy, time-crawling days of my youth. I wanted to live in that time again. And since that was impossible, I wanted to hang, suspended in time, for a while longer.

"Happy to do it."

And when the thirty minutes that followed were over, I was indeed happy that I had taken time from my normally selfish existence to spend time with that extraordinary man. Sitting there in the warm, fragrant air that settled pleasantly on our faces as we rocked on the hard Mississippi dirt, I discovered a man who had fought in Vietnam in the days when the war was new, then returned home to marry his childhood sweetheart, Velma, who died of cancer when their son was ten. He told me how his love for her and her constant letters had instilled in him the will to survive the war and come back to her.

"Every night 'fore I went to sleep and first thang every morning, I looked at her picture. I loved that pretty little thang—she wouldn't of weighed a hundred pounds, soaking wet—with every fiber of my being. 'Bout killed me, too, when I lost her." He shook his head and looked off into the distance. "But I just had to thank the good Lord for the time he give me with her. Ain't any way for a man to be blessed more than that. No, siree. No way. At least I had that love and that's a whole lot more than a bunch of folks can say."

My throat tightened but before I could segue to tears, he moved on to talk of other things. He inherited the battered store from his daddy, who had gotten it from his daddy.

"I don't do too bad here," he said, shooing away the snaggletoothed cat, who had followed us outside. "Don't take much, though, for us to live. Never has. Place's paid for and so's the little bit of land and the old farmhouse where we live. I ain't never gonna be one for understandin' where people get all that money to build them big houses and own two or three brand-new cars." He shook his head in puzzlement.

I knew. I understood even if he didn't. I chortled sarcastically. "Homer, a lot of people live neck deep in debt just to have that lifestyle. Every dollar is spent before it is made." I thought of my friend, Howard, who lives in an eight thousand-square-foot house and is always trying to beat checks to the bank. I looked around at the existence that would be considered simple and humble by most, yet it was the richest of all. Homer had no financial worries and plenty of time. Who could ask for more?

Homer gazed off into the waning afternoon light and, again, shook his head. "Jack, that's my boy's name, he works as a substitute rural mail carrier for the United States Postal Service." He grinned proudly. "Got 'im benefits like insurance and retirement. Proud to see my boy do good. Better than me."

I reached over and patted his leathery hand, which was spotted with large freckles. "Homer, you've done mighty good, too. You fought for your country and you came home to the woman and the land you love. And you raised yourself a good, hard-working boy."

"God-fearing, too," he added. "It sure would do my ol' heart good, though, if that boy could get himself published. It's all he ever wanted in life. Back when his mama died, little Jack would take to his room and just write for hours. I think, surely to God, that it's the only thang that spared him. He loved her so." I saw his eyes mist but pretended not to. I knew he would hate the betrayal of the tears. "We both did. I just wish . . ."

His voice trailed off but there was no need to finish it. It was that moment that I resolved to do whatever I could to help Jack find his dream. I reached down for my purse, pulled out my card, scribbled a number on the back and handed it to him.

"Homer, here's my card. The number on the front is my office number but on the back is my private number. Tell Jack to mail his book to me and I'll get it to some folks in New York." It was possible that his son was an undiscovered William Faulkner and that this could work out beautifully for all involved. Well, it *could* happen.

"Dadgum!" Homer exclaimed happily, slapping his knee. "Thanky, Miss Abby. That's a mighty fine offer."

I held up a cautionary finger. "No promises. God only knows what will happen. In this business, sometimes it takes a lot of rejection before you get acceptance. But I promise this: I will do everything possible." I stood up and smoothed my skirt.

"Homer, I sure hate to be going but I need to hit the road." I reached out and offered my hand. His felt rough and scaly. Hands like that helped to build our country into a great one, but too often, people without calloused hands, like me, forget that. We don't stop to think about men like Homer and the importance of their contributions.

You're a doggone fine woman," Homer bellowed. "Purtty, too. Just remember there's two ol' boys down Mississippi way gonna be much obliged to ya."

"I hope I do something worthy of havin' y'all obliged to me!"

Our good-byes said, I slid into the rented gray Ford and pointed it in the right direction toward Bliss. I thought how close I had come to not knowing what a fine man Homer was because of my own self-absorption and stinginess with my time. I had about forty miles to reflect on Homer and Jack before my cell phone finally registered a "Network" signal. When I'm on long drives and get tired of talking to myself or thinking, I call people just to talk.

"Hello?" Mama said after the eighth or ninth ring.

"Why'd it take you so long to answer the phone?" Normally, she's sitting right on it and grabs it on the first ring. Sometimes, though, she likes to be demur and answer it on the second ring as if she's not anxious to talk to anyone who'll talk to her.

"I'm studyin' my almanac," she replied. "I need to weed my pansies and I'm tryin' to figure out when's the best time to do it."

My mama, just like my daddy did, lives by the guidance of the *Farmer's Almanac.* She's always trying to find something. It's her second favorite book, the first being a thick, one-volume medical encyclopedia, which she calls her "doctor's book." For years, she's been diagnosing—wanted and unwanted—illnesses for everyone in the family.

She has about a 50 percent accuracy rate, which is pretty amazing when you consider that she really doesn't have a clue as to what she's doing. When she pronounced Aunt Bess to be pregnant at the age of fifty after two days of being sick at her stomach and various other clues, Mama had no doubts.

"It's a change-of-life baby," she declared, then marched over to the cedar chest from which she pulled out yarn and her knitting needles. Within a few hours, she had a solid start on a beautiful, soft yellow layette.

"I do hope in the good Lord's name that Bess won't be like all those youngsters today and have to go findin' out the sex of the baby before it gets here," she commented, clicking her needles together furiously. "That's why I'm makin' this yellow. Maybe she'll get the hint."

Two days later, the layette set was almost finished and Aunt Bess was lying in the emergency room at the county hospital with IVs feeding her and slowly bringing her back to the land of the living after being officially diagnosed with food poisoning. A greatly relieved Uncle Harold paced the floor around her bed, repeatedly muttering, "Thank you, precious Lord. Thank you, sweet Jesus."

That just about put an end to Doctor Granny and her homemade doctoring. Now, she mostly keeps herself in practice by working on herself and Kudzu, the last willing patients she can find. We welcome the times when her nose is stuck in the almanac as opposed to the doctor's book.

"I didn't know that you had to look up when to weed the garden," I remarked.

"Well, Daddy used to tell me that if you plucked the weeds on the right time of the moon that they wouldn't come back. But I never knowed exactly when that was," she explained. "Then, the other day, someone told me that you pull the weeds when the signs are in the bowels." I had lived with that all my life, watching both of my parents plan their lives around the almanac diagram that shows which part of the body that the planet was in on which day. They used it to determine the best times for planting, harvesting, cutting hair, surgeries, tooth extractions and now weeding. Once when Mama needed to have a molar pulled, it took weeks for her to coordinate the signs of the moon with Dr. Martin's schedule. Once accomplished, though, the wound barely bled and was closed up tight within two days.

"Hmmm. Looks like that's gonna be another five days. I sure hope it don't come up a cloud that day. I need to get that garden weeded. My yard's beginnin' to look like those trashy Dewberrys live here."

I sighed, which, of course, she didn't hear because she was still caught up with the date that the moon would move into the bowels on the almanac diagram. After a moment, she turned her attention to me.

"Where you at?"

"I'm almost to Bliss, Mississippi, after getting lost." I paused for a moment before speaking again. "Mama, you know what I learned today?"

"What?"

"I learned that every person has a story, if you'll just take the time to dig down and find it." I saw a sign that announced that Bliss was only ten miles away. "Sometimes you find those people and those stories in the darndest places. But always, you just have to slow down and take the time to see it."

Mama, I knew, didn't understand. But I did.

Chapter 4

I turned the ornate doorknob, shiny from decades of wear, and pushed gingerly on the white-painted, solid wood door with the large panel of heavy beveled glass. It didn't budge from the other identical door it was attached to, so I tried again, using a shove from my hip. This time it worked, allowing me entrance into the mahogany-inlaid foyer with its view of the wide winding staircase that twirled upward with a beautiful dark railing and a dark-green-and-gold-tapestry that decorated the steps. A large crystal chandelier hung majestically from the ceiling above, sparkling with brilliance and the grandeur of long ago.

My first glance at the interior of the place where I would spend the next two nights was one of thrilled delight, but of course, the exterior with its huge Grecian columns, wide porch with white wicker rockers, swings and the small balcony that hung directly over the front doors was equally enthralling. I just wanted to hug myself with the Southern coziness of it all, just wallow in the years that had gone before and soak luxuriously in the history that permeated the place. I knew it was there. I could smell it in the mustiness mixed with lemon-scented furniture polish and a potpourri of floral scents like jasmine, honeysuckle, gardenia and magnolia. Finally I was in Bliss, the place I had fought so hard to visit a few weeks earlier when I was in Jamie's office to work on the tour. My mind flashed back quickly to that afternoon.

"Bliss, Mississippi?" the cynical Jamie had hissed in a mixture of sarcasm and astonishment. She slumped dramatically in her chair while a wide-eyed look of disbelief stretched across her face.

I twisted uncomfortably in my chair, grimacing inwardly at the confrontation on which I seemed destined to embark. I don't like battling. I want everything to be smooth and easy, but when necessary, and I knew it was about to be necessary, I can rise, albeit reluctantly, to the occasion.

"You think *what*?" she continued incredulously, poking a long, thin finger in her ear and rotating it rapidly in another theatrical gesture.

I swallowed and took a deep breath. I had not expected it to be an easy sale. "That we should add Bliss, Mississippi, to my tour schedule." I shrugged casually as if it were no big deal. I was mindful never to let the bright-eyed, friendly smile slip the least little bit.

Jamie, unmoved by my friendly demeanor, shook her head slowly, trying to absorb the situation. Directly behind her, windows ran the length of her tiny office, an office in a sky-touching building in the center of Manhattan, a building owned by mega media giant Horizon Media, a company which in addition to a movie studio, television stations and newspapers owns the publishing company that publishes my books. Jamie had been working on the book tour for two months and had already managed to line up appearances on two morning shows and that coveted spot on *Larry King* though I took credit for *The Tonight Show.* Things were shaping up beautifully. Bliss, Mississippi, a tiny township of less than five thousand, did not quite fit into those grandiose plans. While a thunderstruck Jamie stared at me, I distracted myself momentarily by looking out the window. Rising up from its place of prominence on Fifth Avenue was Saint Patrick's Cathedral, its gothic grandeur looming over Jamie's right shoulder.

Finally, she spoke. "Abby Houston, you cannot be serious." She paused for a moment as glorious, spontaneous revelation suddenly filtered across her face, beginning noticeably at one ear and ending at the other. She snapped her fingers. "Oh, I get it!" She slapped a hand with ragged cuticles and nails bitten to the quick against her forehead. "You're *trying* to be funny!" A Cheshire cat–like grin sneaked into the corners of her mouth, and she pointed a sad looking finger at me. "You're doing what you people in the South call 'jerking my chain.' Okay. That's funny." She tried to punctuate the remark with an amused chuckle, but the best she could manage was a tired, obviously indulgent, extremely unconvincing ha-ha.

In an earlier time of lower self-confidence, I would have squirmed uncomfortably and caved in. I, like many rural Americans, suffer under the illusion from time to time that anyone in New York is smarter than anyone from any other part of the country. But for the record, just so you'll know, I've met a couple of idiots there, too, so I know for a fact that they don't *all* live in the South. Idiocy, as best I can tell, has some mighty deep roots in parts of Manhattan, too. I did not squirm or cave in, though. Bolstered by the monstrous success of four bestselling books, one which Hollywood had recently turned into a mockery of my very soul, I did not flinch or feel awkward. I was, instead, very brave, although it took all the courage I could summon.

"No," I said evenly, smoothly. "I am not jerking your chain."

I like Jamie. At first glance, we're a mismatch of personalities, looks, attitudes, ideas and, above all, cultures. I am soft and feminine, always trailed by a vaporous wisp of floral-scented perfume and deeply attached to Luscious Peach, my favorite lip gloss. Jamie dresses in no-nonsense, solid fashion like many New York women, preferring comfortable black slacks and black baggy sweaters or shirts, perfume is never, ever an option, and her lips are cosmetically virginal. She has never allowed herself the unadulterated joy of Luscious Peach. That makes me very sad for my dear friend.

Our approaches to life in general and situations in specific are as varied as our philosophies on lip gloss. She is concise, quick and direct in her demands while I gently pave the way to my requests with the sickening overuse of the words "please," "if you don't mind" and "thank you." In short, we are the perfect, stereotypical casting of the wisecracking New York broad and genteel Southern belle. Make no mistake about it, though. Both definitely have a use in society. There are times that her tough, no-bull approach works much better than my honeyed one. Then, there are times she will call the sweetness into action and say, "You need to handle this one by doing that Abby thing you do. Long Island's not working."

It is fair to say that, secretly and openly, we admire each other despite the vastness of our differences. So we're a good team, a successful team. That's a given. We just don't always see eye to eye, as in the case of Bliss, Mississippi.

My words, coupled with the tone of my voice, sank into her Long Island intelligence. Her pale blue eyes narrowed and she pursed her thin, colorless lips together. She flung a pitiful-looking forefinger in my direction after she had run it through her baby-fine, short blonde hair, which is another nervous habit of hers.

"Look, Red," she began. "This is a big book for us with a big marketing budget and you're a big author. Notice the common adjective in that sentence? BIG. Big is what Bliss, Mississippi, is *not*! I know this because I have never heard of such a place. I also know this: I cannot justify sending an author of your status to such a tiny, lost-in-God-knows-where-in-the-South, Mississippi."

I didn't blink. But I did lose my smile. This is a serious sign. It means that the steel is about to overtake the scent of the magnolia. It's never a pretty sight. Suddenly, I didn't have to search for courage. Somehow it magically appeared without being summoned.

"I am going to Bliss, Mississippi." I said it firmly with a measured beat between each word. I also carefully pronounced the "g" on the end of "going" and did not lazily make "I am" into the contracted "I'm." When I go to the trouble to properly articulate my words, that's another serious sign. Jamie, who after five years of our working together knows me well, recognized the graveness of the situation. She pulled in the lower edge of her bottom lip between her teeth and began to chew on it. She was confounded. That's a Southernism. A proper, refined Northerner would say "perplexed." She released a long, deep sigh. She'd recently taken up yoga so she breathes a lot in annoying situations.

"Why?"

"Because Susan Marie Jackson, who owns the bookstore there, has always been good to me and my books. She has supported me from the beginning when I first met her at a bookseller's convention. I've been promising her for three years that I'd do a signing at her bookstore, and I'm bound and determined to include it on this tour." Funny what several months on the *New York Times* book list will do to the confidence of a person when making such demands. But I had one final point to make. I scooted forward in my chair, pressed the perfectly manicured fingers of both hands together and placed them on the edge of her desk.

"Jamie, there are three things that I am always going to keep until the good Lord calls me home. That's my daddy's Bible, my mama's pin cushion and my word." I paused, hoping that I had thrown the last necessary punch. Her shoulders slumped and she released another long, mournful yogalike sigh. I probably should have stopped there, but I continued, "I always keep my word to you and you appreciate that. So just think how much it will mean to Susan Marie." My smile returned to punctuate the sentence in an effort to soften words that I prayed silently were not too harsh.

She rolled her chair closer to the desk, folded her arms and placed her elbows on her desk.

"I just have one question."

"Yes?" It was the sweetest sounding "yes" you could ever hope to hear.

"How in the world did you guys ever lose a war to *us*?"

I tossed back my head and laughed, delighted that Jamie appeared ready to throw in the towel with a friendly flourish of her hand. She collected her brows together in a deep furrow and tilted her head to the side. "Can I ask you something?" she asked.

"Sure."

"Why is this so important to you?"

I sighed thoughtfully and looked away. "I'm chipping away at a debt that I doubt I'll ever be able to repay." I looked back at her as the furrow grew deeper and she flung an open-handed palm in my direction, inviting me to continue. So I did. "Small bookstore owners like Susan Marie gave a career to a little ol' obituary writer from Dexter, Georgia. They hand sold my first book, practically begging people to buy it. That grassroots effort put me where I am today and I can't forget that. If I sell a thousand books at a big bookstore in a big city, it barely makes a bleep on their balance sheet. But if I sell a hundred books at a tiny store in a tiny town, I've help pay the overhead for a month. It's not a lot but it's the least I can do."

She chuckled—this time it was genuine—and pushed up the sleeves of her black turtleneck. Jamie wears mostly drab colors, but with me, the brighter, the better. On that particular day, I was wearing a spice orange silk sleeveless top and matching slacks, both of which were embroidered with an edging of deep-burgundy-colored, tiny flowers and seed pearls of the same shade.

"Okay," she said cheerfully, nodding with a new understanding. "So let's get down to work." She flung open a desk drawer and began rustling through its contents. "Where's that atlas?" She stopped and looked at me. "Or is it possible that you know exactly where Bliss is? Hey, that rhymes!"

"I think it's near Memphis." I spread my hands to illustrate that I really had no clue.

"Memphis is near Mississippi?" She said it in a tone that expressed complete surprise. I seldom know when she's teasing.

I grinned and nodded. "Which probably explains how Elvis got to Memphis from Tupelo." With a fellow Southerner, I would have stopped there, but with Jamie, I felt it prudent, even necessary, to go one step further. "Elvis was born in Tupelo."

"Oh." She looked up from the atlas she had managed to find. "I've heard of Tupelo." She chewed her lower lip for a moment, then asked, "What's the name of the bookstore in Bliss? I'll need to call the owner and set it up."

I smiled. "It's called Bliss Your Heart."

Her eyes widened and then she shook her head. "Of course, it is," she mumbled under her breath but not soft enough that I did not hear the sarcasm that fully dressed each word. "I suppose Santa Claus spends the off-season there, too."

And that, in a nutshell, is how I negotiated my way to Bliss, even if I did get lost getting there. I stood just inside the door, remembering, when I heard a friendly, welcoming squeal of delight. "Well, Lawdy be, if you aren't just the cutest little thing! Look at you, all decked out in that vibrant shade of pink."

I turned right in the direction of the Southern drawl and saw its owner, rising up from behind an antique writing table that had generously carved legs and a delicate appearance. She stood up, pulling off the small half-glasses that perched on her nose and letting them dangle from a crystal rope that hung around her neck. She was somewhere close to sixty, with strawberry blonde hair that was teased into a bouffant that was oddly appropriate for her. She was about my height, maybe five-foot-four or five-foot-five, and was so robustly round that she reminded me of the snowmen I used to build when I was a kid. "Honey, *that* is your color!" She moved from around the desk and started hurrying toward me. "There are not too many people who can pull off such a bold pink. But, sweetie, you and I are two of 'em!" She laughed in a tinkling chime that signaled that we were now pledged together in eternal sisterhood. She was dressed in similar colors, fuchsia and deep green, but hers were in the form of a floral-printed dress. Lilly Pulitzer, I figured, making us a showdown of trendy versus timeless. In five years, she would probably still be wearing that dress while my outfit would have long been discarded and forgotten.

She stretched out a hand and smiled exuberantly, exuding the spirit of hospitality for which the South is renowned. "I'm Charlotte Williams. Welcome to the Magnolia Blossom Bed and Breakfast!"

Her light green eyes sparkled with joy, with the offer of warm, from-now-till-forever friendship. Closer, I could see the smattering of soft, golden freckles on her full cheeks and ample arms. I liked her immediately. Of course, some of it most assuredly had to do with the bragging she was doing on me. I'm a bit like my mama in that aspect—the more you brag on me, the more I take to you right off the bat. But bragging aside, I liked her because of the kindness that bounced in wide arcs around her and created warmth and compassion.

I took her hand to shake it firmly—I believe strongly in firm handshakes—and returned her joyous smile. "Hello. It's nice to meet you. I'm—"

She cut me off with a delicious laugh. "Oh, honey child, I *know* who you are! Welcome to Bliss, Mississippi, home of the biggest Abby Houston fan in the world. That would be *me*, Charlotte Williams. I absolutely adore everything you write. I saw you on *The Tonight Show* and I nearly fell out of my bed laughing. You were nothing short of perfectly adorable." She touched my shoulder playfully. "I just finished your new book. Looky here!" She danced over to the desk and picked up my newest tome and held it up. "See! I bought the very first one in this town. I made Susan Marie promise that she'd call the minute it arrived." She turned the book over and looked at my photo that covered the entire back. "But I must say, as pretty as this picture is, it doesn't do you justice."

Charlotte Williams and I were becoming fast friends. Still, I blushed. I'm slightly uncomfortable if someone brags too much. That's where Mama and I differ. You can never boast about her enough. With me, there is a limit. I like compliments just as much as the next person, but I'm well aware of my limitations in both the talent and looks department. "Thank you," I said, looking down almost shyly. She caught the look and interpreted quickly. "Okay, enough said about that." She put the book back on the desk and came back over to put her arm around me. "Come in and sit down for a minute before I get you signed in and squared away. Would you like a glass of lemonade or sweet tea? We only have sweet tea here at the Magnolia Blossom, let me warn you about that!"

I chuckled. "Oh, I can tell I'm gonna love this place!"

Charlotte led me into the living room, where matching over-stuffed chairs covered in Valentino-inspired red silk duoponi with taupe-colored cut fringe sewn into the seams sat on either side of the large fireplace below a mahogany mantle. The room was absolutely lovely, appointed with luxury and style. A red-and-gold oriental rug lay on the wood floor in front of the chairs, separating them from a sofa in the same silk duoponi, this time woven in a red-and-taupe paisley design. Thrown casually onto the luscious chairs were custom-made pillows in the same paisley silk. The tall windows that ran from floor to ceiling were draped in a lightweight taupe silk trimmed in fringe with tassels that were two shades darker. The drapery fabric was so luscious that I fantasized a strapless evening dress made from it, imagining how perfectly the full skirt would billow around my legs and flow gracefully with each movement. I love fabric that feels seductive to the skin and color so tantalizing that it makes me shudder with pleasure. It didn't seem strange to consider wearing a dress made from the curtains like Scarlett O'Hara.

I sat down in one chair while Charlotte settled down in the other. My chair faced toward the huge French doors that led to the outside terrace, which was planted in a haze of magnolia trees that hung heavily over the bricked patio and walkway. In the spring and early summer when that multitude of magnolias is in bloom and those doors are swung open wide, the sweetness of the fragrance that permeates the room must be, at times, overwhelming. I can close my eyes now and smell that room as it smelled then, a comforting sense of honeyed beauty and serene peace. The only thing sweeter than a magnolia is a honeysuckle vine, and though I could not see any, I felt certain that somewhere at the Magnolia Blossom Bed and Breakfast, vines, of the sensuous plant were woven carefully and strategically in its gardens.

My pleasure of the succulent beauty betrayed me in the form of a heavy sigh of wonderment. I saw her smile knowingly, so I said, "This is the absolute loveliest place I have ever seen. There is a sense of peace and comfort that floats through the rooms and adds to its sensory seduction." When my sister hears me say something like that, she says, "Oh, give me a break. Please stop being so dramatic!" But Southerners who are deep and true in their heart's feelings about our culture have an unexplained love of rich, expressive words and phrases. I don't know how I managed to get stuck on the obituary desk for all those years where the simplest words are the best. All I can say is that I was chosen for the job, not called.

She laughed again, a tinkling sound of charm and gratitude. "Oh, Abby, you must, you simply must, say exactly that to my husband. Charlie, bless his heart, just doesn't understand the magic of this place. He's a lawyer so he always views things in such a lawyerly fashion. It just slays me completely sometimes. He's pragmatic and argues that we could live somewhere else in grand style for much less than this place costs and that, with what we save, we could also have a home by the water in Bay St. Louis. I am completely unmoved by any such argument." She tossed the idea away with a wave of her hand.

I gasped. "But surely not a place with as much charm and enchantment."

"Exactly. I inherited this place twenty years ago from a great-aunt on my daddy's side. She and her husband never had children, but I spent many afternoons after school and Saturdays with Aunt Mattie, learning the ladylike art of needlepoint and how to properly serve tea. I loved her madly and when she grew old and sick with a weak heart, I came every day to fuss over her and read to her. She loved Southern classics although she detested Faulkner. She said she met him once and he was nothing but an uncouth drunk. My Aunt Mattie had rather an imperial attitude but I loved her anyway. So when she died, she left this house, her literature and poetry collection and ten thousand dollars to me. The rest of the estate, which was considerable, she left to Ole Miss, her husband's alma mater."

"Was this a family home?"

Charlotte nodded. "Yes, indeed. My great-great-grandfather built this house in 1848. That's one reason it's so important to me. Aunt Mattie used to say, 'Unless you know where you come from, you don't really know who you are.' "

Few words are truer. I know the heritage from which I spring, circumstances that were often poor and desperate. My ancestors on both sides were mountain folks, mostly struggling farmers, hopeful preachers or resourceful moonshiners. Both my parents, separately before they ever met, managed to escape that lineage of hopelessness and move to towns where the prospects were brighter. I try not to get too big for my britches by remembering the humble existences of those whose blood runs through my veins. We can't choose the circumstances we're born into, but if we're lucky, we can change them. That was me and I never forget it, although some people would never suspect the poverty of my family, only one generation removed. That's the only thing I hate about the good life I've unwittingly managed to acquire in recent years. People who didn't know me when I was queen of the obituary writers assume that I am different from those with less glamorous jobs and simpler lifestyles. Well, I got news for them, I'm just one very blessed person who isn't anything special at all. If you don't believe that, just ask my ex-husband.

I have a couple of other old boyfriends I could give you as references, too, if necessary.

It's a funny thing about success. It brings many new suitors to your court, seeking your friendship while others, less confident, shy away. It especially happens with men. I don't care what men say or how they try to deny it, but the truth is that the male gender, for the most part, does not deal well emotionally with a successful woman. In their eyes, a woman's success, especially if it's more significant than theirs, puts everything out of whack in the universe.

"I agree completely," I remarked, smiling at Charlotte. "Both sides of my family come from the Scotch-Irish who settled in the foothills of the Appalachians. I very much have the traits of those people—hardworking, stubborn, resourceful, a bit on the stingy side." I winked playfully. "And I love to hear a good story."

"And you tell a good story, too!" She crossed her plump legs in a slightly awkward maneuver and reached behind to pull the paisley pillow from her back. She wrapped her arms around the pillow, cuddled it to her chest and continued to talk. "The first year we were here, I spent the entire amount that Aunt Mattie left me on upkeep and repairs. That led Mr. Practical Charlie to inform me that I either had to find a way to make this money-eating monster pay for itself or we'd have to sell it and move to a place that we could afford. Of course, he figured I couldn't find a way to do that, but he gravely underestimated me when I put my mind to something. Against his protests, I turned it into a bed and breakfast and it has worked out wonderfully. It makes enough to pay for the upkeep, including those absolutely horrific power bills, and for hired help to do the cooking and cleaning. I break even every year and that's all I'm interested in doing. As I told Mr. Charlie, 'It's not my place to make a living for this family. It's yours!'" She laughed delightedly. "You know, Abby, one thing I really appreciate in your books is your sense of history, the respect you pay to what has gone before us. That's very important."

"I think so," I concurred. "History molds us into the kind of people we become. Which is what your Aunt Mattie was saying. Listen, I can't wait to see my room. If it's anything like this, I'm going to be in heaven."

She clapped her hands together once and stood up. "Well, get ready to hear the angels sing! Let's get you registered."

I followed her to the desk, where I filled out a little paper with my name, address and phone number and gave her the credit card that my publisher had provided for my travel expenses. As I signed the credit card form, she said in an apologetic tone, "Abby, I so wanted to take you to dinner tonight but I have a spousal conflict. Charlie, in addition to being an attorney, is also a member of the state senate. The board of education is hosting a reception tonight and Charlie is the guest of honor. I've been in such a turmoil as to what to do. But I just don't know how I couldn't go with him and show my loving support." She winked. "I've spoiled him rotten. His every whim is my command."

I waved away her concern. "Charlotte, please don't give a second thought to it. I am very accustomed to eating alone when I travel so it doesn't bother me one iota. You're right in putting your husband before a stranger. I would expect nothing less."

She reached over, took my hand and gently squeezed it. "I may be a stranger to you, but you're not to me. I feel as if we've been friends forever. I have read the words that flow from your soul, young lady. I know your heart and I very much like what I see." She cocked her head to one side and asked thoughtfully, "Are you married?"

"I'm divorced." I said it without the embarrassment I once felt. Yet I still felt compelled, as I always do, to answer, "I'm divorced." A simple "no" won't suffice. I simply must make certain that the questioner knows that I did manage to land a husband once. Sad, I know. But you wouldn't be quite as judgmental if you had my mother for *your* mother. Like many women whose husbands chose another, my self-image was pretty battered after the divorce. I know that's the reason why I spend so much time and effort on my clothes and appearance. I'm trying to find some prettiness in me somewhere even when it feels like putting a lovely shade of paint on walls that are old and cracked. There's only so much you can do. Even though I put on a brave face for Mama, I often fall into that trap of many women—I judge my feminine successfulness by the ring finger of my left hand.

There was no judgment, however, in Charlotte's expression or voice as she went on, "Then you know exactly the terrible dilemma I was faced with about tonight. I've been in an absolute quandary over it, just sweating bullets of the most enormous kind. Sweet darling, I'm sure you know that men are just big babies who cannot negotiate the rocky courses of this world without our precious little hands holding theirs and leading the way. It is a fact of life, I swear it is."

I love people who are dramatic, and it was a certain fact that, although I had known her for less than half an hour, Charlotte was one of the best I had ever met. Dramatic people are never boring, so I knew that for the next couple of nights I was certain to be entertained by a drama diva. Again, I waved away her concern, overstated though it was. "Charlotte, please, don't worry about it one moment longer." I glanced at my watch. "What time are you supposed to be there?"

"I'm meeting Charlie there at 7:30."

"It's almost seven now, so why don't you show me to my room and give me a recommendation for dinner? You don't want to be late."

We chatted about nothing of consequence as we climbed the broad staircase, built to accommodate the huge hoopskirts of the women who had traveled its steps. At the top, she turned left and led me to a door that she swung open with a grand flourish. That room certainly deserved a "ta-da!" The ceiling was twelve feet high with a large fan in the center that spun around lazily. An enormous four-poster bed was the focal point, so high off the floor that a two-step stool in the same walnut wood was situated next to it for help in climbing on top. A fluffy down comforter floated lightly on top, covered with a custom-sewn duvet in a Laura Ashley floral. A quick glance and I knew that the four pillows at the head of the bed were the most perfect sleeping pillows known to the tired traveler—25 percent down surrounded by 75 percent feathers. Wood floors, walls papered in a tiny print that matched the duvet and flowing drapes were the canvas of the showplace that would have been perfectly at home in the pages of *Southern Living*. The armoire, I suspected, discreetly housed the television and offered drawers for storage, while a small loveseat and chaise, in coordinating fabrics, of course, were poised comfortably to the side of the large French doors that swung out to a small balcony.

"Oh my goodness!" I squealed delightedly and ran over to throw open the doors. I stepped onto the balcony that overlooked the back garden, a miniature Eden. A small pond with a fountain that flowed with a simmering rhythm was just below my balcony. Yes, the backyard was crowded with magnolia trees and other lush greenery such as gardenia, jasmine, oak and late-summer flowers. Charlotte had followed me onto the balcony and I turned back to see her look of quiet pride. "This is spectacular!" I told her. A warm flush of peace crept over me and suddenly I was looking forward to the fall of darkness and the sweet sleep I was certain to find in the midst of this beauty and calm.

"It is pretty, isn't it?" she asked quietly. "Gardens are my passion. I'm the president of our local garden club and a nationally accredited flower-show judge." She winked and smiled conspiratorially. "That means that I am incomparably able to recognize the excellence of any flower in any state!"

"I am sufficiently impressed," I assured her with a lighthearted laugh. I stole another look at my watch. "Charlotte, you better get going. Don't let me detain you. I don't want Charlie mad at me before he even meets me!"

"Listen, Charlie Williams knows better than to start any party before *I* get there." She tapped a finger against her chest. "But you're right. Being late is so inconsiderate of others. I just detest people who are always late."

As I stepped back into the room, my nostrils were pleasantly attacked by a floral ambush. I looked around the room until I found the tremendous bouquet of flowers on the writing desk. Next to the flowers was a white gift basket brimming with candy, snacks, gourmet coffee, a mug inscribed with gold, flowing script that read "Magnolia Blossom Bed and Breakfast, Bliss, Mississippi," note cards, a small bottle of perfume and fruit.

"Oh, Charlotte," I mumbled, shaking my head in wonderment at such hospitality. "This is too much."

"Just a simple little thank-you for all the reading pleasure you have brought me in the evening's late hours as Charlie snored his way through another night! These flowers, mind you, came right out of our own gardens here. They smell so much more vibrant than ones from the florist, you know."

"I would expect nothing less from a nationally accredited flower-show judge." I winked teasingly.

"And you will get nothing less, I assure you. Now, about dinner, what do you have a hankering for? We have several very nice, locally owned restaurants here in Bliss. We frown on chains. Italian, American, elegant Southern? What is your pleasure?"

I thought of all the fancy meals I had gorged on in the past week, and my mouth began to water for something really special. "Honestly, what I'd really like is some good, old-fashioned down-home cooking. Crowder peas, mashed potatoes, fried okra. That kind of stuff."

"Then Maggie's Southern Diner is just the place for you. In fact, you can walk there from here." She looked down at the tottering high-heeled sandals and frowned. "Maybe not in those shoes, though."

I folded my arms and playfully raised one eyebrow. "Don't underestimate my ability," I warned with a smile. "I often amaze myself at the kind of terrain I can conquer in heels!"

"Well, okay then! Just walk those three-and-a-half-inch babies three blocks uptown, cross at the gas station in front of the courthouse. You'll pass Susan Marie's bookstore—by the way, she called and said you could come to the bookstore at eleven in the morning, and she'd take you to the country club for Rotary—then pass the beauty shop and the next door is Maggie's. Got that?"

"Got it. What a lovely evening to walk, too."

"Enjoy it. Rain's supposed to move through in the morning. I've gotta scoot. Need anything else?"

"How could I?"

"Right answer because it shows I've done my proper Southern duty! If I don't see you when I get home tonight, I'll see you in the morning for breakfast. What time would you like to eat?"

"Nine?"

"Perfect. I love guests who don't get up early. By the way, there's only one other guest tonight, but he's a salesman who stays with us once a month and he'll be gone early in the morning. He never eats breakfast here. So it'll be just you and me."

"See you then. And, Charlotte, thanks for what I know is going to be a magical experience."

Even I didn't know how prophetic those words would prove to be. I had no clues to the true magic that was about to engulf me in the town of Bliss, Mississippi.

Chapter 5

I glanced at my watch and decided to make a quick call to Mama since there was a one-hour time difference. I knew it would be too late when I got back. Not because she goes to bed early and sleeps but because she goes to bed early and talks on the phone with her friends until late. I knew I'd never get through after nine.

In the earlier call, I had gotten so distracted by my somber reflections about Homer and Mama's diligent studying of the almanac for the moon in the bowels that I had forgotten to ask about Kudzu.

"What are you doin'?" I asked when she answered. My mama never says "nothin'." She always gives me a full detail of whatever she's doing when I call and the back story as to why she's doing it.

"I'm lookin' something up in my doctor's book."

"Is something wrong with you?"

"No."

Too little information made me suspicious so I prodded further. "Are you sure?"

"No, I'm fine." The answer was vague and sounded distracted.

"How's my baby?" I had really called to ask about Kudzu anyway, so I decided not to waste any time getting to the real purpose of the call.

"She's fine." Her voice was tiny, unsure. "I guess," she added.

My ears sprung up at those last two lines and the manner in which they had been delivered. "You guess! What do you mean *you guess*?" Immediately, I pictured Kudzu in a variety of predicaments from car accidents to snakebites to lost in a field of kudzu somewhere.

She answered with a question of her own. "You don't reckon there's nothin' in Tums that could kill a dog, do you?"

"Tums! Mother, tell me right now what you're talking about," I demanded. I always call her Mother when I mean serious business.

"Well, you know how I just have an awful time with acid reflux. You remember that Dr. Loudermilk stretched my esophagus but that didn't help that much. Not like it was s'posed to anyway. I still nearly die with it and he ain't been much help in findin' a way to fix it. He give me them pills that cost six dollars apiece and said it was the best thing I could take. But every time I think of how much one of 'em cost, I nearly choke when I try to swallow it. It's worse at night, so bad at times that I cain't hardly stand it."

"Mother!" I exploded from the fear that was building inside. *"Tell me what's wrong with Kudzu.* We can talk about *you* later."

"Well, now I knew that the dog would be more important to you than your poor mama 'bout to die."

"You're not about to die," I replied dryly. "I want to know what's wrong with Kudzu."

"That's what I'm tryin' to tell ya. Because I have acid reflux so bad at night that the good Lord callin' me home would be a blessing, I keep a roll of Tums by my bed. It's the only thing that gives me any relief at all."

I could see where this was all heading. "So Kudzu ate the Tums on the nightstand?"

"Right. And when I went in yonder to check on her, there she was, standin' on the bed with the wrapper hangin' out her mouth and all the Tums gone. She ate a full roll. You don't s'pose they'd hurt her, do you? I'm tryin' to find it in my doctor's book, but it don't say a thing about dogs eatin' Tums." Imagine that glaring oversight. What were those medical wizards thinking?

I thought for a moment. I knew that chocolate and antifreeze could kill a dog, but never once had I heard anyone mention a dog dying from antacids. I didn't want to take anything for granted, though, so I thought about the ingredients. Finally, I answered slowly, "I don't think so. I certainly hope not. She is kinda small, though, to eat that much of anything medicinal." Then Mother's lack of guardianship during my absence dawned fully on me. "Wait a minute. Why were you not keeping a diligent eye on her?"

"I only turned my back for a minute!" she shot back defensively. "I cain't watch her every second!" She was getting agitated, and that made two of us.

"Why can't you watch her every minute?" I considered it to be a quite reasonable question. "You don't have anything better to do."

"Well, I'm not goin' to!" she snapped. I couldn't see it but I knew that her chin was jutted out in a stubborn, most unbe-coming fashion and her jaw was set in an angry clench. I had a lot more to say about her shortcomings as a nanny, but there were more important issues at hand like whether Kudzu had been fatally poisoned or not.

"How's she doing right now? Is she moving around?"

"She acts like she's fine. She just went outside awhile ago and took off in a fury after a groundhog that was settin' in the yard. Didn't look like to me anything was wrong with her."

I breathed a sigh of relief. "Well, if she was chasin' the groundhog, she's probably gonna live."

"That's what I think, too." She paused slightly and then chuckled. "I guess she needed them Tums after all that chicken she eat."

"*What* chicken?" Without a doubt, Mama regretted letting that piece of information slide out. Just before I left, I had given her a stern lecture about Kudzu's diet—or rather lack of one—when I was traveling. I had gotten one myself recently from Dr. Marlin, her vet. When he weighed Kudzu, he announced that she was three pounds overweight. When I protested, he pointed out how shapeless she was and how he had to press through a couple of inches to get to her bones. Then I said, probably too brightly to his liking, "Well, three pounds isn't bad at all."

He cut his eyes over to me as he checked her heartbeat. "Abby, three pounds on her is like thirty pounds on you."

I hate it when someone uses my vanity against me. Let's just say that I got the point loud and clear. Still, I had to defend myself. "Well, it isn't me, Dr. Marlin. *I* only feed her dog food. The problem comes when I travel and she stays with my mother, who feeds her God knows what. I did smell pork chops on her breath one day when I picked her up."

"Well then," and he said it very, very kindly. "You need to get control of your mother."

"I'll tell you what," I leaned across the examination table and tapped a dark-rose-colored nail against the stainless steel table. "Why don't *you* get control of my mother about it? And when you get control of her about Kudzu's eating, I've got a few other things I need you to get control of her about."

I did try to reason with her before I left, but of course, it did no good. I knew that even before she slipped up and told me about the chicken. I repeated the question. "Mother, what chicken?"

"I gave her some fried chicken fingers because the poor kid was starvin' to death." She wasn't defensive, merely informational.

"She's not a *kid*." I couldn't believe I was saying that. "She's a dog and dogs, particularly those who have a better pedigree than I have, do not eat fried chicken."

"They do when they're out at Maw-Maw's house. I'm not gonna sit here and have her stare so pitifully at me and know she's starvin' to death."

I gave up. I took comfort in knowing that at least Kudzu was happy while I was gone, even if she was fat and getting fatter by the chicken leg. I heaved my heaviest sigh, the one reserved for only Mama, the one she loves to hear because she knows that I am retreating.

"I'm going to get something to eat now," I said in a resigned tone. "I'll talk to you sometime tomorrow."

"That'll be good. Just know that Kudzu is doin' just fine. And, meantime, don't worry none about her eatin'. I'm of the mind that we need to fatten her up a bit so that she'll be on equal footin' with that groundhog when she catches him."

I rolled my eyes and shook my head in exasperation. The thought of Kudzu entangled in a battle with a groundhog was more disturbing than the Tums or the chicken. She is too prissy to win out with a hardened, outdoors creature who has to dig for food rather than have it fried for her personally. It would have been another useless war of words so I ended the conversation abruptly.

"I'll check in tomorrow. See ya."

It was a couple of minutes shy of 7:30 when I meandered down the front steps of the Magnolia Blossom Bed and Breakfast and past the picturesque white picket fence to the tree-lined sidewalk. Mississippi can be terribly humid, especially when rain is moving in, but the air smelled clean, fresh and free from moisture, and the temperature on the early-September evening was near perfect. A slight breeze lifted my hair and the leaves rustled faintly in the massive oak trees. In the dusky twilight the skies were azure blue and it occurred to me that the radio forecast of rain was wrong.

I met a young family out for a stroll. A small girl with long, tumbling blonde curls, dressed in a short-sleeved pink gingham dress with a smocked bodice, pedaled a tricycle with her tiny feet shod in white sandals, surely one of their last outings, because when Labor Day passed in a few days, it would be a faux pas to wear white. A hand-holding couple trailed behind her, laughing and encouraging her, and a yellow Lab trotted along a few feet in front. Their happiness rang through the air and hung there, drops of their joy falling on me as I approached them.

"Hello," I said with a smile as we came within a few feet of each other.

"Good evening," the couple said in friendly unison as the little girl squeezed the horn on the handlebars of the red bike and then threw her hand up to wave.

"You look very pretty tonight," I commented as the little girl slowed down on the sidewalk to make certain there was room for all of us.

"Thank you, ma'am," she replied politely and then added

proudly, "My mama made my dress." She pointed to the pretty blonde lady behind her.

"Really?" I asked, stopping and then looking over at her mother. "Did you do the smocking, too?"

The hand-holding couple stopped, too. "Yes, ma'am, I did. I took a class in it and it's really not as hard as it looks."

"I know," I agreed. "I took a class in it years ago when my niece was small and I made her a dress, too. It looked almost like that one except hers was blue."

"Pink is Caroline's favorite color," the lady offered, looking lovingly at her daughter.

There was really nowhere for such a conversation between strangers to go so we stood there for a second, just enjoying being friendly until I said, "Well, have a good evening. It sure looks like you're having fun."

The man put his arm around the pretty lady and smiled down at her. "Oh, I always have fun when I'm with my girls." He turned back to me and nodded as a matter of courtesy. "You have a nice evenin', too."

We all continued on our previous courses but my mind stayed with them for a moment longer as I strolled toward the town's square. Sometimes, every so often, when I meet families like that, I feel a touch of melancholy at the reminder that I'm not part of a couple or a family with children. That feeling was a little stronger than usual as I sauntered along the storybook street of white-framed houses with wide porches, some with Grecian columns, all with lawns of lush, thick, bright green grass. I thought of my lawn at home, where the summer's drought had killed the grass in huge patches throughout the yard. My friends constantly chastise me for not hiring a lawn-care company to take care of my yard, but I always hate to hire someone to do what I can do myself. I feel the same way about a housekeeper. I can put my dishes in the dishwasher just as good as anyone can. So I cut my grass, plant my flowers, water my shrubs and let my grass die all by myself. Encountering such a lovely family in such a lovely place made me feel a little lonely, though. As usual, my mind fast-forwarded to forty years down the road when I, should I live that long, would probably find myself in a home alone just like Cousin Zoey. More than likely, when that time arrived, I would regret that I had never suffered through nine months of discomfort followed by months without sleep so that a child of mine could one day be inconvenienced by *my* needs. As it stood now, it would probably be up to my niece Claire to take care of me, and Lord knows she's going to have her hands full taking care of her own mother. Melinda is not easy under the best of circumstances. I made a mental note to buy Claire a really expensive gift in Memphis. It's never too early to get firmly into the good graces of the one who will select your nursing home and make your funeral arrangements.

It occurred to me that it was a good analogy: the beautiful, perfect lawns against my withering, imperfect one, the lives of the people in those houses against my life. Editors in New York like analogies and symbolism, so I've learned a thing or two about that stuff in the past couple of years. The melancholy of it all stung my eyes and the mist from those thoughts pooled in the corners and threatened to dribble down my cheeks. "Snap out of it," I commanded under my breath. "You are very blessed. You can't have *everything* in life."

My smart aleck other side replied, "I don't."

To distract myself from thinking of idyllic family life, I got busy waving to the folks who sat on their front porches and who would throw a hand up as soon as I was close. Without a doubt they all wondered who the stranger in the hot pink sweater and high heels was, but stranger or not, they each treated me to a warm greeting. "Evenin'. Nice out tonight, isn't it?"

One little boy was playing in a tire swing, something I had not seen in years. When he saw me, he called out, "Watch how high I can go!" He pushed harder until he was sailing high into the limbs of the tree, and I demonstrated proper awe for his bravery before moving on. I passed the gas station, full service, not a convenience store, where two men sat on a bench and another sat on an upturned wood cola case. One tipped the bill of his Chevrolet Racing cap while the other two tossed a hand in my direction.

"Howdy, ma'am," said one man, probably the proprietor because his blue work shirt had "Woody's Service Station" monogrammed on it.

"Good evening, sir," I responded.

"It hard to walk in them high heels?" another asked curiously.

"Just takes practice," I replied lightly. They all shook their heads with puzzlement as I walked on by.

I stopped at the traffic light in front of the bakery, and as I waited to cross, I surveyed the town. Before going to the Magnolia Blossom earlier, I had driven down on Main Street for a quick tour of the downtown area. Like many small towns in the South, it had a stately Georgian-style brick courthouse in the center of the town, with Main making a circle around the tree-shaded municiple building as well as leading out of the center of town on both sides. It was an interesting circle within a square with stores and businesses with various facades of brick, stucco and wood. Most buildings had some kind of awning or roof that covered their entrances while three or four, including Morgan's Mercantile, had coverings that doubled as balconies for the upstairs area. Huge wood and brick planters with a variety of small trees and seasonal flowers dotted the walkways, a pretty, finishing touch to a homespun vision. I took a deep, contented breath and surveyed the serenity of it all. The peacefulness vanished with the chiming of my cell phone. I pulled it from my purse and pressed the button. "Hello?"

"Are you blisssssss-fully happy?" the voice sang out in a teasing tone

"As a matter of fact, I'm probably close to it." I saw a wrought iron bench under a massive oak tree next to the courthouse and sauntered over to it. As I sat down, I continued the conversation. "Jamie, you wouldn't believe this little town. It looks like something out of Hollywood."

"Is that good?" she asked skeptically, her Long Island cynicism seeping through.

"In this instance, yes."

"Well, I remember that phone call I got while you were out there, making your mark as an up-and-coming movie star, and as I recall, there was nothing good in the things you said. Why, I didn't even know that you sweet little Southern girls talked like that! Until that phone call, I thought it was against your religion to complain and malign."

I blushed. I remembered that call well. I was livid with some changes they had made in the plot of the book that I wrote, and I had not been, shall we say, a gracious lady. "Isn't it time for you to go home?" I asked, to change the subject. Seven-thirty in Bliss meant 8:30 in New York.

"I am home!" she responded cheerfully. "Cleaning up Chinese takeout as we speak. So it's a pretty town, huh?"

"It reminds me of a movie set I saw in Hollywood. I felt like I was in an Andy Hardy movie until I saw a gang of carpenters who were turning it into a city slum."

"A slum?"

"Yeah. For a movie. One of the carpenters showed me that the buildings were only facades. When you opened the front door of one of the houses, it dropped off sharply into concrete.

But, Jamie, this is real. It's unlike anything you can imagine without seeing it."

"Well, I'm glad to know that it's worth it to you. Especially after that pounding I took from my boss for sending you through Bliss. I leaped buildings in a single bound to get that approved."

My heart darkened. I hated to think of Jamie in trouble over my insistence to come to Bliss. "Really?" I asked, then swallowed. "Did you get into serious trouble?"

"Let's just say it wasn't the most *blissful* moment in my tenure there."

"Jamie, if you had told me," I started before she interrupted me.

"You would have done what?" she asked. "Certainly not backed down in your promise to Susan Marie. Right? What would have come from my telling you?"

"I could have defended you. Or I could have offered to pay for this side trip myself." The Scotch-Irish in me winced at that thought, but doing right is more important than money, even if it does ouch.

She blew hard through her lips, making a childish sound. "After all the money that your books have made the company, they can indulge you this one time. Trust me. But just for the record, you owe me."

"Now, wait a minute! I came here because I owed Susan Marie and wanted to pay that debt and get it off my shoulders. If I owe you, then I just traded one debt for another. I'm no better off than when I started."

I knew she was grinning mischievously on the other end of the phone. "Right. And now that I know for a fact how diligent you are in paying such debts, I know that I will be paid back appropriately."

The light came on. I was being set up and it had taken this long for me to figure it out. "What is it?" I asked flatly.

"Well, CNN is doing a feature piece on women behind successful women. You know, like teachers, mentors, sisters, mothers."

"No!"

"Abby."

"No," I repeated in the firmest tone I own. "I am not going to let them interview my mother. No way. *No way*."

"Abby, you owe me."

"I don't owe you that much. I don't owe *anyone* that much."

"Why not?"

"You know why not. There is no telling what will come out of that woman's mouth." I had once spent two weeks waiting in sheer agony after a magazine reporter called her behind my back and Mama told her everything she ever knew about me, including how chubby, homely and lonely I had been as a child. When the story finally appeared, the reporter had mostly been kind to me except for the quote from Mama where she said, "Every mama loves her children, no matter what. But there was a year or so when Abby was almost as ugly as homemade sin. Thank the good Lord, she growed out of it."

"That magazine article wasn't that bad," Jamie protested.

"I was spared by the grace of God," I responded. "With no help from you, I might add." Across the courthouse lawn, I noticed a bald, lumpy man looking at me. When he caught my eye, he threw up his hand, smiled and waved. I returned the gesture.

"What could I do?" she asked, agitated. "I have no editorial control over such stories."

"You could have warned me about big-city reporters," I shot back. "Then, I could have unlisted mother's phone number." The guy got up from the bench and ambled down the sidewalk. He stopped when he got to a red pickup truck and leaned against the front end. He folded his arms and looked around, as though he had all the time in the world. I tuned out Jamie's indignant response so I could think briefly about how I envied that man, living a simple life like that in a town like this. How did life get so out of control for so many of us? When did we stop taking a moment just to look around and actually see the sky, trees and flowers?

"So?" Jamie's impatient tone returned me from the moment of fantasy, in which I envisioned myself living like that man, my newest hero.

"So what?"

"You'll let the producer talk to her?"

"Jamie."

"Abby."

I sighed and closed my eyes. I was weary from the travel, especially after getting lost, and frustrated from the conversation with Mama, a frustration that was now being aggravated further by the conversation with Jamie. I took the easy way out.

"I'll think about it." I didn't mean it but I needed to renew my strength to fight again another day.

"Really?" Jamie sounded perky.

"We'll talk about it in a day or two." I paused a moment, then said so softly that either Jamie did not hear or did not comprehend because she was savoring her victory, "Or a week or two."

"Abby, thank you! I promise that this is the thing to do. Just wait and see."

You just wait and see, I thought to myself, because there's no way on God's green earth that I'm putting my mama on the national news. Aloud, I said, "Well, I hate to end this conversation but there's some old-fashioned Southern cooking calling my name."

"Okay!" She was still very cheerful and, though she did not know it, falsely optimistic. "I'll check on you tomorrow. Have a wonderful dinner."

"Bye." I clicked off, stood up, smoothed my skirt and looked around at the picturesque town as I tiptoed toward the sidewalk, keeping my heels from sinking into the grassy earth. I thought again of Hollywood, where everything seemed so perfect. I knew that it wasn't perfect in Bliss because real life is never perfect. Still, it looked as though it was as close as possible. This time I could taste reality in the air. I smelled the sweet fragrance of sugary cakes and pies floating from the bakery, then the metallic air produced from the inventory at the mercantile, and the leather-and-paper smell from Bliss Your Heart, Susan Marie's store. I closed my eyes for a moment and allowed my senses to fully absorb the ambiance of small-town living. It was a nice moment until I was jarred out of my daydream by the rapid circular clicking of rubber against concrete. My eyes flew open to see a blur coming at me in the form of a preteen-age boy wearing long shorts and a baggy shirt, balancing precariously on a fast-moving skateboard. I danced forward a few inches, which allowed him to miss me by just that much as he swooshed by.

"Sorry, ma'am," the towheaded youngster called as he skidded past. "I didn't want to hit no gravel! Thanks for movin'."

"No problem!" I tossed a wave in his direction.

He finished our conversation, slight though it was, with a big smile. Then he glanced down for just a moment to stare at my high heels. While they are admittedly stunning, it surprised me that they caught the eye of such a young boy. I had only a moment to be flattered because I realized he was heading smack-dab toward an old woman with a sleepy-eyed brown-and-white beagle tagging along beside her. He had his back to her, and when she saw him, she seemed to freeze in fear. There she stood, a slight bit of a woman in sensible black Hush Puppies, a black skirt that hung to her ankles, an expensive charcoal gray twin-set and a strand of pearls. Her gray hair was knotted into a

French twist so neatly that not one wisp fell around her face. When she saw the bullet of a boy speeding toward her, she clutched her purse to her chest as though it was a shield of armor that would protect her. She looked frail and vulnerable. I wanted to run to her, throw my body in front of her and protect her, but I knew that I couldn't outrun the boy. Not in those heels anyway.

"Watch out!" I screamed. I have to hand it to him; he had fast reflexes. He turned with lightning speed, saw her, used his hips to swerve and managed to miss her, though he did lightly brush the beagle's side. I only know this because the animal started howling and running down the sidewalk toward me. Worried that he might run into traffic, I stooped down and blocked him with my arms and body to keep him from running into the street. Stunned, he fell back, sat down hard and just looked at me with bewilderment in his big, brown eyes.

"Elmer! Oh, Elmer, come back here," the old woman called anxiously. The dog didn't budge. He didn't take his eyes from me. As the woman hurried toward us, I, still stooped down, reached out to let him smell my hand so he would not be afraid. Then I said, "Bless your sweet heart. Are you all right, angel?" I gently stroked his color-blotched hair while he responded to the words of kindness, moving toward me and licking my hand. Within seconds, he was in my arms, happily licking my face.

"There, there, there!" I said, laughing, fighting to keep my balance as I perched in a crouched position on the stilettos and he jumped up to stand on his back legs with his front paws in my lap. "Aren't you just the sweetest thing?"

The woman stopped and glared at me. She put her hands on her bony hips. "I would thank you to remove your hands from my dog."

I stared at her in stunned silence. How could she have missed that daring feat when I threw my body in front of the scared animal to save its life? Either she didn't see it or she didn't care, because when I didn't move fast enough, she snarled again.

"Young woman, did you hear me? Elmer does not like strangers. It unsettles him."

I looked down at the dog, joyously licking any piece of my flesh he could find, and thought that he certainly didn't look unsettled. Aloud I said, "He appears to be thanking me for saving his life." I smiled sweetly and she glared hatefully.

"Your help is not needed."

Nor appreciated, I thought to myself. I stood up. "I'm sorry. I was just trying to help."

She turned sharply on the heels of her sensible Hush Puppies, commanding, "Come on, Elmer. We need to have a word with that young man."

Elmer didn't move so I gave him a little push on his backside with my foot. He turned to look at me pitifully as if to say, "How could you do that to me?"

"I'm sorry," I whispered to my new best friend. With my hands, I shooed him away. "Go now. *Please*." I didn't want another chastisement from the old woman who was anything but frail and vulnerable. She threw another mean look over her shoulder.

"Elmer!" she hissed sharply with such a finality that the beleaguered beagle finally moved slowly to trail along behind her. I had missed the walk signal and had to wait for another, which gave me the opportunity to see the old woman encounter the hapless kid who had made the foolish mistake of skating back toward us. He would have been best served to leave town and never return. Oh, the young. There are some things that only experience teaches, and I am quite sure that once she was through with him, he knew better than to hit, run and then return. She stopped him and grabbed him by the ear, her black purse swinging from her arm and the forefinger of the other hand wagging a mile a minute. She was telling him off to a fare-thee-well. I don't know who I felt sorrier for—the dog or the boy. I finally decided it was the dog, since he had to go home with her while the boy would eventually be set free.

"Well," I thought to myself as I crossed the street, "I guess every town's got at least one mean old biddie. Even Bliss, Mississippi."

♡

In front of Susan Marie's bookstore, I bought a copy of the *Bliss Observer* from the paper box. As I closed the box, I looked up to see a huge poster of my face staring back at me. Across the top of the poster was the name of my new book and then a banner that announced the day and time of my signing. To accompany the window display were a dozen or so copies of my book stacked in a very fetching way. I smiled a bit with pride, I admit, but mostly with gratitude that Susan Marie had worked so hard to promote my appearance. I folded the newspaper in half and then wandered on down the street to the diner a couple of doors down. I pushed the glass door open and saw a woman, in late middle age, dressed in khaki slacks and a dark green polo shirt emblazoned with "Maggie's Southern Diner," hurrying with great purpose to and fro. She first saw me as she scooted toward a booth while carrying two plates of food, still steaming from the heat of the stove.

"Hello!" she called out with a smile so big that I felt welcome immediately. "Just bring yourself on in and sit down anywhere that appeals to ya. I'll be right with ya."

"Thank you." It was a small, rectangular area with a counter and bar stools that ran down the right-hand side, red vinyl-covered booths down the left side and a row of tables for four filling the space in the center. Bottles of ketchup, mustard, dispensers of sugar, shakers of salt and pepper and shiny steel containers of napkins sat within reaching distance of each seat. About a dozen people were scattered hither and yon among stools, booths and tables. I love booths. They're my favorite and given a choice, there is never a choice: I always take a booth. They're more comfortable than those straight, hard chairs, and you can spread out if you feel the need. I selected a booth halfway back and sat down to face the door. Since I'm a writer who must make up characters for a living, I try to take advantage of each situation as a possible research expedition. Writers of fiction, you must know, decorate fact with enough misleading embellishment to claim creation of it. Once I was complaining to my friend Debra that I was stuck for a good, nutty character to insert into a plot. She always has advice.

"That's easy. Just go to a Waffle House, especially between the hours of 1 a.m. and 5 a.m. and you'll see some real doozies." Now, I don't know how Debra knew the best hours for character trolling at Waffle House but she sure was right. Out of desperation, I hauled myself down to the closest Waffle House—there are five within a twenty-minute drive of my house—and there I found a model for one of the best characters I ever "created." Plus, I got to partake of scattered, smothered and covered hashbrowns and crisp bacon. All in all, it was one of my better research trips.

I glanced at the menu on the table, but certain that there were daily specials, I decided to wait for the nice lady to provide guidance. As I waited, I began looking at the *Bliss Observer,* which, according to its masthead, comes out three times a week. I noticed with mild satisfaction that the listings for the obituaries were prominently placed under the score for the Atlanta Braves/Chicago Cubs game the previous night. Good lead-in—lure them in with a final score, then fade to the final out. The front page included a short story in a box about my appearance at Bliss Your Heart and a story of a car wash fund-raiser for the

Humane Society, accompanied by a photo of two kids with their arms thrown around three big mutts who were looking for a home.

"So, pretty lady, what can I get for ya tonight?" I snapped out of the flashback and looked up to see the friendly woman who had welcomed me earlier. She set down a glass of water. Her sandy brown hair with generous streaks of gray was cut in a chin-length bob and pushed behind her ears. Her complexion was rosy and clear with the tiniest of age lines that spread around her violet blue eyes, lines that multiplied several times when she stretched her mouth into the wide grin that revealed even, white teeth. Without a doubt, she had once been a head-turning beauty.

I smiled. "Do you have any specials?"

"Why, sure we do. For meat, we've got country-fried steak, chicken livers and the best meatloaf your tongue ever touched."

My eyes lighted up. "Meatloaf? Is it really that good?"

She nodded eagerly. "I swear on it." She held a hand up to prove it. "I've been in the restaurant business for nigh on twenty years now, and my meatloaf recipe is one reason I've made it this far!"

"Then sign me up. I can't turn that down. I'll have cheddar mashed potatoes and fried okra, please. And is your ice tea sweet?"

"Is there any other kind?" she asked, grinning.

"Then I'll have sweet tea and I hope it's so sweet that my teeth ache." I put my menu back on the table between the napkin holder and the ketchup bottle. "Would you, by any chance, be the famous Maggie of Maggie's Southern Diner?"

She laughed as she finished scribbling the order on her small green pad. "That's me. But it was the meatloaf that made me famous." She turned to walk off but stopped. Slowly, she turned her head back towards me. She looked at me for a brief second;

then her eyes widened in shocked delight. She whirled around. "You're Abby Houston, aren't you? Oh, my gosh! Oh, my gosh!" She scooted back to my table and slid into the bench across from me. "I love your books! I read 'em *and* I listen to 'em on tape. It took me a second but I recognized your voice before I recognized your face." She tilted her head and eyed me carefully. "You look different. I don't have your new book yet, 'cause I was waitin' for you to get here. Lordy be! I can't believe you're eatin' here! Now, why do you look so different?"

"My hair's longer and a bit lighter red. You know, the older you get, the lighter your hair should be!" I winked.

She ran her hand under the back of her hair. "Oh, honey, I just don't bother. I got three grandchildren and there's no use tryin' to hide that I ain't no spring chicken anymore. Besides, I'm either kin to or grew up with most everybody in Bliss, so they know how old I am anyway!" She slid out of the booth. "Well, let me run and put this order in. My husband Joe is workin' in the back so I'll make sure that he takes extra special care of our celebrity. We don't get that many in here, don't you know?"

"All I know is that I can't wait to taste the meatloaf that made you famous," I called after her as she was hurrying off.

I heard the bell that hung about the door jingling to signal that it had opened. I was watching Maggie as she scurried away so I didn't look in that direction until I heard someone call out, "Maggie May, how's my sweetheart?" I turned my head in the direction of the voice to see an attractive guy—young, very young since he looked to be about my age—with his arms spread wide to announce his arrival. His eyes had a mischievous twinkle and his smile was nothing short of irresistible.

Maggie, upon hearing the voice, stopped in her tracks, my order for meatloaf forgotten, and turned to face him. She plopped her hands down heavily on her hips and narrowed her eyes. There was not one glimmer of the friendliness that I had encountered when I entered the door.

"You no-account rascal!" she snarled. "Don't you come whizzin' in here all charms and smiles, pretendin' that everythin's rosy. *Where in the tarnation have you been?*"

Chapter 6

The handsome man laughed easily at the rebuke. He folded his arms across his chest and the broad smile turned into an impish grin, a look that was also irresistible in its charm as one corner of his mouth went up much higher than the other.

"Now, now, sweet Maggie May. How could you possibly treat such a poor guy so badly? Haven't I always been the apple of your eye?"

I settled down comfortably in the booth, ready to watch the show. This, I thought to myself, is better than the Waffle House. No sooner had that thought flittered across my brain than the mood of the scene changed. Maggie's grimness suddenly melted completely into unabashed joy. She started smiling, chuckling and shaking her head. She motioned him toward her with a wave of her hand.

"Come over here and give me a hug, you ol' lug!" she commanded. "I've missed your mean self."

With two long-legged strides, he slid over to Maggie and grabbed her up in his arms for a bear hug. I figured him to be about six feet tall, making him five or six inches taller than Maggie, and somewhere around the age of forty. His shoulders were broad and strong looking, tapering down past a lean torso to a narrow waist. His hair was short around his neck but rakishly longer on top and was the color of rich chocolate suede with a luster that caught the light around his longish, angular face. When he smiled, which he had done without ceasing since his dramatic entrance, every inch of his face sparkled along with his brilliantly white teeth. He was dressed casually but handsomely in a pair of khaki trousers and an orange polo shirt. I decided he was a man of tremendous confidence, as if I hadn't already figured that out, because only a strong-spirited man would wear an orange shirt. That took courage.

The hug slipped into a casual embrace as he threw one arm easily over her shoulders and she let hers hang loosely from his waist. "You old blue-eyed devil," she said teasingly. "I've missed you somethin' terrible. Where you been? I know it's been pert near a week since I last saw ya."

He nodded. "That's 'bout right. Last Friday, I just up and took off with the family at the last minute. You know, Mama and Daddy's got that house down in Bay St. Louis on the water. So we went down there for a few days of R & R. Got back on Tuesday but was so busy catching up that all I got to eat was whatever was in the vending machines at the office or whatever Lulu saw fit to bring back to me when she went out to lunch. Today, I've been in Jackson all day and just got home. Thought I'd swing by here and get some of your good ol' home cookin' to take home for supper."

"I's gittin' worried. Ain't like you to go so long without stop-pin' in." She released her arm from his waist but I noticed—just happened to notice, mind you—before he dropped his arm from her shoulders that there was no wedding band on the appropriate finger. I was becoming more interested in the situation. He had said something about going off with the family and he was certainly old enough to have the proper kind of family for a man of his age, but I told myself, he could have been talking about family like parents and siblings. Myself answered back, "I told you, dummy, a long time ago that the good ones are taken. Why must I keep repeating myself? And another thing, men don't always wear their wedding rings. Remember that Casanova you went out with in Birmingham? The one you assumed wasn't married because he didn't have a ring on, and because he asked you out, you thought that a married man wouldn't date? Do I have to keep reminding you of these things?" No, I was getting the point, loud and clear.

Suddenly she remembered my meatloaf. "Oops! Hold on a sec' while I turn this order in to Joe and tell him that the prodigal son has returned." She hurried around the counter and through the swinging door to the kitchen. The "prodigal son" sat down on a stool, placed his elbows on the counter, laced his fingers together and looked around him, still smiling.

"Well, hey there, Jimmy Lawrence! I didn't see you. How's things in the insurance business?"

"Just tryin' to stay afloat," Jimmy Lawrence replied and pointed to the man across the table. "I was just tellin' Ben here that the drought this summer took a big toll on my farmers. Can't even begin to tell you how many chickens smothered in the heat. Then, folks' wells startin' goin' dry. It's been tough."

The prodigal son nodded sympathetically and looked concerned. "Yeah, I was just talking to some folks down at the capitol about it today. They're going to try to pass some legislation that will give the farmers some financial relief. I just hope it's enough."

An older couple, both gray and wearied with age and probably worry, were sitting in a booth in front of me. The blue eyes—I couldn't see the color but that's what Maggie said—of the prodigal son rested on them. He swung around on the stool to face them squarely. "Hello, Mr. and Mrs. Murdock. I hear you folks have been having some trouble out on the farm."

Mr. Murdock was facing me so I saw his shoulders slump and he dropped his head. His wife's gray head moved back and forth in a slow shake. "I'll say," the man answered tiredly. "One of my young farmhands turned the thermostat in one of the chicken houses the other night. He thought he was turning the fan up but he turned it off. The next morning I had twenty-five thousand dead chickens laying there, all smothered to death." He rubbed his eyes with his fingers. "Took us three straight days with a backhoe and front-end loader to bury all of 'em."

The smile was completely gone from the prodigal's face, replaced by concern as he slid off the stool and walked over to shake hands with the farmer. "Sir, I sure am awfully sorry to hear that. Y'all gonna be all right?"

"Between the insurance company and the poultry company, we'll come out with minimal losses, but the chickens were only one week away from being picked up so we lost seven weeks of hard work and feed cost and all our profit, too."

Compassionately, he reached over and patted the old man on the shoulder. "Well, if there's anything that I or anyone I know can do for you, you just give me a call. You hear?"

"That's mighty fine of you, son. 'Preciate it much. More than you can ever know."

At this point, had I been smart—and I think we have already established otherwise—I would have dropped my eyes quickly to the *Bliss Observer* lying on the table in front of me and pretended to be completely absorbed in the story about the latest FFA winner in the prize pig showing. But no, oh no, even though he was standing almost within touching distance, I had to be staring straight at him as if I was completely mesmerized by his charm like everyone else in the diner. I had to be looking goopy eyed at his profoundly perfect profile when he turned to his right and caught me red-handed. Our eyes locked for a brief moment as I tried to think how to wiggle out of the embarrassing position because ladies, especially those with cool class, do not stare. He, most surely, was still thinking about Mr. Murdock's grievous loss of twenty-five thousand chickens and the financial devastation of it all. It probably took a second for his mind to switch from chickens to a chick. I managed, though red faced, to smile demurely: that would be a tight smile that shows no teeth and reveals no emotion. Then I turned my attention, quite nonchalantly I'm sure, back to the newspaper. I felt his eyes still on me and I glanced back, looking up through my double-mascara-coated eyelashes with my chin still tilted down. A new variety of smile crossed his face. One I had not yet seen. It was flirtatious, courtly and amused all rolled into one. He gallantly tossed a short, quick nod toward me in a way reminiscent of men who once tipped their hats to ladies. It was incredibly seductive and my heart swooned. I was hoping I hid it but I felt as if he could read each rapid heartbeat. I felt the heat of my cheeks as I again smiled, this time a little less demurely and a lot more shyly. Thank goodness that I was saved by Maggie who came clattering out of the kitchen accompanied by a burly, bald-headed guy in a white apron who was carrying a spatula.

"My man!" the bald-headed guy exclaimed. "We's just talkin' 'bout you this mornin' and how it had been a week of Sundays since we last seen you." He rushed over to the boy wonder and shook his hand vigorously.

"Joe, it's good to see ya. This slave driver over here hasn't been workin' ya too hard, has she?"

Maggie playfully hit him on the arm. "Oh, Spencer, you know better than that! He's the slave driver, not me."

"Hmmm, Spencer," I thought. I decided it was a good name for him and how I would have hated it if it had turned out to be Oscar or Roy Lee. I once dated a guy who was gorgeous but his name was Hoyt Grizzle, and somehow that name just managed to cancel out his good looks. The trio chatted for a minute and I tried to act completely disinterested in what was going on but the cruel truth is that I'm nosey. I do it, though, strictly for the sake of my art.

"I best get back to the kitchen," Joe said, excusing himself. "Give Maggie your order and we'll get it right out."

Spencer walked over to the counter and sat down while Maggie walked behind it and picked up her pad and pencil.

"What's it gonna be?" she asked.

"Make it a cheeseburger, extra cheese, ketchup only, with French fries and lots of pickles on the side. Guess who that's for?" From the side, I could see that he winked.

"I don't have to guess," she replied with a chuckle. "I know who loves pickles in your family."

My heart sputtered. A family. Hmmm. Of course, he had a family. But that sounded like a child's meal. Hopefully it was. A woman would never order extra cheese, especially a woman married to that man. She would be too concerned with the width of her hips. After all, there was a chance that he was divorced. Let me stop here and say that I don't even know why it mattered. I never see anyone who captures my attention so I can't explain why he did. Somehow he did.

"What else?" Maggie asked.

"Got any meatloaf tonight?"

"You know I do. Cheddar mashed potatoes and fried okra?"

He laughed. "Maggie May, you know me too well. That'll be it. I'm going to run over to the office and check my messages, then I'll be back to pick it up."

I almost fell out of the booth. He ordered the exact same thing that I did. Out of eight different side dishes to choose from, he ordered the same thing! "This is an omen," I told myself. "I know it is." I was so excited by the thought that I wanted to holler out, "Hey, how 'bout that? We ordered the same thing! We're a match made in heaven." But I refrained. Good thing I did because Maggie's next words closed the door of opportunity.

"What about Elizabeth? Is she not eatin' tonight?"

"Well, she is but not with me." He grinned impishly again and leaned forward on his elbows in a conspiratorial pose. "Girls' night out. They're going out for pizza and a movie. And I'm sure there'll be a lot of girl talk about us guys."

My heart fell. I had been in love for less than five minutes and now it was over. Completely kaput. "Well," I thought to myself, "that's about par for the course." Five minutes in love and it's all over. That might even be a new record for me. I sighed without realizing it, loudly enough that they both turned to look at me.

"Oh, honey, I'm sorry," Maggie blurted. "Your food will be right out. I promise. It won't be but another minute or two."

Now, what was I going to say? I wasn't sighing over not having my food. I was sighing because this man I haven't even met has already broken my heart? I don't think so. I thought quickly.

"Oh, no, that's not what I was sighing about," I immediately reassured her. "I was just reading this story about the Humane Society, and it made me sad to think of all the poor abandoned and abused animals." I thought it was brilliant although I was astounded and a bit ashamed at how quickly and effortlessly such an out-and-out lie slipped from my tongue. But it was actually quite good. It covered up the truth, portrayed me as enormously kind and loving and had the extra bonus of making it look like I actually *was* reading the paper rather than eavesdropping.

A look of empathy covered Maggie's face and Spencer turned to look over his shoulder. He was smiling at me, although I no longer had a right to care, but it was a bit of a consolation prize to win a coveted smile, one meant for me and no one else. I wanted to luxuriate in the moment, but it was snatched from me when the door swung open with such force that the windows vibrated and the bell shook so violently it threatened to break loose from its nailed perch. Forks stopped in midair, conversation ceased in midsentence, and breaths suspended in midmotion. All eyes turned toward the commotion to find none other than that mean old woman of my recent, most unfortunate acquaintance. Her big, black pocketbook hung from the crook of one arm while the other age-spotted hand clutched a hip bone.

"Spencer!" she screeched toward my once beloved. "I'm looking for you!"

Like the others in the restaurant, he had turned to see Hurricane Hateful when she blew in. His reaction was such that I literally could feel his heart sink. He turned his head back toward Maggie, dropped it, closed his eyes and shook his head slowly. She was not deterred. She marched right over to him and threw a bony finger in his face.

"Mr. High and Mighty, I'm talking to you! Do you hear me? You better pay some respect to your elders."

I saw his back rise and fall as he took a deep breath, collecting himself for the showdown. He forced a smile and turned to face her.

"Hello, Miss Eula," he said in a voice that was void of expression. "How are you on this fine evening?"

"Don't be nice to me, do you hear? It may work with everyone else in this town, but it won't work with me." She moved closer to his face and growled. *"I don't like nice!"* She threw back her head imperially as if nice was beneath her.

"I sense there might be a problem here," he said, a bit mechanically but with tinges of sarcasm slipping in.

"You're darn tooting there's a problem. Kyle Edwards almost run me over with that skate doo-lolly of his. He did, in fact, hit poor Elmer." She flung a finger toward the floor where, lo and behold, stood the poor beagle. Maggie was pouring a cup of coffee for a man who was seated a couple of stools down from Spencer. When she heard Elmer's name mentioned, she stopped pouring, set the pot down and leaned over the counter to see the dog.

"Eula! What is that dog doin' in here?" she demanded. "The health department will shut me down tighter than Dick's hatband if they find out a dog's in this restaurant."

The old woman turned her vinegar-tinged tongue on Maggie. "Let me tell you something, Maggie Stephens. I own this building and if Elmer wants to come in here, he'll come in here anytime he pleases. So put *that* in your little pipe and smoke it!"

I saw fire in Maggie's eyes as she moved down the counter and leaned close to the old woman. "I pay rent for this place, too much rent in fact. But I've been here for twenty-five years and I've never been a day late or a dollar short. Joe and I have tried repeatedly to buy this buildin' and you refuse to sell it. But let me tell you this: as long as I pay, you play by my rules or you can get someone else to overpay you. Me and Joe'll be happy to retire any day."

That mean old woman gasped in horror. Speechless, she stared at Maggie for a moment before turning back to Spencer.

"I want to know what you intend to do with that boy, who most certainly is destined for a life of crime and murder."

"I'll have a talk with him."

"Talk!" She shook her fist furiously in the air. "This situation calls for more than just talk! I want action!" Her voice croaked with anger.

"What kind of action?"

"He should be severely punished. Send him to my house for a month and let him work off his debt to society."

He laughed sarcastically. "Miss Eula, I would rather send the boy to the chain gang for the rest of his life than to send him to your house for a month."

It was interesting to hear someone as young as Spencer use the term "chain gang," a reference to the days of old when prisoners were chained together and sentenced to hard labor. But I did think it was an appropriate analogy. I know I saw steam come from her ears. She slapped a brittle hand down on the Formica countertop.

"Let me remind you that I am not to be toyed with. I'll make you rue the day you went up against me, young man!"

"I will speak to him immediately about this and ask him to exercise extreme caution in the future," he replied evenly and firmly. "Is there anything else I might be able to do for you?"

She glared angrily toward him. "Yes. I want signs posted immediately to prohibit any kind of skating on the town's sidewalks."

Again, he laughed sarcastically. "That's a matter for Gus Holbrook and the town council. But, Miss Eula, how antagonistic is that in a town as hospitable as Bliss? To put up signs forbidding this or that? Our townspeople know not to spit on the sidewalk and not to drop cigarette butts. All that has to be done is to run a notice in the *Observer*, asking the kids not to skateboard, and it will become a nonissue."

"Let me remind you that as the town's largest possessor of property, I am also the town's largest taxpayer and the county's for that matter," she spat back at him. "Therefore, I expect my wishes to be adhered to. I shall appear before the next session of the town council."

He nodded. "I am quite certain that the town council will be happy to address your concerns. I believe that is its policy with all of the town's residents. Meanwhile, I will speak to Kyle immediately." He looked down at the beagle. "Elmer, I'm most happy to know that *you* were unharmed by this unfortunate mishap."

I turned my head to the wall, covered my mouth and sniggered. She, however, was not amused. Fire flashed in the eyes hidden amidst lines and wrinkles.

"Spencer, you can make light of the situation if you wish, but I am an old woman who was minding my own business when a speedster raced around the corner and nearly mowed me down. Had it not been for what are truly remarkable reflexes in a woman approaching eighty, I would have been killed. Outright murdered! And let's not even mention the trauma that poor Elmer has had to endure on this awful day. I will deal with you at another time." The awful woman swung around, snapped her fingers and commanded, "Come, Elmer. We must get you home and give you your Prozac in a timely fashion."

Prozac? For a dog? That's one thing I never heard at the Waffle House. Never expect to hear it, either. She clopped her Hush Puppies furiously across the café's linoleum floor and stormed angrily out the door, followed lethargically by Elmer, who no doubt was anxious to get home and get his Prozac. The floor show over, the other patrons returned to their meals while Maggie wrinkled her nose. She stuck out her tongue as the door closed. It was very childish but appropriate nonetheless.

"Maggie!" Spencer exclaimed in mock horror. "How could you be so mean to such a sweet old woman?" She giggled, then happened to glance over and see me.

"Oh my gosh! I'm gittin' your food now!" She whirled

around and as she rushed toward the kitchen door, Spencer called after her, "Maggie, I'm going over to my office. I'll be back in twenty-five or thirty minutes."

He slid off the stool and strolled toward the door. I didn't miss a second of his departure, either. I'm used to watching men walk out of my life. But, oh, how I hated to see that handsome one go.

Chapter 7

Maggie didn't exaggerate when she bragged on her meatloaf because it was, in fact, the best I had ever tasted. She used a sauce made with A-1 rather than ketchup on the top and the result was succulent. The entire meal was so good that I unashamedly ate every morsel. I didn't even worry about being a lady and leaving something on my plate as ladies should. I decided instead to be a woman with a robust appetite, and I did an outstanding job at it, too. Of course, nothing's more of a compliment to a cook than a clean plate, so Maggie was busting with pride when she came over to the table to pour more sweet tea for me. When I saw the look on her face, I was grateful that I had been so unselfish.

"Now, you saved room for dessert, didn't ya?" she asked.

Of course I hadn't. I didn't save room for anything. But when she told me that her specialty was blueberry pie and homemade ice cream, how could I possibly say no? I love blueberry pie and ice cream, even when it isn't homemade. It is my greatest weakness. So great that when I find I have sinned in some way, I do atonement by giving up ice cream for a while. Most Baptists just like to live with the guilt, but not me. I purge myself of it by depriving myself of my favorite decadence. I swear to you that I was already up to my chin in food, and I pushed it up to my eyeballs when I polished off the delectable dessert. I had just finished and was thinking how miserable I felt when my long-lost love returned to pick up his order.

"Got me ready, Maggie?" he asked, stopping at the cash register and pulling out his billfold.

"You betcha!" She toted a white plastic bag filled with two white Styrofoam cartons to the register. He paid and then turned to talk to a couple who had just walked in. I put my tip on the table and went to the register where I was only a few feet away from the prince of Bliss. He didn't realize that I had stepped in between him and the register, so when he turned back to pick up his bag, he stepped into me, and his heavy shoe crushed my sandaled foot.

"Ow!" I yelled and meant every bit of it. I grabbed my foot with my hand and rubbed the area where the skin had been pushed away and tiny spots of blood had begun to leak to the surface. He took my elbow with one hand and put the other around my shoulders as I tried to balance like a stork on one leg.

"Oh, no! I'm so sorry. Are you all right?" I was within inches of his face and I could see that his eyes, indeed, were blue, a mesmerizing blue that was the blended shade of violet and robin's eggs. Those beautiful eyes were filled with such compassion over my distress. I forgot my pain. I didn't even notice the blood. But my eyes still stung from the sudden pain. I swallowed and nodded.

"Yeah, I'm fine." Slowly I lowered my foot and then gingerly I put my weight on it. It still stung but it was getting better. His face whitened when he saw the blood that was running in a tiny stream down the edge of my size-six, beautifully pedicured foot. At that moment, forgetting the pain, I thought how pleased I was that I had gotten a fresh pedicure in Little Rock.

"You're bleeding!" He looked petrified and Maggie flew toward the kitchen, hollering that she'd get a wet towel. "Here, let me help you over there to sit down." Hopping on one foot and leaning, perhaps more than necessary, on him for support, I made it to the chair that he pulled from a nearby table. "I'm so sorry. I didn't even look. I just whirled around like an ox in a china shop."

"No, please don't apologize. It's no one's fault." Maggie had arrived with the wet towel and squatted down beside me to pull my sandal off and pat the blood away.

"Oh, this is gonna be nice and purple tomorrow," Maggie commented. Joe came out of the back to see what all the commotion was about. "It's nothin'," she assured him. "Just a big, strappin' guy runnin' all over a little gal. And a visitor, no less!"

Spencer's face reddened. "Are you sure you're all right? Does anything feel broken?"

I wiggled my foot and I must admit that I did try to make it look a little seductive as I did so. "Hmmm. I think everything's fine. Doesn't feel broken or torn."

He sighed gratefully. "Oh, thank goodness for that." He turned to Maggie. "Has she paid her check yet?"

"No," she replied with a grin. "I was just startin' to ring her up when you ran her over."

He looked at me and smiled. "Then dinner's on me."

Horror flashed through my mind. Dessert. I had eaten dessert. And any woman worth her weight in lipstick knows that you never eat dessert when you're trying to impress a man.

Lord only knows why I was trying to impress a *married* man. But I was and I didn't want him to see my bill and know how much food I had eaten. "No!" I screamed with urgency. "No, I cannot allow you to do that."

He moved quickly over to the cash register and scooped up the ticket that Maggie had left there. He looked down at it and then grinned. "Blueberry pie a la mode, huh?" He winked. "Good choice. One of my favorites."

I felt the red heat run from my forehead down to my pedicure as my mouth and throat suddenly went dry. I just wanted to crawl under a rock and die. While I was writhing in agony over my lack of foresight in having dessert, he was paying Maggie, who happily took his money. My foot felt better and I slid my sandal back on. I stood up and it did hurt a bit, which would have been fine for a short walk to the car, but I suddenly remembered that I had to walk four blocks back to the Magnolia Blossom. While I was trying to think what I was going to do, Maggie walked over to the door.

"Looks like it's comin' up a cloud out there," she commented.

Spencer nodded. "It sure does. Looks like the sky's going to burst any minute." No sooner were those words out of his mouth than a heavy clang of thunder sounded, followed by a bolt of lightning that turned the dark dusk into pure daylight for a second. Within seconds, large drops of heavy rain began to pelt the earth.

"Oh, great," I mumbled, thinking I had said it under my breath. But oh, no, I hadn't, for both of them looked at me questioningly.

"Honey, what's wrong?" Maggie asked.

I shrugged. "Nothing. It's no big deal."

She folded her arms and gave me one of those looks Mama gives me when she knows I'm not telling her something that she thinks I should. She gestured with her hand. "C'mon. Come clean. What is it?"

"I, uh, walked here from the Magnolia Blossom Bed and Breakfast."

For some reason, her face brightened and her eyes seemed to dance with joy. "That's what's wrong? Well, that ain't nothin'." She extended an arm toward Spencer and tossed her hand with a flourish. "Because Mr. Finesse over here will be more than happy to run you home. It's on his way and even if it wasn't, ain't nothin' too far apart in Bliss."

I should have been thrilled. I *would* have been thrilled, if only I had not seen the look on his face. His head jerked around toward her and his eyes bugged out in a classic expression of have-you-lost-your-ever-loving-mind? He was too much of a gentleman to say anything, so when she said, "Won't you, sugar pie?" what's he going to say? Especially since he so recently had almost crippled me.

I cringed. It reminded me of when I was eighteen and dreamed day and night of going out with Trey Thomas. His mama liked me because I waited on her at the dress shop where I worked. She figured out I had a crush on Trey, so one day when he came with her to pick up some dresses that she had left for alteration, she managed to arrange a movie date for us. He looked that same way, and we went on the worst date of my life. He barely spoke to me all night, and he refused to share his popcorn or to buy me a box. That one date cured me well and good of a crush on Trey Thomas. I did not want to be in a similar situation, even if he was a married man and there was no chance for us anyway.

"Oh, no, no, no," I said firmly, "I won't hear of that."

Maggie smiled sweetly. I knew that smile. I had used a similar one many times when I needed to coax a man into doing something for me. "Now, Spencer, you tell this sweet girl how you won't mind a'tall takin her back to the Magnolia Blossom."

He looked at her for a second. It seemed to be a warning look, the kind that says, "I'll take care of you later." Then aloud he said—while still looking at her, I might add—"No, of course, I don't mind at all. I'll be happy to."

I was dying. I'm telling you that I was dying as surely as if a poisonous viper had slithered up my body and fanged me right in the jugular. "I can't put you to so much trouble. Really I can't." The last words of my protest were drowned out by the thunder, lightning and deafening patter of rain that began to pour uninhibited from the heavens.

Maggie looked out the window and smiled happily at the downpour. "Looks like you ain't got no choice but to go with him."

I looked down at my clothes, the high-heeled sandals and the battered foot. I didn't want to ruin my clothes and shoes, and besides that, my foot was starting to feel pretty sore. I didn't have much of a choice. So I told myself that it didn't matter because I would never see him again anyway and it was the gentlemanly thing for him to do. Wouldn't he appreciate it if someone helped out his wife or mother that way?

"Maggie's right," he said, a smile suddenly stretching across his face and causing it to crinkle into an expression of kindness and warmth. "You don't have any choice but to go with me. I'm parked right outside. Let me run out and get a golf umbrella I have in the car and I'll be back to get you." He grabbed his food, blew a kiss at Maggie and dashed out into the rain.

"Now, don't you worry. I've known Spence since he was this high," she said, holding her hand near her knees. "He used to come in here every day after school and I'd fix him peanut-butter-and-mayonnaise sandwiches. He's a good boy."

I wrinkled my nose. Peanut-butter-and-mayonnaise sand-wiches? Yuck. He seemed so normal. The door opened and Spencer, his orange shirt wet from the dash to the car, came in, shaking off a huge green golf umbrella.

"Ready?"

I nodded and Maggie said, "I told her not to worry none 'cause I've known ya since you's a kid and she'll be okay." She turned back to me. "We know where to find him, if we need to." She winked.

At the door, I paused when Spencer opened it for me. The rain was furious. I couldn't stand the thought of ruining the Jimmy Choo shoes, but I didn't know how to say that without appearing shallow and vain. No comments from the peanut gallery, please. But, don't worry, because I figured out a way.

"Everything okay?" he asked.

"You know, I'm not sure I can hurry fast enough in these shoes with the rain." I looked at him and smiled in a tiny flirta-tious way. I wasn't wasting any big flirtatious ways on a mar-ried man, so I used just enough to get my way. "What with my foot somewhat damaged and all, I think I'll just take off my shoes and go barefooted."

"Honey, you goin' out there without any shoes on?" Maggie asked incredulously.

If you only knew how much these shoes cost on Rodeo Drive, I thought to myself. Aloud I said, "Oh, it's fine. At home, I'm a barefooted kind of girl. Trust me, this is best. I can move faster."

Maggie looked at Spencer and he shrugged. By that point, he was probably just wanting to get rid of me, and he wouldn't have cared if I had crawled to the car on my knees.

"Okay, sweetie." She came over and took both my hands. "I'll be over to see you tomorrow."

Spencer was preoccupied with opening the door for me. He held it for me and I stepped under the awning. He followed, opened the umbrella and took my elbow. "I'm in that black SUV over there." He motioned to a parking space close by, and we made a dash for it. He opened the door and I hiked up to the passenger's seat, trying to maintain a ladylike posture, but it isn't easy in those big things. When he got settled in the driver's seat, he shook the umbrella off and laid it between his seat and the door. As he was buckling his safety belt, he looked up and said, "I just realized that I don't know your name. I'm Spencer."

He offered his hand and I shook it and said, "I'm Abby. It's nice to meet you."

He cocked his head, his handsome head I'm compelled to add, to the side and eyed me carefully. "You look very familiar. Have we met before?" I was suddenly conscious of the manly fragrance that filled the air. It smelled like Polo Cologne. I took a deep breath and I am quite certain that my eyelashes twittered in ecstasy. I love a man who smells good but most don't these days. Mostly, they just have no smell in a world that seems to becoming more generic by the day. But when I smell cologne, it is the biggest aphrodisiac in the world to me. My knees buckle and I kinda swoon, especially when the man looks like the one who was sitting next to me.

Oh, trust me, I'd never forget that, I thought as I was melting into a pathetic puddle. I shook my head. "No, I don't believe so."

"Have you ever been to Bliss before?"

"No. First time here. It's such a beautiful little town."

He put the SUV into gear and turned to look over his shoulder as he backed out. "You must have a twin somewhere because I know I've seen you before." I said nothing as he concentrated on getting out of the parking space in the driving rain. When that was accomplished and he put the vehicle in drive, he asked, "Are you here on business?"

"Yes. I'm just passing through. I'll be here for a couple of nights. I'm really quite taken by this town. Everyone is so friendly and nice."

His chortle was sarcastic and he raised one eyebrow as he asked, "Weren't you in the diner when Miss Eula Corbett came in, pitching one of her usual tirades?"

"Yeah, but there's one of her in every place." I shrugged. "Even heaven."

"Heaven?" He looked puzzled.

"Well, it says in the Bible that Satan was first an angel in heaven. I think he might have even been an archangel like Michael. Anyway, he got to causing trouble and stirring things up so much that God cast him out of heaven and created hell for him. So if it can happen in heaven, it can happen in Bliss."

I wasn't trying to be funny but he got so tickled that he slapped the steering wheel two or three times. He must have laughed for a full thirty seconds. He couldn't stop. Finally, he said, "Oh, that's a good one! I love the comparison: Bliss to heaven, Miss Eula to the devil." He started laughing again. He even grabbed his side with one arm. "Abby, I promise that every time Miss Eula raises Cain about something, which is quite a lot, I'm going to think about you and what you said."

Now, we were getting somewhere. I'd said something so memorable that he was not ever going to forget me. Then I remembered his wife, which, to say the least, cast a pall over everything.

"May I ask you a question?" I asked tenuously.

"Shoot."

"Why was Miss Eula jumping on you about the boy on the skateboard?"

He gave me one of those adorable lopsided grins. "Because that boy belongs to me. Kyle Edwards is my son."

"Oh!" I let that sink in for a minute. Then I realized that until that moment I had not known what Spencer's last name was.

Spencer Edwards. Okay. Nice enough name. "Well, for what it's worth, I did see the entire incident, and it was not as bad as she described. He just got distracted for a moment, but when he saw her, it was *his* reflexes, not her remarkable-for-a-woman-approaching-eighty ones, that avoided the situation."

He chuckled and tilted his head to look at me with interest. "You have a unique way of expressing yourself. That's great. But for the record, I figured as much. Still, he shouldn't be skateboarding downtown near the shops, so I'll have a talk with him when I get home. A gentle one."

"I thought he was a very nice, well-mannered boy. He spoke to me as he came whizzing by."

He nodded and a bit of pride showed on his face. "He's a pretty good kid, I'll have to say. At least he is at ten. Who knows what'll happen at eleven?" By that time we had arrived in front of the Magnolia Blossom. Unfortunately it doesn't take long to go four blocks, even in a hard, pelting rain in the first hour of evening darkness.

"Hang on and I'll run over and get you," he instructed as he opened the door and hopped out. When he opened my door, he offered his hand. I took it and tried not to be so conscious of the feel of my hand in his. I cradled my shoes and purse with the other and took a giant leap to the pavement where my feet landed in a puddle of warm rainwater. Again, he took my elbow and guided me up the front walkway, up the four steps and onto the wide porch with the huge columns, making certain that I was well protected by the umbrella.

"Be sure to tell Maggie I got you home safely, and it wouldn't hurt to tell Charlotte, too. Those are two women in town who I always want on my side." He grinned lopsidedly.

"I will," I promised. "Thanks for going to the trouble. I really appreciate it."

"No problem." He patted me on the shoulder. "Have a nice

stay in Bliss." When he got to the steps, he turned back around. "I still think I've seen you somewhere before." He studied my face for a moment and then shrugged. "Oh well, maybe I just dreamed it. 'Bye."

"Bye," I responded softly. As he reached the gate to the white picket fence, I whispered to myself, "See you in *my* dreams. See you there tonight."

♡

Not a soul was to be seen or heard when I entered the grand foyer of the Magnolia Blossom Bed and Breakfast. The crystal chandelier glistened with soft light. Barefooted, I clutched my high heels to my chest and quietly climbed the stairs to my room, where I ran a hot bath scented with magnolia oil from a cute gift set on the vanity. I soaked for half an hour or so, reflecting over the day's events, then pulled myself out, dried off, and went through my regular evening routine of applying lotion, taking off my makeup and moisturizing my face. The final step was powder; then I stepped into a short blue silk chemise trimmed in ivory lace, with a matching robe.

I tried to watch television but was too restless and too mindless to follow a plot. That should tell you something of my mental condition. Who is ever too mindless to watch television these days? I wandered over to the window and saw that the rain had stopped, so I decided to pour a glass of wine from the merlot included in the gift basket and took it out on the balcony to brood.

And brood I did. Curled up in the towel-covered chair, sipping the mellow mood enhancer, I sat in the darkness with the hazy light from the bedside lamp slipping through the drapes behind me. Something had washed over me since I got to Bliss and I couldn't quite understand how I was feeling. It was a maudlin mess of sentiment and fantasy. It was such a precious town from the way it looked to the way it felt, and the people, with the exception of that awful woman Eula, were gracious and kind. All that had set me up to be swept away by Spencer Edwards, a man I didn't even know. A man who, for goodness sake, was married! The way he had captivated me was so completely alien that I was appalled at the shameful hussy that I discovered raging in my soul.

"Maybe I'm going through the change of life," I speculated as I gazed at the smoky moon. I was being a smart aleck when I said it, but then it occurred to me that it might be true. My heart dropped and I felt sick to my stomach. I nearly choked on the sip of merlot. I couldn't fathom the thought of my youthful womanhood disappearing when I had barely used it. Or maybe I was just going crazy. I poured another glass of merlot, a full-to-the-brim glass. I took a gulp, not a sip. Mama's always saying that crazy runs on Daddy's side of the family and that Melinda and I never know when it's going to sneak up on us. The lust I was feeling for a married man could be the first sign of that family problem that Mama's fretted about all these years.

I had no right to want Spencer Edwards, married or not, because I once made a bargain with God. That's right, I sure did. When my husband traded me in for reduced poundage, I was pretty scared. I was terrified that I couldn't pay my mortgage or meet my bills, so I told God that if he would let me make a living doing something I could enjoy, I'd never ask him to send me love again. I just wanted to survive, and at the time, that seemed like a mighty tall task. He answered my prayer, and I haven't felt it was right to shake off my end of the bargain.

I had just been hoping that God would mark my debt paid and send someone to me anyway. Apparently, he hadn't forgotten. I have plenty of opportunities. I meet men all the time who are interested in me. I even go out on occasion. But I *never* meet anyone who tickles my fancy or captures my imagination. I took another gulp of wine and I shook my head. Yet tonight from across the room, I saw a stranger, a family man who barely gave me the time of day, and my heart wiggled. I took another gulp and thought of my good friend and doctor, Neal O'Kelley, who would love to hear that story. One day when I was in his office for a checkup and was bemoaning my single status, he asked me what I was looking for in a man. I was speechless.

"Weeeelllllll," I began, trying to buy some time. But for the life of me, I couldn't come up with anything. After a couple of minutes, Neal nodded and smiled smugly. "That's exactly what I thought. Listen, you need to figure out *what* you want *before* you start looking."

"Don't worry," I popped back. "I'll know it when I see it." He rolled his eyes and then returned to checking my ears with that doodad. I felt sure I would know it, just like I know when I see a dress or a piece of jewelry or a car I want. My heart quivers, I shiver all over, and I get so excited because I know, yes I know, *that's it*. With all of my travel, I've met hundreds of men, but not once did my heart perk up and pay any attention. So I figured that was God's way of making me adhere to the bargain that was my idea in the first place. After all, if he was going to let me off the hook, surely some spark of desire would spring up in my tattered heart. Surely, it would.

Then Spencer Edwards walked into Maggie's Southern Diner in Bliss, Mississippi, and my heart sat up and took plenty of notice. But he was married. So that couldn't be God. That had to be the evil other, who was making me want to sin in the most awful way.

"Oh, Lord," I mumbled through gulps of wine. "Please help me to tame the carnal desires of my wicked flesh."

Chapter 8

I opened one eye the tiniest of slits and peered at the digital clock on the nightstand that announced the time to be 8:20 a.m. Of course, I was curled up in my usual position, half on my stomach, half on my side, which is one reason I have so much aggravation with my neck since I sleep with it twisted into such an awkward position. I turned over on my back, and slowly the realization of how bad I really felt seeped across my conscious but muddled mind. My limbs felt heavy as though weighted down with iron chains, which was partially owed to the previous night's red wine and partially owed to the restless night I had endured, a night in which I tossed fitfully and dreamed off and on of a man I could not have and therefore should not want. My mind was groggy, a condition that was owed completely to the half bottle of wine I had consumed. I am not much of a drinker. I normally drink only on social occasions. At home, I never buy wine so half a bottle to me is like four bottles to a wino. I wasn't hungover or sick; I just felt lousy.

"Oh, Lord," I groaned miserably, throwing an arm over my eyes to avoid the sunlight streaming through the window. "I have become a loose woman *and* a drunk, all within the course of twelve hours."

I pulled the silky, pale yellow sheet up to my chin and squirmed deeper into the sensual luxuriousness of the soft bed and tried to pretend many things, the first being that I did not have to get up almost immediately to dress for breakfast at nine and the second being that I was perfectly content with my life in every possible way. Stark reality, I have discovered, has a way of hanging on and not letting go, and there are times it can be downright annoying. It annoyed me so much that I finally got up at 8:35 to face it head-on. As I stumbled toward the bathroom, I noticed a piece of stationery that had been slipped under my door. In a beautiful script, Charlotte had written, "A pot of coffee is waiting on the other side of the door. Just in case you can't wait until nine."

I opened the door to find an ornate silver tray with a matching carafe of coffee and a cream pitcher, sugar bowl and cup and saucer, all in the same delicate china pattern, one with roses and gold inlay. There was also a Waterford crystal vase with two pink roses and baby's breath. "Lovely," I breathed as I picked it up. I was already starting to feel better because I respond well to such pampering. I poured a cup of coffee and ladened it with cream that turned out to be hazelnut flavored, one of my favorites. I took a sip and savored it. Two sips later and I headed to the bathroom to wash and moisturize my face. I suspected that Charlotte would be dressed to the nines because anyone who went to so much trouble for a proper presentation of coffee was certainly going to look her best. But I had neither the time nor the inclination to make the same effort, especially when I'd have to come back up to my room and dress for the day's events. I pulled on a pair of black slacks enhanced with Lycra stretch, so ironing was not necessary, a turquoise blue scoop-neck cashmere sweater and high-heeled black slip-ons. I added a pair of silver dangling earrings that had the effect of making me looked more pulled together than I actually was. I combed my hair, twisted it up and clipped it, then added concealer to the dark circles beneath my eyes, mascara, lip liner and lip gloss. I sprayed a mist of perfume and headed downstairs. The digital clock reported that it was 8:58.

The dining room, which was as lovely in its appointments as the rest of the house, was to the right of the staircase, directly across the foyer from the living room. Charlotte was setting a vase of fresh flowers on the antique mahogany table when I walked in. As I had expected, she was dressed in an ivory suit trimmed in matching braid and large, gold buttons. The jacket was long, coming to her fingertips when she dropped her arms, and the skirt stopped just below her knee. It was very becoming on her.

"Good morning!" she called out cheerfully, looking up from the flowers. "You're right on time. It's so courteous to be on time, don't you think?"

"My daddy always said that the rudest thing in the world was to keep someone waiting," I said as I walked over to the table adorned in china and silver that matched what had been delivered to my door. "He said that's the same as saying my time is more important than yours."

She laughed and stood up straight. "My sentiments exactly! Is your father still alive?"

Sadness clouded my face and I shook my head. "No. Unfortunately, we lost him four years ago to heart disease. I miss him terribly." I sighed deeply and changed the subject. I was already morose enough without dwelling on that. "Thank you so much for the tray. It was so thoughtful and absolutely lovely."

"I try to be a wonderful hostess but I have a secret." She leaned toward me and lowered her voice. "I'm not that good with every guest. Just the special ones."

I smiled. "Thank you."

"Please have a seat." She gestured to the one at the head of the table, then picked up a silver bell and rang it. "Lollie will be right out to take our order." She took the chair next to me and was unfolding the peach-colored damask napkin to place in her lap when a young blonde woman, somewhere in her twenties, came in and said timidly, "Miss Charlotte, you ready for me?"

Her hair was dishwater blonde, bordering on mousy brown, and pulled back into a thin ponytail tied with a brown ribbon. Her face was unvarnished, with pale green eyes and colorless lips that blended into her fair but flawless skin, presenting a rather plain young woman. But I could see how a bit of mascara on the invisible lashes, a pretty pink lip gloss and a little blush could transform her into a pretty ingénue. She was so small boned and thin that she looked frail, a look that wasn't helped by the shapeless beige cotton dress she was wearing.

"Yes, Lollie, we are. This is our guest, Abby Houston. Remember that book you loved so much that I loaned to you? Well, Miss Abby here wrote that book."

A spark of light hit her green eyes and she smiled, displaying a row of small teeth with an eyetooth that stuck out further than the others. "Sure 'nuff?" she asked, looking from Charlotte to me. "Ma'am, I loved that book Miss Charlotte let me borry. It just made me feel good all over when I read it."

"Thank you, Lollie," I said, reaching over to take one of her hands. "That's the grandest compliment you could give me."

"Lollie is a big reader. She works very hard at bettering herself." Charlotte's voice was kind and thoughtful. "Loretta,

Lollie's mama, worked for me for years, but she has arthritis and it just got to where it was too hard on her. So Lollie took her place. But Loretta and Lollie have a catering business on the side, and I can tell you without fear of contradiction that they are the two best cooks in this county." She nodded with pride toward Lollie, who blushed. The color in her cheeks revealed exactly what I suspected—a beauty lay beneath that plainness.

"Congratulations!" I said. "I admire people who work hard to make a better life for themselves."

She looked down shyly and mumbled, "Thanky, ma'am." She paused, then asked, "What kin I make ya for breakfast? Eggs any way you like, waffles, French toast, biscuits and gravy? Anything ya want, we got. Ain't we, Miss Charlotte?"

"Yes, Lollie, we do. Abby, I heartily recommend anything that Lollie cooks."

"Then I shall have French toast, crisp bacon and fruit."

"I'll git it right now and I'll bring out some coffee, too. Miss Charlotte, I'll bring your usual."

She disappeared behind the swinging door, which, I assumed, led to the kitchen. Charlotte watched until she was gone.

"She's a good girl," Charlotte commented. "But she's had a tough life. Her daddy ran off and left her mama when she was just a girl and her brother was a baby. Loretta had a rough time but she managed to raise two wonderful children. Had 'em in church every time the doors were open, no matter how tired she was. They grew up with my daughters, so I'm as proud of Lollie as I am of either of my two. Her brother Bobby is on a scholarship at Mississippi State. He's studying agriculture and wants to be a county agent. Lollie's smart enough to have gone to college but she didn't want to. She wanted to stay and work with her mama. But I'll tell you this: as much as that catering business has grown, I expect to lose her one day so that she can focus her full attention on it. When that day comes, it will be a sad, sad day for me, I can promise you that."

"God bless you." I reached over and patted her freckled hand. "The most important thing we can ever do in life is to encourage and help those who aren't as fortunate as we are."

"I agree." Lollie appeared at that moment to pour our coffee from a silver pot, so Charlotte changed the subject. "Charlie had a breakfast meeting this morning and wanted me to tell you that he'll see you at the Rotary meeting. He's president of the club this year. This is the third time in thirty years that he's been president."

"President?" I asked. She nodded as she took a sip of black coffee. "Then he's the one who called my publicist and asked for me. Right? My publicist said it was the president."

She laughed. "That's correct. He has heard me talk about your books so much, and when I started jabbering on and on about you coming to town, he decided it was a good idea to try to inject some life into those gosh-awful programs they usually have. He figured that if anyone could write books as funny and entertaining as you do, then you had to be a good speaker."

"I hope I won't disappoint him."

"I have great faith that you won't. If you can handle television like you do, Bliss's little ol' Rotary club will certainly not be a challenge. I'll be there. I wouldn't miss it for the world."

"Terrific! I'm glad you're going to be there." I had quickly developed a liking for Charlotte, and she felt like a friend I had known for many years. "How did the reception go last night?"

"Oh, Charlie was the king of the evening. Everyone was making over him like silly and he enjoyed every minute of it, as you would expect that he would." She winked in a knowing way. "We were a bit worried about you when the storm broke out, though. We went by the diner to see if you needed a ride home, but Maggie told us that we had already been beaten to the punch."

I felt my face flush, which did not go unnoticed by Charlotte. She grinned. "Spencer's something, isn't he?" I was hoping that it was a rhetorical question and she wouldn't stop for an answer but she did.

I nodded awkwardly, the saliva in my mouth draining away. "He seems to be a very nice man."

"Nice?" she asked, then laughed. "Nice is an understatement for that young man. He's the prince of Bliss, a scion of the town's royalty. His father, most likely, will be the next governor of the great state of Mississippi, and his mother is the heiress of a family that owns thousands of acres of land in the delta. Despite the life of privilege that he was born to, Spencer is solid as a rock, as down to earth as Lollie is. He has an incredible way with people because he is so genuine and compassionate. But then, you probably already know that." She winked again.

The color of my face deepened from red to purple, and I muttered, "I just had a brief encounter with him, and to tell the truth, it wasn't his idea to bring me home. It was Maggie's."

She laughed. "That doesn't surprise me at all. Good ol' Maggie's always in there to lend a helping hand!"

"What does Spencer do for a living?" I asked, trying to act nonchalant and feeling that I needed to ask something, not just drop the subject completely. Okay, yes, I did want to know more about the married man who was tempting me in such a wicked way.

"He's an attorney. He and his brother Chase took over their father's law firm when he retired to focus on politics. Spence graduated with honors from Ole Miss as an undergraduate and went on to law school there." She paused for a second as Lollie brought our food in on a silver tray. She set down a large fluffy omelet and bacon in front of Charlotte. "Thank you, Lollie."

"Yum! This looks delicious," I remarked, looking at the thick, golden brown French toast covered with strawberries, blueberries and raspberries. Lollie blushed, dropped her eyes and disappeared. I waited for Charlotte to continue, and fortunately she did. Unfortunately, I hated to hear what she next had to say.

"His wife, Liz, grew up here in Bliss, the daughter of another prominent family." She took a bite of the omelet and chewed it thoughtfully. "Liz was two years younger than Spence, and you know how that is—when you're a teenager, two years' difference might as well be ten years'. My daughter Margaret Rose had the biggest crush on Spence. Who wouldn't? He was a star student and the quarterback who led Bliss High to the only state championship we ever won. He played at Ole Miss, too, even though every school in the SEC and a couple in the Big Ten tried to get him." I was nervously shoveling food in my mouth while Charlotte talked of Spencer and his family.

"I love SEC football," I said, to say something.

"Charlie lives and breathes football from August to January and all important points in between like the spring game, recruiting season and signing day. We have season tickets to Ole Miss, and if they're out of town and Mississippi State is playing in town, we go to their games. I do whatever Charlie wants. That's the Southern way, you know." Lollie had returned to freshen our coffee. "Lollie, you have outdone yourself with this omelet this morning. It is absolutely delicious."

"And the same can be said for the French toast. It's the best I've ever had." She nodded her acknowledgement and slipped out of the room.

"Now, what was I saying? Oh, yes, Spencer. So he never paid a moment's attention to Liz until she showed up at Ole Miss. He was a junior but he quickly took notice of the most popular girl on campus. She was the most beautiful girl you can imagine and so kind. From the moment she hit Oxford, she and Spencer were inseparable. She was homecoming queen, Miss Ole Miss and first runner-up in the Miss Mississippi pageant, but she should have won. Did you know that Mississippi has had more Miss Americas than any other state in the Union?"

"No!" I replied, genuinely surprised. "How many?"

"Four. And two of them were back-to-back, including Mary Ann Mobley. Charlie says that Mississippi has so many beautiful women that they have to redshirt them for beauty pageants!" She stopped and laughed. "Leave it to Charlie to find an analogy between college football and beauty pageants."

I wanted to know something about Spencer Edwards, but not *everything*, especially as it related to his wife. I was thinking quickly of something to say to divert the conversation when the telephone rang.

"Oh my goodness!" Charlotte exclaimed with annoyance. "That telephone can be such a nuisance. Please excuse me while I answer that." She slid her chair away from the table and stood up. "I wouldn't, except I do *attempt* to run a business, so it might be important." She hurried out to the desk to answer the phone. I sat there thinking about Spencer. Of course he married a beauty queen. Someone as handsome and worthy as he would only marry the most desirable woman in the state. I certainly wasn't in that category, so even if he wasn't married, I would never have been his glass of mint julep. I sipped my coffee and chewed over the information about Spencer Edwards that I had just received. I could just picture the kind of woman he had chosen to marry—slender, probably blonde, with a cute nose and dazzling smile, and so likeable that people fell in love with her the moment she extended a well-manicured hand to greet them. I found myself picking at my food, pushing it around the china plate like a disgruntled child. I hated to admit it, but I was beginning to think that I was developing a crush on Spencer Edwards, the kind that you have after you watch a rugged hero in a good movie. You leave the theater, feeling warm and cozy and thinking how delicious your life would be if you had that man in it. Then you picture yourself holding his hand, feeling his touch against the small of your back, resting your head against his shoulder as he slides his arm around you, making you feel so welcomed in his embrace.

"Well! You're not going to believe this!" Charlotte made a short, quick clap with her hands as she hurried into the dining room, her heels clicking furiously against the hardwood floor. It gave me a start and I jumped out of my silly daydream of hand-holding with Spencer Edwards.

"What?" I tried to act sufficiently interested.

"That was Susan Marie, and her store has been absolutely *swamped* with calls today about you being in town. The *Bliss Observer* ran a story on you yesterday and you know the power of the press! Well, she's had so many calls that she has already placed on reserve all but five books. The poor little thing is desperate to get more books, so she called to ask if I would drive to Jackson to a wholesale warehouse and pick up several boxes for her. Now, how could I possibly say no?"

I was slightly surprised at the demand in Bliss for my new book, but only because one thing I've learned as an author on book tour is that you never know, you can never predict how book signings will go. I have been in huge cities with millions of residents and sold twenty books. On the other hand, I have been in tiny towns where four hundred people showed up to buy my book and have it signed. There is no science or formula to bookstore events. Still, the revelation brought a smile to my face. It is flattering to know that people care enough to want to buy your words and thoughts.

"Really?" I perked up and forgot momentarily about a man

I should not be thinking about in the first place. It was my turn to clap my hands together. "Wonderful! That is so exciting."

She nodded, picking up the silver bell and letting its tinkling sound drift toward the kitchen. It was answered almost instantly by Lollie, who pushed the door open and asked, "Yes, ma'am?"

"Lollie, I don't have time to finish breakfast. I've been called away on an important mission." She winked at me, thoroughly enjoying the adrenaline produced by the excitement. "Would you please wrap one of those delicious raisin-bran muffins you baked yesterday and pour a tumbler of coffee to take with me?" Before Lollie could answer, Charlotte hurried on. "While you do that, I'm going to run upstairs, grab my purse and put on some lipstick. I'll be back down in two shakes of a lamb's tail."

She turned to me. "Oh, Abby, I'm so sorry that we can't finish breakfast together, but you take your time and I'm going to do everything I can to be back in time for Rotary. I'll call Charlie from my cell phone and apprise him of the situation. If I'm not there, Charlie will make certain that you're taken care of, and of course, Susan Marie should be there. But with this turn of events, it's hard to know. Do you know where the meeting is being held? At the Bliss Country Club."

"Yes ma'am," I replied in my normal mode of courtesy. I often say "ma'am" or "sir" to those who are the same age or younger than me. The courtesy was not lost on Charlotte who smiled with appreciation, a knowing glint in her eye. I continued, "I have a complete agenda and I'll ask Lollie for directions."

"I know that Susan Marie was planning to take you, but I'm not sure that she really has the time." She snapped her fingers and her expression revealed that she had just thought of the perfect solution. "Oh, I know, I'll have Charlie stop by and pick you up. Be ready by 11:30 and he'll just swing by here and pick you up on his way." She had already crossed the room and was preparing to dart up the stairs. She wiggled her fingers in a gesture of good-bye. "One way or the other, I'll see you later—whether it's at the club or at the bookstore."

"Thank you!" I called after her as she clattered up the stairs. Alone again with my coffee and French toast, I turned my attention to something more productive than my attraction for a married man. I pondered exactly what I was going to say to the august Rotary club of Bliss, Mississippi.

♡

I finished dressing by eleven, and since I had already read *USA Today*, I was looking for something to do. I took my cell phone off the charger and dialed Kadie, my best friend.

"I only have a minute, sweetie," she answered, without saying hello. I hate caller ID.

"Good morning to you, too."

"I'm sorry but I've got a hair appointment in Atlanta, and you know that few things are more important to a Southern woman than a good haircut and color. Let me tell you this very quickly, though. I saw your mama at Winn-Dixie this morning, and she told me all about you and Steve Marshall!"

"What!" I exploded. *"There is no Steve Marshall and me!"* I had, of course, told Kadie all about Mama's newest matchmaking scheme.

Kadie giggled. "I know that. You know that. But your mama don't know that. She's practically got the wedding planned. She was talking all about how Steve owns all those mobile home parks." Here, she stopped talking and started laughing. "Honey, she's done crowned you Queen of the Trailer Parks."

I started shaking all over with anger. Kadie has been my best friend since first grade, so I hoped that even if Mama had spoken freely with her, she had more sense than to share that with anyone else. Kadie, of course, knows I have a crazy mama. Not everyone else is so well informed.

"Are you sufficiently mad now?" she asked gaily.

"Whatta ya think?" I snapped. I was not amused.

"Okeydokey. I'll just hang up now so that you can call her and I can head up the road to my hair appointment. Bye, Queenie!"

I paced the floor for a few minutes, trying to calm down before I called her. My blood pressure had risen so high so fast that I had a sudden, pounding headache. Mama is the only one who can do that to me. I had taken Mama to her last checkup, so I was in the examining room when Neal O'Kelley checked her blood pressure.

"Miss Cora Jean, you've got the blood pressure of a young woman!" Neal exclaimed. He always makes over her and she loves that. "Those are the best numbers I've gotten today."

I folded my arms and smiled too sweetly to be sincere. "Of course, she does. She doesn't *have* high blood pressure. She *gives* it."

Obviously, I wasn't joking. I took a couple of aspirins, drank a glass of water and dialed her up. She was out of breath when she answered.

"Hello?" she said between pants.

I softened a bit. "What's wrong with you?"

She inhaled deeply. "I was on top of the kitchen counters, putting masking tape around the window screens." Mama uses masking tape for everything from wrapping presents to performing miracles. When I was a little, we had a calf born with front legs bent completely under. As the vet left, he told Daddy that he'd be back the next day to put the calf down. Mama, who overheard the conversation, grabbed a roll of masking tape and headed to the barn. Using twelve-inch rulers from my and

Melinda's book satchels, she tenderly straightened the calf's legs, used the rulers as splints, then taped them securely with masking tape. The next day the vet told her that she was wasting her time, but she stood her ground and refused to let him put the calf to sleep. Within a few weeks, the calf, too, stood her ground with perfectly straight legs.

Then, years later, when the left side of her face drooped from a small facial stroke, Mama pulled her face up and taped it in place with the masking tape.

Neal laughed but admonished her gently, "Miss Cora Jean, I hate to see you disappointed, but that will never work."

But he was wrong. Mama and the masking tape prevailed, and after a couple of weeks, her droop had disappeared. Its healing powers aside, it's mighty annoying to have your Christmas and birthday presents wrapped with torn, tiny pieces of the ugly tape. Mama doesn't use a lot. She doesn't want to treat it frivolously.

Suddenly, I was aggravated over something completely different than what I had called about.

"Mother, I told you that Melinda or I will do that for you," I chastised, biting my words off sharply. "Or Sandy can do it. You know that he doesn't mind."

"I'm not askin' Sandy to do it for me," she retorted in a high-and-mighty tone. "That poor boy's got more than he can handle already. I don't know how he does it all. He came over yesterday, after he closed the station, and cut my grass." She paused. "I'll tell you right now, we could use another man in this family." Her tone turned to one of lecture. "And it ain't up to me to bring another 'un in, either. I brought one in and kept him close to fifty years." Dramatic pause. *"I have well done my part."* The last sentence was performed with imperial righteousness.

Fury swept over me. I knew who she was pointing the finger at. I was mad all over again.

"It is not my responsibility to get married just so you'll have someone to mow your lawn!" I shrilled, feeling my throat pinch together with tension.

"Well, I'd like to know whose it is then, if it ain't yours!"

"Forget it! BYE!" I stormed and clicked off. I hate cell phones at moments like that. It feels so much better—not to mention how much better it sounds—to slam the phone down. I dropped my face in my hands and felt them trembling. In a few minutes, when I had calmed down somewhat, I felt horribly ashamed. How could I fly off the handle like that? And how could I talk to my mama like that, even if she was one of the most cotton-picking, aggravating women in the world?

I walked over and flung open the balcony doors, then leaned against the door frame. I knew the answer, even if I didn't want to admit it.

My heart agreed with Mama. It was way past time to find love.

Chapter 9

Charlie opened the door to the country club, a pretty white building with a wide porch across the front with small columns and windows that ran from the floor almost to the ceiling; then he stepped aside for me to enter in front of him. He was the perfect equivalent to Charlotte, a stately, well-mannered Southern gentleman with a personality that made me feel as if we had been friends for years. He stood well over six feet tall with broad shoulders and a thick, paunchy waist. His hair, a glittery mass of different shades of silver, was full and cut very short. The most prominent features of his face were his friendly blue gray eyes and long Grecian nose. His chin was saggy with age and his neck was becoming a bit crinkled, hanging in slight folds around the heavily starched white shirt that he wore, accompanied by a conservative tie and well-tailored navy suit.

"Hey, Charlie!" A tiny red-haired man in an out-of-date plaid jacket and wide striped tie ran over to pump his hand. The foyer was filled with dozens of people, primarily men milling around a sign-in table and pinning on their Rotary badges.

"Hello, Arnold," Charlie responded with a big, politician-like smile, simultaneously shaking Arnold's hand and patting him on the shoulder. Arnold turned to look at me.

"Well, Charlie, who is this good-looking woman you've got with you?" He smiled at me.

"This is my new girlfriend, but don't tell Charlotte," Charlie's conspiratorial tone was pitch perfect. "She even spent the night at my place last night." He winked and grinned.

Arnold laughed. "You must be the lady author who's speaking to us today." He offered his hand. "I'm Arnold McAfee. Pleasure to meet you."

I gripped his hand tightly and looked him straight in the eyes. It's important, I believe, to connect with someone during the initial introduction. "I'm Abby Houston and it's a pleasure to be here. Thank you very much for having me."

"Our pleasure!" Arnold McAfee responded as Charlie reached over to touch my shoulder. "Abby, please excuse me for a moment while I step over to sign in and get my badge," Charlie said. "I'll be right back."

"Take your time. I'll step over there," I motioned to a less congested area near a sitting area. I strolled over to a far corner filled with an overstuffed plaid sofa and two paisley chairs that matched the deep rich colors of the couch. I smoothed the skirt to the bright blue suit piped with Kelly green that I was wearing and checked the matching bright green buttons to make certain that they all were fastened. My lips felt slightly dry so I decided to add a little gloss. It's fair to say that I'm addicted to wet lips. One day I arrived for a lunch appointment only to discover that by some freak incident I had no lipstick in my purse.

Before I went into the restaurant, I dashed into a nearby drugstore to pick up a wand of color. It was the first time I realized how serious the addiction is—I was practically jerking with apprehension over finishing lunch and having no lipstick to put on. Discreetly, I reached into my purse, my back turned to the crowd, and dapped some color on my lips sans a makeup mirror. I finished the top lip; then just as soon as the wand hit the center of my lower one, I felt a slight touch on my shoulder and heard a soft voice near my ear say, "You don't need that. You're beautiful enough already."

A bit annoyed at being caught in an act of vanity, I jerked around to see the source of annoyance. Spencer Edwards smiled and it was an irresistible gesture of charm and humor. I even thought briefly that there were tinges of flirtation around the edges of the smile, but alas, I knew it was merely wishful thinking. My heart dropped with embarrassment at being caught in less than a perfect pose, the likes of which Spencer had yet to see from me; then it began to pound thunderously, practically snatching my breath away. I swallowed, snitching a couple of seconds in an attempt to regain my composure. I searched for words. During those brief seconds, I took note of the casual but handsome way that Spencer was dressed in an expensive navy jacket, a blue-and-white striped button-down with the collar of a navy tee shirt showing and light, stone-colored slacks.

"Well, you know what I say? You can never have too many friends or too much lip gloss." I salvaged the moment as best I could with a flirtatious smile and comical flutter of my eyelashes. It worked, and he laughed.

"I must say that is the first time I've heard that one!" He looked down at my feet, shod in bright blue suede pumps with precariously high heels. "Well, it looks like your foot has recovered from my clumsiness of last night." I relaxed, thrilled that he was looking at my best feature. My feet are really the only thing that I halfway like about myself. They are a well-proportioned size six and are particularly fetching in a pointed, high-heeled pump. I was happy that I had splurged on the ridiculously expensive shoes while shopping in Dallas. Unconsciously, I shifted my feet into a model-like pose with one heel clicking against the toe of the other.

I looked down and said, "Oh, yes, it survived but—not to make you feel guilty or anything—it *is* sore today, and it's also the loveliest shade of blue green. That's why I wore this outfit," I said in a teasing tone. "I wanted to match my bruise." I looked back up at him and winked. Again, he laughed.

"You are a true Southern woman." He smiled and nodded his head with what was either approval or understanding or perhaps both. "Every true Southern woman I've ever known is fanatical about matching everything." His smile turned mischievous and he opened his mouth to speak, then closed it again quickly. Only he knew what he was thinking, but the look on his face and my own crazy imagination sent me tumbling backwards into paralyzing awkwardness. I shifted from one foot to another and scratched the area above my right brow that always itches when I am nervous or perplexed.

I thought quickly and came up with a remark that was nothing short of brilliant.

"So. How was the meatloaf last night?" As soon as the words left my mouth, I regretted it. I remembered that the only way I could have known his menu was if I had been eavesdropping on him and Maggie. It hadn't been discussed between us. Dang it, I thought, there goes my image of being cool and aloof.

He caught it. I saw it when his eyes widened slightly. I heard it in his voice when he stuttered, "Uh. Uh, it was fine. Good. Always is at Maggie's."

Thank goodness we were saved from further repartee by Charlie who sidled up to me, put his arm loosely around my shoulders and said, "Spencer, you aren't over here trying to cut in on my girlfriend, are you?"

A look of discomfort flashed across his handsome face, and there seemed to be the slightest hint of red across his cheeks. "Uh, no," he stammered, ashamed, I guessed, of having flirted with a strange woman while his wife was probably home baking cookies for a Cub Scout meeting. He cleared his throat and regained his composure. "Your girlfriend? And, pray tell what does Charlotte think of this arrangement, and of the fact that you are openly flaunting it at the Bliss Rotary club?" One side of his mouth turned up in the most delightful way as his eyes twinkled with humor.

"It was Charlotte herself who made the introduction. But to be quite frank and forthcoming, this dalliance will end—breaking, no doubt, Ms. Houston's heart—when the president drops the gavel to end this hallowed coming together of the Bliss Rotarians. That is the approximate time that I anticipate Charlotte's return from a brief but necessary trip to Jackson." Spoken like a true member of the bar association. I rolled my eyes comically. Again, the precious tinkling sound of Spencer's laughter fell upon my ears.

"I suspected as much!" He tilted his head back and looked at Charlie. "By the way, where were *you* last night when it was raining cats and dogs and this lovely woman needed a ride back to *your* house?"

"Being feted by Bliss's finest, which I noticed, oddly, did not include you." He raised a teasing eyebrow toward his sparring partner. "But I feel confident you have an appropriate excuse, and I am completely prepared to forgive you. Nonetheless, I heard that in my absence you leapt to the rescue. A fact that surprised me none at all." He winked. I had no idea what that wink meant, but I decided to speak up and enter this conversation that was about me but, at the moment, wasn't including me.

"He *rescued* me *after* he nearly sent me to the emergency room with a broken foot! He was trying to assuage his guilty conscience. Nothing more." I flittered my hand airily to dismiss his gesture.

Charlie looked quizzical. "Broken foot? What are you talking about?"

Spencer spoke quickly. "Nothing." He cut his eyes over at me with a warning look. "Women, including the most beautiful ones, exaggerate. By the way," he turned to look me squarely in the eyes, "last night when I said you looked familiar, why didn't you tell me that it's *your* face on that huge poster hanging in the window of Susan Marie's store and that you're the one I've seen on television twice in the past week?"

"Now, how would I know that you had seen me on television?"

"Because," he shot back, "you seem to me to be the kind of woman who knows *everything*." He grinned but I feared that it was more of a dig than a compliment. Around that man, I was abnormally insecure about the most insignificant things. I decided to bluff and pretend to be the picture of emotional perfection.

"How observant of you to recognize that so early in our acquaintance!" I said it in a coquettish voice, punctuating it with a flutter of my eyelashes and a sweet smile.

"Okay, you two," Charlie said, taking my elbow and steering me toward the dining room from which heavenly smells of home-cooked food drifted. "Let's make our way through the buffet line so that Abby can have some time to eat before she speaks. You can flirt later."

Once again, my cheeks burned and I felt a kick in my gut as I realized that my overt behavior had betrayed my attraction to Spencer. I suddenly had no appetite and I silently vowed to act more professional with the man who was twisting my heart all which-a-ways. I selected my food meekly as we moved down the buffet line. Charlie was behind me, but fortunately, Spencer had chosen to go to the other side of the line so we were separated by a steamy island of turkey and dressing, green beans, creamed corn, mashed potatoes and other vegetables. I made a salad, took a spoonful of potatoes and waited for the man in the tall white chef's hat at the end of the line to cut a slice of roast beef for me. He dropped a large dollop of horseradish sauce beside it on the plate. At a table behind him, I picked up a glass of water and piece of lemon, then turned to find Spencer standing behind me. He smiled, and uncomfortable, I looked down for a second.

"Abby, I'm glad I got to see you again. I'm going to sit in the back of the room because I have to scoot out early for a meeting." With a throw of his head, he motioned to a table in the back, near the door. "If I have a chance, I'll stop by the bookstore later. I'd like to get a signed copy of your book for my sister who lives in Meridian."

I'm embarrassed to say that my heart quickened. To me, it was a powerful jumble of words: he was glad to see me again, he wanted to buy a copy of *my* book for his sister, and most importantly, he might come by the bookstore.

I fought the nervous lump in my throat and I tried to sound nonchalant. "Good." My voice sounded weak from the tightness of my neck muscles. I wanted to clear my throat but fought the notion. I was working hard to bluff my way through the exchange. "I hope you will get to come by."

"Me, too." He looked deeply into my eyes and there was a moment of connection. It felt powerful, at least to me. "The only problem is that I promised my son I would stop by his football practice this afternoon and you know how that goes." Well, there went the connection; he just had to go and remind me of his family. "Thank God for that," I thought to myself.

"Oh, yes," I replied, struggling to act casual. "That's much more important. But if you can't get by and you still want a copy, just call Susan Marie and tell her who you want it signed to and I'll be happy to leave it for you."

His eyes darkened briefly and his brow gathered in a collection of furrows and lines. He nodded with his lips pressed together tightly. "Uh, yeah. Okay. That's what I'll do." Charlie popped up again.

"Spencer, why don't you join us at the front." He smiled teasingly, glancing back and forth between us. "So that you two can continue your conversation."

"Sorry, Charlie," Spencer replied in a perfect mimic of the old television commercial. "But I've got to leave early so I'm going to sit in the back. Otherwise, you wouldn't have to ask twice." He looked at me and smiled and I smiled back. Another moment of connection. Another sinful foray interrupted by Charlie, who I decided was the guardian angel God had assigned to the case to keep me out of trouble with a married man.

"Then, okay, Miss Abby, let's take a seat. See you later, Spence."

Holding the plate of food and the glass of water with the slice of lemon floating in it, I followed Charlie, turning to look at Spencer as I passed. "Bye." That's all I said. Just "bye." And though I knew it was wrong, I sure was hoping that it wasn't good-bye forever, that I would see Spencer Edwards later at the bookstore.

There wasn't a head table, just a small table at the front that held the podium and microphone, so I followed Charlie to a large round table to the right of the speaker's stand. Four people were already seated at a table that held seven, and Charlie introduced me. I met Keith Roberts, the district attorney; Bess Moorehead, the director of the Humane Society; Judy McDonald, the executive director of the chamber of commerce; and

Irene Howorth, clerk of courts. A few moments later, we were joined by a banker named Joe.

After the saying of grace, the standard chitchat for such events ensued, including life in general, then specifically life in the charming town of Bliss and the harrowing life of an author on tour. Charlie tossed down a few bites of food quickly and excused himself to take care of some "presidential duties." Upon his departure, the chubby district attorney, who looked too old to have small children, began to tell the story of his eight-year-old son, who, along with his cocker spaniel, had encountered a disgruntled skunk a couple of days earlier.

"It was the most atrocious thing you ever smelled!" He wrinkled his nose, closed his eyes and shook his head with disdain. "My wife sent me to the store to buy a case of tomato juice. We had to use it on my boy first. Then we moved on to the culprit." He paused between bites of fried chicken and pointed at Bess. "I'll tell you, Bess, you almost had one more resident over at the Humane Society."

"No, I didn't," she retorted. "My job is not to *take* dogs from good homes but to *put* them in good homes!"

Everyone chuckled; then Judy from the chamber turned to me and asked, "Abby, do you have children?" I saw her glance down to my left hand.

I shook my head. "No, but I do have a dog, one which has yet to tangle with a skunk but she loves to chase groundhogs and squirrels." I'm always uncomfortable when people, especially women in small towns rooted in families, ask me about children. There's a bit of me that feels like a monster because I've never felt compelled to add to the world's population. I hoped that answer ended the conversation but it didn't. Irene, the clerk of courts, added in a sad tone, "What a shame! Children can add so much to one's life."

It seemed earnest to pretend that it was, indeed, an unkind

fate that had jerked the possibility of motherhood from my grasp. To be quite honest, I had been keen on having children early in my marriage, but the longer I waited, the less it seemed right for me. After my divorce, I was so grateful that I was not tied to my ex for the rest of my time on earth. I frowned slightly and glanced downward at my plate. "Yes, they can. But I've been divorced for a few years, and there doesn't appear to be any prospect of marriage on the near horizon, so that's probably one experience I'll never have. I can't complain, though. Life has been so good to me in so many other ways." I smiled tightly.

A bolt of electricity seemed to shoot through each of the three women sitting at the table. Each jerked her head back, sat straight up and looked at the others. Silently, they conveyed their thoughts, and slowly, one smile after another spread across their faces as each nodded slightly. The men, of course, were completely oblivious to the obvious conspiracy that was forming until Judy spoke up.

"You're not married!" She could barely contain her glee, expressing it as a joyous statement of discovery rather than a question.

Unsure of what was transpiring, I shook my head slowly, trying to think how to sidestep any hidden land mines.

"How wonderful!" Bess clapped her hands together in delight.

"This is our lucky day!" Irene exclaimed. She looked around the table. "*This* is exactly what we've been looking for!" She swept a hand toward me like those women do who show refrigerators on game shows. "And to think, she came to *us* here in Bliss. The Lord has delivered her to our very doorstep. Our prayers have been answered!"

While the women rejoiced, the two men, suddenly aware of what plan was being hatched, looked at each other and woefully shook their heads. That gave me no comfort whatsoever.

"Uh-oh," Keith Roberts groaned. I know enough to know

that when a well-educated man, elected by the people to serve as district attorney, relaxes enough to stray from sophisticated language to the slang of "uh-oh," it isn't good. He raised an eyebrow and looked across the table to me. "Abby, I find it pertinent to advise you that your single status has just been placed in serious jeopardy."

"Wh-wh-what?" I stammered, fidgeting in my seat.

"Oh, honey!" Bess cried out. "Have we got the perfect man for you! He is so wonderful!"

"It's our mayor!" Irene announced. "Mayor Alexander is the most darling man you've ever seen in your life. And he already has children so you would have a ready-made family and you wouldn't have to worry one iota about ruining your lovely figure! See how the Lord works things out when you trust in him?"

"It's perfect!" Judy concluded, nodding her head with approval. "Absolutely perfect."

I was ready to jump up from the table and bolt out the door, but I assured myself that I could handle it, that I could dance around it and get out of it without hurting their feelings. I knew they were well intentioned about finding an intended for their mayor and I didn't want to dampen their enthusiasm. I just didn't want to be part of the plan. I wish I had a dollar for every person—make that every *woman*—who has thought she had the perfect man for me. Needless to say, he never is, but there is a part of me deep inside that always hopes maybe, just maybe, a magical introduction will occur and I'll be swept away by a handsome prince. For that reason, I always "play along" briefly to find out a little about the new target. You never know when I might hit the bull's-eye. Still, there is a fine art to the game. I have to be careful not to be too interested so I can skitter away gracefully.

"Your mayor isn't married?" I asked, casually sipping my water.

All three women shook their heads woefully. "No," Judy answered, waiting reverently for a moment before continuing. "His wife died a few years ago."

That's unusual. Normally the guy is divorced—usually two or three times—or he has never married and still lives with his mama. This was the first time anyone ever offered to introduce me to a widower. I probed a little further.

"Oh, no. How sad." I shook my head sympathetically.

Bess elaborated. "It was the saddest thing you ever saw. It devastated him and broke every heart in this town. They were the finest couple you could imagine and she was an angel. The year she died, she was president of the Goodwill Circle, taught primary Sunday school class *and* volunteered at the hospital."

"Was it an accident?" I asked, beginning to think from her resume of activities that she was older, which meant he was older. I never knew a woman under sixty to be president of a Goodwill Circle. Women approaching retirement age, whose children have grown out of their authority, like to be in charge of something, and calling other women up to tell them which casserole or cake they should bring for a family in distress is a great way to exert control.

Bess shook her head but Judy answered. "Aneurysm. She complained of a headache when she got up that morning and by lunch, she had expired."

Aneurysm. Okay, that did it. I knew then that they were trying to set me up with a man old enough to be my father. Look at the facts: the man was a mayor, which meant he was stately and old enough to be concerned with social and political issues; his wife, at the time of her death, was president of the Goodwill Circle, a Sunday school teacher and a hospital volunteer. Younger women are normally in the church choir and the Junior Service League. And if that's not enough evidence, how often do you hear of a young woman dying from an aneurysm? I began to skitter away.

"I'm so sorry to hear that. It sounds like such a tragic loss." I was going to wait respectfully for a moment and change the subject but Irene piped up.

"Mayor Alexander is a Rotarian and he rarely misses a meeting so he should be here." She craned her neck around as I quickly tried to think of a way out. A frown clouded her face withered by years. "Hmmm. He usually sits right over there at that table but he's not there." She looked at her accomplices. "Have you seen him today?"

They shook their heads in perfect unison and joined Irene in the search. After a few seconds, to my relief, they admitted that he wasn't there. Judy smiled beatifically. "Don't worry," she assured me. "I'll call him when I get back to the chamber, and I'll do everything I can to get him over to the bookstore this afternoon!"

"Great idea!" Bess agreed, reaching over to give Judy a congratulatory pat on the back.

"Oh, please, don't worry him with me," I said. "I'm sure he's so busy that he doesn't have time to come to a book signing!"

"Trust me. We'll see that he makes time for this!" Bess winked.

My shoulders slumped slightly in defeat, and Keith, apparently noticing my despair, said, "Now, ladies, something tells me that our guest of honor has no trouble finding her own men. I say this with the greatest of love and respect for your matchmaking brilliance, but I don't think she needs your help." He smiled diplomatically like the perfect politician. Except he wasn't perfect. The perfect politician would have stayed out of it. I was happy for that imperfection.

"Oh, we're not worried about *her*," Irene threw a thumb in my direction. "We're worried about the *mayor*!"

I chuckled nervously and Bess turned to Keith. "You know that he is an absolutely wonderful man. Wouldn't you want him to date your sister?"

"Not on your life!" He blew a bellowing gust of wind through his mouth, his cheeks blustery red. "I think too much of the man to do that to him!"

Laughter sprinkled itself around the table like grains of sugar falling into a cup of coffee. I felt a hand settle on the back of my chair and looked up as Charlie leaned down. "You ready?" he asked. I nodded. "Okay, I'm going to introduce you now. Then give 'em thirty minutes of your best stuff!"

For half an hour, I entertained two hundred of Bliss's finest citizens. I told stories, all true, of my family and Southern life, and then tied it into my latest book. I told, of course, about Cousin Zoey, *The Tonight Show* and the three dozen roses that Burt had sent. Some people laughed so hard that they wiped tears from their eyes. And while I talked, I often looked straight at Spencer Edwards. Like the others, he smiled and laughed and I even thought that I saw approval radiating from those wonderful blue eyes. I hoped I did.

I finished by asking them to stop by the bookstore and see me that afternoon, and if they couldn't, "Would you please tell everyone you know about my new book? Not for me," I hastened to add, "but for my *poor, widowed mother's sake?*" I punctuated it with a sad, pitiful look. Gales of laughter swept through the room and I milked it for several seconds before continuing. "You see, in the South, mothers determine their worth as mothers by if and how well their daughters marry. So the fact that I'm not married means that my Mama's not looking too good right now. But she has high hopes." I finished by telling the story of Mama making a list of all the eligible men she knew with the intent of calling them and telling them about my book, in hopes that my newfound prosperity would increase my marketability as a wife. More laughter ran through the dining room as I concluded, "So please buy my book so that we can keep my Mama's hopes alive!"

I stepped back from the podium, blew a kiss and then grabbed my heart with appreciation as the crowd jumped to its feet and gave me a thunderous ovation. I waved good-bye and stepped back to my table.

"Well, Abby," Charlie said after returning to the microphone. "I think we can say that's the best program that the Bliss Rotary has ever had!" More thundering applause. "Now, folks, be sure and stop by and see Abby at Bliss Your Heart books today. I know you'll want to tell her in person how much you enjoyed this program, and of course, Susan Marie will be happy to sell you a book or two while you're there!" Charlie concluded the program with the recitation of the Rotary Four-Way Test and the Pledge of Allegiance. As soon as the meeting was dismissed, the three women at my table huddled together, no doubt for a strategic meeting of the Bliss chapter of the Dolly Levi Society, while Keith came over to shake my hand.

"Great job! I enjoyed that so much." He smiled broadly and put his hand on my shoulder while his other still clasped my hand tightly. "You know, I think the ladies may be onto something. You'd make a fantastic first lady for the town of Bliss." Amusement spread across his face as he winked. I smiled to show my appreciation at his kindness and, at the same time, to hide my complete rejection of any notion that I was the least bit interested in a man whose age far exceeded mine. Even if I did like the idea of being first lady.

Chapter 10

Susan Marie dropped an armload of books, copies of my latest tome, onto a table and rushed toward me, her arms spread wide open. The tiny woman, about two inches shorter than I and at least twenty pounds lighter, scooped me up into a hug that had the force of a professional football player's. Then she stepped back and took a strong, appreciative look at me, peering over the small oblong-shaped reading glasses that perched on the end of her pixielike nose. She brushed a wisp of mahogany-colored hair behind her ear.

"First, let me say that you're a sight for sore eyes! Girl, you look stunning!" She put a hand on one hip and pointed at me with the forefinger of the other. "Second, I honestly believe that I'm going to be able to pay the mortgage on this shop for the next year with all the books you're selling for me today." Before I could answer, she hurried on. "And thirdly, I heard that you were an absolute smash at Rotary today! Thank you very much for that! The phone hasn't stopped ringing since the meeting ended. Thank God for Charlotte. If she hadn't gone to Jackson and picked up those books, I would be sick about all the sales I'd be losing. I still don't think I have enough." As Susan Marie bubbled, a group of several women, including Charlotte, had moved forward to surround her. I reached out and took her small hand and squeezed it tightly.

"Susan Marie, I'm so happy to be here. I promised you that I would make it one day, so thank God and New York, I'm here!"

She clapped her hands together and glanced heavenward. "Oh, yes! I'm grateful to both. By the way, your publicist has already called to check on things, and I told her how well Rotary went." She stopped and looked puzzled. "She seemed genuinely surprised at the response and the number of book sales we've had before the event even began."

I thought of my cynical friend, Jamie Gray, the one who had argued against the stop in Bliss. "I bet she was," I murmured with a light chuckle, but when Susan Marie's expression begged for further explanation, I changed the subject. "Well, it looks like you've got a herd of cheerful helpers here."

"Including one who is a jealous wife," Charlotte spoke up in a playful tone and feigned a look of annoyance. "I hear my husband's been bragging all over town about his new glamorous girlfriend!"

I smiled broadly, suddenly realizing what had truly astounded Jamie was not the rapid book sales, although that had certainly gotten her goat, but rather the fact that Susan Marie had not been at Rotary, yet she was able to give a full report. I glanced at my watch. The meeting had broken up only thirty minutes earlier; still Susan Marie had her report and Charlotte knew that her husband had been playfully telling fellow Rotarians that I was his new girlfriend. Small towns like Bliss knew the power of wireless communication long before it became a high-tech gimmick. In New York, however, I knew people in my publishing company that Jamie had never met.

"How can you work in a place and not know everyone?" I asked incredulously when we were having lunch while I was in New York.

She looked up from her crab bisque and tilted her head, puzzled. "They work on other floors, some for other imprints. There's no reason for us to meet."

I couldn't imagine being in the same building, working for the same company and not knowing everyone. "At home, we'd be exchanging garden tips and recipes."

She turned her upper lip into a snarky curl. "At home, they'd be related to you, probably through several people." Jamie, bless her heart, had no idea how a small Southern town like Bliss works and how a stranger is just a friend who had not yet been introduced. I'm sure she was surprised to learn that the town was turning out in droves to support their local bookstore and that news travels fast among friends.

I put my arm around Charlotte, whose face had split into a wide grin. "I tried to get him to run off with me, too, but he said he had to be back in time for dinner so I called it off." I looked pitiful and said sadly, "Story of my life—the good ones are already taken by someone else and the bad ones are taken with me!" I laughed and giggles rippled through the group of women.

"Well, honey, have we got the perfect man for you!" A woman dressed in a denim jumper with gray hair set in an old-fashioned roll and tease was pointing an unvarnished fingernail in my direction. "Our mayor! Oh, we just love that man so much, and we've all been looking for him a good wife! Haven't we, girls?"

A chorus of gleeful affirmative answers simultaneously sprang up while my heart sank down. Oh, no, I thought to myself, why can I not learn to keep my mouth shut? I knew immediately that just as surely as the news of my Rotary success had spread, so had the news that I was single and that my mama had placed a "For Sale" sign around my neck. The crowd of women moved in closer and I tried to hide my panic. Again, I didn't want to hurt anyone's feelings, dampen any good intentions or cast myself in a bad light by raining on their parade. I'm always mindful of good public relations when I'm out on book business, so I knew that dissing their beloved mayor would not be good P.R. I swallowed hard, trying to buy time, then smiled feebly. Then, before I could answer the mayor's zealous followers, my salvation from the uncomfortable moment sprang up behind the cheerleading squad. It was an impatient voice, one that hovered somewhere between a shrill and croak, its timbre ancient with age and iced with animosity.

"*Excuse me*! Is anyone working in this establishment today, or is everyone just lollygagging around?"

Varying looks of aggravation, annoyance and appropriate chastisement crossed the women's faces, and slowly but obediently they dispersed at the command. When the group spread out and Susan Marie hurried to the cash register, I realized that the voice belonged to none other than Bliss's she-Satan. Eula Corbett scowled meanly at the women before turning her attention to Susan Marie, who began busily ringing up several books. Lying on the floor, looking as sad as a basset hound, was the Prozac-laden beagle, Elmer.

"Susan Marie, when are you ever going to get in a new book by Reverend Billy Graham?" she snapped hatefully. I saw Susan Marie's jaw clench as she focused on punching numbers into the register. She took a deep breath and managed to say in an even tone, "Whenever he writes one, Miss Eula." She took a pause and then continued, "He's getting up in age and I don't know *if* he will write another one."

"Piddle! That good man of the Lord is the same age as me, and look at me. I'm fit as a fiddle." That's because, I thought grimly to myself, the mean ones fight harder going down. They don't have as much to look forward to as the good ones. Susan Marie released a long breath, then turned to face Miss Eula with a forced smile.

"His son has a new book out. Have you seen it?"

"Pooh! I'm not interested in any newfangled religion by the young generation!" She snatched the bag of books from Susan Marie's hands. "You young people need to get back to the basics of the gospel and forget all this new age voodoo!" Susan Marie ignored miss Eula's "gentle Christian kindness" and asked sweetly, "Is there anything else I can do for you, Miss Eula?"

"No!" she snapped and turned abruptly on her sensible black low heels and headed toward the door. "C'mon, Elmer," she commanded the beleaguered beagle, who lethargically pulled himself up from his resting place. As Elmer dragged himself behind in her footsteps, he looked up and saw me. His ears stood up and happiness spread over his face and then slithered across his body until it reached his tail and sent it wagging energetically. He let out a small bark that sounded more like a hooray and trotted toward me. I squatted down and greeted him with a pat on the head and an enthusiastic "Hey there, boy!" His wet tongue made a sweep from my chin up my cheek, and I pulled my face away from the slobber, laughing. "Careful, buddy! You're gonna take all my blush off."

Miss Eula was almost to the front door when she heard the commotion. She swirled around and glared at me. "Oh! It's *you* again! Did I not tell you yesterday to leave my dog alone?"

I was stunned. I didn't know how to answer the wicked woman so I said nothing. She walked closer to me, her black purse swinging from the crook of her arm.

"Answer me!" she ordered.

"Yes ma'am," I mumbled meekly. "I believe that's what you said."

She crossed her arms and scowled. "My Elmer has a delicate constitution and exposure to strangers is extremely upsetting." She looked down at the dog. "Come, Elmer. We must depart immediately."

Elmer ignored her and continued to look at me adoringly. He laid his chin on my knee and gazed at me with absolute worship. Despite her meanness, I did not remove my hand from the top of his head. The poor baby needed some kindness.

"Elmer!" Her voice and her temper were rising but Elmer continued to ignore her. Huffing, she unsnapped the clasp on her purse and pulled out a leash. Angrily, she reached over and attached it to his collar. Then she pulled his head from my knee with a strong jerk. He coughed from the violent action of the collar around his neck, but she paid it no mind. She pulled him a couple of steps toward the door, and as she opened the door, she turned back to me. "You wear too much makeup, young woman! You look like a floozie! I would strongly recommend that you remove some of that ridiculous eye makeup immediately." The door slammed behind her and I wished it had knocked the heck and maybe some of the meanness out of her. I knew I wasn't wearing too much makeup, so her words didn't sting, but they did cause a veil of embarrassment to creep across my face when I remembered the group of women in the store.

Charlotte spoke first as I stood up and smoothed my skirt. "Oooohhhhh, that woman just makes me so blasted mad!" She ran over and put her arms around me. "Abby, please don't pay her any mind. She's just a bitter old maid that has plenty of money and no friends. She can't stand anyone, particularly other women. Especially attractive ones."

Susan Marie, looking like she was about to cry, rushed over.

"Abby, I'm so sorry. Here you have gone out of your way to do me a favor and then to be treated in such a shabby way by someone from Bliss! It's inexcusable. Even if it is the meanest woman in the state of Mississippi. You can tell how awful she is. Why, even her own dog doesn't like her!"

I smiled, wanting to soothe the situation and put it behind us. "Don't worry. Unfortunately, I've already had a couple of encounters with her, so it's not just me. She treats everyone that way." I shook my head thoughtfully. "She must have had a sad life to end up with an attitude like that."

The woman in the denim jumper with the teased hair spoke up. "My mama has known her since they were girls, and she said she once was the sweetest angel you ever saw."

My mouth dropped. "*That* woman?"

She laughed. "Yes, *that* woman. Her daddy, Mr. Clyde Corbett, owned most of this town. Before he died, he sold many of the buildings. We bought the one where our drugstore is. Still, he left her with several other buildings, thousands of acres of land and a bank full of money. In fact, he owned the bank. There were two of them children. She had a brother, Clyde Junior, who was killed in Iwo Jima during the war. That nearly broke the entire family, but the final blow for her came when her fiancé was killed at Normandy. Folks say that, at first, she was just pitiful. Then she got mean. She gets meaner with every year that passes. If she lives much longer, she's going to be so mean the devil won't have her!"

Charlotte crossed her arms, raised one eyebrow and looked at me. "Her fiancé's name was Elmer." She rolled her eyes. "Every dog she's had since World War II has been named Elmer. That one that just left is Elmer the fifth or sixth."

I could not stop the smile that was tugging hard at the corners of my mouth. Eccentricity is such an admired trait in the South, even among mean people. "Have they all been on Prozac?"

A lovely teenager with shiny blonde hair pulled back into a ponytail spoke up. "My uncle's her vet and he says they've all had to have some kind of sedative for nervous conditions."

"I bet they have," I muttered.

"By the way," Susan Marie said as she walked over to the table where I would be signing books and set about finishing what she was doing when I arrived, "that Elmer is a girl dog, not a boy."

"You're kidding."

"Nope. When the last Elmer died suddenly, she couldn't find a litter of beagles that was ready to leave the mama, that had a boy in it. And of course she wasn't willing to wait so she just took what she could get, but she pretends he's a boy. That was one unlucky day for that poor dog."

I walked over to the table and set my purse under it while the other women scattered around to finish setting up for the event. "Well, it just goes to show that everybody has a story and that that story shapes who she becomes." I thought again of Homer and his story, which I had learned only after taking the time to listen. My heart softened slightly, ever so slightly, for the old biddy.

I saw dozens of books with white slips of papers attached to them on the table. "Are these preordered books that I need to sign?"

"Please. You can sign them now or after the event." Susan Marie looked up from the box she was unpacking. "Did you get to meet my troop of wonderful helpers? It takes an entire town to put on a book signing of this grand proportion." When I shook my head no, she introduced all the women. The one in the denim jumper was named Mary Louise, and she set up a table full of finger foods while Charlotte was searching frantically for cocktail-sized napkins. The book signing was due to begin in fifteen minutes.

"Suse, there's not a napkin in this store!" Charlotte threw her hands up in desperation. "I'll just run down to the Hallmark store and pick up several packs."

"Thanks. Just tell 'em that I'll run down there tomorrow and pay for them," Susan Marie instructed as Charlotte hurried out the door. Mary Louise came over with a tray of cheese straws and offered me one.

"Hmmm," I said munching on the staple of Southern hospitality. "These are delicious."

"Kay Ann Alexander, who owns the bakery up the street, made them. She also has a small floral shop that connects to the bakery." Mary Louise smiled conspiratorially and added, "She's a first cousin to our mayor that I was telling you about. Her daddy and his daddy are brothers." To myself, I thought, "Oh, here we go again," but I smiled. "Really?"

She nodded. "That's a wonderful family. You couldn't ask for a finer family. I always say that the apple doesn't fall far from the tree, so it's very important that a man come from a good family." She looked over at a woman with mango-colored hair and big fat earrings that looked like red lollipops dangling from her ears. "Evelyn, wouldn't you say that Mayor Alexander comes from the finest family in Bliss?"

Evelyn nodded eagerly and rushed over to join the conversation. I busied myself with applying fresh lip gloss and searching my purse for my favorite pen. "Yes, dear, they're the finest people in Bliss." Sadly, she cast her eyes downward and sighed heavily. "That's the saddest story. He adored his wife and they were such a sweet couple. He was devastated when she died so suddenly, but it's been about six years now so it's high time that he find him someone else. I'll tell you this: you couldn't possibly find anyone who would treat you any better than that man would."

I smiled weakly as the women continued to chatter about

their mayor being the ideal man for me, talking sometimes to me but mostly to each other. I began signing books that had already been purchased, reading each slip of paper for my inscription instructions, and thought of the man in Bliss who had really captured my attention. Spencer Edwards had sat in the audience of the Rotary presentation and smiled approvingly, joining the laughter of his fellow Rotarians. Once when I looked directly at him, he had winked, causing me to stumble momentarily in my train of thought, but I recaptured my balance and forged on. I knew he was there for my entire speech, but sometime before the meeting adjourned, he slipped out. Although I knew he was leaving for a meeting, I was still disappointed not to see him again before leaving the country club. My sinful, wicked heart wished that he would find the time to come by the bookstore, but my mind pointed out that it would be best to start forgetting him as soon as possible.

The door of the bookstore began to open and close in rapid succession, and within minutes, a line with dozens of people, mostly women, had formed. The first in line was a gorgeous woman, probably in her thirties, with light chocolate-colored skin and a captivating smile of beautiful teeth.

"Oh, I just love everything you write," she gushed, reaching out to pat my hand. "We own a little cottage down on the gulf, and when a new one comes out, I just haul off for the beach, take your book and treat myself to a great joy."

I looked up and smiled. "Thank you. What's your name?"

"Lulu." She laughed, displaying her divinely white teeth. "It's actually TaWanda but when I was a little girl, I was quite a pistol. One day, my daddy said to my mama, 'We got ourselves a real lulu in this little girl.' Name stuck and that's what they all call me."

I chuckled. "Oh, that's funny." I was signing her book as we talked. She leaned over quite close and in a soft voice said, "My husband told me that you were at Rotary today." I nodded. "He's done quite taken with you as is every man in Bliss. Now, we women, we loved you already for the pleasure your books bring, but those men!" She clucked her tongue and shook her head, "All's it takes with 'em is a little charm and a little beauty and they're done gone over the moon 'fore you know it." Before I could reply, she continued. "He tole me that you ain't married. That true?"

"Yes." It was a tiny word for a big mouth.

She leaned a bit closer. "Well, we got us the best mayor in this town that you ever saw. That man's as fine as a pot of black-eyed peas, collard greens and crispy corn bread on a cold winter's night." She winked. "I'm just thinkin' you oughta meet this man 'fore you leave town. He's widowed."

"Well, maybe I'll get to meet him," I said, just trying to be nice.

"Tell you what I'm gonna do. I'm gonna leave here and march myself right over to the courthouse and tell 'im to get that behind of his'n over here to meet 'cha." She tapped a red-painted fingernail against my hand, then drew back. "And, honey, it is a fine behind, too!" She roared a deep belly laugh.

"Now, Lulu, I appreciate that much, but don't go to no trouble on my behalf."

"Trouble! Honey, it ain't no trouble whatsoever. After all the pleasure you done give me what with your books and all, it's the least I kin do. Plus, I'd be doin' the mayor a favor, too. And you know, it never hurts to stay in good with them what can help you!" She grabbed up her signed book, winked and then flounced out the door. That was just the beginning. It is not an exaggeration or an embellishment from a writer's overactive imagination when I say that every woman, and even a few men, who came through that line, made a glorious pitch for their mayor. Within an hour, I knew that he had lost his wife six years earlier, had the two incredible children, lived in the biggest house in Bliss, was a trusted advisor to the governor, had once spent the night at the White House, dedicated time to orphans, mowed grass for widows, was chairman of the deacons at the Baptist church and had won his first mayoral election by 93 percent, the largest margin of victory ever in the state of Mississippi. After that, no one had run against him in the next election, knowing that it simply was no use. A woman named Shaye, who owned Chez Bliss, "the best upscale restaurant in town," offered a romantic dinner by candlelight at a corner table, promising, "It's all on the house. And I can promise that when you leave, you two will be feeling very romantic." She winked and I blushed.

I was weary from trying to sidestep their efforts and rapidly growing weaker. I knew there was no way that I was going to escape the town's efforts. I was going to have to meet the god of Bliss, and since I was spending the night again at the Magnolia Blossom Bed and Breakfast, I was probably going to have to have dinner with him. If he wanted to, that is. My heart sank at the thought. I knew one thing, though—I wasn't going alone. Charlotte and Charlie would just have to go. But I was thinking as the townswomen worked so hard on his behalf, the man had to be downright pitiful or else he wouldn't need so much assistance in finding a date. Usually, though, it's easier for an older man to find someone because men die younger, leaving widows behind. I couldn't figure out what was going on, but there had to be a reason that the town's well-meaning matchmakers flocked like ants to a picnic when a halfway decent single woman showed up. Even Bess, Judy and Irene from Rotary stopped by, each to tell me that she had spoken with the mayor, and he assured her that he was coming by the bookstore to see me. No way out.

Another from the legion of matchmakers stepped away from

my table, and I looked up to see a nice-looking, neatly dressed man. Silently, I breathed a sigh of relief, knowing that I would have a slight reprieve.

"Hello, Abby," he said, offering his hand. "I'm Brian Jordan." I shook his hand and said cheerfully to the slender blonde, "Hello, Brian. It's a pleasure to meet you."

"I just wanted to tell you that you were great at lunch today. That is the best program we've ever had at Rotary. I went home and called my dad and told him that he really missed it by not being there today."

"Thank you."

"I'm not just saying that. You absolutely won everyone over. The whole town's talking about it. I saw you on *Larry King* the other night, too. That was really cool."

"I appreciate you saying that. Now tell me, your wife must have sent you over here to pick up a book for her."

He shook his head and laughed. "No. She's coming over to get one for herself. She's a schoolteacher so as soon as she gets out of school, she'll be over here. Her name is Sheila." He stopped and smiled broadly. "And she's drop-dead gorgeous so you'll be able to spot her as soon as she comes in."

I thought that was nice, a man who would talk so glowingly of his wife. "Well, Sheila is very lucky to have a husband who adores her like that."

"She's got him all right. I'm a lucky man." There was a moment that nothing was said; then he cleared his throat. "Uh, I'd like to get a book for my mama. Her name is, uh, Linda. With an i."

I signed the book and handed it to him. He looked at me for a second, then expressed his appreciation and turned to leave. But he stopped and turned back to me. "Uh, if you don't mind me asking, how long do you plan to be in Bliss?"

"Until tomorrow. I have a book signing in Jackson late tomorrow afternoon."

"You're here tonight?"

"That's right."

He stepped closer to the table and leaned forward slightly. "You've got to go out with our mayor while you're here!" he blurted out in an urgent tone. For a brief second, I was stunned into silence and then I started laughing. It was all so absurd that it was suddenly hilarious. He looked genuinely puzzled as I continued to laugh. Finally, I crossed my arms and leaned back in the chair. "I have never seen anything like this! Every person who has come through this line today has tried to set me up with the mayor." Brian looked a little white around the edges. Matchmaking, apparently, did not come as easy for him as it did for the women. "Let me ask you something," I continued. "Why is the mayor not over here, asking for his own date?"

Brian didn't miss a beat. "Because he's very sensitive. He wants to go out with you but he's afraid to ask. So I'm his front man." A smile teased my lips but the earnest gentleman continued quite seriously. "I've come to make sure you'll say 'yes' before he asks. Will you go?"

I shrugged. "I don't know. Maybe. *If* he asks me, himself." I was beginning to see a way out. If he was that nervous about asking me, maybe he wouldn't ask me and then I would be spared.

Desperation filled the guy's eyes. "But you have to go! You have to! He's my best friend in the world, and I can tell you that he's the greatest guy in the world. Please say you'll go. My wife and I'll double with you. We'll have a wonderful evening. Or you can go with just him, whatever works for you. Please?"

I chuckled. "I won't promise that, but I will say this: I have got to meet the man who is so beloved that an entire town would rally around to find him a date. Brian, please ask him to stop by for an introduction."

Brian sighed heavily, disappointment clouding his face. "Okay. I'll see what I can do."

Something occurred to me. "Brian, does he know that you're over here asking me for a date on his behalf?"

He shook his head slowly. "Uh, no."

I was amused. The situation was getting funnier by the moment. "What if I say 'yes' but he doesn't want to go?"

"Oh, he'll go!" Brian's voice returned to an enthusiastic pitch. "I promise that." For a brief moment, his face saddened. "Since his wife died, he's been so lonely and sad. It just kills me. Of all the people in the world, he deserves happiness."

"Tell him to stop by and we'll see." I wagged a finger playfully in his direction. "But no promises, understood?"

He smiled faintly. "Understood."

About thirty minutes later I heard a clatter of commotion behind me. After two hours of continuous signing, my line had dwindled down to two or three, but the bookstore was still filled with people drinking hot spiced tea and socializing. At the thunderous sound, I, along with everyone else, turned to see the back door flying hard against the wall as a big, blustery man, somewhere between fifty-five and sixty, with a red face and gray hair cropped close in an old-fashioned crew cut, burst through the door. He walked in with lumbering steps like those of a strapping linebacker when he's dressed out in pads. Susan Marie was standing near the door and greeted him. I smiled, nodded and turned back to the book I was signing.

Charlotte handed a cup of steaming spiced tea to a lady and then turned to face the door. She put her hands on her hips and said with a smile. "Well, it's high time that the mayor of Bliss showed up for one of this town's most auspicious occasions!"

I froze, pen in midair. Then, my heart started thumping rapidly. Great, I thought. He looks just like what I was expecting, which was to say he was too old and too wrong for me. I was going to ignore him but Judy and Bess were still in the store and they rushed over to me.

"Abby," Bess whispered, unable to contain her excitement. "*There he is!* The mayor's here!"

"Mayor Alexander, you just come right over here and meet the renowned Abby Houston," Judy commanded with the authority of a woman bound and determined to end the single-hood of two strangers.

I glanced sideways to see the large, older man headed in my direction. My throat was dry and I was trying desperately to think of a way out of the date that the town wanted us to have. I knew I was trapped. But he stopped a few feet away to speak to Charlotte. Then my heart really spun out of control. The gigantic girth of the man had hidden Spencer Edwards, who, apparently, had come in the back door behind him. I was in a bodacious mess, faced with a man I wanted to adore and a man I wanted to ignore. Spencer, a smile dangling on his handsome face, walked straight to me. He grabbed a nearby rocking chair, pulled it up beside my chair and plopped down. He put an elbow down on one armrest and leaned toward me. With his face only inches from mine, he said, "Hello, beautiful!" He winked, a bit wickedly, I thought.

"Hello," I replied nervously, the emotion brought on by my attraction to him and the fact that I was uncomfortable with a married man flirting openly with me in front of everyone. I finished signing for the last person in line and turned to face him.

He gave me that heart-stopping, lopsided grin. "Good to see you again."

"Again!" Judy and Bess chorused.

"You two have met?" Judy asked, completely stupefied.

I nodded. "We met last night at the diner."

Bess crossed her arms and looked at me sternly. "Why didn't you tell us you had already met the mayor?"

I blinked hard. "The mayor?" I shook my head slowly, in complete puzzlement. "I don't know what you're talking about. I haven't met the mayor."

Spencer Edwards started laughing, his chair rocking to the rhythm of his laughter. I gaped at him in complete bewilderment. I stared in puzzlement so long that he stopped rocking. "What?" he asked, that delicious smile spreading salaciously across his face and a teasing twinkle glimmering from his blue eyes. He leaned very close until I could smell the fragrance of his cologne. "You didn't know that I'm the mayor of Bliss?"

Chapter 11

My mind was so muddled that I was momentarily incapable of putting two logical sentences together. Thoughts began zipping rapidly, piercing my mind like little bullets. Was I in a dream where my ultimate fantasy seemed to be reality? But no, I quickly decided, this was a joke and I was so not amused that it wasn't funny.

My eyes narrowed. "You're not the mayor."

He was really enjoying his role in the joke. A teasing smile tipped his lips upward, and I just wanted to smack him right across that finely chiseled jaw. "Oh, yeah? Well, I beg to differ with you, pretty lady, but the popular vote by the fine citizens of this municipality says differently." He tilted his head proudly. "They elected me as their leader by an *overwhelming* margin, I might humbly add."

"*Arrogantly* add," I retorted with a huff. He merely lifted an eyebrow and grinned. I was vaguely aware that conversation in the store had stopped and all eyes and attention were riveted on us. I didn't care. Nothing was going to stop me from getting to the bottom of the situation.

"If you're the mayor, why didn't you tell me last night?"

He stopped rocking and leaned toward me, resting his elbows on his knees. "Why didn't you tell me that you're famous?"

"If I were really famous, I wouldn't *need* to tell you!" Aha! I had trumped him. He couldn't beat that one. He acknowledged surrender of that minor battle with a jaunty tilt of his head and a forefinger thrown in my direction.

"Good one!" To my further infuriation, he applauded.

I glared at him. I refused to go down easily. Buoyed by the success of my last retort, I confidently moved in for the final blow. I leaned over until my face was only inches from his. "What's your name?"

"Spencer," he replied glibly.

"I know that!" I snapped. In all honesty, it was the only thing I knew for certain. "What's your last name?" I knew it was Edwards and that the mayor's name was Alexander. I was confident that I had snagged him in the web of his own deception.

He chuckled. "Spencer Tolbert Alexander." A dramatic pause. "The fourth."

The blood drained from my face. "Alexander?" I whispered.

"But *you* can call me Spence." He winked. "Feel free to dispense with the formalities of 'Honorable' or 'Mr. Mayor.'" He tossed the formalities away with a nonchalant wave of his hand.

"I thought your name was Edwards." I said it so softly that I could barely hear it.

"Edwards?" His flippancy disappeared and he looked stunned. "Where on earth would you—?"

I cut him off. "Last night at the diner when that Eula woman made such a spectacle over your son and his skateboard, she called him Kyle Edwards. Why would you have a different last name from your son?"

He banged his head against the back of the rocking chair and slapped his forehead with his hand. "Ohhhhhh," he moaned lightly. "Now I understand where the misunderstanding came from." He shook his head and then looked at me. "As I'm sure you know, being the bright lady that you apparently are, in the South, an inherited name ends with the fourth. That would be me. So Kyle's name is Kyle Edwards Spencer Alexander. The Edwards comes from my *late* wife's family." My face reddened with the emphasis that he was not married, and I know that I heard some light giggles in the spellbound audience. "Her father is the town's most prominent family physician, Dr. Mac Edwards. Miss Eula thinks a lot more of the Edwards family than she thinks of the Alexander family, probably because Mac's daddy and Miss Eula's daddy were close friends. Or maybe because when I was ten years old and her paperboy, I used to throw her newspaper in the bushes more often than on the front porch. It will probably come as a great surprise to you, but that woman is quite capable of holding a grudge into the vastness of eternity. Whatever the reason, she always refers to him with 'Edwards' attached to his name." He ended the explanation by rolling his eyes.

I couldn't speak. What was there to say? I had made a classic mistake. I had assumed. I felt like a complete fool. Thankfully, Charlotte spoke for me.

"Spencer Alexander, do you mean to tell me that you drove this woman home last night and you didn't even give her your last name?" She came storming over from her perch of observation by the romance novels. "Where on earth are your manners? If I didn't know better, I'd think you were raised in a barn!"

His Honor looked like a small boy chastised by his teacher.

His smile vanished while I struggled to keep one from my lips. She had beautifully managed to put him in his place. He was uncomfortable, which made me a bit more comfortable.

"Well, uh, well, uh, I-I-I-I didn't realize I hadn't told her. Gee, Charlotte, I didn't do it on purpose." Like a small boy, he tried to deflect the blame. "Hey! Why don't you get onto her for not asking?"

Like a mother, she reached over and popped his hand. "It is not her place to have to ask, *Mr. Leader* of the Community! She is a visitor to Bliss and she should not have to bear the responsibility of figuring anything out. It's simply not hospitable."

Smiling, I settled back in my chair. I was enjoying Charlotte's noble rise to my defense. He cast an embarrassed glance in my direction, refusing to let his eyes meet mine. I enjoyed that only briefly, though. I much preferred him as confident, verging on cocky.

I spoke up. "It's no big deal. I feel silly for assuming. It's just odd how I tripped into so many misconceptions." I thought of some of them—assuming his name was Edwards, that the mayor was much older—and then something else flashed into my mind. I remember his conversation with Maggie about Elizabeth and her night out with the girls, and Charlotte had told me at breakfast that his wife was called Liz, certainly the shorthand version of Elizabeth.

"Who's Elizabeth?" I asked.

The light of pure, sublime love filtered immediately across his face. He glowed. My heart lingered in the balance, waiting for the words. "My daughter. She's almost twelve. She's named after her mother." I was relieved. He leaned back in the rocker and stretched out his legs. "As you can see, I was quite generous with my wife when it came to naming our children." His playful arrogance had returned and I was delighted. "I'm just a generous kind of guy!"

Mary Louise chimed up. "I can vouch for that. Spence gives time, money and emotion to every good cause in town." That opening line delivered, she turned to me. "That's why he needs a good woman to help him out. One who's like him—energetic, kind, generous. And of course, we all think she should be just as pretty as you are." She turned her palms up and spread her arms. "You're so perfect that if we had written down a list of what we wanted for Spencer, we could haven't done better! It's like a miracle has been delivered this very day to Bliss, Mississippi."

A murmuring of agreement filtered across the room. I blushed crimson. Spence blushed more. I dropped my head and picked up a book to sign generically for store stock. To his credit, he gathered his thoughts and quickly found his voice. "Now, Mary Louise, that is a mighty big burden of salvation to put on any one woman," he said in an easy voice, so funny that even I, in my embarrassment, had to chuckle. His shoulders relaxed at the sound of my giggle. "Abby, I know, being the in-demand star that you are, that you're on a very tight schedule. But could you possibly work it into your schedule to get married while you're here? Won't take but a minute." He weaved the fingers of both hands together and then pointed toward me, using both forefingers. "I have some connections down at city hall, you know. I think I'd be able to arrange for a quick processing of the marriage license."

I slid easily into the game and played along. I looked at my watch and pretended to be counting the hours. "Let's see. Hmmm. I think I would be available between nine and ten in the morning before I leave for Jackson at noon. Will that work?"

He snapped his fingers. "That'll do it." He turned to the gaggle of gawkers. "We'll expect to see each and every one of you there. With an appropriately expensive gift, I might add. Sorry, but there's not enough time to have invitations properly engraved."

Susan Marie put her elbows down on the counter and put in

her two cents' worth. "Why, of course we'll have the reception here; it's so fitting. We can set up the cake table over in the cookbook section. How appropriate is that?"

A small ripple of polite laughter spread through the store, but suddenly I wasn't having fun anymore. I was trying to be a good sport, but I actually was quite serious about Spencer Alexander, and I didn't think that all the presumptuous silliness was helping my cause. He was seeing me more as a source of amusement, of public entertainment, than as a woman that he would be interested in romancing. "Oh, my goodness!" A thought tore through my frazzled mind. "He's not married! This man I am so attracted to is not married. After all the anguish I've suffered over my attraction to a married man, he's *really not married*." A chill of excitement swept through my body and settled down in the center of my abdomen. I don't know what's there exactly because it's too far down for the heart and too far up for the stomach, but it's that erogenous zone where good and bad feelings go to get our attention. It kicked me there and I felt a frosty spot that overwhelmed my gut. It made my heart wiggle. I was also happy to discover that I wasn't a bad person, a wanton woman lusting after the flesh of a married man. I was, I suddenly realized, a very intuitive woman drawn to an attractive, successful man who, most importantly, was not attached. The room was buzzing with conversation but I submersed myself in my thoughts for a moment and loitered in a place of supreme anticipation. "Something could possibly come from this," I thought to myself. "That's why I'm not going to tease about this anymore. Somehow he has to take me more seriously. Besides, I'm leaving town tomorrow so there isn't much time." I pulled my lower lip in and chewed on it thoughtfully.

"Hello, Miss Houston?" A gentle, timid voice pulled me back to the bookstore. "I looked up and saw a familiar face, a face, though known to me, that I couldn't immediately place. He wasn't handsome, far from it, but he was enormously pleasant looking because of the sweetness that radiated from his plump red Santa Claus–like cheeks. Had I been asked to guess his age right then, I'm sure I would have said around fifty because his weight and lack of hair made him older. Upon closer inspection, though, I would have realized that his face possessed few lines and no wrinkles, so he was probably five to ten years younger than I thought.

"Hello!" I said brightly, greeting him warmly as I always do with people kind enough to spend their money on my books. Too, I was sure I recognized him, so I added, "It's good to see you. How're you doing?"

His red cheeks blushed darker and he pushed several books toward me. "I wanted to get these signed. I bought ten the other day and got you to sign them, but then I realized that I had forgotten several people. My cousin loves you, so does my best friend's wife, a lady I work with and my neighbor who gave me both of my cats. I don't know why I didn't think of them sooner but I need more books!" He grinned so widely that his bulbous cheeks pushed his eyes together in tiny slits. Of course! I knew him from a previous book signing. Now, where was it? I asked myself, trying to remember the places I had been. My mind was stuck for a moment. I couldn't think or remember the last few days, especially since my mind was wrapped tightly around the honorable mayor sitting to my right. Then it hit me.

"Wait a minute!" I put my pen down and pointed my finger at him. "You were at a book signing a few days ago." I laughed and said teasingly, "I always remember multiple book purchases." He proudly threw out his chest, which also pushed his jellylike belly out further.

"That's right." He nodded happily. "Now, do you remember where it was?" I looked thoughtfully, trying to remember, so he added, "But don't worry if you don't. I know that you meet a lot of people and there's no reason you should remember a guy like me." He said it in a bit of a sad tone as if he was used to not being remembered. I felt a pang through my heart. I hate to see kind, wonderful people rejected by society because they don't possess beauty, position or power.

"Oh, I remember *you*," I said quickly and winked. "It's just that I've been in ten cities in twelve days and they're all running together. After a while, all places and bookstores blend together. It has nothing to do with you." His cheeks burned redder and the smile grew larger. Then it hit me. "I know! It was Little Rock, wasn't it?"

He nodded vigorously and the shine from his bald head danced brighter with the light from the room. "I can't believe you remember."

"Your aunt loves my books," I added as more began to roll back into my memory. "And she is retired and lives in Cashiers, North Carolina." I was proud of myself, so I crossed my arms and leaned back in my chair with a look of triumph. He was amazed. I knew I had just made the day for someone to whom others rarely gave the time of day.

"Miss Houston, you're just unbelievable!" he exclaimed. "I can't believe that you remember me, but it means a lot that you do." He looked down at the floor and muttered in an embarrassed tone, "Thank you so much."

I uncrossed my arms, leaned forward and put my elbows on the table. "What in the world are you doing in Bliss, Mississippi?" I asked in what was undeniably an incredulous tone.

"Hey!" Spencer chimed up, the rocker squeaking to a stop. "Bliss happens to be the garden spot for the state of Mississippi, I'll have you know." He added playfully, "So watch your tone. It's not like we're the end of the world!"

I cut my eyes toward Spencer, then looked back at the gentleman and rolled them. "Pay no attention to him. He happens to be the worshipped leader here in Bliss but you can call him Spence. Don't worry about calling him the Honorable or Mr. Mayor."

The guy chuckled and stretched out his hand to Mr. Mayor. "Hi there. I'm Walter Hackett. Pleased to meet you."

The mayor stood up, as a matter of courtesy, and appropriately welcomed the visitor to the garden spot for the state of Mississippi. "Mr. Hackett, we're most pleased to welcome you to our town. We hope you will have a fine time, partaking of the hospitality of this most gracious town." He cleared his throat. "Uh, we do have one citizen who is, shall we say, a little challenging. But perhaps you will have the fine fortune of avoiding a misfortune with her while you're here. Otherwise, I have complete confidence in our townspeople to make you feel mighty welcomed here. What brings you to Bliss?"

Walter dropped his eyes and shifted his weight from one leg to another. I didn't think it was possible but his cheeks reddened further. "Uh, I, uh, came because of Miss Houston."

"What!" I exclaimed. "You came all the way to Bliss because of me?" I glanced over at Spence, who, after recovering from the announcement that it was me and not the beauty or hospitality that had brought the visitor to town, was looking quite impressed.

He nodded. "Well, I sure hated it that I didn't get these books the other day and I wanted to get 'em signed."

"How did you know that I'd be here?"

"Your publisher's Web site. It has your complete schedule on it." He opened one of the books and pushed it toward me. "Could you please sign this to Samantha, Miss Houston?"

I obediently began to sign, commenting as I did. "Well, I'm quite impressed, Walter, that you would drive all the way over here to get these books. For future reference, you can always call the bookstore, order the books over the phone, I'll sign them, and the store will ship them to you. The shipping will cost a lot less than the gas! By the way, please call me Abby."

Walter, no doubt, was an overzealous fan who probably had a crush on me. I had seen it a few times before, and they, almost always, looked like Walter. They never looked like Spencer Tolbert Alexander IV.

"Thank you," he said quietly, looking down at the floor. "I didn't mind driving, though. It was nice to get away."

"Where do you live?" Spencer asked.

"Zionsville, Arkansas. Betcha never heard of it."

The man I was certain knew everything did not disappoint me. "Why, I sure have! I've even been to Zionsville. Had the best sausage gravy at a little diner there, right in the middle of town."

Walter nodded. "Yeah. That's Hazel's place. She's awfully good. I eat breakfast there most mornings."

Spencer's expression turned to one of perplexity. "Zionsville's quite a haul from here. It's way on the other side of Little Rock. It must be six or seven hours away."

"Six and a half."

"You drove all that way just to see *her*?"

"Hey! What's that supposed to mean?" I cried in a mock voice of implied insult. "I happen to be famous. Remember?"

Spencer snapped his fingers. "I keep forgetting. What's a six-and-half-hour drive to see a celebrity?"

"Right," I replied. I picked up another book. "Walter, how do you want this signed?"

He told me and for the next several minutes, I signed books while Spencer and I chatted with Walter. The books signed, he picked them all up, offered his hand to me to shake and said, "Abby, you're awfully nice to be so nice to me. Thank you very much."

"Walter, you're the one who's so nice! Thank you for driving all this way just to see me. Now, remember, if you ever need any more books, just call a bookstore where I'm going to be and I'll sign them when I get there." I snapped my fingers. "Wait a minute." I grabbed my purse from under the table and rummaged through it until I found a notepad. I scribbled a name and phone number, tore the page out and handed it to Walter. "Here's the name and number of the manager at the bookstore in my hometown. Just give him a call and place the order. I stop by once a week and sign books for him. He'll ship 'em to you."

Walter Hackett looked as if he had been handed the keys to the world. He gingerly held the piece of paper as if it was a Faberge treasure from the Czar Nicholas era. I thought it was my imagination but the man honestly looked like he had tears in his eyes. He gulped. "Miss Houston, I mean Abby, thank you very much. Thank you. I can't tell you how much this means to me."

I waved away his appreciation. "Think nothing of it. I'm happy to do it. Now, you have a safe drive home, okay?"

He nodded. "I will." He stood there for a moment awkwardly, and when nothing further was said, he waved good-bye. "Guess I better pay for these and get out of your way."

"You're not in my way," I said as he meandered toward the cash register. Spencer sat back down in the rocker and looked at his watch.

"Well, it looks like the book signing has officially ended. It's now four o'clock."

My heart winced. I hated for it to end and to have to bid adieu to Spencer Alexander. "Yeah," I said a bit sadly. "It's over."

He leaned closer, putting his elbows on his knees. "My spies keep reminding me that you're staying in town again tonight." He glanced with amusement toward Charlotte, who immediately busied herself by straightening a box of bookmarkers on the cash wrap.

I nodded, my heart speeding up. I tried to act calm, not wanting to raise my hopes. "I'm here tonight. I leave in the morning for a book signing in Jackson."

"Now, I know that you're a big Hollywood star and I'm just a small-town mayor," he began.

"But you're the mayor of the garden spot for the entire state of Mississippi," I interjected. "That's probably the most important mayoral position in the United States."

"That's right." He nodded and tried to squelch the smile of amusement that was tugging at his lips. "So when you put it that way, that puts us on more equal footing."

"Yes, it does," I agreed.

"So in that case, would you possibly consider having dinner with me tonight?" That grin slid lopsidedly up his face and a burst of rapturous happiness flooded my body. I hadn't felt that way since I was a teenager and Skippy Chastain had asked me for a date. For a moment I couldn't speak. My eyes locked with his mesmerizing blue ones, and before I could say a word, ecstatic cheers rang through the bookstore. It shook us both out of the moment, and we looked around to see the townswomen, including Maggie who had just come in, high-fiveing, clapping and dancing little jigs of delight. The joy was so intense that I looked to see if my mama was leading the celebration. She wasn't. But I was confident that back in Georgia, her "mother's intuition" had her raising the roof with exaltation. We looked back at each other and laughed.

"How could I possibly say no when it means this much to the town?" I asked aloud while adding silently to myself, and to Mama and me.

Chapter 12

I was so happy that I could have danced in four-inch heels all the way back to the Magnolia Blossom Bed and Breakfast. The feeling that slid sumptuously from my head through my heart to my toes was so scrumptious that it felt foreign to my body. I had long forgotten how glorious attention from the right guy felt. Light of foot and giddy of heart, I floated out the door with Charlotte, who was driving me home so that I would not have to dance down the street.

Without a word we both slid into the big silver Mercedes she was driving, but when the doors were closed, before she put the key in the ignition, she turned to me and let out a squeal of delight. "Wheeeee!" she exclaimed, clapping her hands together. "I can barely believe that two of my favorite people are going out! Oh, this is simply the most exciting news I could imagine."

Despite the fact that I was silly with delight, I attempted to force an expression of "business as usual." "Yes," I answered, reaching over to fasten my seat belt thus avoiding direct eye contact. "It was quite nice of him to invite me out, wasn't it? I suppose he's doing his proper mayoral duty by showering a visitor with hospitality."

Charlotte wasn't fooled for one Mississippi minute. She raised a motherly eyebrow and looked at me with a cut-out-the-nonsense stare before slipping the key in and turning it. "Quite nice? Okay, little Miss Priss. You can try that business with everyone else but don't think for a second that it'll work with me. I saw how your big brown eyes lighted up when you found out he wasn't married."

I swallowed and looked out the window, watching a mother scold a small boy who was wearing a navy baseball jacket. Out of the corner of my eye, I saw a red truck with a white camper top attached to the truck bed. Briefly, it skittered across my mind that I had recently seen another red truck with white camper bed somewhere, probably on the trip to Bliss the previous day. But I didn't dwell on such an unimportant thing. I turned my mind back to the conversation at hand. "Was it that obvious?" I asked in a small, insecure voice as she backed out of the parking space.

"Not to everybody. Probably not to anybody but me and, most importantly, not to Spencer at all. I just have a knack for things like this." She shifted and eased the big car forward. "It never occurred to me that you didn't know that Spencer was widowed. Especially after I heard that he brought you home last night. I knew that Maggie was up to matchmaking when I heard that she had insisted that he drive you back to the inn. That's why I was filling you in on the details at breakfast this morning."

"Yes, but you left out one *single* detail."

She laughed. "And it was the most critical one since that tiny detail meant he's single. He's dreamy, isn't he?"

I nodded. "Charlotte, I get asked out often but I rarely see anyone who captures my imagination. I can't tell you how many years it has been since I've actually been excited about a date!" I sighed happily. "I feel like I've won the lottery. I saw a man who tickled my emotions and he actually asked me out!"

She smiled. "But let's talk about something more important than that."

I looked puzzled. I couldn't imagine what could possibly be more important. "What?"

"What are you going to wear tonight?

She was right. At the moment, nothing was more critical.

♡

As soon as I flipped off my high heels, I ran a hot, sudsy bath, then crawled in to soak and relax. After the bath, I slathered my body in lotion, pulled on a thick terry bathrobe with "Magnolia Blossom Bed and Breakfast" monogrammed on the left side and lay down under the lightweight down comforter to rest. I was too keyed up to sleep but I rested my eyes and body and whispered a grateful prayer that Spencer Alexander was not married and that he had asked me out. I also whispered prayerful thanks that I was capable of feeling such girlish enthusiasm. I sadly had thought that was an emotion of the past.

After resting for a half hour, I decided that I was in such a good mood that I wasn't mad at my meddling mother any longer. I decided to humble myself and call her. I was so happy that I didn't mind the humbling at all. Still loitering in bed, I called from my cell phone.

"Hey," I said in a weak, softened tone.

"Hey." Hers was stronger without a hint of pouting. She didn't sound mad at all that I had ended our earlier conversation so abruptly. Of course, I knew her well enough to know that she certainly didn't think she had done anything wrong. So she had no remorse or concern.

"What's goin' on?"

"I'm just readin' the obits." That's Mama's favorite afternoon activity. She can't wait to get the newspaper, settle down with a cup of coffee and carefully study the obituary page. "I guess I'm gonna have to get ready after while and go to the funeral home."

"Who's dead?"

"Do you remember Jake Samples? I don't know that you do because you's just a little girl. But we used to pick him up every Sunday morning and take him to church. He was an old man and he didn't have no other way to go and he didn't have no children. So he'd put on a clean pair of overalls and sit down outside on his front-porch steps every Sunday and wait on us."

"So he died?"

She ignored me. "I'll never forget—you know old men like that always thought they had to pay you for everything you did for 'em—so one Sunday, we brought him home and he said to your daddy, 'Brother Harrison, if you got a minute, come with me. I wanna show you something.' So your daddy went around back with him and Mr. Samples showed him a new litter of pigs. He said, 'Now, y'all been awfully good to me so I wanna do somethin' for ya. Pick you out a pig. You get the pick of the litter. You can grow it into a fine hog that'll feed your family for a while.' And you know what your daddy did?"

I like to hear stories of my daddy. He always did such honorable things. "What?"

"He picked the tiniest little runt in the whole bunch!" She paused for my reaction.

"Really?" I expected no less.

"Mr. Samples said, 'No, Brother Harrison. That ain't good

'nuff. Pick y'un another 'un.' Your daddy said, 'Now, Jake, you told me to take my pick and that's my pick. Are you goin' back on your word, or are you gonna let me have the one I want?'"

My eyes misted. That was my daddy. He knew that the old man could get more money for the others, so he chose the one he wouldn't have been able to sell at all. I swallowed down my emotion, then spoke. "So Mr. Samples died?"

"Heavens no!" Mama was incredulous at the question. "Why, that old man's been dead twenty years at least. Maybe twenty-five."

I rolled my eyes. "Then, what did that story have to do with going to the funeral home tonight?"

"Well, I guess since you don't know him, you won't remember Idelle Nix, who lived next door."

"I've heard the name. Did she die?"

"Oh, no! She's in the nursing home with Zoey. Been there for a long time."

My patience was straining. "I'm going to ask one more time. Who died?"

I might as well have not uttered a word. "Idelle was married to an old man who wouldn't nothin' but a drunk. Bad drunk. But they had a girl together and she married a Jarrard who was my cousin Chloe's son."

I rolled my eyes. "And?"

"Chloe's second husband—not the daddy to that boy—he died. He's been goin' downhill for a long time." That crooked road detour of verbal splatter made perfect sense to her and none to me.

"Mama, you told me all that just to tell me your cousin's second husband died?"

"Well, I wanted you to understand real good who I's talkin' 'bout."

I was mentally worn out and physically aggravated. One

good thing had come from it: I was in no mood to tell her about Spencer Alexander and our date. Instinctively, I knew it was better not to tell Mama because she'd worry me to death about it, but I was aching to share the good news. At least, I was *before* she got me off track. But if the date turned out like most of my dates, it would be easier if I didn't have to relive it with Mama and answer all her questions.

Most of all, I didn't want to get her hopes up. Mine were already up, which was enough of that.

"I can't decide what I'm gonna wear," Mama said, and that began a rambling of all the outfits that were possibilities. I half listened as I always do when she starts with that, then seconded the notion of her black dress trimmed in turquoise. Not because I particularly like it but because I wanted to get off the phone and start dressing.

Four times, Mama asked if I was certain that outfit would be okay, and four times I assured her that it was. The fifth time, I ignored the question and asked, "How's Kudzu?"

"She's fine. I'd be fine, too, if you cared half as much about me."

I rolled my eyes. "Well, if you licked my cheek and happily ran around in circles, wagging your tail frantically when you saw me, I'd care that much about you, too."

She couldn't help it. She had to laugh. "Well, don't count on that happenin'!"

"Don't worry. I'm not. Okay, I've got to run."

"What are you doin' tonight?" There it was. The question I was going to have to slide around.

"Goin' to dinner with some of the folks here," I replied in a voice that was the verbal equivalent to a shrug. Then I moved to an urgent tone. "Listen, I'll talk to you tomorrow. Okay?"

"Okay. Talk to you then. Be sweet."

♥

At 5:45, I pulled myself up to begin dressing for the evening. Spencer was to pick me up at seven, so I wanted to give myself plenty of time to prepare meticulously. I turned on the radio and sang along with Elton John as I laid out my clothes—a long-sleeved black sheer top with a matching camisole. The top was embroidered with flowers of pale pink and dark pink. The skirt was deep pink lace with a black lining that peeped through the lace. To finish off the outfit, I pulled out high heel slip-on sandals beaded in hundreds of pink and black seed pearls. I much prefer the way a best-selling author dresses as compared to an obituary writer. I was putting on my makeup when I heard a slight tapping at the door.

"Abby?" Charlotte asked softly. I opened the door and saw a bouquet of flowers so enormous that it completely hid the proprietor of the Magnolia Blossom Bed and Breakfast.

"Oh my goodness!" I gasped at the gorgeousness of the pink, white and yellow flowers. "Are those *mine*?"

She moved them to the side and leaned way over to stick her head around a bulging gladiola. "They will be, if you'll move aside and let me set this heavy thing down! I'm about to drop them." After she set them down on the desk, she heaved a heavy sigh and turned to me. "Now, I know I'm a bit out of shape but darn if those aren't the heaviest flowers I've ever carried up a flight of stairs."

"Those are the most beautiful flowers I've ever seen in my life." I shook my head in wonderment while Charlotte tilted her head and looked at me questioningly.

"Do you suppose that Kay Ann has any flowers left at the shop after making that arrangement?"

I giggled and ran over to pull out the card. I read it silently and then aloud. "Looking forward to dinner. Spencer." My heart speeded up. "Oh, Charlotte, isn't that so thoughtful?"

Charlotte smiled beatifically. "That young man is really

something!" She put her hands on her hips. "But, Miss Priss, I have a few other surprises for you, too. Come downstairs with me for a second." She saw me glance down at the terry robe, but she waved her hand to dismiss my hesitation. "You look fine. No one's here but us and even if Charlie comes in, he's seen a woman in a bathrobe many times. Trust me."

Barefooted, I pattered down the stairs behind her, following her to the antique desk used for registration. The top of the desk was covered with packages—a box of Godiva candy, a huge basket of fruit, a small vase of short-stemmed yellow roses with baby's breath, a white bakery box tied with string, a gift basket filled with food items like cheese straws, cookies and gourmet coffee, and a couple of other boxes stamped with the names of local stores. Bewildered, I looked at Charlotte, who laughed and spread her hands.

"Don't ask me! These have been arriving for you on a steady basis since we returned. I knew you were resting so I didn't bring them up. Good thing, too. Otherwise, I'd have climbed those stairs a dozen times."

I walked over and began pulling cards from the gifts, and without fail, the name following each inscription was Spencer's. The yellow roses did not have a name on them, but based on the other evidence, it was safe to assume that those, too, were from the mayor of Bliss. The stash also included a delicate china figurine from the gift shop, a box of nail polishes from the beauty shop and an adorable teakettle from the hardware store. Charlotte was as amazed as I was.

"Spencer sent you all of this?" She shook her head. "I have two things to say. First, that boy's got it bad. Second, where did he find the time to do all of this? We barely beat most of this stuff home!"

"Wow," I whispered with awe. I opened the box from the bakery, which was filled with white iced bonbons topped with multicolored sprinkles. "I have to say that I've never been courted like this before!"

"I have to say that I have never seen *anyone* courted like this before!" For a minute or two, we both stood there, looking at the stash and shaking our heads. We were too stunned to speak. Finally, Charlotte spoke and issued a command that made perfect sense.

"You'd better run along upstairs and finish dressing. A man that goes to this much trouble deserves the most beautiful woman possible."

I didn't argue. She was right, of course.

$\heartsuit$

I was still fiddling with my hair when the phone rang at precisely seven o'clock. I made a face in the mirror to show the right side of my hair just how annoyed I was with it that it refused to behave properly like the left side, then walked to the nightstand and picked up the receiver to the 1940s-style ivory-colored phone.

"Hello?"

"Hey, gorgeous!" At the sound of his voice, my heart thrilled, and knowing how much he was taken with me gave me complete confidence in that thrill. "Are you ready for your big night out in the big town of Bliss?"

I was but my hair wasn't. I decided, though, not to mention that. "That I am," I replied, with a smile in my voice. "I'll be right down." I checked my lip gloss, gave my hair one last desperate fluff, grabbed my purse and left the room. As I tapped down the stairs in my high heels, I saw the handsome object of my affections waiting at the bottom of the steps, his back turned, looking over the stash of gifts on the desk. Halfway down, I smugly asked, "Aren't those the loveliest gifts?"

He turned and when he saw me decked out in the black and

pink outfit, he gave a short, startled shake of his head. "Holy Moses!" he muttered under his breath. His widened eyes told me first that he liked what he saw; then his mouth told me. "You are absolutely beautiful!" He stretched out his hand, and when I reached the third step from the last, I took it and felt a magic tingle from my fingers up my arm. I couldn't speak for a second, so taken was I by the moment. I stepped off the last step and looked up at him. My heart was pounding in my ears. I wanted to kiss him. Right then and there. That's saying a lot for me because I have a mantra that I always follow with dates—I don't hike, bike or kiss on the first date. Something told me deep inside that if Spence Alexander asked, I would do all three all at once if he wanted. He broke the intoxicating moment by speaking first. He cleared his throat.

"Uh, what is all that stuff?" he asked, gesturing toward the loot with a throw of his head.

I laughed. "Gifts from an admirer. A very handsome one, I might add."

His face clouded from the "ouch!" his heart seemed to be feeling. He looked perplexed and hurt, neither of which I understood since he was the admirer. For a couple of turns, he looked from me to the gifts and back again.

"Seriously?"

"Yes, silly. Why are you teasing me? Except for those yellow roses, they each had a signed card. The most beautiful, though, was that huge arrangement of flowers. Incredibly spectacular. They're in my room, along with a box of Godiva chocolates from which I did sneak one piece."

"There's more? You got a big arrangement of flowers?" He shook his head. "Someone sure thinks a lot of you." Halfheartedly, he added, "Of course, I can certainly see why."

I moved closer and fingered the lapels of the dark charcoal-colored suit he was wearing. "Thank you for thinking so much of me. All teasing aside, I love everything you sent me. It was so romantic."

"Wait a minute." He stepped back and looked at me hard. "You think that *I* sent this stuff?"

I rolled my eyes playfully. "I think that because that's what the cards said!" I walked over, picked up a card from the Southern-belle figurine and handed it to him. "You can stop pretending now."

He read the card and shook his head. Then, he walked over to the desk and picked up a couple of other cards. His mouth dropped; then finally he spoke. "Abby, I'm so sorry to tell you this, especially since it has obviously put me in such good favor with you, but I didn't send this stuff."

My heart squatted sadly into a pitiful pile, then rolled over with a slow thump. I was so disappointed after having felt so good just a few moments before. After that kick in the stomach, I began to feel the drawing up of my muscles, a surefire signal of embarrassment. I wanted to cry. First, from disappointment and then from the fool I had just made of myself. I hate to admit it but I even had thoughts of my mother. I swallowed.

"You didn't send these things?" My voice was so tiny that I didn't recognize it.

Silently, he shook his head. "I don't understand." He began picking up the boxes and reading aloud the names of the businesses. Then he stopped. "Wait a minute!" A dawning of understanding rose across his face. "Kay Ann, Margaret, Lizzie, Cindy. You know what all of these businesses have in common?"

"What?"

"They're either owned or managed by women, women who are busy-body romantics and are eager to give this old guy a helping hand!" He smiled broadly. "Women, who have been trying to matchmake me for years."

"Are you saying that these women, without your knowledge or consent, sent me all of these gifts?"

He started laughing. "Yes ma'am. It's obvious that they didn't get together and discuss this plan, but each one, on her own, sent over a gift that would make you think better of me. Lizzie McCain spends most of her free time trying to find the perfect woman for me." He walked over and took me by the shoulders. "Abby Houston, you're an extraordinary woman. I dare say that there's not another woman in the world who can lay claim to being courted by an entire town!"

The embarrassment and hurt turned to a gentle touching of my heart. I was charmed at the thought of a town that loved one man so much that they would go to this much trouble on his behalf. "You mean to tell me that I'm dating an entire town? Oh, Spencer, that's the sweetest thing I've ever heard." I looked at the man who was greatly loved by so many and I knew then, if an entire town could love him that much, so could I.

Chapter 13

A beaming man with chubby cheeks splashed with red, the shade of high blood pressure, threw open the door of the restaurant from the inside just as Spencer reached for the knob.

"Come in!" he called out heartily as his grin grew larger. "I am so honored that you lovely people have chosen to dine at Alfredo's on your first date! This does my battered soul good."

By that point, it was obvious that the only person who did not know about my date with Spencer was Mama. I was hoping I would have a chance to tell her before she saw it on CNN.

"Fred!" Spencer pumped his hand vigorously. "I haven't seen you since yesterday!" To me, Spence winked and added as an aside, "Small town. We all run into each other quite frequently."

"And apparently, you all talk frequently, too," I replied dryly with a teasing smile tipping at my mouth. Spencer got the inside joke. He chuckled and nodded, then moved forward with the formal introductions.

"Abby Houston, meet Fred Alford." We smiled at each other, I offered my hand, and he held it delicately, bending over it in a perfect imitation of European-style. He kissed it lightly.

"Madam," he said in a long Southern drawl, making it almost comical. "It is our grand pleasure to welcome you to the finest Italian dining in Bliss, Mississippi, and, it is believed, the best within a seventy-two-mile radius."

I laughed and Spencer, shaking his head, added, "The *only* Italian restaurant within a seventy-two-mile mile radius. Fred keeps track by radar. Until last month, it was eighty-seven miles but one opened up down the road a ways. You may notice that Fred combined his last name and first name to come up with a fitting name for this fine establishment."

"You're quite a clever man!" I exclaimed brightly, swinging along with the mood.

A dark look crawled across his face, stretched to the point of playful exaggeration. "Alas, to all people I am indeed clever. To all, that is, but my wife!" On cue, a large woman with her blonde hair pulled straight back in a bun hurried around the corner and stopped when she saw us.

"Speak of the angel now," Fred said with a teasing lilt in his voice.

"Sweet Spencer!" she cried out, rushing over to reach up and squeeze his face. "I'm so happy to see you!" Then she held out her arms, inviting a hug which she promptly received. Women, I have noticed, enjoy hugging the mayor of Bliss, which leads me to believe that when he is campaigning, he doesn't kiss babies. Instead, he hugs their mamas.

"Hello, Twinky," Spencer said. "Have you been keeping Fred straight?"

"Huh! As though I could." She pulled back from the embrace

and shook her head. "But what's a gal to do? I married him for better or worse. Only thing is that I didn't know the worse included a restaurant that keeps me running like a maniac." She glanced my way, her face turning into a beam of light. "Spence Alexander, is this the lucky woman I've been hearing about all afternoon?"

He laughed easily and I squirmed uncomfortably. "First, I don't know if she's lucky, and second, I don't know if she's the one you've been hearing about."

She ignored him, slid over and gave me a great big hug. "Honey, I've heard all about you down at Sadie's beauty shop. It was the talk of the afternoon. All about how you're a big, famous author and how you just swept into town and swept this big ol' hunk off his feet." She held my shoulders firmly in her grasp as she talked. "Why, sweetheart, we're all just so proud of you." She winked good-naturedly. "There has even been talk of giving you a medal."

In situations like that, you can either wither in embarrassment or roll with the punches. I decided to roll. "A medal?" I snapped my fingers. "Thanks for reminding me." I turned to Spencer and said very seriously. "Did you bring me the key to the city?"

He slapped his forehead. "I knew there was something I was forgetting!" He started digging into his pockets. "Darn! I usually have a spare one with me." He shrugged. "Well, I guess you'll just to get someone to let you into the town until I can get a key made for you."

Twinky plopped her hands on her hips and affixed the mayor with a steely look. "Look, big guy, don't be worrying about no key to the city. You need to be worrying about giving her the key to your heart! That's the one that appears to have been lost."

Spencer paled but recovered quickly with an easy smile. "Oh, I haven't lost that key. It's in a safe-deposit box over at the First

National Bank of Bliss. I'm just waitin' for Fred to kick the bucket so I can dig it out and use it on you."

Beautifully done. With one slick comment, he had side-stepped the moment *and* made Twinky feel special. She was so flattered that a warm glow lowered its radiance over her from head to toes. I knew that glow. One just like it had drifted over me and attached itself as we left the Magnolia Blossom Bed and Breakfast. He smelled absolutely wonderful with a manly cologne that hinted of woods and muscles. I was inhaling the scent deeply as he opened the door for me, and when he touched the small of back, my entire being weakened. On the veranda he had stopped for just a moment and eyed me with such admiration that I felt awkward.

"Hmmm," he said quietly in a way that was seductive but not rude or brash. There's a special art to saying "hmmm" in the right way. After a few seconds, he took my elbow to guide me down the stairs and said, "Abby, I believe you're the pretti-est girl we've seen in Bliss in a very long time." My heart flut-tered and though I was already entranced, I became mesmerized to the point that I lost the little intellect I had. On the short ride to the uptown restaurant, I jabbered stupidly and said absolutely nothing that was brilliant, memorable or witty.

I knew how such charm could tongue-tie a woman, so I un-derstood when Twinky looked completely at a loss for words. Before she could speak, Fred stepped in and said, "Woman, we got to feed these kids." He grabbed a couple of menus. "Let me show you to the table we have for you."

"I'll be over to check on you!" she called softly after us.

The smell of cooked tomatoes, garlic and steamy pasta filled the air as we followed Fred through the dark-wood dining room crowded with white cloth-covered tables, each with a glass-covered candle in the center, glistening silverware and sparkling glasses. The mayor, of course, was obliged to speak to each

table. Some folks got a handshake, others a smile, others a toss
of the hand and a mention by name. As we zigzagged the
course, I became aware that a quietness was slipping over the
room as conversations halted. Fred led us to a corner banquette
that was covered in elegant, tufted red leather. It was a round
booth that swung around in a semicircle so that we could sit
side by side rather than face each other across the table. On any
other date I had had since my divorce, I would have been disappointed. I would have wanted a table to separate me from my
date. But not on that glorious night in Bliss, Mississippi, with
Spencer Alexander as my date. I wanted to sit as close as possible. Fred pulled out the table and I slid in from one side while
Spencer came from the other side to meet me perfectly in the
middle. A large hand-cut crystal bowl of water glistened in the
center, filled with floating orchids and violets.

"What beautiful flowers!" I exclaimed.

"Yes," he sighed. "Gorgeous. They're compliments of Lulu
and her husband who wanted you two to know they were
thinking of you."

Spencer rolled his eyes comically. "I'll have to speak to her
boss about how much he's paying her that she could afford orchids." To me, he added. "I believe you met Lulu today, but did
she tell you that she's my assistant?"

I giggled. "No, somehow in the big pitch she was making
about you, she didn't find a place to slip that in."

He grinned. "She was my paralegal at the law firm, and
when I took over as mayor, she insisted on lowering her stan-
dards and following me. She's a good 'un, though. I make up
the difference between what the city pays her and what they
should be paying her."

Fred, uninterested with Lulu's pay scale, was ready to get on
with business. He cleared his throat and in the silence of the
room, it reverberated through the rafters.

"Yes, Fred?" Spencer was visibly amused.

"Enjoy!" Fred commanded. "I will tell you that the Veal Oscar tonight is delectable." He stopped and smiled wickedly. "It's a good choice because it has no garlic in it." I guess we both looked puzzled because he added in an authoritative tone, "Neither one of you will be having garlic tonight." He pressed both hands to his chest in dramatic form. "I will not be responsible for tainting your first kiss." He stopped. More wickedness slipped into his smile. "It will be the *first* kiss, won't it?"

That was it. I wanted to crawl under the table. From the look on Spencer's face, I thought he was going to beat me there. I couldn't think of anything to say, and Spencer, for the first time since I had known him, couldn't throw back a cunning comment. He cleared his throat, put the menu in front of his face and said in a quiet tone, "I'll keep that in mind. Thank you. To start off, bring us a bottle of my favorite merlot."

"Immediately, sir!" Fred saluted crisply, winked and turned to leave.

I spoke up. "And if you don't mind, would you please bring us a basket of garlic bread to start with?"

Fred whirled back around, his round face redder and his eyes almost as round as his face. It was priceless. It was so funny that Spencer and I collapsed in laughter, falling against each other as we laughed. We laughed for so long that we couldn't catch our breath. Fred, seeing nothing comical in the comment, heaved a deep sigh and walked off. Our laughter had turned to quiet amusement shared with sly glances when a disgusted Fred returned a few minutes later with a basket stacked high with bread. It smelled so strong of garlic that I coughed involuntarily, and Spencer pulled back and silently mouthed, "Whoa!"

"I won't interrupt," Fred commented dryly. "I'll come back and get your order in a few minutes."

We shared a conspiratorial smile as Spencer pushed the basket across the table. "Do you think Fred left any garlic in the kitchen?" The look on his face was priceless and comical at once. Again, I threw back my head and laughed. Then, simultaneously, we both looked around the restaurant and saw that the other patrons, who had initially tried to be discreet, were all staring unabashedly.

He leaned over and whispered in my ear, the light weight of his breath dancing around delightedly on my earlobe. "I don't think we're doing a very good job of being inconspicuous tonight."

I dropped my head over until it gently touched his face. I savored for a brief second how it felt for my cheek to touch his warmth. I wanted to be lost in the moment, to just forget everyone else around, to linger in a feeling I didn't want to lose or to ever forget. Unfortunately my common sense won out, and in a pitch-perfect performance, or so I pretended to myself, of a titillating Marilyn Monroe, I purred seductively, "Peas and carrots. Peas and carrots. Peas and carrots." I punctuated the dramatic delivery with an alluring smile. I lowered my head and glanced upward through my lashes, which I fluttered flirtatiously.

His sweet blue eyes still danced with the merriment of the previous moment, but his smile was filled with puzzlement.

"Peas and carrots?"

My seductiveness melted into silly, soft laughter. Shaking my head, I explained. "I spent a few months in Hollywood while a movie was being made of my first book. I even had a tiny part where I played an over-the-hill, worn-out waitress. That's another story. Anyway, you know when you see background actors talking among themselves behind the stars? I always thought they were having actual conversations, but I learned that they're usually just saying 'peas and carrots' over and over to each other! It looks good on camera. Since I couldn't think of anything brilliant to say and all eyes were on us, I decided it was a good time to try a little Hollywood magic."

Spencer hit his head against the back of the booth, pounding it back and forth as he laughed, one of those deep-from-the-belly laughs, the contagious kind that swept me up, and there we were again—laughing joyously. We weren't laughing because it was genuinely funny but because we were happy. We had to breathe, though, so finally, given the choice between air and jolliness, we chose the life-sustaining element.

"Abby, you're something." He touched my hand lightly, briefly, studied me carefully and smiled with approval. "I knew you were a famous author but I didn't know you were a movie star, too."

I shook my head. "I'm not even a twinkle. They were paying me to be a consultant on the movie, and since I was already there, they tossed me another bone." I shrugged nonchalantly.

A sobering thought crossed his mind and it showed plainly on his face. "You're going to leave Bliss tomorrow and we'll never see you again." For the first time, I saw him frown. A deep furrow drew his brows together tightly. "By this time next week, you won't even remember this little town or any of us at all."

There's always two sides at war in those who find fame in their art of choice, whether it's movies, television or writing. There is the side that the public perceives and the true side that reveals who you really are. A casualty of success is often that the true person disappears in a maze of misconceptions. The public often chooses the public persona, so more often than not, it's simplest just to give up and become that person. I can see how easy it would be to get caught up all in the glitz and glamour and in thinking that you're something more special than you are. Thank goodness I had lived a lifetime before I found success. I just knew that I had been truly blessed and that a pen's stroke of good luck had taken me away from a life of death and deadlines. Spencer, though, had already formed his own misconceptions, and I knew from experience that as misinformed as those opinions might be, they're mighty hard to change. The person who holds them reacts with distrust, innocent though it might be, when you try to set the record straight. My heart sank because I knew those misconceptions wouldn't be easy to change.

"Spencer, that's not true. I'm not that kind," I said softly, doing little to veil the hurt on my face or in my voice. "This wonderful town is special to me and I, uh, I—"

"Okay, folks, here you go!" Fred interrupted. He tossed a white cloth over his arm and began attacking a wine bottle with a small corkscrew. "We have here the finest merlot that Alfredo's has to offer. The proceeds from this sale will go to pay the power bill this month."

I don't know a lot about wine so an expensive one is completely lost on me. I looked at Spencer, who looked at me and then to Fred.

"Is that the wine I ordered?" I won't say that panic flashed on his honor's face, but there was definitely a bit of anxiety leaking out around the eyes.

Fred lifted one eyebrow. "Now, now, no need to start worrying about your pocketbook." Pop. The cork was freed. Fred picked up one of the fat glasses he had brought out. "These are those fancy, special glasses that allow you to fully experience the bouquet of a fancy wine. I only bring these out for the expensive bottles. Needless to say, they don't get used around here much."

"Fred?" Spencer still did not have a complete answer. Fred ignored him a bit longer while he poured a small amount.

"Taste this," he instructed.

Spencer took a long whiff, obviously pleased, then took a sip that he rolled in his mouth for a moment. "Hmmm. That's a

beautiful wine." He nodded. "Almost as beautiful as my date."
He smiled, and again, I melted.

"You're going to think it's even more beautiful when you find
out that it's free."

We both blinked.

"Yep, that's right. The Morgans sent it over." Immediately
Spencer's eyes began searching the room. "No need looking for
them. They're already gone. Just said to tell you that it's mighty
good to see you laughing so much. Ready to order that Veal
Oscar yet?"

"Sorry, Fred, but we haven't had a chance to look at the
menu. Come back in a second?"

"Take your time. These other folks are enjoying staring at
you so much, they just keep ordering more food so they can stay
here." Fred grinned. "Best night we've had in right near a year."

"Who are the Morgans?" I asked when Fred left.

"Old friends of my parents. The Morgan family has owned
the cotton mill in Bliss for over a hundred years." I heard a quiet
ringing.

"What's that?"

"Huh?" Suddenly, he frantically began digging in his pocket.
"That's my cell phone. I never carry it, but the kids are out
tonight." He fumbled as he flipped the phone open. "I'm sorry.
I'm a worrywart. Hello?" Within seconds, his shoulders relaxed. "Hi Marie. Yes." He glanced toward me. "Fine." He
smiled. "I think so." He shook his head. "I guess." He rolled his
eyes. "I hope so." He chuckled. "I'll let you know. Let me get
back to dinner, or neither of us will ever know."

He was still chuckling as he flipped the phone shut and slid
it back into his jacket pocket. "My housekeeper."

"Is anything wrong with the children?" I took a sip of the
wine.

"She wouldn't know. She's at home with her family, but she

needed to know something very important, and I'm sorry to say that I don't have the answer. Perhaps you could tell me, fair lady."

"What?"

"How do you like me?"

Before I could answer, a flash exploded in our faces.

Chapter 14

I t took a few seconds to recover from the blinding flash of light. We both scrunched our eyes tightly and shook our heads rapidly as if that would help anything. Finally, the room began to come back into focus and there we saw standing before us a man around fifty with black-rimmed glasses and a goofy smile. He was holding a very official-looking professional camera.

"Howard! What in the dickens are you doing?" Spencer sounded more annoyed than he looked.

"Hey there, buddy!" Howard answered cheerfully. "Y'all havin' a good time?"

"Howard, you didn't answer my question." Spencer had lowered his voice because, once again, we were performing at center stage. The patrons at Alfredo's, surely for the first time in the history of the restaurant, were being treated to dinner theater.

Howard, still grinning like a friendly nut, replied, "George sent me over here. Said to get a photo of y'uns for the front page of the next issue."

Spencer fell back against the cushion and, from what I could figure out, was rendered speechless. He shook his head slowly and just looked at Howard, who continued to grin happily. Seeing that the man at the table was going to be little help in clearing up the muddy situation and since I was as confounded as he was, I spoke.

"What front page?"

Howard straightened his shoulders and puffed out his doughy chest. "The front page of the *Bliss Observer*, proudly serving the residents of Bliss, Mississippi, since 1869. We publish three times a week and on special occasions when the need arises." He leaned toward us and whispered confidentially. "There was much ballyhoo and discussion at the office about whether or not to put out a special issue on this, but George said—no offense to you, Miss Houston—that there probably wasn't enough interesting stuff to fill an entire issue. So we're just going to put the two of you on the front page and run a special pull-out section." He cocked his head to the side with unabashed pride. "We sold out the advertising on it in one hour flat. First time that's ever happened. Not one single merchant turned us down, and when the space was gone, we had others begging to be included." Since we couldn't find our voices, Howard continued. "So if you don't mind, I'll tag along with y'uns the rest of the night and get the photos and story."

I couldn't comprehend clearly what he was saying. It sounded, though, like my date with the town's mayor was such a news event that the local paparazzo was hovering to get the story and photos. Perplexed and showing it with my mouth hanging open, I turned to Spencer, who mirrored my look. Wordlessly, he thumped his elbows down on the table and began to rub his forehead. Then, he dropped his hands and looked up at Howard, who was quite unperturbed by our astonishment.

"Howard, ol' pal, here's what you're going to do." Howard nodded eagerly, anxious, no doubt, to hear his instructions. "You're going to pack up and go home."

Howard's grin disappeared. "But, but, I can't do that! George'll fire me!"

"You leave George to me. I'll call him first thing tomorrow and straighten this out." Spencer's voice was firm but kind. His captivating wit then returned. He arched an eyebrow and grinned. "Thanks, though, for pointing out to this lovely lady that my love life is so desperate that when I do manage to get a date, it's not only front-page news; it's worthy of an entire special advertising section." He wagged a finger toward the news reporter. "You know, Howard, this isn't making me look any too good."

Howard flushed. I tried but was unable to suppress a giggle. Spencer shrugged comically. "After this, I'll be lucky if she stays for dinner. And if she leaves, then there goes the special section and all those advertising dollars." He turned his palms up to demonstrate his helplessness.

Not another word needed to be said. Howard, apologizing profusely, began backing away but, in the bargain, stumbled into Fred, who was carrying a platter of food. I gasped as I watched Howard lose his balance and take a sliding tumble while the platter of meatballs covered in red tomato sauce flew in a great splash of red into Fred's face and all over his white shirt and navy blue tie. Fred then dropped the platter, which landed with a clink on Howard's head. Again, conversation in the restaurant stopped as all turned to look at the proprietor, dripping with tomato sauce, and Howard, lying in the middle of the floor, rubbing his head with one hand and picking a meatball off his camera with the other.

"I think," I said, putting a hand on Spencer's slumped shoulder, "that this is the most interesting date I've ever had."

♡

Somehow, we managed to order and finish dinner that night. We even had the Veal Oscar in order not to upset the rattled Fred further. We ordered coffee but Fred informed us that we would also be having Twinky's freshly made tiramisu because she had created it with us in mind, and therefore, it would be hurtful to her if we refused. Of course, I couldn't be impolite when she had been so kind, so I agreed to suffer the delectable sweetness for the sake of courtesy.

"Hey there, pal!" A familiar voice interrupted our chitchat as we waited for dessert. It was the guy I had met earlier at the bookshop, who told me he was best friends with Spencer. Beside him stood a pretty, slender blonde with green eyes and a shy smile.

Spencer grinned from ear to ear and slid out of the booth to stand and greet them both. He shook hands with his friend and kissed the blonde lightly on the cheek.

"Abby, this is Brian Jordan, my best friend since kindergarten, and his wife Sheila." Mutual affection glowed happily on all three faces.

"I know Brian! I met him this afternoon at the bookstore." I held out my hand, shook his and then offered it to Sheila. "I signed a book for your mother-in-law this afternoon. I hope she enjoys it."

"To tell you the truth, I am going to start it tonight before I go to sleep. I love all your books but I got tied up at school this afternoon and didn't get to the bookstore. I'm going to buy one for me, though. I just wish I had gotten it signed by you." She smiled and then dropped her eyes. Spencer slapped Brian on the back.

"You didn't tell me that you went over to the bookstore." Brian and I winked at each other, an exchange that did not go unnoticed.

"Wait a minute. What's going on between you two?"

I laughed. "Nothing. It's just that Brian is another of your big fans."

Spencer groaned. "Oh, please tell me that you weren't over there, too, pleading on my behalf."

Brian grinned. "Okay, I won't tell you."

He threw up his hands helplessly. "I have no dignity left."

"Yes, but you do have a date, something we've all been praying for, for a long time. Finally, the prayer chain can rest." He grinned playfully. "Besides, you not only have a date; you have a beautiful date. So it's well worth a loss of dignity."

"Doctor, I agree." Spencer bowed his head in concession.

"You're a doctor?" I asked.

"The most important kind." He paused dramatically. "I'm a vet. I took over my dad's practice when he retired."

"Hey, we're just about to have coffee and dessert—a fresh-made tiramisu created by Twinky's own hands. Won't you join us?" Spencer asked.

Both quickly began to protest. "We were just out for an evening stroll and thought we'd stop by and see how things are going. We're only going to stay for a minute."

"Well, if you want to know how things are going," I pointed out, "you'll need to sit down for coffee and dessert." We had a good story and it was worth sharing. "That's a story we can't tell quickly." I winked at Spencer. "Besides, Doctor, I'm in desperate need of counseling."

"You are?"

I nodded somberly. "I need to know if Tums will hurt a dog who's already had a bellyfull of fried chicken."

"Sheila, have a seat, my dear," Brian instructed. "I need to tend to serious medical business."

♡

Life smelled perfect when we stepped onto the sidewalk outside Alfredo's. I took a deep breath and filled my lungs with the sweetness of the September air in Bliss, Mississippi. It was the fringe of summer so there were no magnolias, honeysuckle or jasmine to enjoy, but still in the air hung the sweetness of the fruit of life, the likes of which I had not sniffed in many years. We said good-bye to the Jordans, a delightful couple, despite the fact that we had branded them as out-and-out fibbers. Brian had not been truthful when he claimed that they were just out for a stroll and had stopped in to see how we were doing. Rather, they had driven to the restaurant planning to pay for our meal as a surprise gift. Sheila, however, explained that after Brian made necessary financial arrangements, he couldn't resist coming in to see us.

"You know men." She sighed. "They can be terribly nosey."

"I'm not nosey!" Brian protested in mock despair. "I just have my best friend's interest at heart."

"Of course you do, dear." She patted his hand. "I won't tell them that we stood behind that big potted plant and spied on them ten minutes *before* we came over to the table."

Although I enjoyed being alone with Spencer, I enjoyed just as much getting to know him through the eyes of his childhood pal, college roommate, fraternity brother and next-door neighbor.

"It's a two-for-one deal," Sheila explained. "With one, you get the other. Thank goodness they chose different yet helpful occupations. It would have been a terrible waste of such a close friendship for both to have been lawyers or veterinarians. At least this way, we can swap our services!"

We watched as the Jordans drove away. Then Spencer gently

placed an arm around my shoulders and asked, "What would you like to do now? But before you answer that, let me warn you that entertainment in the town of Bliss is a bit slim."

I didn't care. I needed no other entertainment than to just sit quietly, look into his blue eyes and enjoy being in his presence. It sounds silly and it doesn't at all sound like me. I had unintentionally turned into a bit of a curmudgeon about love. I didn't want to be disappointed. I also didn't want to be greedy. The good Lord had blessed me with so much already, I didn't want to parade around with my little hands out, asking for more. I was practicing restraint.

"Let's go for a walk," I suggested.

He eyed my high heels. "Can you walk in those?"

"Not only can I walk in them; I can run in them, too. Fast. Do you think you can keep up with me?"

He grinned. "I think I can but I don't want to brag too much up front. I learned that lesson in my last campaign." He took my elbow and steered me away from the center of town. "Let's find out."

The early evening air was kissed with a soft, pleasant breeze, and the barely dark sky was decorated with glistening stars of tremendous magnitude and an awe-inspiring full moon.

"I love the moon when it's full," I said quietly as we sauntered along. "I guess that's because my daddy loved it, too. You know, he died on the night of the biggest, most gorgeous full moon I have ever seen. A few minutes after he died, I wandered over to the bedroom window and saw it. I just felt that the magnetic pull of that beautiful moon was too much for him that night. He had to go."

Tenderly, Spencer put his arm around me and drew me tightly to his side. He took a long breath and his chest moved noticeably from the heaviness of the sigh. I knew he was thinking of how death had touched and changed his life. I wasn't bothered by that. Instead, I felt it drew us closer because hurt like that makes the heart more tender.

"How long has your dad been gone?"

"About four years. He was sick for a couple of years. I think, in a way, that makes it easier. You're a bit more prepared, although you're never completely prepared for death. It's tough, though, to watch them die. But as Tennessee Williams said through Blanche DuBois, 'Funerals are pretty compared to death.'" Aware suddenly that the conversation was too maudlin, I changed the subject and my tone immediately. "Hey, are we going anywhere special or are we just walking?" I asked brightly.

He dropped his arm from my shoulders, picked up my hand and slid it into the crook of his arm. "You're on parade," he winked.

With a quizzical look, I shook my head, "Parade?"

"See that house on the corner?" With a throw of his head, he motioned toward a lovely two-story white Victorian with blue shutters. "Second floor, window on the right. Notice how the lace curtain is pinched up on one side? That's Ida Mae Pittman in a wasted effort to be discreet. Over at the service station, the old men are pretending to play checkers, despite the fact that it is well past bedtime for all of them." He turned his head and looked across the street. "Over there at the diner, Maggie, Joe and God knows who else have made several trips to the window. In other words, the eyes of this town are upon us, eager to know how we're getting along."

"Does everyone in this town know we have a date tonight?"

"Most everyone. I fear there might be a few who don't, so I'm parading through the streets in order that those possible few who didn't know will know before they lay their heads on their pillows tonight. And for the multitude who do know, they can see firsthand what a lovely couple we make!"

I threw my head back and laughed robustly. "You are too funny!"

"Well, I have to turn this thing around after the fine citizens of this town have made it clear to you how pitiful I am. That's why I was uncomfortable when Maggie wanted me to take you home."

"Why?"

"They're always, always, trying to fix me up with someone. Once, Maggie tried to set me up with a married woman!'

"No!"

"Yes! But Maggie didn't know she was married because the woman was from a town about an hour from here. I mentioned it to a friend who lives there, and he said, 'Is her husband in favor of you two dating?'"

I had to laugh. It was too funny. Spencer shook his head comically and joined my laughter.

"Well, I have to say you're certainly a good sport about this," I said with a wink.

He spread his hands. "What else can I do but joke about it? I'm a desperate man clutching at straws to preserve a modicum of dignity."

My head barely reached past his shoulder, so I strained to lift my lips closer to his ears. "I'll tell you a secret," I offered in a conspiratorial tone.

"Okay," he answered eagerly, leaning his cheek against the top of my head.

"I don't date that much myself."

He stopped suddenly drew back and stared at me with surprise saturating his face. After a brief moment, the surprise melted into firm disbelief. "You are indeed a well-mannered lady. But you don't have to go to such extremes to make me feel better."

"I'm not. I'm being truthful. Much to my mother's chagrin, despair and dismay, I date on a very select basis."

The light from the nearby street lantern fell softly on his face as he searched mine for the truth. "You must have men beating down your doors."

"No. Not only are they not beating down the doors; they're not even knocking," I replied with a shrug, though the latter was a bit of a fib.

He folded his arms and half smiled. "Then, there's either something wrong with all the single men over in Georgia or there's something wrong with you. Which is it?"

"Probably a little of both." I winked. "Did I tell you that I eat my French fries with mayonnaise on them? You wouldn't believe how many men are absolutely repelled by that precious little idiosyncrasy."

Mock horror filled his eyes. "Shame on them for throwing away a perfectly good woman over such a silly thing."

"That's what I think, too."

We heard a car slowing behind us. Turning, we saw a city police car. It stopped and the officer opened the door. As he was stepping out, I whispered, "I hope you have diplomatic immunity."

"Evening, Mayor!" The officer was a dark, skinny kid in his early twenties. He scooted around the front of the car and ran over to shake hands with his honor.

"Hello, Rickey! Good to see you. How are you liking it on the force?"

"Love it. It's the greatest job in the world." The young man beamed with enthusiasm. "Thank you so much for giving me a chance."

Spencer slapped him on the back. "Glad to do it. We're lucky to have you." He reached over, took my arm and pulled me closer to them. "Rickey, have you had the good fortune of meeting Miss Abby Houston yet?"

"No, sir!" He offered an eager hand to me. "Howdy do, ma'am? We're mighty pleased to have you in Bliss." His smile was contagious. "I saw you on *The Tonight Show* the other night. I always watch when I get off duty. You were really good."

"Thank you, Rickey." I changed the subject as I often do when the talk centers around my "other" life. "How long have you been with the police department?"

"Comin' up on six months next Wednesday." Happiness jumped in his eyes. "Best six months of my entire life. I have the mayor here to thank for it. All the folks on the city council thought I was too young, but he insisted on giving me a chance." Hero worship of Spencer was as plain as the row of straight white teeth in his mouth.

"Best hire I've made since I've been mayor," Spencer claimed. He wagged a finger in Rickey's direction. "I'm expecting big things of you. Don't forget."

"Yes, sir." He beamed. "I won't let you down. Well, I best get back to patrolling the streets. Just wanted to say 'hey.' Where you folks headed?"

"I thought I'd take Miss Houston over to the park and let her see the gold-and-pumpkin-colored mums in all their glory."

"Oh, ma'am, you're gonna love our park. We have lots of town activities over there. Every Fourth of July, there's a big picnic with a band and games for the kids. It's bunches of fun." He shook the mayor's hand again and tipped his hat to me, a courtesy that is rare in kids today. I was impressed. "Better get back to work. Have a nice evenin'."

"What a nice young man," I commented as we watched the police car pull away.

"Uh-huh, he is. Had a hard time growing up, though. His daddy was the town drunk. I don't know that he ever had a completely sober moment in his life. One night, toting a bottle of cheap whiskey in one hand, he staggered onto the train tracks and passed out. The engineer didn't see him until two or three seconds before he hit him."

I grimaced. "How sad."

"Yes, it is. Rickey's mama worked three jobs to keep her family going. By the way, Rickey is Lulu's nephew. His mama and Lulu are sisters." He cupped his hand around my elbow. "Let's cross the street here. Over there is the pride and joy of Bliss— our city park."

It was as lovely as promised. Gorgeous fall flowers had begun to bloom, large oak and magnolia trees stood grandly throughout the park and a rippling creek gurgled through the center with three or four bridges, including one covered and one arching, that stretched over the bubbling water. To the right of the entrance was a large gazebo with a built-in bench and to the left was a children's play area with swings, slides, seesaws, sandboxes and all the kinds of things that make kids happy. The park was lit for romance with old-fashioned street lanterns and spotlighting that lay flush with the ground along the lush green trails. It felt safe but looked dreamy.

I sighed contently. "Oh, Spencer, how beautiful." He reached for my hand and squeezed it tightly. We stood there hand in hand at the edge of the creek with only the rippling water for sound, drowning out, or at least I hoped, my pounding heart. He glanced over my shoulder; then suddenly he moaned with guttural anguish.

"Oh, no." He threw his head back in despair. "I knew it was too good to last."

He said it just as a force of some kind hit me below the knees, causing me to lose my balance. As I toppled headfirst toward the creek, Spencer's strong hold on my hand kept me from landing face-first in the water. For a moment, I dangled sideways before he pulled me up into his arms. At last, I was where I had wanted to be since I first saw Spencer Alexander. I was in his arms. My joy, though, was short lived. It was cut to the quick by an indignant, familiar screech.

"Land alive! It is a shame and a disgrace to see such a sight with my own eyes. And in a family place, too! You two should be arrested and put under the jailhouse!"

"Spencer," I mumbled wearily. "Would you just throw me in the creek now and spare me from any further humiliation?"

Chapter 15

The force that had nearly knocked me down danced and yipped merrily around our feet. Elmer was happy to see me, a fact she demonstrated by enthusiastically licking my ankles while her companion, who was not joyful in the least, came charging in our direction as fast as her spindly legs would travel.

"Spencer Alexander, you are a black mark on the honor of this town!" She stormed to a stop, stomped her foot angrily and plopped her hands on her skinny hip bones. "How dare you, a man of your high-ranking position, bring this, this, this *floozy* to our park, a park named in memory of my fine and decent father, and make love to her out in the open for all the citizens of this town to see."

The "black mark" on the town's honor took his time to see that I was steady on solid ground before turning to the daughter of the "fine and decent father."

"Miss Eula," he began calmly. "Isn't it a bit late for you to be out?"

She flung her bony finger in his face and stepped closer. "Don't try to get out of this. I won't have it! When I'm finished reporting your escapades to the upright citizens of this town, you'll be finished politically." Another thought apparently crossed her mind, so she dropped her finger, folded her arms and smiled smugly. "You may even be turned out of the church for this before all is said and done."

Turned out of the church! I hadn't heard of such a thing since I was eight years old when the pastor and some of the deacons of our church had called a conference to discuss turning out Arlene Gaddis, a well-known "loose" woman who was due to give birth to a child without benefit of matrimony. I remember the heated debate that had raged until my daddy, the chairman of the deacons, had risen to have his say. When he finished, he had put everyone in their proper Christian place. The proposed vote was rescinded; the newly humbled left the church that night and never again was there a mention of turning anyone out. I didn't even know churches still did that. I kept quiet, though. I thought it was best that the "floozy" not draw more attention to herself than absolutely necessary.

Spencer pursed his lips and huffed before speaking. "There was nothing going on here. Abby nearly fell into the creek when Elmer ran into her. I simply caught her and kept her from falling."

"Huh! Do you expect me to believe any such? Why, the whole town's talking about how silly you've gone over this ridiculous woman!"

My feelings were starting to hurt. Spencer, though, was getting angry. "Miss Eula, you're completely out of line. You owe Abby an apology for saying such mean things. She has done *nothing* to deserve this. You can talk about me all you like. You usually do. But I will not—*do you hear me?*—I will not stand by and listen to you run down a woman who has done nothing but be nice and charming to each person she has met in this town, including you. Which to me shows what a fine person she really is, because a *floozy* or a *ridiculous* woman would have set you straight already for the way you've talked to her." He caught his breath, then started up again. "You're the ridiculous one here. You torment and ridicule everyone in this town, including poor Elmer." On cue, Elmer whined soulfully. "You know, Miss Eula, it's pretty bad when your own dog doesn't like you." He stopped but he never dropped his eyes from hers. They stared eyeball to eyeball for a moment as I fell more in love with the hero who had ridden up to save me from the evil witch. Finally, she reached down and grabbed Elmer by the collar, jerking her away from my feet where she lay in silent worship.

"C'mon, Elmer," she snapped hatefully as the poor dog moaned and yipped pitifully. A few feet away, she turned to throw back at Spencer a look filled with hatred. "I promise you, young man, that you will live to rue the day you talked to me in such a disgraceful way." She marched off through the park, still tugging at the resistant canine.

We stood in silence, watching her go. Finally I spoke. "Well, I think it's safe to say you just lost a vote in the next mayoral election."

A sarcastic chuckle escaped his throat. "I never had her vote in the first place."

"She voted for your opponent?"

"No. She wrote in a candidate."

"How'd you know it was her ballot?"

His grin returned. "Because she's the only one in town who would vote for Elmer."

♡

While the night grew darker, my mood grew lighter. Spencer took my hand and held it with purpose. We strolled through the park. Or rather, Spencer strolled and I floated. At the playground, he stopped at a set of swings.

"Have a seat," he offered with a smile, pulling the swing up for me. He took the one beside me, and while rocking back and forth, we talked. I looked across the park and the town square that surrounded it and I sighed deeply.

"It's so lovely here."

He nodded. "It's peaceful, something that cannot be bought at any price. Is your hometown like this?"

"Not hardly," I replied. "We have too much traffic, too many people in line at the bank or post office and too many strangers." I couldn't resist teasing by adding, "And if I were out on a date tonight, the only person interested would be my mama." I held my hand up. "But mind you, she'd be as interested as all the people in Bliss combined."

"I'm embarrassed." He dropped his head shyly. "I didn't know that most of the women in town were going to turn up at your book signing to beg you to go out with me. Even my own best friend! Then, look at all the gifts and the attention." He shook his head. "You probably think of me as a charity case and that you've done your good deed for a month. Maybe the whole year."

I stopped swinging. "I think of you as the most fun date I've ever had in my life."

He perked up immediately, returning to the confident, charming man who had captured my heart. "Wait a minute! You never gave me an answer."

"What answer?"

"Remember when Howard interrupted us with his camera? I had just told you that my housekeeper called and wanted to know how you like me."

I snapped my fingers. "I remember that."

"So what's the answer?" He winked. "Now, pay no attention to the fact that the wrong answer will crush me completely. I wouldn't want you to feel pressured."

Keeping in mind that we were sitting in the middle of a play yard, I decided to answer as a child would. "I like you this much," I said, spreading my arms in a circle as wide as I could stretch.

"So if we were in class and I sent you a note that said, 'Do you like me? Check yes, no or maybe.' You would check?"

"*Yes!*" I practically screamed in an imitation of childhood exuberance. "*I would check yes!*" We started laughing. He stopped the gentle movement of his swing, grabbed the chain of mine and pulled my swing close to his. In sync, we moved slowly toward each other, negotiating around the cold metal chains of the swings. I tilted my face toward his as his lips touched mine gently. His lips lingered there while we bathed in the feeling produced by the combination of moonlight, soft Southern nights and perfect kisses. He withdrew his lips from mine for a dreamlike second, then leaned back in to gently pull my top lip between both of his, surrounding my mouth with sensuous warmth. He ended our first kiss with a short series of quick, gentle pecks. My heart thumped with slow, thunderous beats while my toes and fingers tingled like thousands of pins were piercing my flesh. I was smitten. I felt like a very young teenager. Just plain silly. It was glorious.

"Hmmm," I murmured with my eyes still closed. "That was lovely." He answered by kissing me tenderly again. With that kiss over, he slid out of the swing, then pulled me to my feet. He drew me into his arms and held me close against his chest, stroking my hair gently. I knew that finally I had found the place I belonged. Wordlessly, he put his arm around my shoulders and we walked until we reached the gazebo. He gathered my hand in his and led me up the steps. Without conversation, we sat down on the bench and I slid into the safe harbor created when he put his arm around me.

"Abby, I've had a wonderful time tonight," he said quietly after a few minutes of silence.

I nuzzled my head against the soft spot inside his shoulder. "Me, too." I sighed contently.

"I didn't realize how lonely I was," he said it more to himself than to me. "I'm so busy with the kids, my job and other obligations that I haven't stopped to think that I might be missing something. My dad's getting ready to announce that he's running for governor so that's been a complete zoo. The pace of my life is hectic from the time I jump out of bed in the morning and hit the ground running. I guess there's just no time to think about what I feel."

"I know that's true of me," I said. "I create things to distract myself from thinking about being alone. I love my life and I'm blessed with adventure and neat opportunities. But sometimes I think, 'I'm in the prime of my life and there's no one here to share that with me.' Then, I get annoyed at myself for being greedy and wanting *everything* when I already have been given so much in life."

He shifted his position on the bench, turning his body more toward mine. That caused me to shift, too, until my back had found a comfortable nest against his ribs. "When Liz died, I discovered how stupidly self-absorbed I had been. I took for granted all she brought into my life and how comfortable she made me. The funny thing is that if you had asked me while she was alive if I appreciated her for all she brought to me, I would have said, 'Yes! Most definitely I do.' But I didn't. I couldn't. Not until I was left alone to find out the hard way. I miss waking up in the middle of the night and hearing someone's soft breathing next to me. Three o'clock in the morning can be extremely lonely." Sadness crept into his words as he talked. "Then, there are so many other reminders. I can't braid Elizabeth's hair. I tried once and she ended up looking like a disheveled Pippi Longstockings."

"Wait a minute!" I cried out in protest. "That was one of my favorite books when I was a kid."

He held up a hand in surrender. "Nothing against Pippi. This is about my ineptness at trying to be what I'm not." He paused before he began reflecting again. "Before Liz died, I had never made a pot of coffee in my life. I still can't make it as good as hers." He thought for a second. "You know what else I miss?"

"What?"

"Spam."

"Spam?" For the life of me, I couldn't see how anyone could miss a pop-top can of processed meat.

"Yep. I love fried Spam sandwiches."

I pounded my head against his shoulder. "Oh, no," I moaned. "But I'll say this, you should have met my daddy. You two would have really hit it off. He loved fried Spam with mayonnaise on soft, white bread not toasted."

He chuckled. "That's me to a T. It used to be the only thing I could cook, so when Liz was busy, I'd pull out a can and fry up a pan of Spam. In all the years we were married, I never once, not once, went to the pantry and discovered we were out of Spam. There was always a can there. Now, half the time, I go to get a can and I'm out." He shook his head.

"But you have a housekeeper. Doesn't she shop for you?"

"Yes, but for some reason, no matter how many times I tell her, she can't remember to buy Spam."

I waited a moment before replying. "That's because she doesn't love you," I commented softly.

"Huh?" I felt him turn his head and look down at me. I moved my head and looked up at him.

"She doesn't love you like a woman in love," I continued. "A woman in love remembers the little things that are important to her man."

"See?" he asked, leaning his cheek down against the top of my head. "Those are the things I'm learning."

"Once you're alone, you figure out that you can't underestimate the importance of having someone who knows you well and cares about those little things. It's emotionally nurturing and comforting. I had lunch about a month ago with my best friend from high school and her husband. Karen had gotten caught in traffic, so she called and told Dan to go ahead and order for her. So there he goes down the menu, ordering with an expertise for her that is not to be believed. Mixed green salad. Ranch dressing on the side. Salmon, well done. No capers. Mixed vegetables sprinkled with olive oil. Water. No ice. Lemon only. It was remarkable. I thought about it all afternoon. It was really sad to think that there's no one in the world who knows me that well."

"I know that you like mayonnaise on your French fries," he offered helpfully. "I don't understand it but I know it."

"There's a start!" I said brightly. "My own mother doesn't even know my phone number! I've had the same number for ten years. Yet every time she goes to call me, she has to look up my number. How sad is that?"

"That's pretty bad," he admitted with a smile. "My mother, on the other hand, has my number on speed dial."

"Well, listen to this. I don't eat eggs. Never have. *Ever*. When I was about four, I took a big bite of scrambled eggs, spit it out and that was that. Mother, though, can never remember that I don't eat eggs. Sometimes, she'll cook a big country breakfast for supper and call me to come over to eat. When I get there, she'll turn around from the stove with an egg in one hand and ask, 'How do you want your egg? Fried or scrambled?' For the one thousandth time, I have to remind her that I don't eat eggs. It'll be forgotten the next day, and she'll call—after looking up my number, mind you—and say, 'I just made a platter of deviled eggs. Why don't you come by and get some to take home with you?' I'll reply, 'Because I don't eat eggs, which I told you last night.' She comes back with, 'But they're good for you. You should eat 'em.'" I threw up my hands in despair and sank down against his side. "That's the way it is. Sad but true. My own mama doesn't even pay attention to me."

He chuckled lightly and, gazing up toward the sky, asked, "When you divorced, were there things you found that you missed?"

"Absolutely. Like you, I miss having someone in bed with me. I miss having a reliable escort. I hate sitting in church alone on Christmas Eve when everyone else is surrounded by family. When I put on a beautiful new hat on Easter I miss having someone say, 'You'll be the prettiest girl in the Easter parade.' Before my husband, my daddy used to say that," I recalled wistfully. "However, I miss my ex the most when it's time to take the trash out." Spencer chuckled. "No, seriously. I hate it so much. I put it off until bags of garbage are everywhere in the garage, and I have to put it in my car and take it to the dumpster. But you know," I said thoughtfully. "I wouldn't trade the trash for him."

Spencer chuckled. "Abby, you're too much. I have laughed more with you tonight than I have in the entire time since my wife died." He kissed the top of my head. "It feels good, too. I'd forgotten how good it felt to be lighthearted and to have fun."

"What's your favorite movie?" I asked suddenly, curious to know more about my knight in sports coat and khakis.

"*Bridge over the River Kwai,*" he answered instantly. "What's yours?"

"*Breakfast at Tiffany's,*" I answered as quickly.

"What's your favorite color?" he asked.

"Anything bright. What's yours?"

The repartee stopped. With his left hand, he gently picked a strand of my hair and twirled it with his fingers. "The color of your hair," he whispered softly. The words pulled me back into a trance of enchantment. I looked up at him and he leaned down to kiss me again. In the midst of the heart-racing kiss, I became aware through my barely closed eyes of a blue, revolving light. I pulled my lips from his and asked, "What's that?"

He opened his eyes in time to see a police car pulling up to the curb several yards from the gazebo. Though void of a siren, the blue light was spinning furiously.

"Oh, no," he groaned, rubbing his eyes with one hand. "*What* now?"

Chapter 16

Rickey was grinning ear to ear as he popped out of the police car and scooted around in front of the head-lights. He was carrying a parcel in one arm.

"How y'all doin'?" He called out as we hurried down the steps of the gazebo toward him. He tipped his hat to me.

"Rickey, what's wrong?" Spencer asked anxiously. "Has anything happened to my children?"

"Nothin's wrong," he shrugged happily. "I just brought this by to y'all." He held out the box, which was a small brown wicker picnic hamper.

Spencer took it and eyed it quizzically. "What's this?"

"Don't know except that it's a gift from somebody. Pete Marshall was supposed to send it over from his store while y'all were eatin' at Alfredo's. He thought his delivery boy had taken it, but when he closed the shop tonight, he saw it. He was plumb sick over it. I saw him down at the Dairy Queen, and when he told me about it, I told him I knowed where y'all was. So we went to the store, got it and here I am." Pride filled his face.

"Why do you have the blue light on?"

Rickey shifted his weight from one foot to another before bashfully answering, " 'Cause I thought this was a good excuse to use it. But now I didn't use the siren. No, sir! I know better than that. But, Mayor, I've been on this job for six months, and I only got to use my blue light once before." His voice squeaked childishly as if he were talking about a red wagon rather than a police car. "That was when Susan Marie's cat escaped from her store one day and took off through town with Elmer flyin' after her. Miss Eula was pitchin' a conniption fit, screamin' and car-ryin' on as to how Elmer was gonna be mowed down and killed by some car. So I put on the blue light and went after Elmer. I finally caught him, too, but it took an hour. He kept escapin'."

"She." I thought I should clear up a crucial misunderstanding.

"Huh?" He looked puzzled.

"Elmer is a *she*, not a *he*."

"Well, I didn't know that," he admitted, thoughtfully scratching his forehead. "All I know is that dog shore didn't wanna come back."

"I can understand that," I remarked dryly.

Spencer thrust out his hand and shook Rickey's firmly. "Of-ficer, thank you very much for rising above and going beyond the call of duty." He threw his head in the direction of the attention-getting blue light. "And thank you for doing it so dis-creetly, too."

I think Rickey blushed invisibly. "Huh, yeah. Thank you, sir." He tipped his hat to me again. "Ma'am, hope I didn't in-trude on nothin'." My face blushed noticeably but he pretended not to notice. He ran around to the driver's side, threw his hand up as he slid in and immediately turned off the blue light. We waved good-bye, and as we watched him drive away, Spencer put his arm around me. I felt I was part of a couple. It struck me that I couldn't remember the last time I had felt that I was one of two.

♡

We settled back into our cozy place in the gazebo as the bull-frogs croaked loudly and the water from the creek rippled by in a rhythmic lullaby. Dreams hung heavy in the air of Bliss, Mississippi, that night.

Spencer balanced the picnic hamper on his knees and, preparing to open it, shook his head in wonderment and snickered. "No doubt about it, you certainly have been an economic boom for Bliss." He chuckled again. "There's gonna be a lot of merchants in this town sad to see you go."

Go. It was something I hadn't thought about all evening. But I did have to go. The time of my departure was only a night's sleep away. When the clock struck twelve o'clock the next day, I, like Cinderella, would be driving away, my beautiful fantasy pulling apart and drifting like mystical stardust coating the skies of Mississippi. My heart dropped. That's the unfair aspect of happiness. Sadness and worries are always lurking around the corner, waiting to pounce on it and distract us from the joy at hand. It's a quirk of the human spirit. If we don't have something troubling us, we go looking for it. This night had seemed like the most fun of my entire life. My last few years had been filled with wonderful surprises and adventures, but nothing could compare with the evening I was sharing with Spencer.

"Glad to help." I tried to sound gloriously flip or, at the least, brave.

With a wink and that beautiful lopsided grin, he remarked, "I should make you our director of economics."

I shrugged playfully. "I just want the key to the city."

"And you deserve it. Have no fear, my fair lady, I shall see that you receive it." He turned pensive for a moment, his hand resting on the lid he was about to open, his eyes penetrating the blue painted floor of the gazebo. I waited a minute before I spoke.

"Anything wrong?"

He shook himself out of it. "Uh, no." He turned to look at me solemnly. "I was just thinking of the other key I'd like to give you." I searched his face, trying to figure out what he was saying. Slowly the wheels of my mind turned until, at last, I remembered Twinky talking about the key to his heart. A big lump jumped from my heart into my throat. I was nervous and didn't know what to say, so I pretended I didn't know what he was talking about.

"Key?"

"Yeah. Remember back at the restaurant what Twinky was saying?"

"Oh, yeah." My act of nonchalance was pretty good if I do say so myself. Since he didn't elaborate, I thought it pertinent that I push the issue. "So?" I was remarkably articulate.

He smiled sadly and dropped his eyes. "But I can't."

I felt water rush to my eye and I blinked quickly to push the droplets back. With significant effort, I found my voice, tiny though it was. "Why?"

He looked away, seeming to focus on a border of azalea bushes. "You're too big for me, Abby. You're a big star with a sensational life that puts you in the presence of presidents, kings and movie stars. You're on television, in movies and on the pages of magazines. I'm just a small-town mayor who is widowed and has two children. It's a dull, uneventful life compared to yours. Your orbit is far past mine. I'm on earth and you're on the moon." He stood up, walked over to the railing and looked up toward the glistening sky. "What in the galaxy could I possibly offer *you*?"

His words fell heavy on my heart. I knew what he could give me. I was certain that he could give me more than the sum of all the things he mentioned. How, though, was I to convince him of that? I rose and tiptoed over to where he stood, lifting the spiked heels of my sandals so that they did not clatter disruptively on the planked flooring. I placed my hand on his arm and turned him toward me. I drew all the sincerity that choked my heart upward into my eyes. I was not acting. I did not have to.

"Spencer, please don't look at me that way. Please. I'm not a star. I'm a simple country girl who used to write obits for a living until an incredibly fortunate event landed in my lap. I'm nothing special. There are millions of people who have written books much better than mine, but theirs are still tucked away in their desks because they weren't as blessed as I was. It's a one-in-a-million chance."

"I disagree," he said firmly, looking at me directly. Uncomfortable, I shifted my weight. I dropped my head and then he said, "I think you're unbelievably special." He took my chin in his hand and lifted it so that I was, again, looking directly into his eyes. "Don't ever let me hear you say again that you're 'nothing special.'"

"Thank you," I whispered, not knowing anything else to say, and almost wishing that Miss Eula would come rushing up to change the mood and the moment.

"Abby, tonight you reminded me of how outrageously happy life can be and should be. I feel like I've been drinking unsweetened tea for years and tonight you added the sugar. That sweetness is an intoxicating touch."

I laughed lightly at the analogy. "Well put, sir, since we Southerners are known for our addiction to sweet tea." I paused thoughtfully before continuing. "Spencer, all the other days of my life have paled in comparison to this night. I want to feel like this every day. It would be so sad to only know this exuberance for a few hours."

He gently lifted my hands and held them in his. "Abby, how can we make this work? You live two states away from me and we have completely different lives. How can we pursue this path that we stumbled upon?"

"First, we have to agree that this is not a dead end. We're at an intersection where two lives meet. We may have to clear bushes and trees out of the way and sidestep some potholes, but we're reasonably smart people, so we can figure this out." I tried to laugh lightly. "As they say back where I come from, just follow the dirt road until you come to the first blacktop!"

He smiled. "That's what we say around here, too!"

I loosened my hands from his grip and spread them wide, palms up. "Well, see there? We have a lot more in common than you give us credit for!" He pulled me into his arms and held me tightly as though he never wanted to let me go. I squeezed him just as closely. After several moments of holding me, he kissed me again.

"Sweet Abby," he said, taking my hand and leading me back to our seat. "I don't have a clue as to how we're going to figure this out. But I know this: somehow we must find the right road. We have to."

I nodded, so happy to know that hope prevailed and that Spencer, like me, wanted to test the durability of what we were feeling. I was giddy with excitement and glowing with optimism. I acted cool, though. I know how men are. You just can't let them know they're winning, or next thing you know, they start running. I wanted to jump up and down, clap my hands and click my high heels. But I didn't. I just squeezed his hand, kissed him on the cheek and said, "Let's see what's in the basket, shall we?"

"Good idea. After all, it's been over an hour since we ate."
He flipped the lid open and pulled out a bottle of expensive
champagne. "Well, what do you know? Just what we need just
when we need it! Now, we can toast to figuring out how to get
to the blacktop from the dirt road."

"I don't know a lot about champagne but that bottle set
someone back a pretty penny." I touched the expensive engraved label.

"Yeah," he agreed. "It probably cost more than my first car.
I wonder who sent it." He dug in the basket, bringing out champagne glasses, gingham napkins, a long narrow box of crackers,
a package of hard cheese, a large bunch of grapes but no card.
"Oh well," he shrugged.

"That's the kind of gift that a person should definitely get
credit for." I smiled slyly. "Maybe it's from Miss Eula."

"Yeah, when pigs fly." Then, his eyes widened. "On the other
hand, maybe we shouldn't drink this. If it's from her, it probably
has arsenic in it." He pulled the foil off and stood up as he began
to work the cork. Pop. It was off and spewing everywhere.

"I feel like that champagne looks," I said, holding the two
glasses while he poured the exuberant liquid. He set the bottle
down, took his glass from me and looked at me for a long time.
I was fairly certain that I could have boiled an egg in that time.
Anxiously, I bit the inside of my lip knowing that what he said
could be so telling of how he felt about us and the future. I felt
the way I had when my tenth-grade math teacher called me to
tell if I had passed or failed the class.

Finally, he spoke, holding his glass aloft. "Here's to fate when
it behaves as it should and brings someone special into your
life." Pause. His eyes did not move from mine. "Here's to hoping that fate continues to act as it should."

Good. Those were words of promise. I relaxed a bit. Clink.
Our glasses gently kissed each other. My mind was racing over

what he had just said, analyzing, hoping he meant everything I wanted him to mean. It's ridiculous how many answering machine messages from guys I have played over and over, dissecting every inflection for "hidden meanings." We each took a sip of the extravagant champagne. Tenderly, he pushed my hair from my face.

"What are you thinking?"

"That a ten-dollar swallow of champagne doesn't taste that different from a ten-cent swallow."

It was the dumbest thing I could have said. It was, in fact, the stupidest thing I have ever said in my life and I've said some pretty idiotic things over the years. But I was scared. Fear suddenly punched me in the face. I had loved the feeling that was sweeping over me. It was as luxurious and as welcomed as a warm, soapy bath after a hot summer's day spent at work in the garden. I had just been pushed to the edge of sublime joy, but I was terrified to step over the edge and fall freely. Hurt. It's the worst four-letter word in our language, and it had been a part of my vocabulary for too long to be forgotten in one evening. Spencer had just taken a step forward, and I had cancelled it out by taking a step back. He looked mildly puzzled, but to his immense credit, he said nothing. If he had stepped back from me that way, I would have crumbled emotionally and then pondered on it for days. He smiled knowingly, and I knew I was safe when he stepped closer and put his arms around me, careful not to spill a drop of the expensive grape juice. I laid my head against his chest, my face turning toward the picnic hamper. My eyes rested on something small, square and white lying beneath the bench. I focused on it, still fearing the torrent of emotion, turning to something insignificant instead.

"I wonder what that is?" I said, pulling out of his grasp and walking over to it. I knelt down and picked up the tiny envelope. "It has your name on it." I handed it to him.

"It must have been in the basket," he said. He set his glass down on the railing.

"See there?" I asked, teasing. "I knew that no one in their right mind was going to send over a bottle of champagne that expensive and not take credit for it!"

He smiled as he pulled a card out and held it closer toward the street lantern. In the soft light, I saw his face change as he read it. The carefree look of happiness rinsed out into one of somberness and the stain of worry emerged. With his change of expression went the mood, suddenly hanging as heavy in the air as the look hung on his face.

Uneasy, I shuffled my feet and asked in a tight voice, "Who's it from?" I tried to say it nonchalantly but the words were painted with ugly tension. I thought I had the right to know yet I dreaded the answer. What I got in reply surprised me.

He started gathering things together to pack up the picnic hamper. He glanced at his watch and said in a stony tone, "It's getting late. We need to go."

My heart sank. I leaned down and scooped up the cork. Pop, I thought, another bubble bursted.

Chapter 17

I wouldn't say that we walked back to the car in complete silence, but it was about as close as you could come to it. The familiar voice of my intuition told me something was very wrong and my heart was heavy. We tried to talk, at least in polite conversation, but it was forced and strained. Our easy laughter and high spirits had evaporated into the Mississippi night. He didn't take my hand or put his arm around me, so I withdrew and walked beside him, with several inches separating us. A little earlier, it had felt like Christmas morning, when you tear into the gorgeous gifts, laughing merrily at all you have been given and all the love they symbolize. But Christmas day had unexpectedly turned into the day after, the cheery anticipation had vanished, there was nothing left under the tree, and the sky seemed exceptionally gray and overcast. The glitter of the gifts had gone, and the time for returns and exchanges had arrived.

He opened the car door for me, but as I started to get in, something caught my eye. I shrugged it off and climbed in. I was looking over my shoulder through the rear window when Spencer slid in under the steering wheel.

"What is it?" he asked, turning to look in the direction of my stare.

I shook my head and turned back to settle into my seat and snap my seat belt. "Nothing." He noticed I was still pensive and pressed further.

"You sure?" He put the car into reverse and began to back out of the parking space in front of Alfredo's.

"It's just the weirdest thing. See that red pickup over there with the white camper top?" I motioned to a parking place about twenty-five yards away.

He nodded, switching the gears and easing forward. "What about it?"

"I've seen that truck three or four times in the last day. Since I got to Bliss. Just seems odd that it keeps popping up."

"Just a coincidence. It's a small town so you notice things more than you do in larger places. Plus, it's an older pickup. You don't see many of those these days."

"You're absolutely right," I agreed. "But you know what? When something like that keeps catching my attention, I always feel like there's a reason." Had I been in a more talkative spirit, I would have elaborated with a couple of examples. But truth was, I didn't feel like talking much. I had backed away, and now he had done the same. At the moment, I was concerned that one of us had run a stop sign and was speeding away from the other.

We were pulling up to the Magnolia Blossom Bed and Breakfast when the next words were spoken, and quite frankly, it sounded like Spencer was talking just to ease the heaviness of silence.

"I don't know who that truck belongs to." He turned off the ignition and looked at me. "Never seen it before."

I opened my door and stepped to the pavement. He waited for me at the front of the car, then placed his hand at the small of my back and guided me. My heart jumped weakly, hopeful that we might be recovering from the spinout. He opened the gate of the white picket fence and stepped back. Other than that miserable twig of an olive branch, nothing improved as we walked up the steps. On the veranda, we stopped and looked at each other quietly for a moment.

"When are you leaving?" he asked.

"Around lunch or shortly after. I have a book signing in Jackson at six and I want to give myself plenty of time to check into the hotel and rest some."

He nodded. "You'll be careful?"

"Of course." The knot in my throat was growing larger with each second.

He put his arms around me and hugged me. But it wasn't an embrace like before. It was one of good friends saying good-bye. Not one of future lovers. The next thing he did really took the cake. *He kissed my forehead!* After those sweet, tender, intimate kisses in the gazebo, he kissed me like a father kisses his little girl. That really burned me up. I was starting to swing from sad to mad. I have never known a man who enjoys seeing that side of me. I was fighting down words of anger when he said, "Abby, I've had a wonderful time tonight. Thank you." He squeezed my hand and began backing away to make his escape. "We'll stay in touch, okay?"

I nodded. I had swung back to sad and was about to tear up. I watched him walk down the steps. Suddenly, I couldn't let him walk away like that. I hurried to the edge of the veranda.

"Spencer?" He turned around. "What's going on here?" I spread my hands, palms up. "I don't understand."

Uncomfortably, he shoved his hands in his pockets and looked down at the ground. "I don't know what you're talking about."

Feeling the onset of defeat, I sank down on the first step. I rubbed my forehead with both hands and then wearily looked up at him. "Something feels different here than it did a half hour ago. Something *is* different. And it happened when you read that note. Please tell me what's wrong."

A small piece of resistance seemed to fall away. He climbed the four steps and sat down beside me. He picked up my trembling hand. "Abby, I just realized that I was moving too fast."

What? I couldn't believe I was hearing that. Normally, a guy saves that line until the third or fourth date. And usually he says "we're" moving too fast. I've never known a man who would own up to doing it on his own.

"Too fast?"

"You're something special. Probably too big for me and this little town. It just kinda hit me that I needed to slow down. I foolishly got swept away with the fun of the evening."

I didn't really know what he was saying. So I asked. "What does that mean?" My voice was so weak and small that it sounded strangely unfamiliar.

He looked away. "I don't know."

That wasn't much help at all. We sat quietly, the harmonic sounds of the crickets growing louder in the silence that hung between us.

"Abby," he said, standing up but not looking at me. "I can't talk about this right now. I just need to be alone and think. I'll call you later."

I looked at him blankly until he turned toward me. I tried to think what I had done wrong to bring this about. Or what I could have done differently. Sadly, I knew strategic planning does not work in love. That darn fate was fiddling around with me. Again.

I wasn't playing games or being strategically smart when I stood up, smoothed my skirt and straightened my shoulders. Anger had suddenly seized me, threatening to rage out of control. Yet I held my composure. I appeared cool and calm but my retort was firm.

"Don't bother."

His mouth dropped open, something I noticed for only a brief moment before spinning around on my spiked heels and stomping ungracefully into the house.

Chapter 18

I didn't sleep well that night. I was a jumbled mess of stinging emotions. Over the past twenty-four hours, I had skidded at high speed from admiration to infatuation to exhilaration to devastation. I wanted to cry but I refused to shed a tear, which would have been admitting how much I hurt.

But I did pray.

I'm ashamed to say that in those woeful prayers I didn't ask for help or comfort. I particularly did not pray for "your will be done, not mine" because I did not feel generous of spirit. There's no sense lying about it now and trying to pretend I was noble. Instead, I asked "why?" I was especially interested in knowing why God would tease me like that. Why he would let me think that I was onto something, and then jerk it away? I wondered if he was having a good laugh at my repeated naïveté. I couldn't begin to understand. I was to blame, too. I had broken my cardinal rule about men. I, for a brief moment, had let down my guard and tottered out on the delicate high wire of trust. Then I had fallen and slammed to earth with such a violent force that I was bruised all over. Even my heart felt bloodied. I writhed in agony and wondered, as I have on several occasions, why there isn't a medicinal solution to hearts that are suffering.

I got no answers to my prayers that night, and felt no easing of the pain as the hours of darkness crept toward the light of dawn. I wadded myself in a ball, clutched a pillow to my chest and finally fell asleep, feeble pleas for help falling from my lips onto what appeared to be deaf divine ears. The sleep, if you want to call it that, was only slightly better than none at all. By six, I was wide awake so I lay there until seven, thinking, trying to make sense of a senseless situation. At seven, I pulled my weary, heavy body from the bed and prepared caffeine with the coffeemaker that Charlotte had put in my room. Ping, ping, ping. As the black droplets hit the glass carafe, I paced the bedroom, holding a hand against my chest as if trying to soothe the ache that lay within. I found a Gideon Bible in the nightstand and whispered, "Please fall open to words that will help."

I found myself looking down at the pages of Ecclesiastes, my eyes falling immediately to a scripture that pronounced, "Two are better than one. For if they fall, one will lift up his companion. But woe to him who is alone when he falls."

I slammed the sacred book shut with an almost hateful force. I was not amused. I glared upward to the heavens. "*This* is *not* funny."

Again, I prayed. This time I prayed with total humility because all arrogance, all I've-got-a-good-life-and-everyone-should-be-this-lucky was completely gone. In the course of twenty-four hours, I had soared; then I had fallen to terrible depths. Since Terry Houston dumped me, I had been playing at believing that there was no lack in my life. I dressed myself up—

mighty good, too—and tried to pretend that only the outside mattered. But what I really needed—what I ached to have—couldn't be bought, nor could it be impressed by a spot on the *New York Times* best seller list.

Then I did something that I know was not an answer to prayer. I do not think for one moment that the Lord directed me to it. He knows better than that. He knows that my mama is rarely helpful in my moments of distress. He knows that I have to be emotionally stable to deal with her. So I know it didn't come from him. Apparently, it came from desperation. Like a drug addict ripping through a neighbor's medicine cabinet, I was emotionally clawing for help.

I grabbed a tissue, wiped my dribbling nose and called Mama.

"What are you doin'?" I asked in a wounded voice.

She didn't hear the hurt. "I'm cleanin' out from under the bed. I oughta wait and let you do it when you get home. It's your child that made the mess."

"How?"

"She has carried every tissue or paper towel she can find—gone through the garbage can, mind you—and taken them under the bed and torn them to smithereens."

"Mama, she's a little dog," I began wearily. "How can she possibly get into the trash cans?" I knew too well Mama's penchant for rolling up paper napkins and tissues, then absentmindedly tucking them in the edge of her chair or sofa. Mama believes that idle hands are the devil's workshop, so she has a nervous habit of twisting and tucking while she's watching TV or talking to company. No doubt that Kudzu was digging the paper out from the hidden spots and then ripping it up.

"Well, I don't know how she does it but she sure enough does," she responded in a haughty tone. "I sure don't do it. Why would I tear paper up and throw it under there? Just to entertain myself when I have to clean it up?"

I dropped my head in my hand and, again, doubted my decision to call her. But I was desperate. I'd do anything to stop the pain. I started to cry silently, brushing away the tears.

"How was the funeral home last night?" I asked, chasing the words with a sip of coffee.

"Oh, it was great!" she replied enthusiastically. "I had the most fun and everybody was tellin' me how good I looked. Melinda did my hair for me. She cares how I look. You don't."

I rolled my eyes. I wasn't in the mood.

"You wouldn't believe how many people I saw that I hadn't seen in forever," she continued. "I sat there and talked for three hours! Horace McGee finally had to run me and Verna Reynolds off so he could close the funeral home down last night." She stopped for a beat. "I miss the old days when we used to sit up with the dead. And they used to take the bodies home, too. So it was more comfortable. Used to be that the only time you could catch up with folks was when someone died and you sat up all night talking. But I had a good time last night anyway."

In the South, funeral home visitations are large social events. Normally, though, people act a little more restrained when they talk about it. Unlike my mother, most don't talk as excitedly about the funeral home as they do about the bowling alley.

"Guess who I saw?" I knew from her tone that I didn't want to know.

"Who?"

"Charlene Marshall!" She said it with such glee that if she hadn't been holding the phone, she surely would have clapped her hands.

I blew the aggravation through my lips. At least it was Steve's mama and not Steve himself. I didn't say a word. I was too busy counting to ten. My tears, though, had completely disappeared.

"Well, don't you want to know what she said about Steve and his divorce?"

"No."

"Yes, you do."

"No, I don't."

"Since I know you really do, I'm gonna tell you anyway. Even if you are actin' so unbecomin'."

I took a deep breath, pulling it slowly in through my nose and then releasing it, equally slowly. I learned this from the Pilates instructor at the gym. She swears by it as a relaxation tactic. She probably has a reasonable mother, though.

"This is good news," she chirped cheerfully. "Since Sue Ann was dumb enough to run off and leave him—and left her kids behind, too!—Steve ain't gonna have to give her any of the trailer parks."

"*Mobile home* parks," I corrected, knowing that Steve's developments were on the high end and some included community swimming pools, playgrounds and clubhouses.

Her clatter continued on. "That was a big deal because them trailer parks bring in a lot of money. Now, the judge did say that it wouldn't be right for her not to get something and he couldn't just give her nothin' 'cause they've been married for almost twenty-five years."

I rubbed my eyes, trying to erase her double-talk from my mind.

"She's gonna get a flat settlement of fifty thousand dollars, her clothes, half of the furniture and her car." Mama chuckled. "Why, I bet just one of them trailer parks alone brings that much in, in less than six months! Charlene said that Steve's tickled to death. And since a divorce in this state can be finalized in thirty days, he'll be all free and clear by the time you git home. Charlene thinks it's a grand idea, too. You two gittin' together, I mean. She said you're the only one that she'll know for a fact ain't after him for his money but only 'cause you need a husband."

My sorrow gave way to rapid anger. I wanted to fling the

phone across the room and break something. I could just hear that conversation at the funeral home. The nerve of Charlene Marshall talking about me needing a husband! And my own mama acting as though she was exactly right about it, too.

"I want to tell you something and I want you to listen very closely," I said between teeth clenched so tight that my jaw was aching. "I wouldn't go out with Steve Marshall if he was the last man left in the world. Especially when his mother thinks I *need* a husband. That is the most insulting thing I have ever heard in my life. I can't believe you didn't defend me."

"But she's right," she replied calmly, without a hint of apology in her tone. Even in my fury, I could hear a soft, gentle logic in her voice. She couldn't have slapped me across the face and gotten my attention more. My shoulders slumped and I dropped my head. Large tears began to drip down my cheeks, again.

"Listen, Abby, don't you know that I know my little girl? I know how lonely you are inside. Don't you realize that more than anything in the world, I want to see you happy? You're mighty blessed and I thank the good Lord for that every day." Her voice softened further. "Not until your daddy died did I realize how I had it made all those years, having a man to love me and help me through life. I took it for granted. He used to get in bed, put his arm out and I'd lay on it and we'd talk ourselves to sleep. Money can't buy that. I want my little girl to have that."

I swallowed my tears. "Mama, I'm sorry. I guess I'm just a little touchy about the subject."

"That so?" she laughed lightly. "I hadn't noticed."

I smiled weakly and though she couldn't see, I knew she felt it.

In a shaky voice, I made a big admittance. "You're right. It's exactly what I need."

With a sit-up-and-take-notice vengeance, my desperate, matchmaking mother returned. "I knew it! I knew all along. That's why I got Steve's phone numbers for you while I was at the funeral home. I got 'em right here. You want his cell phone number now?"

Anger sputtered in my throat. *"No!"*

"Hmmm." She was thinking. "Maybe it would be best to wait 'til his divorce is final and all this dust settles."

I couldn't bring myself to play along and say something like, "You're right. Later would be better," so I said simply, "Whatever." I sighed heavily and then finished with, "I need to get down to breakfast and get on the road. I'll call you tonight or tomorrow morning."

"Okay. I'll tell that precious Kudzu that her mommy called. She's a little blue today. I think she's ready for you to come home."

"Tell my baby that I'll see her soon."

I hung up, had a good heart cleansing with a ten-minute cry and then resolved that it was time to move on.

♡

About an hour later, dressed, with all of my things packed and my tears dried, I ventured down to the dining room where Charlotte sat sipping a cup of coffee quietly. I saw worry in her eyes the moment she saw me.

"Good morning," she gently greeted me, rising up to hurry over to me. She took both hands and squeezed them. "How are you this morning?"

Something in the way she said it told me she knew. Of course, she did. I was learning that in Bliss, emotions are not sacred and events are not secret. All is shared. Still, I pretended differently.

"I'm fine," I lied, infusing a degree of false cheerfulness into my words. "This has been the most wonderful time in Bliss. I hate to leave."

"No, you're not," she responded firmly.

"Not what?" I looked perplexed.

"Fine."

I tilted my head in absolute puzzlement. She took my hand and pulled me toward the living room. "Come along, little chickadee. We need to talk." I dragged my feet behind her but she yanked me along harder. We sat down on the sofa, our knees touching as we faced each other. I pasted a stiff smile onto my face and tried to exude contentment.

"I know you're not fine because Spencer called me this morning." My smile vanished. My mouth went dry and my throat choked. "He told me what happened last night."

I blinked. "Huh," I snorted, sarcasm rearing its ugly head. "I'd be interested to hear that, because I don't know what happened."

She wet her lips and looked at me with motherly compassion. "He told me that you told him not to call you."

I clenched my jaw tightly and daggers, I am sure, jumped from my eyes. "Did he tell you why?" I didn't give her time to answer. I rushed on. "Did he tell you what a terrific evening we were having, and then suddenly he shut down and, without any explanation, pulled away?"

"Honey, he's confused. You're not the first date he has had since Liz died. There have been a few others here and there, but you are the first one who made him feel something he hasn't experienced in many years."

My smitten heart wavered, but I knew what I had to do. I had to pull up the drawbridge, put the guard up and stop hurt from ambushing me again.

So I shrugged nonchalantly.

"Charlotte, it was just a one-time deal. Nothing serious." I sounded so convincing that I almost believed it myself. "I'm leaving Bliss in a few hours and I'll probably never see Spencer again. But it was fun last night. He's a wonderful man."

She lifted a brow and eyed me skeptically. "Abby, you don't have to put on a brave act with me."

"It's not an act." I looked straight into her eyes and did not blink.

She laid her hand gently upon mine. "Falling in love is fun. It's one of the most exhilarating experiences we can ever know. It's also terrifying. You can't have the joy without risk. You have to let your defenses down and take the chance. Otherwise, you'll live a life that is nothing more than mediocre."

Her words were true. I knew they were. But after the night of pain I had spent, I wasn't willing to take them to my fragile heart. I closed my eyes and shook my head.

"Not interested." I dismissed the idea with an airy wave of my hand. "What's that old saying, 'He travels fastest who travels alone'? That's me. I have a lovely existence. I don't want to be distracted by a relationship that isn't going anywhere. I don't have the time."

Sadness filtered across Charlotte's face. Before she could reply, the doorbell rang.

"Excuse me a second." She crossed the room and opened the door. "Hi, Janie! Please come in."

A large arrangement of red roses filled with baby's breath proceeded through the door, followed by a woman dressed in a long cotton skirt and tunic sweater that fell almost to her knees.

"My goodness! There must be three or four dozen roses there!" Charlotte exclaimed. "Did my precious Charlie send those?"

"No, I'm afraid not," Janie answered. "These are for Abby Houston." Hearing my name, I rose from my seat and quietly moved toward the mountain of blooms. "Is she here?"

"Here I am." I took the flowers from her, though they weren't easily handled. "How beautiful," I obliged halfheartedly with the expected comment. I suspected they were from another of Bliss's little romance elves.

"Kay Ann has just outdone herself," Charlotte offered.

"Please tell her that I said she's still the best florist in the entire state of Mississippi."

"I will," Janie promised. "Miss Houston, I hope you enjoy those. Now, I'd better run. I've got several deliveries for the hospital." The door closed behind her and I set the roses down on the antique registration desk. A card, tiny among the forest of red, sat in the midst of beauty. I stared at it.

"Aren't you going to open it?" Charlotte asked.

I shrugged. "Why? It's just another tactic among the townspeople to put two people together who have no business being together. Besides, it's meaningless if it comes from someone other than Spencer, on his behalf. I know everyone means well but—" I shook my head and whispered softly, "It just isn't the same."

She reached over and jerked the card from the roses. "Humor me." Her voice was kind but firm. "Read it anyway."

I opened it and silently absorbed the words. "Sorry about the detour. I took a wrong turn but am back on the right road. Love, Spencer."

It really was from Spencer, not someone else. I pondered the words quietly. After a moment, I tore the card up.

"Let's eat breakfast," I said a bit too brightly to be genuine, tossing the card in the wastebasket. "I'm starved."

Chapter 19

A bit of sad reserve hung darkly over the dining room table as we munched on breakfast, served again by the shy-smiling Lollie. I pretended nothing was wrong and Charlotte gamely played along, though I could tell she was saddened over the turn of events. I was, too, but I wasn't about to admit it.

I took my last sip of coffee, touched my napkin to the corners of my lips, then laid it down on the table.

"Well, I guess I could get going now," I announced, looking at my watch to see it was almost 9:30. I had planned to stay until lunch, but there was no reason for that now. Charlotte's eyes sprung wide in surprise.

"Oh, surely not!" she exclaimed. "Abby, dear, please don't go yet. Why the hurry? You don't have to be in Jackson until late afternoon. You have plenty of time."

I smiled tenderly and placed my hand on hers. "Charlotte, I'd love to stay but it's time to be going." My eyes said what my mouth could not. "Besides, I feel like doing some shopping. I think I'll stop at some antique stores and such along the way."

A half hour later, I was precariously coaxing my luggage down the flight of stairs in high heels.

"Oh, honey! Let me help you!" Charlotte flew up the steps and grabbed the suitcase while I clung to the large shopping bag filled with the gifts from the day before. "Charlie is always off playing golf when I need him most," she grumbled good-naturedly. At the bottom of the stairs, she hugged me. "I hate to see you go. Promise me you'll come back someday."

With watery eyes, I pulled back from the hug and smiled. "Promise. How could I not come back one day to such a charming little town filled with such wonderful, loving people?" I took a moment to gather myself. I swallowed, then continued, "By the way, you can keep the flowers that Spencer sent this morning. I hope you enjoy them."

"Abby, you may not want to hear this, but I'm going to say it anyway. If you leave here without calling Spencer and straightening all this out, you'll be making a big mistake. One that will probably hurt you both, and one that I feel certain you'll regret the rest of your life."

I sighed heavily. Stubborn resolve resonated from my eyes and in my words. "No," I replied firmly. "Charlotte, I adore you, but I stepped out in the water, and when I started to sink in its depth, I ran back to shore. I won't do it again. I won't risk being hurt another time. Spencer is obviously not ready for this."

"He wasn't ready last night, but he may be ready today!" she replied brightly, hope hanging tight.

"Maybe? *Maybe? MAYBE?*" my voice cracked. "And what if he's not? What if he thinks he's ready today, then tonight he decides he's not? Or worse than that, what if he decides next month when I'm already gaga, over the moon in love? What about that?"

She pinched her frosted pink-colored lips together and looked at me for a long moment before replying. "Honey, you know there are no assurances in love. There are none in life. Sometimes, you have to roll the dice and take the chance."

"Not with my heart." I shook my head firmly.

The memory of the look on her face will stay with me for a long time. It was a mixture of sadness, surrender and wisdom that is earned, not learned. "If you don't take a chance, you won't have a chance."

"Charlotte, what are you talkin' about?" I was trying to be patient.

"If you don't put your heart at risk at some point—either now or later—you will never have a chance of growing old with someone, of having someone there when your health begins to slip and time begins to grow short. I'm sure you're happy with your fun, glamorous life now. But when you don't have all these fun distractions to entertain you, what then?"

She had hit me between the eyes. I staggered emotionally, but physically I did not flinch. Maybe I had learned something in Hollywood, after all.

She was a dedicated foot soldier in the war of love. She did not stop. She kept coming. She reached over and took my hand in hers. "Honey, the only people who don't outlive the need for love are the ones who die young."

I blinked and the threatening tears retreated. Charlotte was hitting too close to home. Since my divorce, my constant prayer had been that I would not die alone.

"I know you're scared. But so is Spencer. Love deserted him, too. He didn't have any choice in the matter, either. Don't distrust him just because he feels the same way you do."

She made sense. But I'm not a gambler anymore, not when it

comes to love. I don't want to feel the whip of pain that it can lay on my heart.

"You're right," I said. It was obvious that Charlotte wasn't expecting that reply but she was delighted. She straightened her back and smiled triumphantly. I continued, "Charlotte, I know your intentions are good. I know that and I appreciate it. But you're talking to the wrong person." I set my jaw. "I am not changing my mind. I can't stand the thought of another broken heart. End of discussion."

She nodded, swallowing slowly. It was funny but I could actually feel the lump that had formed in her throat. I hated to disappoint her. Still, I had to be selfish and do what was best for me. The only problem was that I wasn't too sure I knew what was best.

♥

I did everything I could to avoid thinking about Spencer Alexander and the events of my stay in Bliss. I stopped at two antique stores and tried to stamp out my sadness with antique costume jewelry, a passion of mine. I also used a trick I had discovered when I was nineteen and Spooks Randolph had broken my heart. I was sweet and virginal and determined to stay that way. Spooks, a football hero, could have his choice of girls, so after chaste dates, he was on his way. I discovered that whenever Spooks crossed my mind, I couldn't let him linger. I would immediately replace memories of him with thoughts of other things. I tried the same thing again as I drove toward Jackson that day. This time I found it much harder than it had been with Spooks. Thoughts of Spencer weren't so easy to dismiss.

I was trying valiantly, though. In search of a distraction, I picked up my cell phone to call someone, anyone, as I drove away from the second antique shop. I turned it on and was greeted by a flashing notice: "You have one new message." The time/date feature announced it had come in at 6:08 p.m., the previous evening.

Just after I turned it off from talking with Mama, I thought to myself. For some reason, the message hadn't shown up when I used the phone to call Mama earlier that morning.

Jamie's playful voice greeted me. "Helllloooo, Miss Object of Someone's Affection!"

My heart pittered its way up to the center of my throat. "How does she know about me and Spencer?" My mind zipped through various scenarios, trying to figure out how she could possible know. Then my heart sank from my throat and found its way to my stomach. If Jamie knew, she had probably already put out a press release on it and called the gossip columnists. I could see how she could find a news angle in it—"Town comes calling to find a wife for its widowed mayor."

"Oh, Lord," I whispered, then realized I had missed part of the message, so I hit a button that rewound it to the beginning and listened carefully.

"Helllloooo, Miss Object Of Someone's Affection!" She paused to laugh gleefully. "Have you been keeping something from me? I thought we were best friends. Thought we had no secrets. Then, I have to find out about your secret lover from someone else. I'm so sad. Simply devastated."

Let me point out here that Jamie was neither sad nor devastated. She was gently mocking my Southern female tendency to, as she always puts it, "overdramatize." I shook my head. I was in no mood to be humored.

"Well, I'm disappointed that I couldn't discuss this personally with you. But ring me up when you have a moment, and we'll discuss this piece of ardent fan mail I got for you." My ears perked up. She wasn't talking about Spencer at all. She chuckled, then continued, "I have to say this is the best love letter I've seen in all my years of collecting fan mail for authors. Everyone else in the office thinks so, too! Ciao!"

I frowned at the phone. Because of the bad mood I was in, it annoyed me that Jamie was flouncing around the publishing house reading my private mail. That, of course, shows my irrational state of mind. Readers sometimes send letters to authors in care of their publisher. So it wasn't private at all. It was community mail.

With aggravation, I sighed heavily, then, with irritation, turned the phone off again. I was in no mood to talk to Jamie and play happy. I wanted to sulk. That message had managed to put Spencer all over my mind again. Dang it.

I was seduced back into those wonderful hours when it seemed that love was knocking again. I thought of the flirtations, the gifts, the laughs and, of course, the kisses. I was swept back into the emotions I had experienced in the gazebo when he had held me in his arms and I felt that I had found the one place in the universe where I belonged. Yes siree, just twelve hours before I thought I had found my destiny in Bliss, Mississippi, in the arms of a man that I hadn't known two days earlier. Wrong again. Story of my life as it pertains to romance. I struggled to pull myself out of those flashbacks that were producing nothing beneficial. I thought of my sparkling new necklace, earrings and large brooch created from four different shades of blue stones. I planned to use the pin on a navy wool hat.

I was so caught up in trying not to remember that I almost missed it. I reached down to hit the scan button on the radio when I saw something, from the corner of my eye, up ahead. I glanced over. My heart flopped heavily as it always does when I see a motionless animal on the side of the road. If it is a dog or a cat that is wearing a collar, my sorrow is doubled when I think of the sadness that its owner will feel over losing a friend.

I try not to look at these things. It only makes matters worse. So I didn't. But after I had passed it, something—don't ask me what, but I believe I know Who—made me glance into the rearview mirror. I saw the injured animal, surely a dog by the size of it, lift its head for a moment and then let it fall again.

"Oh, my goodness!" I exclaimed aloud. "The poor thing is still alive!" That has never happened. Never have I seen an animal, hit by a car, that was still alive. Suddenly, my mind started spinning. What should I do? Should I go back? If I went back, where was I going to take it? I didn't have a clue where I was or where a vet's office might be. Too, I was in a rental car without benefit of a blanket or towel. How was I going to get the dog in the car without ruining the velour upholstery, questionable though it was in elegance? And if the dog was large, how would I ever be able to lift its heavy body into the car? How could I get it into the car without causing it further pain? Then the big question lingered over my head. Why on earth would I want to expose myself to an emotional involvement that could just end in more pain? I know me. I knew that if I got involved and that dear dog died, I would be beside myself with grief. That's the kind of grief I don't want under any circumstances, particularly when my heart was already laden with it.

"That's it," I said firmly to myself. "You're not going back. You don't need this. You best just stay out of it."

I didn't like that answer, though. I glanced down at the clock near the radio dial. Well, one thing was for certain, I had enough time. I didn't have to be in Jackson for several hours, thanks to the fact that Spencer broke my heart and sent me hightailing it out of town early. For the next few miles, I argued with myself. My biggest hang-up was opening myself up to more hurt. More compelling than that, though, was that a precious, innocent creature needed me and I had the power to help. Finally, I cast my selfishness aside, made a U-turn on the nearly deserted highway and went back. I braced myself, thinking that if the dog had died by the time I returned, I would be crying all the way to Jackson. Within four or five minutes, I found the spot, although the dog was obscured somewhat by the grass. I eased the car over on the shoulder of the road and put my emergency flashers on. As I opened the door, I heard the most pitiful moaning, a tiny whimpering. My heart sank. Still, I forged ahead, not certain of what I would find, and got out of the car. Thank goodness, there was very little blood. That would have stopped me dead in my tracks. I didn't need blood to stop me, though, because something else did. The poor baby opened its eyes and when it saw me began to lethargically thump its tail. It wasn't much of a thump but I got the point.

"Oh, my gosh!" My hands flew to my mouth in surprise. I darted over and fell to my knees, picking up the dog's head and placing it in my lap. "Oh, sweet baby," I cooed, gently stroking the face. "What happened to you?"

The wounded animal looked at me with dark eyes full of pain, then the whimpering stopped, and Elmer closed her eyes.

Chapter 20

At times like that, I am never sure what is the right thing to do. Then, after it's over, I wonder if I did the best thing possible. I did at that moment of crisis the only thing I knew to do.

Pulling the car onto the road, I kept an anxious eye on Elmer, who was wrapped in a sweater I had hastily pulled from my suitcase. I had cushioned the seat for her with a pile of several cotton tops. After I arranged the makeshift bed, I kicked off my high heels and gently lifted her from the ground. I cradled her shaking body as I took her to the car. She yipped in pain as I picked her up, but it was obvious that there was too little energy or life left to allow much of a response from her. Once I was back in the driver's seat, I poured water from a bottle into my cupped hand and held it under her nose. She did not open her eyes or her mouth, so I took my finger, moistened it with the liq-

uid and ran it along her gums. I didn't know what to do. I had
no idea where I was or where a vet might be, but I knew I could
lose valuable time trying to find one. So I did what I thought
was the only thing I knew to do. I headed back to Bliss.

"Honey, honey," I crooned to the barely breathing animal,
reaching over with one hand to stroke her head as I drove with
the other. "How on earth did you get all the way out here?
You're at least forty miles from home."

I might add that forty miles was also a stretch of Mississippi
flatland where there was no cell phone signal. I kept checking
the phone but had no luck until about seven or eight miles from
Bliss. Finally, I got directory assistance, got the number for
Brian Jordan and called his emergency number. The answering
service took my number, and within a couple of minutes, Brian
was on the phone.

"Abby?" he asked, obviously puzzled. "Is something wrong?

"Yes, Brian. Something terrible. I'm on my way to Bliss with
Elmer. I found her on the side of the road and she's been hit by
a car."

"You found Elmer?" he exclaimed.

"Yes."

"I'll meet you at my office," he replied, taking charge.
"Where are you now?"

"I can see the city-limit sign. I'm about a mile from the Magnolia Blossom. How do I get to your office from there?"

He gave me directions and said that he could be there as
quickly as I would since he was in his car, running errands.

"How is she?" he asked.

"Not good at all. Barely here. I'm sure she's in shock."

"I'll see you in two minutes."

Brian's truck was parked at the office when I pulled into the
parking lot. He came flying out the front door, pushing a little
table. He took a quick look and shook his head in concern. "It's

not good," he commented, as he picked her up and placed her on the cart. "Probably internal injuries. But we'll do everything we can. I called my assistant. She's on the way to assist during surgery." Tears brimming in my eyes, I watched as he pushed the broken dog through the door. He looked back at me. "Abby, this would be a good time to pray."

♡

I sat for what felt like hours on the hard bench in the waiting room. It looked like most veterinarian clinics—all tile, with nothing that could not easily survive tantrums, vomit, urine or diarrhea. I propped my elbows on my knees and buried my face in my hands. When the entrance door squeaked, I looked up.

"How's Elmer?"

"In surgery right now." My voice was flat with no inflection of emotion.

Sheila sat down beside me and put her arm around me. "Are you all right?" she asked tenderly.

I shook my head. When I looked at her, tears spilled down my face. I turned my eyes toward shelves of pet food. "Sometimes I wish my heart, like that song says, was made of stone," I whispered softly.

"Oh, sweetie, you don't wish that, either. You just think you do." She removed her arm from my shoulders and took my hands in hers. "If you didn't feel things so deeply, you wouldn't be the successful writer you are."

I shrugged. "What good is money or success when your heart hurts so much? I can't buy a cure for an aching heart." The tears welled up again and I tossed a hand toward the operating room. "I just can't bear to see a poor, helpless creature like that in such pain."

Sheila smiled compassionately. "Which poor creature in pain are we talking about? Elmer or you?"

Her words weren't meant to be unkind, but they touched a place in my heart so raw and tender that the tears unashamedly poured from my eyes. Once I released the gate that had long held them back, I could not find the key to close it again. I cried until the front of my blouse was soaked with moisture and the skin on my face was void of it. I had just begun to dry up when Brian emerged from the surgical room. When I saw the look on his face, I began to cry again.

♡

Brian rubbed his eyes wearily and walked over to the bench. Heavily, he sank down beside Sheila.

"Honey?" She, like me, was afraid to ask the question. We waited a long moment but it appeared that Brian was not going to answer the question until it was asked outright. So I, scared though I was, did.

"How's Elmer?" I asked in a voice so small that it was barely louder than my breathing.

He blew tired air through his lips. "I don't know." His shoulders drooped. "She was dehydrated so we've pumped her full of fluids but that's only one problem. Internal injuries, loss of blood and a hip that was badly dislocated. I've patched her up the best I can."

"Is there any good news?" Sheila asked hopefully.

"Yep. She's stabilized. That's good. She has to do that before she can begin to heal."

That sounded good. "So? Will she make it?" I choked.

"Maybe. But it's a long maybe. Don't get your hopes up."

I wanted to cry again but I had already depleted the liter of water I had drunk that day. Brian fell forward, propped his elbows on his knees and stared quietly at the floor for a moment. He looked over at me, and a sorry sight I was, too, with streaked makeup, mascara washed away, red blotchy skin and swollen eyes. Questions darted through his dark eyes, but he kept them to himself. Instead, he asked, "How did you find Elmer?"

"I was driving to Jackson. Saw her on the side of the road but didn't know it was her. I just saw that an injured animal was still alive because she raised her head briefly. I turned around and went to help and discovered it was Elmer. Brian, she was almost forty miles from here. How did she get there?"

"I don't know. She's been missing since about eleven last night. Miss Eula said she had taken her for a walk in the park." He checked himself and my red face reddened more as I remembered the event and wondered what she had told Brian about it. "She said that she didn't have Elmer on a leash but she thought she was right behind her. When she got home, Elmer was gone."

"Elmer couldn't have walked forty miles overnight, could she?" I asked.

He shook his head. "Naw, not at all. She had to have some help. The only thing is, if someone had taken her, why didn't they keep her? Why would they just put her out somewhere?"

No one had the answer to that, so we all shook our heads quietly. Suddenly, Sheila spoke up.

"Hey! Has anybody called Miss Eula to tell her that Elmer's been found?"

Brian slapped his forehead. "Man, I hadn't even had time to think about it. I've got to call her now." He jumped up.

"Must we?" I asked with dread. My day was already bad enough without encountering the wicked witch of Bliss.

He smiled sympathetically. "She's worried out of her mind. Someone finally had to send for the preacher early this morning, and of course, he came runnin'. He hasn't left her side, and about eight, they started the prayer chain. Looks like it worked, too." He crossed the room to the phone on the reception counter and turned back with a large smile. "I know she hasn't been kind to you, Abby. But you're a hero. *You* found Elmer and brought her back. Why, Miss Eula is liable to put you in her will now." His grin broadened. "You may end up owning most of Bliss."

I rolled my eyes. "Right. I'm sure that is gonna happen."

The call connected. "Hello? This is Brian Jordan. May I speak with Miss Eula, please?" He put his hand over the receiver and mouthed quietly to us, "It's the preacher's wife." In a moment, he said, "Miss Eula, I have some news for you. I have Elmer here at the clinic. She was—" He didn't finish. He pulled the receiver away from his ear and looked at it with puzzlement for a moment. "She hung up on me." He motioned toward the door. "We should see her whirling through that door as fast as her little, skinny legs will carry her in about four to five minutes."

"Whoopee." I deadpanned. "I can hardly wait."

I didn't have to wait long, for true to Brian's prediction, Hurricane Hateful swept in, in a few minutes, trailed by a short, plump woman and a scrawny, balding man.

"Where's Elmer?" she demanded. Twelve hours of sorrow had obviously not humbled her.

"In ICU, with my assistant," Brian answered, grabbing her by the arm as she tried to storm past him. "Wait a minute. You can't go in there."

"I most certainly can and will," she retorted with the haughtiness of a woman who always gets her way.

"No, you're not. Elmer is in critical condition and does not need any excitement or agitation." I was growing to like Brian more each minute. I always appreciate a man with backbone. They can be mighty hard to find.

She puffed up like a mean ol' bullfrog. "What's wrong with Elmer?"

"She was hit by a car. I had her in surgery for almost two hours. She had internal injuries and I had to fix a dislocated hip. She's stable now and if she is going to make it, she will have to remain quiet for a while."

She settled down a little and Brian offered his hand to the bald man. "Hi, preacher. How ya doin'?" He tipped his head to the woman. "Hi, Miss Doreen. Good to see you." This was the moment that Miss Eula Witch turned around and saw me. Fire flew from her eyes.

"You! You awful woman!" she spewed. "It's all your fault!"

I recoiled and Sheila stood up. "Miss Eula, I will not let you talk to Abby that way. You have no idea what this woman has done."

"Yes, I do! She's the reason that Elmer ran off. She can't leave him alone. We saw her when she was cavorting shamelessly with the mayor in the park. I'll tell you that what I saw was a shame and a disgrace. Right after that is when poor Elmer disappeared. It was probably too much for his innocent eyes, what he saw."

I was so embarrassed that I wanted to climb under the bench. The preacher lifted his eyebrows in judgment. I didn't know what to say. I was ravaged with emotion, wrung dry, but she hit a raw nerve. Somehow I found the strength to pull myself up from the bench and walk over to her. I threw my finger toward her as though it was loaded with gunpowder.

"Let me tell you something," I started, anger darkly edging my words. "I have had it with the way you talk to me. You are the most horrid woman I have ever met. It is you, not me, who is the shame and the disgrace. How dare you speak to people the way you do! Who gave you that authority? Poor Elmer is so beleaguered by you that if I hadn't found her forty miles from here, I would have thought that she had run off! If I were a dog and I belonged to you, I would certainly run away."

In the course of the few brief seconds that it took for those words to come out, her expression changed rapidly from anger to astonishment to disbelief. I paused to let her reply. I looked her straight in the eyes and didn't blink. It took a second before she opened her mouth.

"Wait a minute," she croaked. "What do you mean you found Elmer forty miles from here?"

Brian moved to my side and took over. "Miss Eula, Abby was driving to Jackson when she saw an injured dog on the side of the road. She turned around, went back, discovered it was Elmer and put her in the car, called me and drove Elmer back. If it hadn't been for Abby finding Elmer when she did, Elmer would most likely be dead by now."

I don't know what we expected. Perhaps a softening of a hardened heart or a small word of appreciation. We got neither. Instead, she turned on her sensible heels and stormed out the door with the preacher and his wife scampering after her. I should have felt bad for my caustic tongue. But I didn't. I wished, instead, that I had said more. I even thought of running after her and firing off a few more choice words. Somehow, I found restraint and stayed behind.

Sheila started laughing and Brian soon joined her. I didn't see humor in anything.

"Abby, bless your heart! You really told her off!" Sheila was bent over, holding her stomach as she convulsed in laughter. "I wouldn't take a million dollars for having had the pleasure to see that!"

Brian put his arm around me and hugged me. "Good for you. I'm proud of you for standing up to her."

Daddy used to say that something good comes out of everything that's bad. It wasn't much in my estimation, but after a day of pining after Spencer and finding poor Elmer in such miserable shape, at least I'd given the old woman with the wicked heart a bit of comeuppance. A tiny smile tugged at the corners of my mouth.

"Do you still think I'll make it into her will?"

"There are some things," Brian said somberly, "that no amount of money can buy. That would be one of them."

I looked at my watch. "Oh, my gosh, I've got to get going. I didn't realize it was so late. I have a book signing in Jackson in a couple of hours. I need to check into the hotel and try to straighten myself out beforehand."

That opened the door for Brian to ask, "Are you all right?"

I nodded and said a bit too brightly, "I'm fine."

"That's funny," he replied. "I talked to Spencer this morning and he wasn't doing fine at all."

I pursed my lips together tightly and glanced down. "I don't want to talk about it."

"I understand. But you need to know that Spence is a mixed-up guy. He didn't expect to meet someone like you who would just sweep him away. He's at war with himself."

"That's a battle he needs to fight himself. As for me, I'm waving the white flag. I'm bloodied enough without getting involved in another war. I have battle fatigue."

Brian smiled sadly. "I guess that'll teach me to get into a war of words with a writer. I find myself poorly armed against you. So you're going now?"

"Definitely." I hugged Sheila. "Thank you for being here and being so kind to me. I hope we'll meet again."

"Me, too. Before I met you, I felt we had been friends for years. That's the power of books."

"Spoken like a true teacher." I smiled. "Brian, will you please keep me posted on Elmer?"

"That I will," he agreed. "I'll call you on your cell, if that's okay."

"It is, indeed." I opened the door. "Take care of yourselves." I waved good-bye.

"Come back to Bliss sometime, okay?" Sheila looked sad, so I nodded.

"And y'all come to see me. I'd love to have you in Dexter."

"You may be sorry that you said that!" Brian warned with a laugh.

"Never. You can't ever have too many good people as friends." The door closed and I walked to my car, looking down at the ground. I didn't look up until I heard someone say, "Miss Houston?"

It took only a moment for me to recognize him. I walked toward him and offered my hand. "Walter, right?"

He grinned shyly and looked down. "I can't believe you remembered my name. I only met you that one time yesterday at the bookstore."

"I always remember people who make multiple book purchases!" I was trying to act happy. "Plus, don't forget that we met in Little Rock. We're old friends by now!"

He beamed. "I thought of some other people that I need you to sign a book for."

"I signed some and left them at the bookstore. I'm sure that Susan Marie still has a few."

He answered me but I didn't hear his words. I was distracted by what I saw behind him. A red pickup truck with a white camper top.

Chapter 21

"Miss Houston? Did you hear me?"

I snapped out of the distraction caused by the sight of the red truck. "I'm sorry, Walter. What did you say?"

"I said that I already bought the books at the bookstore. I was wondering if you would personalize them for me?"

I tried a poor attempt at a slight smile. "Sure. I'll be happy to." I glanced at my watch. "I need to hurry, though. I have to get to Jackson for a signing. Do you have them with you?"

He grinned. "Yes, ma'am. Right over here at my truck." He motioned to the red truck and began walking that way. Not wanting to waste any time, I followed him to the driver's side. He opened the door and pulled out a stack of six or seven books. Something felt strange. I had an unsettled feeling but I didn't know why.

"It's the strangest thing," I commented as he handed me a pen and I opened the first book. "I've seen a truck like this several times over the past couple of days. So strange."

"Please make that one to Jan. She's my next-door neighbor. I feed her cat for her sometimes." I started to sign and he continued. "Yep. I love this old truck. Folks ask me all the time why I don't buy me a new one but I don't need one. This 'un fine."

As I reached for the second book, something suddenly occurred to me. How did Walter know where to find me? How did he know I'd be at the animal hospital? Click, click, click. The thoughts zipped through my mind like a camera taking fast-action pictures. Had Walter been following me and I had been so preoccupied that I hadn't noticed?

"That's one for Randy Joe. We go huntin' together."

As I wrote the name, the picture became crystal clear. Walter was stalking me. My heart speeded up and I tried to think of an excuse to step away. I was blocked in between the door, the seat and Walter, who was standing behind me.

"Uh, Walter. I need to get my own pen. I prefer to sign with it." I laughed feebly. "I know it's silly but it just writes better. I'll scoot over to the car and get it." I moved to slide between him and the truck when I felt something round and solid poke me sharply in the back. Walter leaned closer and whispered, "Get in the truck right now."

I stalled, my heart and mind both trying to outrace each other. He pushed the hard object, certainly a gun, rougher into my back. I froze. Nothing I had ever seen or heard of in Dexter, Georgia had prepared me for such a perilous moment in time. The only kidnapping in the history of my hometown happened when George Adair snatched Marva Jones' cat after she dumped him in favor of a water meter reader. He thought that a ten-year courtship was owed more respect than that. It was a sad day for George made sadder by the fact that the terrified cat, which, by all reports, had never liked George anyway, got loose in the car and clawed him wildly. During the catfight, George lost control of the car and plowed into the big magnolia tree in front of the post office. That's all I knew personally about kidnappings but I did know that high heels could not outrun bullets. I was certain of that.

"Miss Houston, please!" His tone was urgent. "Get up in that truck now. Please don't make me hurt you. I couldn't stand to do that." He grabbed one arm and with overwhelming strength picked me up, dangling me by an elbow, and shoved me into the cab of the truck. He jumped into the seat, pushed me over further, slammed the door and started the engine. He hit the gas, spun the truck around and I, half lying, half sitting, saw the dust that arose when one tire dropped off the pavement and churned through the thick gravel. With uneven, unpleasant bounces, the truck jerked over a small gully, hit the highway and took off at a high speed, tires screeching as it went. I pulled myself upright and slid over as close to the door as possible. The thought of a seat belt never crossed my mind. It didn't matter, though. It would have been hard to be in much more danger than I was already in. As the truck speeded away from Bliss, I found I was shaking as fast as it was moving. I knew that would be no help so I tried to get hold of myself. I tried to calm down.

"Walter," I began softly, "where are we going?"

He didn't take his eyes from the road. "You'll see soon enough. Don't worry. I'll take good care of you, Miss Houston."

I tried again. "Walter, I'm going to be in so much trouble if I don't make it to Jackson for that book signing. You wouldn't want that to happen, would you?" He glanced quickly over to me, then back to the road. "Would you take me to Jackson?"

"Well, I might could." He thought for a second; then he rejected the thought with a vicious shake of his head. "No, no, no. I can't do that. That would mess up the plans."

"The plans?" My throat and mouth were growing drier by the moment.

"Uh-huh."

"What plans?"

"Our wedding plans."

♡

I've always heard that a person's life flashes before him as he's dying. I don't know if that's true but I know that my life, the good and the bad, replayed in my mind as the miles and the minutes ticked away. I could live—and die if it came to that— with most of what I saw except for one thing: the way I had run away from Spencer and never tried to straighten things out. Never mind the fact that if I had worked things out with Spencer, I'd never have been kidnapped in the first place. It's that chain-of-events thing. Where one thing done differently changes the outcome of many things. Of course, I would have left Bliss much later and all would have turned out differently. As much of a knife to my heart as that was, it did not compare with the fact that I had run away from a man I was beginning to love. Here was the kind of man I had dreamed of finding all my life, and when I found him, I had taken the easy way out. Who knew if I would ever be able to right that wrong? Who knew? I closed my eyes, leaned my head against the window and thought of the only thing that brought me comfort—me in Spencer's arms, safe from harm and far removed from worry. As if I were ten years old again, I slipped into a fantasy world and found a dreamy reprieve for my frazzled mind. I kept my mind there and away from the bothersome thoughts of Mama, Kudzu, Melinda, Claire, Sandy and all the others I loved and might never see again.

"Miss Houston?" Walter asked gently. "Are you okay?"

I didn't hide my sadness. I heard tenderness in his voice so I

hoped that my hurt could overcome any evil that might be dart-
ing around in his round, bald head. "No," I replied quietly. "I'm
worried."

"About what?"

I looked at him like the nut he was. "What do you think I'm
worried about?" I smarted back with words full of sarcasm. I
was too tired to be intelligent and not aggravate him.

"Elmer. I think you're worried about Elmer."

I jerked my head around and looked at him with suspicion.
"How do you know about Elmer?"

"I'm really sorry about that. I didn't mean for her to get hurt.
By the way, why is a girl named Elmer?"

My mind started clicking again. Things weren't adding up.
"Walter, I'm confused. You're a stranger to Bliss. How would
you know about Elmer or that Elmer's a girl?"

He smiled sweetly. "I did it for you." Then, awkwardly, he
added, "Sweetheart." His chubby cheeks reddened at his bold-
ness. He took a breath and continued. "That old woman was so
mean to you." He shuddered violently, his face flashing to crimson. "It just burned me up the way she talked to you." He
looked over at me. "You're so nice and you don't deserve that.
After she acted like she did with you last night in the park, I decided that I'd teach her a thing or two."

"You were in the park!" Oh Lord, Walter had seen the spectacle of me falling into Spencer's arms. "How embarrassing,"
was my first thought. "How stupid that I care what a kidnapper thinks," was my second.

"As soon as she turned her back, I grabbed the dog and took
off as hard as I could run."

"Walter!" I gasped. "You took Elmer?"

He grinned proudly. "Yep, I sure did. Did it for you. That's
how much I love you." My mind flashed back to seeing the red
pickup when Spencer and I left the town square. "I put Elmer in

the truck and took her about an hour away and put her out. I didn't mean for her to get hurt, though. I thought that she would eventually get home, but it would take enough time to worry the old biddy sick. If I didn't like animals so much, I'd done more."

I dropped my face in my hands. I was the one who was sick with worry about all the trouble and distress I had brought to such a wonderful little town. My head popped up as a horrible thought crossed my mind. If he had seen how Miss Eula talked to me, then he had seen me in the park with Spencer. And if he had seen us in the park during our romantic moments, he might have done something to Spencer out of jealousy. I opened my mouth to ask but I was afraid to know. After ten minutes or so, I had to ask. I plunged in.

"Walter, do you remember Mayor Alexander, who you met at the bookstore?"

Walter's jaw tightened. He turned a grim look toward me. "That man likes you."

I was not consoled by Walter's expert opinion on Spencer's affection for me. "Is he okay?"

He shrugged. "Naw, I don't think so. I think you should be careful of him. He might not be on the up and up."

Great. Walter was also a judge of dubious characters. He, of course, had overlooked himself. "No, Walter, what I mean is, has the mayor been harmed in any way?"

"You mean like Elmer?"

We were getting somewhere. I nodded with a knot in my throat. Walter chewed his lip for a moment before answering. It is safe to say that it was the longest moment of my life up to that time.

"Would you like it if he was?"

"Walter!" I was close to tears. "Please tell me! Did you do anything to the mayor?"

With sadness pouring over his face, he shook his head. "No. I'm sorry, Miss Houston, but I didn't." He looked pitiful. "I wouldn't let you down for nothin'."

I knew then that I was dealing with a mind warped but not broken. "Why would you think that I wanted anything done to him? Where would you ever get such a notion?"

" 'Cause last night when he took you back to the place where you were stayin', I saw y'all have words; then you stomped off. I knew he musta made 'cha real mad or somethin'."

I was incredulous. "You were there?" The story was growing more bizarre by the moment.

"Uh-huh." He nodded. "You went inside; then he got in his vehicle. But he didn't leave right away. He sat there for a while."

"He did?" In spite of myself, I brightened. Maybe ol' Walter and his snoopy stalking was worth something after all.

Walter's face lighted up. He knew he was being helpful and he enjoyed it. "Yeah. First, he laid his head over on the steering wheel and just sat there like that for a while. Then, he sat back in the seat and just sat there, staring out toward the house."

"How long did he stay there?" I was liking what I heard. Who would have thought it? Me and Walter in cahoots together.

"Dunno. I stayed about twenty minutes or so, but I had Elmer with me. She was sleepin' so she didn't see nothin'. I realized I needed to get on up the road and put her out somewhere. He was still there when I left." He looked over at me. "Miss Houston?"

"Abby," I replied weakly. If I was going to be in the possession of a kidnapper, I preferred to be on a first-name basis.

He blushed. "I don't feel right about that."

"About what?"

"Callin' you by your first name. It wouldn't be right."

For crying out loud, I had been taken hostage by a courteous kidnapper. One who was too courteous to use my first name but, on the other hand, saw nothing bad mannered about holding me captive. That's just my luck.

"Okay," I responded. No sense quarrelling over that. "What did you want to ask me?"

"I just want you to know that I wasn't mean to Elmer. I stopped at the Piggly Wiggly and bought her some Little Debbies and milk, and I give them to her before I put her out."

"Walter, do you know that Elmer was hit by a car, and though the vet has done everything possible, there's a strong chance that she will die? In fact, she's more likely to die than to live."

His bottom lip blubbered. This was a good sign. If he was upset over Elmer, then I was probably safe.

"Miss Houston, I didn't mean her no harm. Honest." Tears stood in his eyes. When he looked over at me, he ran off the side of the road and barely missed a mailbox.

"Walter! Watch out!" Geez. He was a kidnapper *and* a bad driver.

"I'm sorry!" He clutched the steering wheel with two hands. "I'm not gonna let you get hurt." He didn't look at me. He kept his eyes on the road. "You're too precious to me."

With a heavy heart, I sat quietly as the miles drifted by and shades of dusk were falling. It was time for my book signing in Jackson to begin. At least someone would begin to miss me and maybe a search would begin. A couple of hours later, I had no idea where we were when Walter turned off the paved road onto a little dirt road crowded by overgrown bushes and trees, many of which scraped the truck as we pushed past.

"Walter, where are we?" I asked nervously, the approaching darkness doing nothing to ease my anxiousness.

"We're goin' to the little cabin where we're gonna spend our honeymoon. I just know you're gonna love it."

Honeymoon. Not even the thoughts of how happy my mama would be that I was going to have one could lighten my mood.

Chapter 22

Shack was more what it was than a cabin. I've seen lean-tos in the deepest part of the Appalachians that didn't look much worse than that did. It was tiny, with kudzu growing over the rotting wood on one side, edging its way up over the rusty tin roof. It had a screen door with wire that had rusted to the darkest shade of ruin. A narrow porch, high enough for a small child to play under it with the rats and snakes that surely resided there, ran the length of the front with gaping holes in a couple of places. The plank that had once represented the second step had broken and was hanging lopsidedly toward the ground.

It was the second time I ever regretted having on high heels. The first was when I realized I couldn't jump from a moving truck and make a getaway.

He turned the engine off and turned his sizeable girth toward me. "Miss Houston, I know it's not much, but one day I'll build you the kind of house you deserve." He reached over and took my hand in his pudgy, sweaty one. Repulsion ran from my hairline to my toes but I tried to cover it up. Making him mad was not one of my aspirations in life.

"Where are we?" I managed to squeak out, my throat dry from anxiety.

"The middle of nowhere, which is located near the Arkansas line." He grinned happily. "Nobody'll ever find us here."

Great. Just what I wanted to hear.

"Is this yours?"

"It belongs to my first cousin, Buddy Junior. Actually, he's more like my adopted brother. We grew up together. It's his huntin' place. Me and him come up here sometimes. Lots of deer in these woods. There's a bear that hangs out close by. We seen him a bunch of times."

Wonderful. I liked hearing that, too. Escape wasn't looking too good, and I was beginning to wonder where the moat with the alligators was. He reached over and brushed his hand quickly against my cheek. Sickness floated over me and I felt lightheaded. I clutched the armrest, trying to steady myself.

"I've loved you since the moment I saw your picture on the cover of your first book. I've got a whole scrapbook full of articles on you and lots of videotape from every time you were on TV. I got me one of them fancy satellite deals where you just put in someone's name and it tapes 'em every time they come on the TV. I got quite a collection."

My eyes filled with tears but I made up my mind that I wasn't going to cry, unless, of course, I thought it might help my situation. In that case, I was going to be all for it. I just didn't think this was the time. So despite the fact that I was miserable and scared, I kept the tears within my eyes. Instead, I tried a ploy that had worked quite well with a few unwanted suitors. Of course, none of them had kidnapped me. They had just taken me to the Dairy Queen for a hamburger. Still, I decided to try it.

"Walter," I began, stifling my repulsion and taking his hand, "you can do so much better than me." It wasn't true, of course, but I was, after all, trying to escape. "I would just disappoint you. And heavens know, I wouldn't want that."

Distress leapt into his face and when he turned more in his seat, I saw the glimmer of the gun that he had put in the side pocket of the door. That jerked a knot in my plans.

"There ain't no way on this earth you could ever disappoint me. No way! You're the best." He leaned forward and I stiffened because I thought he was going to kiss me or at least try. Instead, with a bumbling awkwardness, he patted me on the head. Like a dog. *He patted me on the head like a dog.*

I didn't know whether to be comforted, insulted or amused. It was almost time for the tears. But not quite. I took a deep breath and tried to speak calmly.

"Walter, why don't we go in and rest? I'm so tired and worried about not keeping my commitment in Jackson."

He relaxed, nodded and opened the door. "Stay right there and let me come around and git 'cha." He grabbed the gun and ran around the front of the truck. He opened the door, took my hand and helped me down. Holding my arm firmly to the point that he pinched my elbow, he steered me toward the door. The air was crisp like a night on the front edge of autumn, with a smell of fading greenery about to turn golden. It reminded me of high school football games on those early-fall evenings, and under any other circumstances, I would have taken a deep breath and been happy to be alive. I guess, come to think about it, I should have been happy to be alive then, too.

"Miss Houston, you be careful now. I wouldn't want you to fall."

"I guess I didn't wear the right shoes for the deep woods."

"No, you didn't. But don't you worry none. Soon as possible, I'll go into town and git 'cha some decent shoes and comfortable clothes. I'll git 'cha whatever you need." Walter was such a paradox—a disillusioned kidnapper with lovely manners. Though it was rude to kidnap me.

When we reached the treacherous steps, I had to step over the second step, not easy in a straight skirt and high heels. Walter, though, held firmly to my arm and helped me up. I'm sad to report that the inside of the cabin looked no better than the outside. It was stark: two rooms with the front room serving as combination den and kitchen. There was a fireplace, a raggedy couch in a gosh-awful green-and-orange plaid, a brown cushioned chair, a black worn footstool, a table with a lamp that had a big red glass belly and in the "dining" area an old aluminum table with an atrocious green vinyl top and four matching tattered chairs. It was a nightmare in which *Gunsmoke* met the *Brady Bunch*. I am proud to report that it did have electricity. I didn't see a bathroom, though, and that worried me.

"Walter, where's the bathroom?"

He looked sheepish and dropped his head slightly. "Uh, well, Miss Houston, we don't have one. But there's a place down back you can use."

"You mean an outhouse?"

He nodded. For the first time in my life, I didn't have a desire to go to the bathroom. That's quite an accomplishment since there're probably few bathrooms I have passed up in my life. I drink a lot of water; plus I, apparently, have a small bladder. These two things combined make me a regular to the bathroom. It's an annoyance to Mama, who must have a bladder the size of Texas so she is rarely inconvenienced. When we go somewhere together, she'll always say, "Do you need to go the bathroom? Because if you do, you need to go before we leave." And to think that I thought I would escape such instruction when I became an adult.

I dropped down on the sofa with the sponge squeezing through the rips in the fabric. I dropped my face in my hands. I was in a heck of a mess. It was a bit like locking myself out of the house in the pouring rain without a spare key or telephone around. I knew there had to be a way out; it was just figuring out what that was. Since we had screeched out of that parking lot, I had been trying to think how I could get away. So far, I hadn't thought of a good way because I had two major problems: high heels (though I never thought I'd consider them a problem of any sort) and being in the middle of the woods in the middle of nowhere. I missed my cell phone. I was so sorry that it was still on the passenger seat of my car where I threw it when I hung up from talking to Brian, en route to his office. "Of course," I thought glumly to myself, "there probably isn't any cell signal here anyway."

"I'm sorry, Miss Houston."

Walter was standing behind the sofa, looking like a pitiful puppy. Puzzled, I looked at him. "What?" I asked. After all, there was so much that he could have been apologizing for.

"That there isn't a bathroom." He dropped his head. "I guess I didn't think about that."

I waved my hand in dismissal. "Don't worry about it." I sighed wearily. There were bigger things to cause worry. Walter walked toward the kitchen, and suddenly it occurred to me that I hadn't seen any food. Perfect. The thought made me smile. My mind began flittering away. Either Walter could go to the store alone and I could escape, or he could take me with him and I could run away then when other people were around.

"Walter," I said sweetly, thrilled with my new plan. "We don't have any food."

He grinned. I knew then I wasn't going to like the answer.

"Oh, Miss Houston, don't you worry none about that. I got a whole truck bed full of groceries. We could stay here for weeks and weeks and never run out of anything to eat."

My heart fell to the ground. Oblivious to my disappointment, he continued. "You hungry? Betcha are. Let me just run git the stuff out of the truck, and I'll fix you up somethin' good to eat." He picked the gun up from the table and casually waved it in my direction. "Now, you stay put. Don't move."

I looked down at the spiked heels I was wearing and thought glumly, "Don't worry."

♡

I pushed my food around my plate, taking only a small bite from time to time.

"You don't like it?" Walter looked worried. He had fried up a pan of sausage and scrambled eggs and made biscuits and sawmill gravy. Normally, I would have eaten every bite except for the eggs and gone back for more. I love home cooking, especially Southern-style breakfasts.

I smiled faintly. "It's fine. I'm just not much hungry."

The furrow across his brow grew deeper. "Now, Miss Houston, don't make yourself sick." He studied me for a moment. "You still worried about Elmer?"

Oh, yeah. Elmer was all I had thought of for the past few hours. I had never despaired over myself. I frowned. "Walter, I'm still very unhappy about Elmer and what happened to her."

He dropped his head. "I'm sorry. I was just tryin' to help you."

At that point, I thought of how he should get together with my mother. They would make a great tag team in their concerned but distorted efforts to help me. Seeing that his guilt over Elmer was strong, I pushed it further. Guilt, I had a feeling, could be used against Walter to my advantage. "Well, you didn't help.

You hurt me. I've been very sad today over Elmer." I found myself talking to Walter like a small child. In a way, though, he was.

He didn't say a word. He picked up his plate still scattered with eggs and bits of broken biscuit covered with gravy. He walked over to the trash can and brushed the food into it. "You finished?" he asked.

Probably in more ways than one, I thought. I nodded and pushed the plate toward him. I wasn't offering to clean up. After all, I wasn't a guest. I was a hostage. The least I could get out of it was to let Walter wait on me. While he scraped my plate, I propped an elbow on the table, dropped my chin into my cupped hand and sulked. Pouting had turned into sulking. This was a serious situation. Too serious for mere pouting. I became interested in Walter's belly, which spilled over his belt and jiggled like jelly as he went about his kitchen tasks. "Poor Walter," I thought about my kidnapper, "must really be lonely and sad." I often think that about folks who are overweight. That's because when I'm frazzled or blue, I feel like, "Bring on the ice cream! The Mexican food! The biscuits, gravy, fried green tomatoes, potatoes and macaroni and cheese!" Show it to me and I put it in my mouth. But when I'm happy, I could go days without food. I felt sorry for the man who had dropped me into a tank of misery, thinking that his overeating must come from a place of deep hurt and despair.

While Walter washed up the dishes, I thought of the dadgum situation I was in. Walter seemed harmless but Lord knew when that could turn. I once went out with an accountant named George Hazel, who was benignly forgettable; then one day as soon as tax season ended, he became the most unforgettable man in Dexter. Took off all his clothes except for his Bugs Bunny boxer shorts and paraded around the Confederate-soldier statue downtown with a handmade sign that read, "Your tax money is being used to support Martians on welfare."

He ended up in a state-supported mental institution, which, of course, provided a heyday of mirth for Melinda.

"See what happens when we leave it up to you to pick out your own dates?" she asked with a cluck of her tongue.

Something like that could happen to Walter any second, and I, for one, wasn't discounting it. As I moped about my captivity, my eyes fell to rest on a fat, black stick lying several feet away. That's just like a couple of guys, I thought faintly. Just leave a big ol' stick in the middle of the floor to be tripped over. Having been married, I was familiar with that kind of mind-set. I continued to sulk with my eyes on the stick because it was better than looking at the atrociously ugly furniture. That would have made things even more depressing, and I certainly didn't need any help with my depression.

Then, the stick moved. I jerked out of my sulk and sat up straight. When I saw its head lift up, I dove from full-fledged sulk into full-fledged alarm.

"Walter!" I called softly in an urgent whisper. He turned from the sink where he was drying a plate.

"There's a snake!" I pointed to the long black beast. Then I gulped, leapt up and climbed on the table where I crouched in a quake, high heels and all.

As calm as you please, Walter placed a finger against his lips, quietly laid down the plate and eased his hulking frame across the floor. I did not know that that much weight could move so gently. The ancient planked floor did not creak as he slipped up behind the varmint. I couldn't imagine what he was going to do. If it had been me, I'd have been looking for anything to take its head off swiftly. I've killed snakes before and I know how it's done.

But not Walter.

My kidnapper sneaked up behind it and, with incredible lightning-fast reflexes, grabbed it behind the head in a grip that would not allow the snake to turn and bite, jerked it up, dashed—yes, and dashed is what he did—out the door. He returned in a few minutes, dusting his hands on his jeans.

I slid out of my nervous crouch, lowering myself into a sitting position on the tabletop. I was impressed. Who would have thought it? I looked at Walter and shook my head slowly.

"That was something," I admitted. "You pick up snakes often?"

He dropped his eyes bashfully. "Only when they need to go back into their natural habitat."

"What?" I was puzzled.

"That was a black snake. It didn't mean no harm to nobody. I just wanted to put it outside and let it slip back into the woods."

My eyes widened. "Why?"

"Why what?"

"Why wouldn't you just kill it?" I shuddered. "It's a snake."

His head popped up and he looked at me with amazement. "I couldn't kill it." He shook his head frantically. "No ma'am. No way. It's just a poor little creature that wouldn't hurtin' nobody. I ain't got no right to hurt a little critter like that." He rubbed at his eyes with one hand. "That's why I'm feelin' so sad. You know, Elmer and all that." He sniffed.

I blinked. Walter, I then realized, was a piece of work. It was also at that point that I knew I would be okay. I was safe. If Walter wasn't going to hurt a snake, then he certainly wasn't going to hurt me. I put my elbows on my knees, leaned forward and looked at the odd man. I studied him quietly for a moment; then I thought of Homer back at that little country store in the middle of Nowhere, Mississippi. I thought of how much he had taught me in such a short time, and how from him I had been reminded that every person has a story and that story is what shapes him into what he becomes.

Homer's story had captivated me, and now, here I was being held captive by Walter. There was a lesson in there somewhere. I brushed the hair back from my face, slipped off the table and walked over to my gentle captor. I took his pudgy hand. He looked surprised that I had willingly touched him, but from deep inside, it felt right to me.

"Walter, come over here to this fine lookin' assortment of living room furniture and let's have a seat," I said as I led him toward the ugly couch.

He sat down at the end and I settled into a sunken spot halfway down the sofa, a comfortable distance away from Walter but not too far. I slung one arm over the back and let the other fall into my lap.

"So, Walter." I looked at him and smiled. "Tell me all about yourself."

Chapter 23

Puzzled and speechless, Walter stared at me for a few moments. Again, gently I urged, "Please, Walter. I want to know about your life."

Slowly, he shook his head; then he scratched the top of his bald head. "Ain't nobody ever asked me about myself." He pondered the significance of the moment; then gradually his face stretched into a smile, the kind like the delight of a child who sees a shiny new bike in the driveway on Christmas morning.

"You really want to know?" He asked in a hopeful tone. "Or you just joshin' me?"

I smiled warmly. Honest to goodness, it did not occur to me to be nice to Walter in hopes of luring him into letting me go. I have always believed in the power of nice. Always believed that by being nice to people, you're treated more favorably in life. In short, people are nice to people who are nice to them. But for at least once in my life, it never occurred to me that by being nice to Walter, I could coax him into what I wanted—my freedom. Instead, I sensed a deep loneliness in Walter, and based on what I had learned from Homer, I wanted to know from where that loneliness sprung. Maturity and understanding—just like Santa Claus with expert radar—had found me in a remote, back-woods location in Arkansas.

I didn't have to wait long. Once I reassured him that I did want to hear about his life, he opened his mouth and almost drowned me with the flood of words that poured forth. I am sure that, metaphorically speaking, Noah was in a mere sprin-kling of raindrops compared to me. Over the course of the next couple of hours, I watched as a man who had brazenly broken the law, who could be called an outlaw, was transformed into a vulnerable heap of mush. At first, I had to play the role of re-porter and ask the questions, but then he segued effortlessly into the avalanche of emotion that he had stored in his heart for over thirty years.

"How old are you?" I began.

"Thirty-nine," he replied shyly. I hope my eyes didn't bulge. He sure looked older. I would have marked him at closer to fifty.

"Where were you born?" I asked.

"Mississippi County, Arkansas. Around an hour, more than less, west of Memphis. It's in the delta."

I nodded. "Mississippi County," I repeated softly. It wasn't lost on me how well educated I was becoming from people and events associated with places named Mississippi. "Did you grow up there?" There was no mistaking the sadness that crossed his eyes. He gathered his brow into a furrow.

"For a while. 'Til I was six."

"Then your parents moved?" I prompted.

He shook his head, then looked over to a far corner decorated with a spider's web. "I moved but they stayed put." He sighed sadly. "They're both buried in the county cemetery."

Ouch. I felt the pinch on my own heart. "Did they both die when you were six?"

He swallowed, then nodded. "They died together. At least that's what the coroner said. Said they died so close together that they was no way to figure out who went first."

Silence hung heavily in the dusty room. Finally, I plunged ahead. "What happened?"

"Car wreck. A bad 'un. They got hit head-on by a couple of boys who had had themselves too much to drink. Some moonshine that they had bought across the county line." He sighed again but this time when he did, I felt a release that tumbled toward emotional freedom. He stood up and walked over to the black, potbellied stove. He shoved his hands deep into his pockets and continued talking with his back toward me.

"Miss Miranda, who lived next door to us, had come over to babysit me that night. Mommy and Daddy were going over to Memphis for something. I didn't know what then; all I knew is that they promised they would bring me a toy home." My ears stayed focused on the word "mommy," an unusual pronunciation for a grown man. Then I realized that it was normal for a six-year-old, which was how he last knew her, so "mommy" was what he had last called her. He continued, "When I got grown, they told me that Mommy had a doctor's appointment in Memphis. That's where she grew up so she used to go back over there a lot. She found out that day that she was going to have a little baby." His voice slid toward childish with the last words, then returned to normal with the next. "She and Daddy went out for dinner at the Peabody Hotel to celebrate. They were less than a mile from home when the accident happened." He shook his head. "I remember that before they left, I had a tummy ache. I didn't feel good but they thought I was just puttin' on a show to keep them from their trip. I didn't want 'em to go. Begged 'em to stay. Cried and pleaded. But Mommy hugged me and said she loved me and I would be okay. She said, 'Now, you be a little man for Miss Miranda. Okay?' "

He turned and looked at me. "I heard it, you know. Heard the tires screechin', metal crashin' and the boom of it all." He shuddered at the miserable memory. "Woke me up from a dead sleep. I was so scared. I sat straight up in my bed and started screamin'. Miss Miranda came runnin' and told me that it was just a bad dream. She was watching television and never heard it. She gave me a glass of warm milk and I went back to sleep." He hung his head. "I never slept that good as a child again. You just get scared to go to sleep because you don't know what will happen during the night."

I thought about my mama in all her aggravating glory and about the comfort of my daddy when he was alive. I couldn't imagine having grown up without the love, nurturing and teachings of the two people who had brought me into this world. I stood up and crossed the room until I was close to Walter. With teary eyes and heavy heart, I patted him on the shoulder in a consoling way. After a moment, he walked back to the sofa and sank down with a thud. I stayed at the potbellied stove and listened as his story continued.

"Next morning, I put on my little cowboy boots with my pajamas and ran down the stairs. Mommy was always in the kitchen making breakfast, and she'd say, 'Do you want oatmeal, cereal or eggs?' I always wanted Capt'n Crunch cereal 'cause it came with prizes like spy rings. I went running into the kitchen but Mommy wasn't there. Miss Miranda was there and so were lots of neighbors and my granny and papaw from Memphis. Something wasn't right. I just knew it." He looked at me earnestly. "How can a kid like that know something ain't right?"

I shrugged. "Children are smart. Usually smarter than adults when it comes to natural instinct. I guess the good Lord just gives it to them to help take care of 'em."

He nodded silently, then went on. "I said, 'Where's my mommy?' Papaw came over and said that he had something to tell me. Said it was something that we needed to talk about man-to-man. He took me outside to my swing set in the backyard and he told me. First, I screamed and cried. Then, after a while I just got on my swing and I swung all day, high as I could go. They couldn't get me to come down. I thought if I could swing high enough, I could swing into heaven and be with Mommy and Daddy."

Well, that did it. My tears started falling and soon I was wiping away black tears darkened with the tint of what mascara remained from my previous tears. For a couple of minutes, neither of us spoke. The big hulk of a bald-headed man sat like a withered cantaloupe, drawing himself into as tight a ball as possible. Outside an owl howled into the night and the light wind whistled through the trees. Finally, someone had to speak. So I did.

"Walter," I began gently as I sat down in the faded plaid chair next to him. "Where did you go to live after your parents died?"

He fell back against the sofa and let his head drop down on the top. "My uncle Big Buddy and Aunt Jolene took me in because they had Buddy Junior, who was about my age. Everybody thought it'd be best if I lived with them. That's how I wound up in Zionsville, on the other side of Little Rock."

"That was sweet of them," I commented.

He nodded. "Yep. Me and Buddy Junior have always been real close like. We used to play cowboys and Indians." He raised his head and looked at me with tears glistening in his eyes. "But you know what, Miss Houston? It wouldn't the same. I always knew that I wasn't really Big Buddy and Aunt Jolene's child. I was an orphan without no parents. People around town always treated me different."

"In what way?"

"Like I wasn't really one of them. Like they just pitied me and was tryin' to do their Christian duty by seein' after me." He wiped away a tear. "I ain't never had nobody who loved just me. After my folks died, I never again had anyone who loved me without thinkin' about it."

I looked puzzled but didn't have to ask for clarification because he continued with only a slight pause. "What I mean is that everybody else tried to love me because you're supposed to love orphans." He shrugged. "I just wanted to be loved for no reason at all."

Whoa. Talk about taking a step back. If I could whistle, I would have. I would have given the kind of whistle that rings of amazement, of the dawning of long overdue reality. But since I can't whistle, I merely sat there, looking like the kind of fool I was and thinking that it took a lonely, simple-thinking man to show me what I most needed to know. I wish I could mark that spot, that hidden place in the Arkansas woods, with a monument that would say, "It was here that Abigail Margaret Houston finally grew up. For on this spot of Arkansas soil, she learned that those who are wise always run toward love and not away from it. They energetically seek love, not shun it. They adore love, not abandon it."

I don't know how long I just sat there and stared stupidly at the last person on earth who I would have ever thought could teach me a life-enriching lesson. I don't know how long because when powerful lessons like that come along in life, you don't time them. You absorb them. While I stared, Walter dropped his head in his hands. After I completely absorbed the lesson of love, I tried to think of something to say. But what do you say to a man who had his world ripped out from under him when he was only six years old? "I'm sorry" is well meaning but hollow, especially after thirty-three years. Without a doubt, he had heard that over and over until it no longer had substance.

Charlotte's words came floating back to me. In an instant, I had learned that she was right. I was running away from love. I had indignantly packed my bags and turned a deaf ear to Spencer's plea for redemption. With all the self-righteousness I could muster, I had painted him with a black hat and waved good-bye with my white hat and ridden off into the sunset away from Bliss, Mississippi.

Then, like Walter, I dropped my face in my hands. Not out of sorrow like Walter but out of shame for my actions. It is safe to say that, in that moment, I also bore shame for the annoyance I had felt for Mama when she tried so hard to find me a husband. It was love, plain and simple, that drove her to meddle, but I, in all my self-centeredness, had never bothered to understand that. I don't deserve to be loved, I thought glumly.

"Thank you," I whispered, unable to bring my voice to a normal decibel.

He looked up, bewildered. "Thank you? What are you talkin' about?"

I didn't really want to speak but pushed myself to find words. "You've shown me the importance of love." I took a deep breath. "Walter, I'll never forget what you said about being loved for no reason at all." My eyes watered. "That's pretty powerful."

"But lots of people love you," he protested, shaking his head.

"Lots of people love me for a *reason*," I corrected him. "They love me because of the books I write or because I can help them in some way or because I'm well known. They aren't the kind of people who would be there to hold my head while I was throwing up." A graphic example but a good one, nonetheless.

"Some people love me because they're supposed to." I thought of Melinda and wondered if she loved me for that reason.

He smiled sadly. "But, at least, they love you. Nobody loves me."

"What about Big Buddy and Aunt Jolene?" I asked.

"Aunt Jolene died a couple of years ago. A heart attack. And Big Buddy hasn't been the same since. Buddy Junior worries 'bout him all the time. He just sits 'round and watches TV or stares at the hummin' bird feeders."

"What about Buddy Junior? I'm sure he loves you."

He shrugged. "Yeah, I guess so. At least, he likes me real good. I'm obliged for that."

We both fell silent again, which is when it occurred to me that I was in a hostage situation because Walter felt no one loved him. In trying to find love without reason, he had reasoned himself into kidnapping me with the intent of making me love him. I rolled my eyes. I couldn't help it. Mama has always said, "The things people will do for love." Somehow those words had new meaning.

Without any prompting, Walter spoke. "I've been trying to get your attention for six months, but you wouldn't never answer my letters."

"Letters?" I shook my head. "I don't know what you're talking about."

"I mailed three letters to your publishing company."

I threw my hand up in a dismissive gesture. "Oh, who knows what happens to those. Some I get but it might be months later and some I never get." This shot through me like a bullet and I jerked straight up. The voice mail from Jamie. The ardent love letter she spoke of. It had to be from Walter. For the first time in hours, I felt hope knocking. If Walter had signed his name, then Jamie would be able to pass along that information to police. I brightened more. It occurred to me that Jamie would be the first to know that I hadn't made the book signing because the bookstore manager would call her to find out why I hadn't shown up. And when Jamie learned I hadn't phoned, she would know that something had happened. Then, with all the vigor of her Long Island upbringing, she would launch a full-scale search for me.

It is safe to say that never had the South needed the North more. Needless to say, Long Island was looking awfully darn good to me at the time.

"Walter, did you sign your name to those letters?" My heart pounded hard. With one heavy beat, it wanted to know, but with the one that followed, it didn't want to know. I held my breath.

"Yes ma'am. Signed 'em all. Gave you my phone number and e-mail address, too."

The relief that swept over me was so enormous that I felt lightheaded. "Thank you, Lord," I mumbled under my breath.

"What?" Walter asked, cupping an ear and turning it toward me.

"I just said, 'Oh, my Lord.'" I replied quickly, though how in the world I thought that quickly, I haven't a clue. "You know, Walter, it happens all the time. People are forever telling me that they sent me mail to my publisher's office, yet I never get it. Well, *never* isn't exactly right. Sometimes I do get it. But I didn't get yours. I'd definitely remember that if I had." I paused. "What did you say?"

"I just told you how I knew we're meant to be together. Miss Houston, I knew it the moment I saw your picture."

I just looked at him. I was very careful not to roll my eyes. But I wanted to. How on earth, I've always wondered, could someone fall in love with a picture? I saw him digging around in his back pocket. He retrieved his billfold, opened it and pulled out a photo. He looked at it and smiled sweetly, then handed it toward me.

"See here, Miss Houston. You look a lot like her."

I took the picture and saw a woman in a faded color photo probably taken with a Kodak Instamatic forty years earlier. It was one of those exactly square photos with the date encoded on the side. Walter had folded it neatly, careful not to crease the face of the pretty young woman with shoulder-length dark auburn hair that was crowned with a small aqua green hat. The color of her short-sleeved dress matched perfectly and was accented by a necklace made of large beads that were a couple of shades darker than the dress and hat. She beamed with one of the prettiest smiles I have ever seen. I unfolded the edges of the photo and saw a nice-looking but not handsome man standing beside her. I glanced up at Walter and back at the photo. There was a resemblance. Yes, if Walter had been thinner and had hair, he would favor the guy.

"Is this your father and mother?"

He smiled broadly without showing his teeth, pushing his chubby cheeks into his eyes. He nodded. "That was the Easter after they got married. I was born about six months later."

"I see a resemblance to your dad," I remarked.

"Yes, ma'am. But he had hair. Both of my granddaddies didn't have hair so I guess that's where I got my lack of it." He rubbed his hand over his head.

I focused on the mother. There was no doubt that she was pretty, though with the 1960s red lipstick and dark brows, it was hard to say how much we looked alike. But her hair and eyes looked like mine and what I could see of her smile was similar to mine.

"Do you think I look like her?"

He nodded so enthusiastically that he looked like one of

those dogs with the bobbing heads that some people used to put in their back car windows. "The moment I saw you, I thought you looked just like her."

Well, there you had it. Didn't matter if I did or didn't. Walter thought I did and that's all that mattered. That, more than likely, was what had gotten me kidnapped. After, of course, he had made up his mind that he was going to marry me. In an odd way, he was trying to reconnect with his mother. That was both good news and bad. The good news was that he wasn't going to hurt his mother.

The bad news was that he wasn't going to let her go.

Chapter 24

I was exhausted. Worn out physically, mentally and emotionally. My head pounded and my stomach hurt from the tension tightly knotted in it. I glanced at my watch and saw that it was close to midnight. It was no time, though, for giving up. I trudged on.

"Walter, is that what attracted you to me? That I look like your mother?"

He smiled happily. "She was beautiful."

I sighed with aggravation. That didn't answer my question and my nerves were getting too short to be toyed with. "Walter, please tell me."

"What?" He looked completely lost.

"Did you want me to be your sweetheart because I resemble your mother?"

He cocked his head to one side and looked puzzled. "I don't

think so. But it did make me like you at first, and it's the reason I bought your first book."

Wearily, I rubbed my eyes, the ones without any mascara left on the lashes. "Please tell me what you're going to do with me."

Walter leaned forward from the sofa, briefly touched my hand, which was resting on the armrest of the "fashionable" chair in which I was sitting, and said gently, "Miss Houston, you're gonna be fine. You'll get used to bein' out here in a little while, and you'll like it much more than being 'round people all the time." He had a point there, but I wasn't going to be that easy of a sale. "When you feel the time is right, we can get married. But only after you feel right about it."

Now that we had a time line of "never in a million years," I felt a bit better. I thought of telling Walter that I didn't love him, didn't have any plans to and didn't ever see it happening. But why do that? The poor guy had been turned away from love for so many years, there was no sense rubbing salt into raw wounds. Like Charlotte said, I was running away from love, while Walter was desperately trying to dig up a chance at it. At least he had the courage to chase it. I was nothing but a coward hiding in the dark shadows of hurt. I plunged forward.

I leaned toward him until my face was only inches from his. "Walter, if you really love me, please let me go." I asked it earnestly, gently but not pleadingly. I was willing to beg when the time came, but I first tried it with a little dignity. A little dignity, by the way, was all I had left.

He shook his head firmly. "I can't."

"Why?"

"If I let you go, you won't come back. Just like my mommy and daddy. I didn't want them to go but they did. And then they didn't come back."

My heart broke. Not for me but for Walter. Love had left him behind like the debris scattered by a spring tornado. In that instance, I thought also of Homer and Spencer who had been wounded by the loss of great love. To the outside world, the four of us might be as different as night is from day, but hurt, the kind that is brought about by love that disappears, is an equalizer to all. We were bonded by the understanding of how heartbreak scars for life.

I just looked at him.

"You wouldn't come back, would you?" he asked earnestly.

I hung my head. I wanted to lie but there was too much honesty developing between my kidnapper and me. When I again raised my head, I saw a solitary tear roll down his cheek.

My heart broke further.

"Walter, I would stay if I could," I whispered softly.

"Why can't you?"

"For one thing because I'm lousy at love. You need someone special. For another, there are too many people depending on me for various obligations." I glanced around the spare cabin. Though it was lacking in modern conveniences, it was tempting to run away to find a simpler life. "I missed my book signing in Jackson tonight, and that has caused a lot of upset and trouble to many people. You don't want to hurt other people, do you?"

Most people would have been selfish enough—and I admit that I would probably have been one of them—to say, "I don't care about anyone else. I only care about what I want." But not Walter. Not the man who grew from the little boy who was intimate with disappointment and upset. With a sad expression, he shook his head.

"I don't wanna hurt nobody, Miss Houston." He paused for a moment. "But I just want to be with you. I just want you to love me." He smiled sweetly. "For no reason."

That was my cue and I took it. "But, Walter, if I stay with you here, under these circumstances, it will never be love for no reason. It will be because you made me stay and I didn't have another option. Love has to choose to be for no reason. It can't be forced."

Perhaps a small part of him understood, but the main part—the part that had dragged me there, enabled by a gun—did not. He straightened his back and said firmly, "If you stay long enough, you won't want to go. You'll have no reason to go."

I slumped and fell back into the chair. This is like dealing with my mother, I thought glumly. Suddenly, that thought electrified me. Hey, I thought, I've got plenty of experience in dealing with unreasonable people, people who want me to get married when I don't want to. That experience will, sooner or later, get me out of the situation. I just have to figure out how to do it. Although, I remembered, I hadn't been able to change Mama's mind about marriage nor had I ever been able to reason with her. What on earth was I going to do?

Walter slapped his hands against his knees. "Well, are you ready to get some shut-eye?"

In one way, I didn't want to close my eyes in that place, but in another, it was tempting to go to sleep in hopes of waking to find it had all been a bad dream.

"Where?" I asked suspiciously.

"You can have the bedroom. There's twin beds in there and I can sleep on the sofa."

The sofa! That was the answer. I'd sleep on the sofa, and just as soon as Walter was snoring—and I was certain that he was a snorer—I'd slip out the door and get away.

I looked at the disgusting couch and shook my head. "I don't know, Walter. That sofa looks pretty uncomfortable for you. I think it's probably built for someone smaller and more petite, like me. Why don't I take the sofa?" Another brilliant idea crossed my mind. "You could push the two beds together and make a comfortable bed for yourself. Why don't we do that?"

He shook his head with the same stubbornness that was keeping me hostage. "Nope. I will not let you sleep on this old sofa. It's awful to sleep on. One time Big Buddy came with me and Buddy Junior so I slept on this old thing. I know it ain't comfortable so I won't let you sleep on it."

Walter's thoughtfulness was starting to get to me, especially since he was thoughtful about all the wrong things and none of the right things. It kinda reminded me of Terry Houston, who used to kiss other women in order to spare me the trouble.

I looked down at my clothes. The straight skirt, the high heels and nothing else that was comfortable for sleeping in. As if he had read my mind, Walter said, "Just as soon as we can, maybe tomorrow, we'll get you some more things like pajamas. I could get you one of my tee shirts out of the truck. Do you want me to?"

Ugh. I did not want to sleep in one of Walter's tee shirts. I shook my head. "No, that's okay. I'll just lie down in these clothes. They're actually very comfortable." Okay, so I did have to lie for once. But I didn't want him thinking that I was in that bedroom without any clothes on. Just to be on the safe side, you know. Out of the blue, I found myself wondering if Walter had ever kissed a girl. I doubted it.

I pulled my fatigue-laden body from the chair as Walter, too, stood up as a gentlemanly courtesy to a lady. He stepped sideways and allowed me to pass easily between the sofa and chair. I patted his arm as I walked by.

" 'Night, Walter. I'll see you in the morning." I was so tired that I didn't want to think further of the hostage situation. But, after the talk we had just had, I was optimistic that I would eventually free myself. We'd talk about it in the morning.

I got to the door of the bedroom and stopped. I thought for a moment, then turned toward him. "Walter, I'm sorry," I said with genuine feeling. "I'm sorry that your life hasn't been happier. You're a nice guy and you deserve better than you've gotten." I meant it, even if I was perturbed with Walter for snatching me and dragging me out into the woods. I knew that, without question, where I was then was because of where Walter had been. If Walter's parents hadn't died when he was six, he wouldn't have become a disillusioned kidnapper thirty-three years later.

His face melted into a muddle of sorrow and he dropped his head. "Thanks for that, Miss Houston. 'Preciate it much."

I closed the door behind me, kicked off my high heels and plopped down on the bed. With my feet dangling toward the floor, I fell backwards, flopped my arms over my head and tried to corral the thousand thoughts racing through my mind. Here's what's funny: I didn't plot an escape or even think about being held against my will. I thought simply of love's lessons that had unfolded to me in the last thirty-six hours. In that time, three men whose hearts had been broken by the loss of those they loved had paraded into my life and demonstrated that I was not the only person who had been deserted by love. My loss was no worse—and actually was better—than theirs. At least it wasn't death that had snatched my love away. Though there were times I would have preferred death over divorce, especially when Terry was cavorting around town freely and I thought of killing him myself. People have more sympathy for widows than for divorcées, even if the wife has been wronged.

First, there had been Homer. Despite the lost of Velma, whom he loved dearly, he had picked up and carried on. Spencer, widowed with two small children, had not let the hurt turn to bitterness. He was just scared. Yet I had penalized him for it and refused to listen to his apology. I felt heartsick. I had thrown away the possibility of finding love with a terrific guy. A guy I was attracted to! I had discovered in my lifetime that those to whom I'm attracted are few and far between. Sometimes—too many times—I am my own worse enemy.

I thought about Walter and the pain of losing his parents as a small child. The devastation of losing his foundation had chewed away at him for years. It had driven him to becoming a felon when he wasn't a bad person at all. He was just a misfit trying to find love because love is what every person, good or bad, strong or weak, needs. That made me think again of Spencer and the shock and despair he must have felt over losing such a young, beloved wife. Why, no wonder he had the skitters. I pounded a fist against my forehead, simultaneously attacking myself for such stupidity and attempting to pound some sense into my thick skull.

My turmoil was interrupted by a thunderous boom. It scared me so badly that I jumped straight up from the bed, my heart throbbing so hard that it made my head dizzy. I looked around the room. I couldn't see where the noise had come from, but it sounded like something had hit the outside of the cabin. I opened the door and ran to the next room, where I found Walter peering out the window.

"What's going on?" I asked.

Walter looked around, frowned and shook his head. "Don't know. Probably just a bat or something flew into the side of the house."

"Just as long as it doesn't fly *inside* the house," I mumbled. Nervously, I looked around the cabin. In a place that old and that run down, there surely were some holes somewhere that something could fly through.

That was it. This time the tears refused to stay put and spilled down my face. I couldn't bear any more. Not only was I scared, my heart ached with pain from losing Spencer and from loving him so much. I was certain there was no way that I would ever see him again. Alarmed, Walter spun his thick frame around and ran over to me.

"Miss Houston, please don't cry. Nothin's gonna harm you. I promise that I'll—" before he could finish, another hard thump hit the house closer toward the back. I stopped crying and asserted myself.

"Walter, that has got to be something besides a bat."

He looked uneasy and headed toward the back, just as something hit the cabin on the other side. He grabbed his gun. "I'm gonna go out to check on this. Stay right here." He charged out the door but I didn't stay put. I didn't even take the time to regret that my only shoes were high heels. I dashed back to the bedroom, grabbed my shoes in my hands, then after giving him half a minute's head start, I darted out the door, down two steps, took a leap over the broken one and ran toward the truck, practically oblivious to the twigs and small rocks that were piercing my feet.

I was probably taking a chance, deciding to run, but I was no longer afraid of Walter or what he might try do to me. Something instinctive told me to run and I did. At the time it never occurred to me that the plan could backfire on me if Walter caught me. I didn't even stop to think of the fact that I was in the middle of the backwoods of Arkansas or that I was barefooted, clutching a pair of spiked high heels or that I didn't have a cell phone. Either I was very brave or very stupid. I still don't know which it was.

I knew he had the keys to the truck, so I guess that I planned just to run into the woods and let the bear get me. I honestly don't know what I was thinking. I was only a few feet past the tailgate of the truck when a long, strong arm grabbed my arm, jerked me back against him and slapped his hand against my mouth to stifle my screams. I fought with all my might, trying to stab a man's hands and face with my spiked heels. For the first time in several hours, I was glad I had them. I heard a slight grunt as he winced at the pain. He tightened his grip and said in a low voice, "Honey! Please stop that!"

When I heard "honey" and the way he said it, I released all the tension and fight from my body. I slumped against him. I knew there was no reason to continue the battle.

Chapter 25

I flopped like a wilted lettuce leaf over the arm that he had spread across my chest. He held me up for a second, then turned me toward him, engulfing me with the strength of his arms. I laid my cheek against his chest as he moved one hand up to grasp my head tightly against his rapidly beating heart. I began to sob quietly, my entire body shaking from the convulsions caused by those tears.

"Baby," he breathed into my ear. "Oh, sweet baby. It's okay. It's all over now."

Those were the sweetest words I had ever heard. Relief flooded every pore of my skin. It was too much at once.

"Oh, Spencer," I mumbled. "How on earth did you ever find me?" The fragrance of his manly cologne filled my nostrils, and I inhaled it deeply and gratefully.

"Shhh," he replied gently. "There's plenty of time to explain that."

An owl hooted somewhere in the deep woods, only to be interrupted by a jumbling of noise that included footsteps rustling through the carpet of fallen leaves and twigs. I heard a radio squawk, "Ten-four. Go ahead."

Another voice responded, "We have the perpetrator in custody. We're bringing him in."

"Ten-four."

I jerked my head just in time to see Deputy Rickey of the Bliss police force and four other law enforcement officers heading toward us with Walter, head hanging low and wrists shackled by handcuffs. I moved out of Spencer's embrace but stayed close to his side, tucked safely—at last—under his arm.

"Evenin' ma'am," Rickey tipped his hat. "Are you all right? Should we call for an ambulance?"

"No," I replied shakily. "I'm just a bit unsettled but physically fine. He didn't lay a hand on me." Well, he had held my hand but I refrained from mentioning that. Even in my haze, something faintly became clear. "Rickey, did you make the noise we heard?"

He grinned. "Yep. I threw myself full force against the outside wall." He rubbed his shoulder and chuckled. "Hit it a little bit harder the second time than I meant to. But we wanted to distract the kidnapper and get him to come outside."

"Hello, Miss Houston," an officer stepped forward to offer his hand. "I'm Sergeant Barnard with the state police. Kidnapping and crossing county lines is a state and federal crime, so we'll be taking the suspect to the nearest jail, booking him on those charges and then moving him to a state facility. We'll also need to get a statement from you. Do you feel up to it now?"

Spencer spoke up. "Sergeant Barnard, Miss Houston has

been through a tremendous ordeal. Would it be all right if I take her back to Bliss, where she can get a good night's sleep, then meet with y'all in the morning? You can interview her in my office. How's that?"

Sergeant Barnard frowned. "That's against procedure. We should talk to the victim immediately while the experience is still fresh."

I smiled ruefully. "Sir, you don't have to worry. I don't believe that I'll ever be able to forget a moment of this experience."

Spencer looked at me with sympathy. At that moment, I thought I could bear no more. I teared up. I wasn't thinking completely clearly but I knew enough to focus my eyes with the big tears in them directly on Sergeant Barnard. I blinked and one big fat tear came spilling down my cheek. Spencer proved to be a terrific conspirator because he moved to take advantage of the moment.

"Sergeant, as you can see, she's worn out. I believe that you would get a much better statement if you would wait until tomorrow when she refreshes herself with sleep and food."

And a bathroom, I thought.

Sergeant Barnard smiled warmly. "Let's compromise. Miss Houston, would you give us a brief statement now? Won't take more than five minutes then tomorrow, we'll talk in-depth. How's that?"

Spencer looked at me for approval and I nodded quietly. The officer was right because it only took a few minutes for me to tell him what happened. He scribbled furiously and I, the reporter that I once was, made a conscious-though-mind-tired effort to be clear and concise.

"As soon as he was outside, I ran for it and that's when Spencer grabbed me," I concluded.

Sergeant Barnard smiled, closed his notepad and put his pen away. "Good. That's enough for now. Thank you very much. We'll get the fine details tomorrow. Would eleven a.m. work?"

"Well, actually tomorrow is Sunday," I replied. "Why don't we take the time off for church and then meet in the mayor's office after lunch?"

The officer laughed. "Yes ma'am, that'll be fine. After all of this ordeal, I imagine you do have a lot of thanks to be giving to the one upstairs."

"Yes, sir, I do."

"Okay, Mayor. We'll see you tomorrow around two in your office." Sergeant Barnard reached out and grasped Spencer's hand tightly. "Thank you so much. We couldn't have pulled this off without you."

I certainly wanted to know what that meant, but Spencer avoided the question on my face and pulled me closer with a tight squeeze around my shoulders. "No appreciation necessary. I did what I had to do." He looked down at me and I declare that I saw love crinkling around the edges of his eyes. It was a lovely sight. There's no two ways around that one.

One of the other officers jerked Walter roughly by the arm and commanded, "C'mon! It's time for you to go where you belong."

As he walked by me, he looked down at me sadly. "Bye, Miss Houston. You take care of yourself, now hear? Don't let nobody hurt you while I'm gone."

"Bye, Walter." I felt sadness seeing him taken away like a harmless animal that had been ruthlessly captured. I tried to comfort him. "Don't worry. I'm sure everything is going to be all right." When he was out of earshot, I turned to Sergeant Barnard. "Sir, please see that he gets the help he needs. He's not a bad person or a mean one. He's just sick." Tears burned my eyes. "He's just lonely and wants to be loved." To myself, I thought, "Like all of us."

His voice was compassionate when he spoke. "We'll do our best but I can't make any promises. He'll certainly be charged.

You can of course speak up for him, and your word would probably go a long way since you're the victim." He changed his tone to more of an upbeat one. "Okay, let me escort you back to the car."

Rickey spoke up. "Mayor, why don't you take my patrol car and drive Miss Houston back to Bliss? I need to stay here and help out with the crime scene investigation. I'll call the chief and have him send someone for me later."

My heart skipped for joy. A long ride home to Bliss, just me and Spencer, plenty of time to say all the things I had regretted not saying and, hopefully, straighten out the situation. Spencer apparently agreed because he smiled and said cheerfully, "Sounds like a plan to me!"

I slipped my shoes back on and Rickey commented, "Well, it's a good thing we came along when we did. You wouldn't have gotten far with those things on!"

"Don't underestimate a desperate woman!" I winked.

Back up the dirt road a piece, two patrol cars pulled onto the blacktop with their blue lights spinning while Spencer helped me into the passenger's side of another. When he slid into the driver's side, he handed me a cold bottle of water, gently stroked my cheek and asked tenderly, "Anything else you need right now?"

"Yes." I nodded firmly. "Could you please take me to the nearest restroom?"

He threw back his head and laughed heartily. He put the key in the ignition. "And there I was, thinking you were going to ask for a kiss."

I smiled demurely and glanced up coquettishly through my lashes. "I didn't think I had to ask for *that!*"

As it turns out, I *didn't.*

♥

We got a lot of things straightened out on that drive. It took over three hours, including a stop for a quick, late supper at a twenty-four-hour restaurant. Life's a funny thing. You can be in the pits of misery, and then, in a blink of an eye, you're on cloud nine. That was me, floating my way back to Bliss as a humbled, apologetic Spencer explained what had caused his abrupt about-face in the gazebo.

"Remember the champagne we got?"

"Of course!"

"You found the note that went with it under the seat?" I remembered. He read the note and everything changed. He had grown distant.

"Yes?"

"The note was from Mac and Mary Jean Edwards, Liz's parents."

I drew in a breath and held it. I couldn't imagine what they would have said about their daughter's husband on a date or how much pain they must have felt as they were reminded of the void in their lives. He looked around at me and shrugged slightly as if trying to free his shoulders from that particular weight. He lifted the edge of his mouth in a half smile.

"The note said, 'Good for you. This is exactly what Liz would want.' "

Slowly, I released my breath but felt the tears that stung my eyes. I saw a tear in his eye as he looked back over at me. He reached across the seat—that wonderful bench seat in that big ol' police sedan—took my hand and pulled me toward him. It'd been years since I had been in a car where I could scoot over next to the guy, but I gladly did that night. He put his arm around me and drove with the other hand on the steering wheel. Unconsciously, I dropped my hand and let it rest on his knee in a gesture that felt so natural.

"Abby, I wasn't looking to be in love ever again in my life. I was focused on raising my two kids and being grateful for the love I had known. Then, this little redheaded fireball dropped in unexpectedly and it put quite a spin on things." He shook his head. "I was scared to walk away from my past and let go of it. I was even more scared to walk toward you because I was afraid of the pain I might suffer if you didn't feel the same way. I panicked and that's why I acted like such a dope."

I reached up and kissed him on the cheek. "I acted no better," I admitted with a grimace that recalled my stupidity. "I ran away from you as fast I could this morning, despite Charlotte's pleas for me to call you. At least you called first thing and tried to straighten it out."

"And sent flowers, too," he pointed out.

"That's right. But I was scared, too. The hurt from the failure of my marriage is something I never care to know again. I didn't want to take a chance. Trust me, though. I've learned a lot in the past couple of days. For the last twelve hours, I have cursed myself for acting so stupidly. I was afraid that I had lost you forever. Just because I wasn't brave when it came to love."

"I understand. You're talking my kind of talk now. But I'm ready to take a chance on us. I'm willing to risk the hurt but I also am willing to believe that there won't be any hurt. Whadda ya say?"

I leaned over and kissed him quickly on the lips. "I say you're talking *my* kind of talk now!" He squeezed my shoulders and I laid my head on his.

"Funny how quickly things can change, huh?" he said with romantic tenderness.

"Thank God for that! I was so afraid that I had screwed everything up and that I would never see you again. In fact, I was afraid that I would never see anyone *else* again!"

"Fame does have its burdens, doesn't it? And you said you weren't famous. I think it has been proven otherwise today."

I sat straight up and looked at him. "By the way, how on earth did you ever find me?"

As I heard his story, I realized how truly fortunate I had been, how a pair of seemingly insignificant events had been my salvation. I was also reminded that good can often be found in the bad. That night, after the note from Liz's parents when Spencer fell quiet, I had noticed the red pickup with the white camper top and mentioned it to him. There is certainly reason to believe that if we had still been caught up in the previous romantic mood, I would never have seen it, and, if I had, would never have interrupted the romance long enough to mention it. Sheila, wise to the struggle that was going on between us, had called Spence on his cell phone as soon as I walked out the door of Brian's office. Thank God for nosey people. Spence got there just in time to see the red pickup with the white camper top squealing away. That, combined with my mentioning it the night before and my rental car abandoned along with my purse, alerted him that I had been taken against my will.

"You know what really tipped us off?"

"What?"

"You left without your lipstick," he announced with a grin.

I cut my eyes over at him and made a face. "Very funny."

"Hey! Don't blame me. It was Sheila who said that no woman in her right mind would leave her lipstick behind."

I had to laugh. It's so true. It also reminded me of how bad I must look. I checked the rearview mirror, and sure enough, I don't believe I've ever looked worse in my life. I didn't have a stitch of makeup left, and the ordeal had frizzed my naturally curly hair into a pitiful mess. The careful job of straightening I had done that morning was long forgotten.

"Yuck! What a sorry sight I am," I moaned, attempting to tame my curls by running my fingers through my hair.

"I disagree," he said. "Considering that I didn't know if I

would ever see you again, you look pretty darn good to me."
That's when I knew I loved him.

I smiled gratefully and prodded him on with his story. "So
what happened after my left-behind lipstick revealed the real
truth?"

"I got on the phone and immediately demanded an all-points
bulletin to be put out."

"You can do that?" I asked in awe.

He pretended to be offended. "Well, I *am* the mayor of Bliss,
Mississippi. I do have a certain amount of pull, thank you very
much. I also happen to have an almost photographic memory,
which you can thank me for later." He winked playfully. "I recalled the license plate completely."

I grinned from ear to ear. "The more I learn about you, the
more I like you."

"Ditto." He squeezed my hand. "Except in this case, the APB
didn't work because no law enforcement officer saw you. But—
and we can be very grateful for this—the state police connected
with the FBI and the Arkansas Bureau of Investigation, and
working together, they very quickly were able to put details of
Walter's life together. It helped that you're a celebrity." I
frowned at the use of that word, but he blithely skipped over my
reaction and continued, "So they knew that the media would
certainly be all over it in a heartbeat, and it would quickly be a
major national story. They didn't want to look foolish."

I folded my arms and looked at him suspiciously. "They
thought of that all by themselves?"

"Well, with a little help they did. They just needed someone
to plant the thought." He grinned. "Your publicist Jamie also
helped."

"Jamie?" I thought I knew why. "Let me see if I get this right.
The bookstore in Jackson called Jamie when I didn't show up;
she called Susan Marie, who called you. Then someone talked

to her; you discovered that Jamie had received an ardent love letter for me. Was that letter from Walter?"

"It was," he said, nodding. "Walter's an interesting guy. He's not playing with a full deck. He had just gotten fired from a job. The FBI profiler said that was enough to set him off into believing this fantasy he had created about you."

"Poor Walter," I said under my breath.

"He lived with his uncle. His parents died when he was young."

That was news to me. In our conversation, Walter hadn't told me that he still lived with Big Buddy. I had assumed he lived on his own.

"It's a good thing he did because his uncle was a big help. He said they saw you on TV the other night, and Walter said that you were the woman he was going to marry. His uncle pointed us to the family cabin. His cousin Buddy Junior, gave us the location, and we followed a hunch that he would take you there. Thank goodness we were right."

I slipped my arm through his and nestled over next to him. "You're my hero," I whispered with all the sincerity my heart felt. I laid my head back on his shoulder, he kissed the top of my head, and I drifted off to sleep. The next thing I knew was the sound of Spencer's voice.

"Okay, sleepyhead, wake up. We're almost there." Foggy, I opened my eyes and shook my head, trying to clear it. We had just entered the city limits of Bliss. "I'm taking you to Charlotte's. They're expecting you."

I rubbed my eyes. "What time is it?"

"Almost 4 a.m."

I nodded quietly but was suddenly jerked wide awake when we came in sight of the Magnolia Blossom Bed and Breakfast.

"Oh, my gosh!" I exclaimed. "What's going on?" There were dozens of news vans with satellites perched on their roofs and

power and microphone cords stretched all over the street and
sidewalks. Portable spotlights were strewn about. A mass of
people were scattered hither and yon, some on the porch, others on the steps, still others just milling around in the yard and
on the sidewalk.

Spencer started laughing. "That, my dear, appears to be your
welcome-home committee. Looks like I was right after all about
this being a national news story." He arched an eyebrow and
said, "Only a *famous* person would get this much attention." I
wrinkled my nose but he ignored it, caught up by the circus in
front of us. "Look! There's an ABC network van and over there
is CBS."

I was so stunned I couldn't speak. As Spencer pulled to the
side and eased to a stop, I found my voice.

"Dang it. I can't believe I don't have any lipstick on!"

He looked over at me and shook his head. "Me either," he
said.

Chapter 26

In all my born days, I have never seen such a clattering commotion as that which stormed into the previously peaceful, quiet town of Bliss. It rained cameras, microphones, recorders and notepads and thundered with reporters representing television and radio networks, wire services, major newspapers, national-news and general-interest magazines and Internet information sites. The *Bliss Observer* printed a special edition, and the *Dexter Tribune* even sent a reporter and a photographer. This from an editor who normally grouses that he doesn't have the money to send a reporter across town to cover a town-council meeting. It was amazing. The storm that had gathered hovered over Bliss for four days, pumping excitement, entertainment and a lot of corporate dollars, thanks to large expense accounts, into the town's economy.

They swooped over Spencer and me as we climbed from the

car that night, begging for enough sound bites and quotes to make their imposing deadlines. I complied, giving them twenty minutes of answers and images of me at my bedraggled worst. While I was doing that, Spencer once again called upon the full authority of his ruling position and summoned uniformed members of the Bliss police force to escort me through the crowd and into the house. Charlotte was waiting with a steaming cup of raspberry tea, sweetened with honey, which I sipped while we all huddled and made plans for the next morning. As a bonus, she had refused to rent out any rooms to the intruding media, explaining that I needed a quiet refuge after all I had been through. We decided that we would go to church as planned, then have lunch back at Charlotte's. I would meet for a debriefing with the various law enforcement units, and then we would hold a press conference in the late afternoon. We were all quite taken aback with how big a news story it had become. Some said it was because I was a celebrity of sorts. Others said that it was because a stalker had preyed on an author, proving that pop culture had exploded to a point that even writers of books were susceptible to a danger once reserved for movie stars. I thought it simply had to be a slow news day. Whatever the reason, the unexpected windfall of publicity pleased my publisher so much that I actually came to believe they were all happy that I had been kidnapped. I was even a mite suspicious, recalling all I had read about Hollywood publicity schemes during the golden age of movies.

"You didn't have anything to do with this, did you?" I asked Jamie Gray, who virtually danced with glee during every minute of the next four days as she scheduled interviews including cover stories in two prestigious news magazines. She, who had once doubted the existence of Bliss, found it and flew in to personally handle the media mob.

"I *wish* I had been this smart," she replied with her typical Long Island honesty.

I may have had to twist Jamie's arm to convince her to let me stop in "Lost-in-God-knows-where-in-the-South, Mississippi," but that was soon forgotten as she claimed all the glory and honor for such a "stroke of genius" in that sky-touching building in Manhattan. I didn't mind at all. My kidnapping had put Jamie on a career fast track and I was happy for her. She became the front-runner for director of publicity for the entire publishing company, a position soon to be vacated by a retirement.

The news story made the front pages of newspapers across the nation, but when it was discovered that I had been rescued by the handsome, widowed mayor of Bliss and that a romance had, indeed, developed, there was no putting a lid on it. Even the tabloids got in on it, digging up my beleaguered ex-husband who claimed to have divorced *me* over the fact that I didn't cook dinner every night. He also claimed that I had loved my dog more than him. That part was true.

Television satellites were set up and live interviews were beamed from Bliss to the morning shows in New York, the late-night shows in LA and *Larry King* in Washington. Even Mama, jubilant over the romance more than the rescue, was interviewed by CNN, Fox News, MSNBC and King himself. Whenever possible, she held Kudzu in her lap because she thought the world "should see your only child." The "child," I noticed, had fattened up considerably during the time I had been gone. Melinda fixed Mama's hair and made sure she was wearing something besides a NASCAR sweatshirt. *People* magazine ran a small photo of me on the cover and then a story focusing on the romance with a sidebar about the kidnapping. Inside there was a lovely photo of Spencer and me with our arms wrapped around each other as he kissed my forehead, my face turned up toward his with an expression of pure contentment. The headline read, "A Bliss-ful Ending." That was so true.

Spencer's dad craftily capitalized on the onslaught of publicity that included his son, taking the opportunity to announce his candidacy for governor. As it was swiftly reported throughout the nation, we all thought that not only would he win, but he would also become one of the country's best-known politicians. Of course, the incredible amount of attention sold books, with my latest vaulting to the number one position on every imaginable list and reviving my last paperback to the point of best-selling status again. The New York brain trust suspended my current tour to leave me in Bliss for several days in order to squeeze out every drop of possible newsprint and then decided to add ten more cities to my book tour. I was exhausted just thinking about it, and though I was stunned by all that was happening, I was very grateful. The commercial success was lovely but I was thankful to be safe again and, most of all, to have found Spencer. That, of course, was the best. After a week of publicity obligations sprinkled liberally with lots of hand-holding, starry-eyed looks, cuddling and kissing, Jamie announced it was time to return to the road. It broke my heart.

"Baby, don't cry," Spencer consoled me sweetly the night before my scheduled departure. We were sitting in the front-porch swing on the veranda of his house, which rested on an enormous lot a couple of blocks behind the town square.

"But, but I don't want to leave you," I sniffed pitifully. Love, at that moment, was more important to me than any amount of money.

He hugged me up tightly to his chest. "You only have to work a couple of weeks and you'll be back."

"*Nineteen* days," I corrected him, pulling back to let him clearly view the agony on my face.

He smiled, then kissed me. "What about if I fly out in a week and meet you somewhere?"

My tears stopped. "Really?" My eyes widened with a childlike enthusiasm.

"Yep. I can do that."

I threw my arms around him. "That would be great!" My mind immediately began working. "Hey, this would be terrific publicity! I bet I could even get Jamie to pay for your flight and hotel!"

"That would be wonderful," he replied with that precious lopsided grin. "But if not, that's fine, too. Nothing will stop me from being with you."

My heart swooned and my soul rested. Finally, I had found the peace for which I had been searching. To my delight, it was wrapped up in a beautiful package of love and romance.

♡

Consoled somewhat by Spencer's solution to meet me in a week, I was able to forge forward in fairly high spirits the next morning as I prepared to leave. I had breakfast with Charlotte one last time, packed the rental car and said good-bye to the few remaining camera guys who were taping my departure for the day's news. They felt like friends because we had been together so long, so I hugged each one good-bye and shared a few words. Then I slid behind the wheel and drove off to say the last important good-bye.

Spencer was in his office performing mayoral duties, but he stood up the moment he saw me and rushed around the imposing oak desk to hug me. Lulu, who hadn't told me that she was his assistant the day I met her at the bookstore, stood in the doorway, saying "Hmmmm-hmmmm. If that ain't the most bodacious sight I ever seen in my life, I ain't knowin' what is. Praise the Lord, it done turned out just like it shoulda."

Together, we walked through city hall, saying good-bye to everyone who had become like family over the course of the mayhem; then, hand in hand, we walked out to the front of the old brick city hall and sat down on a wrought iron bench under a massive oak tree, one of many that stood in the yard. From that perch, we could see three sides of the town square of a place that now felt like home to me. Spencer put his arm across the back of the bench, I slid as close as possible, and we sat there, for a moment, not saying a word.

"Oh!" I exclaimed, snapping my fingers and reaching for my purse on the ground at my feet. "I almost forgot. I have something for you." I pulled out a familiar blue box tied with white satin ribbon and handed it to him.

"Tiffany's?" he asked as he pulled the bow and released the ribbon.

"I borrowed the box from Charlotte."

"Oh, I see."

"But for what it's worth and for future reference, I adore little blue boxes wrapped with white ribbon."

"I'll keep that in mind," he replied, nodding, his hand poised to lift the top. "Any color of blue?" He winked teasingly.

"No. *Tiffany* blue with those little black letters on the top." Chuckling, he took off the top, pulled back the tissue and then broke into roaring laughter.

"Spam! Oh, boy, I'm gonna have a fried Spam sandwich when I get home tonight!" He saw the look on my face and he stopped laughing.

"Remember what I told you under the gazebo when you said that your housekeeper always forgot to buy Spam?" I asked.

He thought for a second and then his face broke into the grandest of grins. He reached over and hugged me tightly. "Yes, baby. You said that a woman in love would never forget the Spam."

"See? I didn't forget."

He leaned over and kissed me quickly but gently. "It's the best present I ever got." He jerked back. "Hey! Wait a minute!" he said, clapping his hands together. "I've got a surprise for you, too, little sweetie."

"Is it as good as a can of Spam?"

"No. But I hope you'll like it anyway." He squeezed my knee. "The city council and the fine citizens of Bliss thought it most appropriate, based on the amount of national attention that you have brought to our town—not to mention the dollars of some whopping big expense accounts—that you should be awarded the key to the city!"

I gasped in delight and my hands flew to my cheeks. "Oh, Spencer! What a wonderful gift!" I tilted my head merrily and said in mock seriousness, "I want a ceremony."

"We can handle that."

"And a parade." I wagged my finger playfully. "I want a parade."

"No problem." He started laughing. "Abby dear, this town loves you so much that I believe you can have anything you want. Just ask for it."

I took his hand and held it tightly. "I have everything I want from Bliss. I couldn't and wouldn't ask for more." With his free hand, he reached into his inside jacket pocket and pulled out a long, narrow box like one that would hold a bracelet.

"That mean that you don't want this?" I snatched the box, tied with red ribbon, from his hand.

"Of course, I want this." I winked. "I didn't say I wouldn't *take* anything. I said I wouldn't *ask* for it. There's a big difference." In a flash, I had opened the box to discover a big key, the long, old-fashioned kind that is used to open heavy front doors on Victorian houses. Gingerly, I picked it up and looked puzzled. "Is this, is this the key to the city?" I looked at him and teasingly admonished him. "Spencer, you told me that you'd give me a ceremony!" I slapped his arm playfully.

"And a parade," he reminded me. "Don't forget the parade."

"That's right," I nodded. I picked up the key and held it in the palm of my hand. Softly, he spoke.

"In the palm of your hand, you're holding the key to my heart." My head snapped around.

"What?"

"The other night at the restaurant, Twinky said I should give you the key to my heart. Well, here it is. And you're holding it exactly where you have me—in the palm of your hand."

My heart leapt with gladness while my eyes teared up. One of those woman things men can never understand is how we can be happy *and* cry at the same time. I threw my arms around his neck and hugged him tightly while he embraced me just as closely. We were so lost in each other that it took a moment to hear the whooping and hollering. In sync, we looked around to see a group of townsfolk who, I would learn, had come to see me off. In a circle of smiles, balloons and signs stood Charlotte, Charlie, Maggie, Susan Marie, Brian, Sheila, Lulu, Judy, Fred, Twinky, Rickey and many others. Elizabeth, blonde, sweet and laughing, stood at the front while her brother, Kyle, the first member of the family I had met, rolled by on his skateboard, pumping his fists in celebratory triumph and grinning from ear to ear. Most notable, though, was Miss Eula, who had grudgingly come to terms with my role in saving Elmer. She had even begun to speak to me in a somewhat civil manner. Wordlessly and without a smile—but not with a frown either—she reached down and unclasped the leash from Elmer's collar. Happily freed, Elmer charged toward me, then took a high flying leap and landed in my lap, covering my face with gleeful, sloppy licks.

"Easy, girl! Easy!" I said laughing, trying to pull my face away from the unabashed affection.

Spencer looked over at the crowd, then back to Elmer. "Well, it looks like I'm not the only one who has fallen in love. Seems like there's a bunch of us. A whole town full, in fact. I don't think I've ever heard of an entire town falling in love."

I kissed him on the cheek and said not a word. What is there to say when you finally find bliss because Bliss found you?